Noah's Story

Noah's Story

An Epic Tale of Faith and Adventure

A NOVEL BY
Paul Christian

*This book is dedicated to my grandfather:
Jens Kristiansen, an old man of the sea.*

Foreword

In this book Paul has produced an entertaining and imaginative account of the life of Noah, one of the Bible's outstanding characters. He has faithfully brought the brief Bible account of Noah to life in such a way that the reader will be able to readily understand Noah's love for the sea, his preparation for building his great ship, the flood and its consequences, and his commitment to serving his God in the face of opposition within his own family and from others. In all of this Noah emerges as a real person, and one from whom we can learn so much for our own lives. I recommend this book to you, and am glad I have had a part in helping Paul in his work. Happy reading.

Ian Clark MA (Hons)
Former New Zealand Diplomat (Germany, Japan)
Thirty years Christian ministry – National Executive, Pastor,
Bible College Principal

Contents

Dates, Times and Measurements
As Used in the Narrative

Date: AM = Anno Mundi, or Year of the World (From the day of creation forward)
Year: One revolution of the sun (365 days)
Month: One full phase of the moon (Approximately)
Week: Seven days (six days of work and one of rest)
Day: 24 hours (sunset to sunset)
Distance: Land – one day's journey (walking) = 30 kilometres (approx.) Sea – one day's sailing = 50 kilometres (approx.)
Short Measure: 1 cubit = .5 metre (approximately)

Bible Prologue

In the beginning, God created the heavens and the earth. The earth was without form and void, and darkness was over the face of the deep. And the Spirit of God was hovering over the face of the waters.

And God said, "Let there be light," and there was light. And God saw that the light was good. And God separated the light from the darkness. God called the light Day, and the darkness he called Night. And there was evening and there was morning, the first day.

And God said, "Let there be an expanse in the midst of the waters, and let it separate the waters from the waters." And God made the expanse and separated the waters that were under the expanse from the waters that were above the expanse. And it was so. And God called the expanse Heaven. And there was evening and there was morning, the second day.

And God said, "Let the waters under the heavens be gathered together into one place, and let the dry land appear." And it was so. God called the dry land Earth, and the waters that were gathered together he called Seas. And God saw that it was good.

And God said, "Let the earth sprout vegetation, plants yielding seed, and fruit trees bearing fruit in which is their seed, each according to its kind, on the earth." And it was so. The earth brought forth vegetation, plants yielding seed according to their own kinds, and trees bearing fruit in which is their seed, each according to its kind. And God saw that it was good. And there was evening and there was morning, the third day.

And God said, "Let there be lights in the expanse of the heavens to separate the day from the night. And let them be for signs and for seasons, and for days and years, and let them be lights in the expanse of the heavens to give light upon the earth." And it was so. And God made the two great lights — the greater light to rule the day and the lesser light to rule the night — and the stars. And God set them in the expanse of the heavens to give light on the earth, to rule over the day and over the night, and to separate the light from the darkness. And God saw that it was good. And there was evening and there was morning, the fourth day.

And God said, "Let the waters swarm with swarms of living creatures, and let birds fly above the earth across the expanse of the heavens." So God created the great sea creatures and every living creature that moves, with which the waters swarm, according to their kinds, and every winged bird according to its kind. And God saw that it was good. And God blessed them, saying, "Be fruitful and multiply and fill the waters in the seas, and let birds multiply on the earth." And there was evening and there was morning, the fifth day.

And God said, "Let the earth bring forth living creatures according to their kinds — livestock and creeping things and beasts of the earth according to their kinds." And it was so. And God made the beasts of the earth according to their kinds and the livestock according to their kinds, and everything that creeps on the ground according to its kind. And God saw that it was good.

Then God said, "Let us make man in our image, after our likeness. And let them have dominion over the fish of the sea and over the birds of the heavens and over the livestock and over all the earth and over every creeping thing that creeps on the earth."

So God created man in his own image,
in the image of God he created him;
male and female he created them.

And God blessed them. And God said to them, "Be fruitful and multiply and fill the earth and subdue it, and have dominion over the fish of the sea and over the birds of the heavens and over every living thing that moves on the earth." And God said, "Behold, I have given you every plant yielding seed that is on the face of all the earth, and every tree with seed in its fruit. You shall have them for food. And to every beast of the earth and to every bird of the heavens and to everything that creeps on the earth, everything that has the breath of life, I have given every green plant for food." And it was so. And God saw everything that he had made, and behold, it was very good. And there was evening and there was morning, the sixth day.

– Genesis 1

Please continue reading the Book of Genesis through chapters 1-14 for the background to this narrative.

AS IT WAS IN THE DAYS OF NOAH

ONE

The Gathering

Year of the World from the Day of Creation
AM (Anno Mundi) 1952

The sun was at its peak high in the clear blue sky. No clouds were there to lessen the sun's intensity as the traveller plodded his way westward along the dusty trail. He was walking to lighten his donkey of its heavy human load at this the hottest part of the day. They would soon find shelter under a cliff or in a cave and rest for a few hours during the scorching afternoon heat, before continuing on during the cooler portion of the day. It had taken the traveller several days to reach this point on the journey, with his donkey as his only companion.

The traveller had been summoned to make the journey by the Patriarch, the Priest of God, who had written to his father requesting this. Once his father had received the parchment he had compelled his son to make the journey.

"If Noach has summoned you," he said, "it must be important. You must go my son, but beware, he will likely preach to you regarding his God. You must be respectful whether or not you accept what he says."

Continuing his journey in the late afternoon, somewhat refreshed after a nap and having eaten some dried food with water from his goat skin bladder, the traveller eventually reached the top of yet another ridge in the rocky and hilly countryside. There before him in the far distance was a vast flat blue sea reaching as far he could see. It was the first time he had ever seen such an amazing spectacle. Below the ridge he was standing on he could make out that he was just a short distance from the edge of the village to which he was heading. The sun was sinking below the distant horizon across the sea as dusk approached.

He walked into the seaside village and port of Ty finding as he did tents scattered about as well as mud brick dwellings here and there, with a cluster of them in the centre of the village. Beyond that was the sea front. Palm trees were growing in abundance in its heart, and around its perimeter were many other shrubs and small trees scattered about. There were the usual signs of evening activity in a small village. Older people were retiring for the night and younger ones were laughing and shouting to one another before their mothers called them indoors. There were goats, sheep and chickens wandering about, with the occasional bark of a dog and the smell of cooking in the air tantalising the hungry traveller's nostrils. The grunting of camels and bleating of sheep and goats as they settled down for the night ahead reminded him of his own village now so far away. The only difference for him was the sight of the tops of ships' masts on the far side of the village in what was most likely the port area. The traveller took all this in, but it did nothing to quell his apprehension at what he had been summoned to.

As he ambled toward the buildings in the middle of the village, he was hesitant to meet the revered man who had sent for him. Why had he been chosen, what could this great man want of him, he wondered? He was simply the eldest son of his father and his grandfather before him.

"It is true that Noach is also my father," he thought, *"as we are all descended from him. But he is so old now. We have grown up hearing about his adventures and the discoveries he has made. What amazing stories he had to share. But what could he want of me?"*

Musing on these things and with some trepidation he walked

into the entryway of a two storey stone and mud brick dwelling close to the market square in the centre of the town. Here, a servant or some member of its household greeted him and spoke kindly to him, seeking to put him at ease. "Come this way up these stairs," the man said. "The master told me to bring you to him as soon as you arrived."

As the traveller entered the room he was shown into, he saw a tall heavyset man standing before a large window. He was silhouetted against the setting sun while looking out over the small settlement. The immediate impression on the traveller was how strong and tall he looked and his long white hair was even whiter than what he had imagined from stories he had been told. As Noah turned to face him he was awed by the greatness of the man, his piercing blue eyes that for such an old man still held a youthful alertness and sense of adventure coupled with great wisdom and knowledge. Now so old yet none of his stature appeared to have diminished. His presence was inspiring.

"Come in, come in my son. Don't be shy. Sit down here and have a drink with me. Here are some breads, cheese, dates and sweet-meats also, the fruit of the vine and field."

They sat on comfortable divans facing each other. Noah smiled as he said, "I have heard much about you and your father from his grandfather and his forbears as they have been great men of God who uphold the truth and are dedicated followers of Elohim our Creator. They have all at times been a great help to me. You are all my sons. Everyone alive today is my son or daughter and I am the only person in the world who can say that," he chuckled.

"It is a great honour to meet you my lord, I have learnt much about you."

"Yes, yes I suppose I must expect that. We have achieved much over the years. Many years have gone by now," he said reflectively.

"But you are wondering why I have summoned you?"

"Yes I was, as was my father who sends you his humble respect and esteem."

"Thank you and you must return his blessing with my blessing when you return to him.

"I have walked with Adonai our Lord nearly nine hundred years. There is much to remember and share with all those who follow me. I have heard of your father but never met him. Is he a God fearing man and you? Are you, my son?"

"Well lord, we respect your, I mean yes we try to do as God would have us do."

"Mmm I see, yes, that is hopeful. Adonai still speaks to me though not as much as he used to. I have made a few errors in my life as we all do and learn from them. None of us are perfect, none of us are as good as He would have us be. I am an old man, a very old man. I suspect now that no one else will live as long as I have. I have seen this new world decline as the years go by and those that are born each generation are not as strong or live as long as the previous generations. Although Shaddai the Almighty gave us a second chance I fear mankind has already failed him once again. Therefore we must do what we can to obey Him and live righteously as examples for the generations that follow however long that might be."

"I agree," murmured the traveller politely, although rather perplexed with what he was thinking were the musings of an old man and consequently not reflecting total agreement.

"This village is not my home. I live far away to the west now, by the sea, on a great peninsula of land. I came by ship to Ty here. We have spread throughout the world in just a few hundred years. I am returning to the lands hereabout, I suppose as a sort of pilgrimage, no doubt for the last time. Here in this very town, a while after we left the Ark, I inscribed our story on the stone pillar that stands in the centre of the square as I did in other villages in these lands. All my voyages in this new world started from here.

"Indeed I have a story to tell you, but that is for later. Meantime, no doubt you are wondering why you are here?"

"Yes I was, I …"

"I intend to go on a journey," interrupted Noah, "and I want to take you with me because I have a task for you."

"Of course I will do what you wish, my lord, but I am rather curious as to what you want me to do," replied the traveller, feeling rather perplexed by what Noah had said.

All he learnt from Noah in response, however, was "Yes, of course, all in good time it will be revealed to you. You are not the only one I have summoned here. In fact, there will be several others who will travel with us. I trust that when you meet them you will be impressed by them. We all belong to the same family, though I doubt you have met any of them before. My hope is that this journey will have a significant impact on you now and for the future, as, indeed, it may well have on all of us. Please don't be unsettled by what I am telling you, having come all this way, when the reason I summoned you here is not really about you but someone else.

He continued, "You do not fully understand yet, but some of the reason for the journey will be revealed to you tomorrow when we gather together. The rest of the reason is at its end. Meantime, stay here with me tonight as my guest. My assistant will show you where you may sleep."

‡‡‡

The village standing on the shore of the great Western Sea had developed into the port of Ty, which serviced all the lands to the east that traded with all those so far inhabited to the north, south and west. Noah had arrived in Ty just seven days earlier on one of his ships, bringing with him several of his household attendants, scribes and other volunteers. All of them were men, since the journey they undertook was deemed by Noah to be very demanding as he shared his fears with them. Consequently none of the younger women elected to accompany their men. It was typical of him that he would not permit them to do anything beyond what they were capable and comfortable with. Nor did he intend that all those who came with him to Ty would be part of the expedition he was about to embark on, because some would be needed to stay in Ty and trade the cargo of the ship they arrived on for the spices and other delicacies not available in Noah's homeland. Once this cargo was loaded and taken back to his estate they would return again several weeks later to take him home once more.

On arrival in Ty Noah purchased a number of domesticated camels and donkeys to carry his belongings and those of his attendants on their intended journey, as well as several horses for them to ride on. He also bought enough supplies for the needs of the entire party to cover the many weeks his intended journey would take. Three days later Noah also left three men at the port to trade and organise the loading of the ship's cargo, then, gathering together the rest of his retinue, he made his way to the inn at the centre of the town on Ty's main trade route to the east. Having found accommodation here for himself and his personal attendants he could now look forward to the gathering he had decided was necessary. He was now ready for the important message he had for all the men he had summoned to meet him.

Meanwhile three aged men stood by the well that was just a few cubits from a large stone pillar in the centre of the village. Their heads were not bent in prayer or reverence but in close conversation, looking, to any observer, as if they did not want any of the people in the market place to overhear what they were talking about. They were not discussing anything illegal or secret, it was simply the way the three brothers had talked together for much of their lives. Often together and never far apart in their younger days, now they seldom saw one another. They had each arrived in Ty from different directions over the past three days and were glad to see each other again after such a long separation. In fact it had been almost ten years since they had all been together in the same place.

Two other men nearby were similarly in deep conversation. One was a distinguished man and the other his grandson. Both were mature men, yet it would be hard to say which was the older or younger. Another man who looked a little younger than the other two stood near them but did not take part in their conversation as he was admiring or reading the inscriptions on the pillar. These three had also arrived separately in the village in the last two days.

Yet another group of men who had just arrived were also standing apart from the rest, two of whom were not talking but watching what was happening around them. And two others with darker features than the rest of the men were laughing together, obviously brothers as they looked remarkably alike. All these men seemed to have come together for some purpose, but were waiting for someone or something to occur.

One man in the first group asked his two companions whether they had any idea why their father had summoned them all here. A second member of the group, a man called Japheth replied, "I have no idea. It's unlike him not to greet us when we arrived. All he said was to meet at this well by the pillar today. But he did add that we are going on a journey of many weeks, so come prepared."

"I hope it's not another sea voyage," the third member of the group, a man called Ham said in exasperation, "which is quite likely since we are meeting here at the old port. Then again, it may be something inland. It better be important for him to have gathered us all here at this time, for we all have come a long way."

"We can count on one thing though," Japheth added, "He's always full of surprises."

"When father speaks or summons us we have learnt over the

years that it's quite likely to be something significant," said Shem, the originator of the conversation, as they all turned and saw the imposing figure of Noah, their father and patriarch, walking towards them.

With a broad smile on his face and his arms outstretched as if to embrace the entire group of ten men, Noah walked toward his offspring, looking like a youthful man of fifty years, rather than one of nearly nine hundred. "Greetings, my sons and grandsons and great grandsons and more, welcome, welcome," he said. "Come, let us go to my lodgings and the place I have prepared for us to meet. We have a lot to talk about."

"Yes father, but why…? a bemused Ham asked impatiently.

"All in good time Ham, all in good time," Noah replied.

Entering together into Noah's lodgings the men congregated in the large room with drapes at the windows immediately inside the entrance. It was carpeted with woven rugs, and oil lamps hung from the ceiling to give light later in the evening. Divans and cushions were scattered about with small tables laden with fruit, breads and wine, giving the room a comfortable, welcoming feeling. It was clearly a warm place to gather and relax in and encourage everyone to be at ease and feel free to speak their minds. This was clearly the very thing Noah desired. Setting the scene, he hugged each one in turn and so did all the others, greeting one another and slapping backs as families do when they know someone well. Only Ham and his sons were more reserved than the others.

As for the traveller, chatting to one of the attendants preparing the food and drink, he was overawed when he saw all the others enter the room at the same time. He stood there as a surprised and uninvolved spectator, watching this camaraderie taking place before him. No one apparently was aware of his presence, and he realised they were all quite a lot older than him.

After a short time to allow the initial pleasantries and making fun of each other to die away and still wondering what this meeting was all about, the loud conversations faded away into silence. All eyes were turned to Noah, waiting for him to address these men who were his family. He stood there for a time, pausing before speaking, looking over the faces of the group of men in front of him. Friends, family members and acquaintances had got used to him doing this when he had something significant to say. Then he called forward his three immediate sons, and even though they looked almost as old as he was, it was as if he was calling up his young boys to be presented to him. They came forward and stood beside their father, though it was clear that Ham was somewhat reluctant to do this.

"Japheth, Shem, Ham, I have called you all here to this place and asked you to invite your sons and their sons, but not your wives to this particular gathering, even though they are important, because none of us would be here without them. We shall meet with them later. I did not expect of course that everyone could come, but I am glad that those of you that could have done so. Perhaps some others will still join us. You all know each other of course, some better than others, and there is at least one other you have not met before. We are family, although we are now greatly spread abroad. I will speak to you all presently as to why I have called you, but for the benefit of our youngest member who is standing behind you and who you all supposed was one of the helpers I will now introduce him to you all."

They turned as one and looked at the traveller whom many had indeed thought was a mere attendant and had therefore simply ignored him. Noah then said for the benefit of the traveller, "This is Japheth my eldest son on my right, with Ham my youngest and Shem who has had the least distance to travel. Also on my right we have Arpachshad, Shem's third born son and Eber his grandson. Then Peleg, Eber's son. Over here we have Gomer, Japheth's eldest and Ashchenaz, Gomer's son. On this side are Cush and Mizraim, two of Ham's sons. Don't they both look so very alike?"

"So who is the goat herder at the back?" asked Ham rudely.

Sighing in exasperation at Ham's discourtesy Noah introduced the traveller. "This is Tarah from the land of Shinar." He then explained how he was related to the gathering. He also mentioned the many grandsons and daughters and their sons and daughters that were not here and just how large the family had become in only three generations, let alone the rest of the family of those not present.

"And Tarah is not a goat herder but a builder," continued Noah, "of some repute I have heard. Now enough of introductions. Let us all eat and drink and be merry. I am sure you have many tales to tell each other. Tonight after supper I will explain why we are all here. Be patient. I hope you will give me the honour of listening to what I have to say later and acting on it." Thus they mingled and chatted together in an amicable way for the rest of the morning.

"I have a bad feeling about this," grumbled Ham to his brothers.

"Oh Ham, let it go, said Shem. We know you have had your differences with father, but I thought we had put all that behind us. He may not be with us much longer. We three may not be long behind him either. People are dying younger in this world than they did in the old world before the flood. Give him the respect he deserves, as he has given us so much. I am sure what he has to say is important and no doubt has something to do with the future."

"You are showing your wisdom and perception again my brother Shem," said Japheth as he patted Shem's shoulder in approval and encouragement.

For the rest of the morning and early afternoon the men conversed together, argued over trivial matters as only they knew how to do and spent time in the market looking at the goods being traded that had come from literally every direction of the known world. After a siesta during the hotter part of the afternoon the attendants prepared a banquet to which the group settled down in the early evening.

As they were about to partake of their supper three more family members turned up at the meeting place, having arrived that afternoon and camped outside the village with all the others. Joktan, son of Eber, Madai and Javan, two sons of Japheth were introduced to the group as they caught up with their immediate siblings, cousins and fathers. Now there were fifteen in the family gathering. Once they were welcomed everyone continued their banquet and one another's company.

Merry with wine, much of which had come from Noah's own vineyards, and full of good food, the men settled themselves down comfortably and waited for Noah to share what was on his heart. They knew it would take him a long time to do this and they could be there well into the night.

Noah eventually rose from where he was sitting and held his arms out in a gesture to quieten the gathering. Once again he paused until there was complete silence.

"My sons," he stated, "I can call all of you my sons, and as I often say and reflect on everyone alive today, they are all my sons and daughters for which I am very proud. We are gathered here for two reasons. I asked you all to come and be prepared for many weeks away from your home and families. A few of you of course have brought your wives, and tomorrow we shall have another feast in their honour in Shem's camp outside the village. But tonight it is a gathering of only the men. More may join us later and I hope so.

"Tomorrow, as I have just said, we will gather with the rest of those who accompanied you, and on the next day we will start out on an extended journey. This includes all of us, or at least as many as wish to come. I will not force anyone to do this, but I hope you will all come. It may very well be the most important journey you have made or will ever make, for I will endeavour to impart to you the care and responsibility you face in your future lives as we continue to repopulate this new world.

"I will tell you where we are headed in due course, but before that the second reason I called you here, I would like each of you, Ham, Japheth and finally Shem to address us. Everything we speak of here tonight and over the days and weeks to come will be recorded. I have brought three scribes and between them we should have a good account of what we discuss and decide. I want you to tell us briefly of your settlements and where you have decided to concentrate your dynasties. For dynasties they are, your destiny. All the earth will flourish and be populated from your loins. Come, tell us what is on your hearts, each one of you."

As Ham was rising from where he reclined on a camel hair sofa, there was a shout at the main door and everyone turned round to see what commotion heralded this interruption.

"Oh, it's you Ludim," chuckled Ham, "late as usual, but then I suppose you have had the furthest to travel. Come in my boy and get some refreshments, and go sit by your father while I expound our destiny as Noach would have me do."

Acknowledging Noah, his patriarch and great grandfather, Ludim hugged his immediate family, greeted his cousins and uncles, then took some food and wine and sat between his father Mizraim and Cush his uncle. The room hushed once again as Ham prepared to speak.

"It has been many years since we left the Ark and settled in our first village not too far from here and there raised our children. My good wife Nae did not come with me this time. Yes, Nae, my dark haired beauty has been a good wife and I have greatly appreciated all she has given me. She stayed here near Ty while my brothers and I went on our first great sea voyage together with our good seaman father and Patriarch Noach, not complaining that we were absent for such a long time. I could be here all night telling about that voyage, but something tells me that will be the prerogative of the great man himself to share with us. I acknowledge you, father, for what you have achieved, what we all achieved together. It is no secret that you and I have had some differences, but again I will not go into that and leave you to speak on that if you so desire.

"Most of us here are old men and for many years now have walked this new land. There are only four in this room who knew the old world. We have come far in this new world, and I am proud of what has been achieved by establishing villages and small tribes in many places. After all, the vast expanse of this world is for everyone to explore and populate. Long ago my brothers and I decided where we would seek to plant our roots.

"I chose the southern lands, especially the large peninsula to the south and the great continent beyond. It is a vast area with much fertile land, rivers, lakes, mountains and great forests. Many animals both wild and domesticated have established themselves there. In fact, I might say it is the closest to the Old World in climate, with similar vegetation and an abundance of animals exceeding those I have seen anywhere else, although I admit that Noach and Japheth have seen more of this world than I have. Ha! Folks are even now calling it 'The Land of Ham.'

"Cush and Mizraim have already established settlements along the great river that runs from the south into the great sea. Ludim, who has just joined us, has come from far to the north of that land along the coast of the Western Sea. Put is another son, and his tribe has settled there too.

"Having stated that, as I said, it is not our intention to live only in those lands. Canaan, my other son, has established himself elsewhere. In fact, Canaan's lands are just south of where we sit. So why is he not here when he lives close by?"

At this point Ham looked over to Noah who raised his eyebrows and nodded in a silent message they both understood.

"Again I must state," Ham continued, "that our family have different views and beliefs to some of you. We will not discuss them here tonight, but Noach has indicated that he will speak about them in due course. You should understand this is the reason Canaan cannot be here with us. Neither unfortunately can Nimrod, my grandson and son of Cush, for similar reasons."

"I wait with anticipation father Noach for what you have to share with us. If you want honesty and openness, which I have come to learn this is what you expect of a man, then I have my doubts that I will agree with you. My sons will make up their own minds. I am also intrigued as to where this expedition you talk of will take us. Again, I will not promise to follow until I have heard you out. That is all I have to say for now."

"Thank you Ham for your summary and your honesty. I do appreciate that," replied Noah.

There was further talk as the group reflected on Ham's words, but when Japheth got up to speak the room quietened once again.

"Father Noach, brothers, sons and nephews it is good to see you all again," he began. "I am glad to be here. I appreciate your last words my brother Ham and understand your view of life. We must acknowledge that there will be differences among us because it is what we are and how Adonai made us. We are different because we each have a unique personality, again no doubt as evidence of the beauty of creation, who we are and what we may become. We are all sons of the same God, yet we have free choice and this freedom enables us to decide our destinies. I understand Ham's view, yet I also appreciate my brother Shem's view as well and respect our father's view of life too. I suppose I take a middle ground and do not wish to see conflict among us. We should endeavour to live in harmony. There is plenty of land for us to occupy. We don't need to squabble and fight over this piece of land or that river, nor whether there is one God or what spiritual forces guide and control us. Let our consciences decide our disputes I say.

"As many of you know I have inherited the adventurous spirit of our father and have travelled further than any of you in this new world. So I look forward in anticipation of what adventure you have in store for us this time father. I know we will not be disappointed when we learn from you what it is. I have already explored far and wide. Sometimes it was on my own together with my wife Adataneses who is always by my side, at other times with my brothers, or the grand voyage I made with father and Shem, and, of course, the latest voyage father and I took together with my sons and grandsons. I have even explored further overland to the north and east with them as well. So I have a larger view than most about how to populate and create settlements in this world.

"To that end, our immediate family have in recent years populated the lands hereabout where we started this new life. We will happily dwell with you Shem, and also Ham and your descendants. We must mix and multiply to continue the integrity of our human race. Beyond that I would wish my descendants to settle in new lands to the north, west and east. There are abundant lands not only in the northwest but also to the east waiting to be populated, and beyond them is another great ocean with many islands.

"We know that because we have been there already. I could speak of the three major voyages we have made, but I perceive that my father wishes to speak about this so I will not elaborate further. The heritage I leave after this life is for my descendants to establish new lands to all corners of this world. Gomer who is sitting here with us and Ashkenaz have also established themselves to the north. Magog, Madai and Javan are to the north and east. Others of their offspring are nearby and also to the south.

"Like Ham I also give credit to my beautiful wife Ada who no doubt is at this very moment in the camp outside the village discussing with Shem's wife the failings of their menfolk and why they need to keep reminding us of our shortcomings, even in our old age. Ada has been an enormous help to me and all of us, and we could never have achieved what we have without her help."

As they consumed more wine the men became more relaxed, and a cheer went up from them as they raised their goblets in praise of Japheth's speech as he took his seat again.

"Thank you Japheth," said Noah. "Yes, you have been a great companion to me and your brothers. You were always the one who encouraged us to go beyond the next headland to see what was there when we were happy to stop where we were. Many new discoveries were made because of your desire to go that much further. I will speak of our travels again shortly. Shem?"

As Shem got up to speak the room became quiet once again. "What would we do without our good wives," he said, smiling, as he swept his arm over the gathering. "None of you would be here without them. I wish to honour both you, father Noach, and also our mother who suffered and toiled and held us all together. I honestly believe without her input in our younger lives and the way she brought us up we would never have achieved what we did in the Ark and in establishing this new civilization and raising our own families."

Nodding his head, Noah interrupted him. "Well said Shem, well said. You are quite right. Your mother has been an inspiration for us all. I have much to say about her, but please continue."

"Sede, my wife, has certainly been an inspiration to me and I am sure my sons agree. Even though I was your second born son, whether it was by God's design or because father was stricter with me, I have from a very young age followed his lead and his beliefs and I have to say like him I am a devoted follower of Shaddai, the Almighty God. No, I am not going to preach, but I simply want to state where I stand. I believe that whatever our Patriarch Noach, our Priest of God, which he is, whatever he says to us tonight and the purpose of this journey before us will be significant. I have no doubt it will be as if God himself is speaking through him to us."

This occasioned a quiet murmur of discontent from Ham's group.

"Yet, as Japheth has stated, and I liked what he said very much, we must put our differences aside at least for tonight and the days ahead and learn to live together even when we think differently. We need to respect each other's worldview and not try to change one another, but I encourage you all to seek God, be true to your walk with him, yet respect each person's various views.

"As for me and my sons, their families and those that are born already, we have sought to settle in these lands from where we first began again in this new world, mostly in the land of Shinar. I have settled close by in Shalem, Arphaxad, Eber, Peleg and Joktan, you have all settled close by or in Shinar, as has our builder over there. Elam, my first born, and Asshur likewise live to the east and Lud and Aram my younger sons have settled to the north of here. However, like Ham and Japheth, no doubt many of their descendants will seek to find new lands to settle in, and I will fully support them in that.

"I look forward to where you plan to take us father. Like Japheth said, we are not likely to be disappointed. I also perceive that this will be a journey of some significance, and I have the feeling you may very well be going to talk about everything that has gone before."

"Wise words my son Shem, and yes, you are very perceptive as always," said Noah. "Thank you for your kind words on my behalf.

"Now I will not keep you here all night as I suspect some of you thought I might. What I have to say will be brief. Well, brief enough. You will return to your beds in good time I promise you.

It was my intention to have each of you speak first, Japheth, Shem and Ham, so that as I hoped you would set before us the outline of what I wanted to share and the purpose of the journey ahead. What I am saying is not just the musings of a very old man, but is really the very essence of what lies before you and describes what you have already achieved.

"I now have some sobering words for all of you. They are not for discussion here and now, but are for you to carefully consider as you make your way back to your camps tonight, tomorrow and the days ahead. Keep your questions and arguments until we are on our journey, but listen to me now.

"We are going to the Ark!"

TWO

Noah's Discourse

It took Noah quite a few minutes to quieten down the bubble of excitement in reaction to his announcement, but eventually the men did settle down and there was silence again as Noah continued.

"I see that got a reaction I didn't expect. I'm not sure what I expected, to tell you the truth. But yes, the Ark. It gave us a new life, the chance to begin again. It's now many years since we came out of her, and relatively speaking we were not in her very long compared to the years before and after the flood she brought us through.

"I believe it will be a worthwhile experience for those of you who have not seen the Ark to view it before it disappears, and also for the four of us to visit it once more. I'm sure your families and the people you have with you will enjoy seeing it for the first time. I hope you will all come. I am sending messages to those of us who are not here that they may still join us, because the journey to it will be a long one, seeing there are so many of us, and so they will have ample time to meet up with us.

"I don't know how much longer Adonai will give me on this earth, so at this time of my life I want to share my story, earth's story, mankind's story with you. I've now lived longer than any of you, and possibly even longer than men or women will live in future. This is why I've gathered you together my sons, all of you, to hear my words. So listen to what I have to say, take note, remember and pass on the truth of what I'm telling you to your descendants. Let these words of mine be told continually down through the ages and never forgotten. To that end I've not been idle these past few years. I've done a lot more than just making wine.

"I've transcribed the words of Enoch, my father Lamech's grandfather, who first wrote down on animal hides and tablets the creation story and the history of mankind from the beginning. And I've added my story from his time to now. I have written it using this revised language that Eber and Peleg have fashioned since the languages were confused, what do you call it? Eberu, isn't it?"

"Yes, my lord," Peleg replied. "We call it that in honour of our father who first composed it. It's what we call an aleph-bet after the names of the first two characters in it."

Eber nodded in agreement with his son's explanation.

"I think it serves us well," said Noah. "I find it's much easier using these lines and scripts than a lot of pictures and symbols. That's what I've done, or at least what my scribes have done. We've made four copies of this extensive work on these deer and calf skin scrolls I have here, one each for you Shem, Ham and Japheth. Take them with you tonight. I will hand over the fourth one at the end of the journey. You in turn must make copies and give these to your sons and daughters and all those who will follow. That way the world to come will know where they originated and how we all started this great adventure called life.

"As we gather together collectively each evening on our way to the Ark I will speak to all of you and expand on what is in these scrolls and more. It will be an account of my life's journey so to speak, explaining all that happened before the flood since Enoch walked the earth, then the times of the end of the old world, the building of the Ark and the arrival of the great flood. I will continue with our time spent on the Ark and the years since, when we have been building and replenishing this new world. This will be my story, but from time to time I will also allow my sons to share some of their experiences if they wish. When we reach the Ark we will hold a dedication of it to Elohim and build another altar as we did at the beginning and thank him for where he has brought us to.

"I hope you will all come on this journey with me. It may well be long and hard at times, but I believe that everyone here will gain something worthwhile from it. For one thing, you will know where the Ark is, so that you can show it to friends and family who have never seen it, and they in turn may do the same for others still, and in this way its story will never be forgotten. Our journey together will end at the Ark and you can then go your own ways. I shall return here to Ty and thence to my home estate. I will give each of you a blessing as you leave, for I may never see you again."

Noah then spoke what was on his heart to them before finishing with a final statement.

"I wish to add at this time that the importance of what I say is in this. Before the flood Elohim spoke to me and warned me of God's judgment coming on mankind. Now, today, he has spoken to me again and given me a vision of what is to come. He impressed upon me the need to share this important message with all of you and anyone else who will listen to what I have to say. So pay attention to me my sons, for your destiny depends upon it. But that is all I will say to you tonight."

Once again there was a hubbub of agitated voices. Many were obviously excited about the journey ahead and seeing the Ark again or for the first time. Others were unsure and wondering if the next several weeks could not be better spent working in their villages. But in the finish there was the realisation by all that here was an opportunity to embark on a journey they might never have the chance to get again. So eventually all decided to make the journey with Noah, and some were even enthusiastic about doing so.

As they continued to discuss all this Shem approached Noah,

"Father," he said, "this is a good thing you are doing and I am with you wholeheartedly on this venture. It seems pretty clear that you have something very important to impart to us."

"Thank you Shem," said Noah, "I knew I could count on you. I believe Japheth will be likeminded. But I'm concerned about Ham because of everything that has happened in the past as you know. I can only trust that this journey may be a turning point for him, but we'll have to wait and see how it turns out."

Looking toward the traveller, Shem added, "Why is Tarah here? He's several generations younger than us, while you have gathered just the first three generations since the Ark."

"I'll tell you Shem, but it's just between you and me for the moment."

Noah then outlined to Shem what the purpose of specifically inviting Tarah was.

"But what has …"

"Yes, Shem, I know. I don't understand it all myself but I am bound as I always have been to follow Adonai's instructions."

"But father, don't you know that although this man and his father are in my bloodline they are idolaters! They don't follow Adonai. They are part of this dreadful new moon-god cult. I believe he is responsible for making terephim idols and selling them. I've seen these awful things myself!"

"I know, Shem, and that's exactly why I've invited him. Hopefully this journey will steer him away from such nonsense and prepare him for what is to come."

"But why would God do such a thing as you say for an idolater?"

"And haven't I asked Adonai the same question Shem? Many times. I don't understand it myself. But as we have learned these many years, the Lord does things that we do not understand and uses men and women for his purposes whom we would never have chosen. No, I am certain Elohim has shown me that this man will precede something significant in the future of the world. As we journey to the Ark it may become clearer to both of us why God has chosen him, yet I feel sure it is not Tarah himself who is chosen but some other person."

"You are quite right father, God's ways are not our ways."

Suddenly there was a small earthquake that shook the building and subsided quickly afterwards.

Noah clapped his hands and brought the room back to his attention.

"We are so used to these earthquakes, but they seem to be receding as the years go by. Let's not dwell on them for now. We have a lot to do and think about in preparation for our journey, my sons. I've said enough for tonight. Now you need to all go back to your camps, get a good night's rest and tomorrow start preparing for our journey. I'll come again in the evening and address everyone at Shem's camp.

"Tomorrow at mid-morning I want you to select a member from each of your camps to come here to me and we'll draft a plan for the journey. I've brought plenty of supplies in my ship, but there are many things you'll need to get ready before we start out. I expect we'll leave the day after tomorrow. Go now, and God be with you."

Gradually each of the three family groups broke up and made their way back to their respective camps. This left the attendants at the meeting to start clearing away and tidying up before they too took their rest. Before he did this as well Tarah approached Noah and Shem with a question.

"Lord, what you are planning is noble, and I look forward to the journey ahead. However, you did say to me that tonight you would reveal why you specifically summoned me. You told me you had a job for me to do."

"Yes, I have. I would like you to take charge of the camels, donkeys and other livestock on the expedition. My servants and attendants will be at your service to assist you."

"But lord, I am a builder, I don't know anything about animals. I have only been in charge of men."

"My father Lamech," replied Noah, "told me long ago when I was old enough to work on my own and wanted to explore the sea, that I needed to gain experience in other areas first. So he sent me on a trek with other young men inland, far away from the sea. He was satisfied this would give me necessary experience before I tackled the great ocean. So you see, although I appreciate you are much older than I was, when my father instructed me, I am giving you an opportunity to extend your horizons."

"I see sir, I think," murmured the puzzled traveller. Then he added, "Well, actually I'm not so sure. You asked me to come just to look after the animals?"

"Ah no, of course not," added Noah. "There is another reason, and I will tell you what it is since I promised to do so last night."

Noah then outlined to Tarah why he had specifically invited him, although he did not reveal as much to him as he had to Shem. He knew that he would not reveal this further reason until much later in their journey.

As for Tarah, he was not at all sure he understood what was required of him as he thought over what Noah had said to him, turning away to go up to his room.

'Perhaps tomorrow after a good sleep and in the days ahead it will become clear to me,' he thought.

He then turned back as Noah addressed him once more.

"Only you, Shem, and I know what I have just told you Tarah," said Noah. "Do not share this with anyone else until the end of our journey. I trust you have enjoyed yourself tonight and met some of your, ah, elder relatives."

"Yes lord," he replied, "there is a lot to take in. I hope I will do you the honour of achieving what you have set before me."

As Tarah left them, Noah put his right arm over Shem's shoulder.

"I have a word for you also my son. Not tonight but at the end of this journey I will have a blessing for you along with Ham and Japheth as well of course. Sleep well. God has great things for you I know." At that Shem made his departure.

Noah, alone now, looked over the meeting room lit solely by the light of the moon descending to the west and casting slivers of light through the open windows across the room with its floor rugs, previously so full of activity, laughter and talk from his progeny, but now so quiet as he contemplated what he had shared and what he knew in his heart lay before him.

'Life was never meant to be easy,' he mused to himself and then prayed, *'What trials and tribulations will you put before me on this journey O Adonai, I pray for a safe, uneventful and receptive family journey. Will I gain their trust, will they accept what I say? Yes Lord, I know what you would say to me – "Say what I give you to say, it is up to them to receive it. You Noach are not responsible for their unbelief."*

"So be it Lord," Noah said out loud.

At that moment as Noah was about to go up the stairs to his sleeping quarters the front door of the house was slammed back on its hinges and a desperate man burst into the darkened room, panting to catch his breath as he had been running.

"My lord," he gasped, "I come from Ham's camp. He sent me to you. A man there has been stabbed!"

The Journey Begins

Noah looked at the wretched man standing before him. He had been so desperate to convey Ham's message to Noah that he had neglected to put his sandals on and had run the whole way barefoot.

"Calm down my man, tell me what happened," a tired and exasperated Noah asked him.

"They found him beyond the camp when one of the men went to relieve himself, my master. He was lying in his blood groaning and could not get up."

"So he is still alive? Do they know who did this?"

"Yes sir, he is alive, but only just. The women are tending to him. We don't know yet who did this, no, my lord."

"Very well. Thank you for letting me know. Tell Ham to send someone when it is light with any further news and let me know if they want me to come. Otherwise, I am sure Ham is capable of deciding what needs to be done."

"Thank you my lord." With that the man ran back to Ham's camp and Noah went on up to his bed.

The sun rose in the morning's early mist, which soon disappeared as the warm rays beat down on the dry and dusty ground for yet another day. No one came from Ham's camp to inform Noah of any further word regarding the injured man. However, just after sunrise a traveller passing through the village gave him a message.

At mid-morning Arpachshad, Gomer and Cush, representatives of the three camps of Shem, Japheth and Ham respectively, together with Ada, Japheth's wife, Tarah and Noah sat down together in the room where they had met in the previous evening to discuss what additional requirements needed to be arranged for the expedition ahead and what part each member needed to play for the journey to be successfully accomplished. Acknowledging each person in turn, Noah then began by asking about the events of the late evening before.

"First of all Cush, what is the situation with the stabbed man?"

"Ah, he will live, but we won't be able to take him with us. He has lost a lot of blood and is very weak. We'll leave him here in the care of some local women and pick him up on the way back. It's a setback, because he is a good strong worker. We could have done with his skills."

"You can perhaps hire a local man to take his place."

"Yes, Ham is looking for a man right now."

"Do you have any idea what happened, who, and why?"

"None, and neither does he. The man went out to relieve himself, just like the fellow who found him. He was grabbed from behind, felt a sharp pain in his side and then blacked out. He didn't wake up until our man arrived to help him and never saw anyone as it was too dark. He was not robbed of anything. It's a real mystery."

"Not good," said Noah. "But all seems to be under control. Now we need to work out what further supplies we require and what all of you will be responsible for. We need to know what each camp has on hand and I will tell you what I have brought with me. We can, of course, barter and hunt for food on the way and there are many places to obtain water so we won't have to carry everything from here. We should have plenty of extra camels, horses and donkeys in addition to what you have all brought to carry us and our supplies."

"Now, you men, you think you have it all worked out," interrupted Ada, "You don't see things as women do. You need some female input."

"Haha, I am so glad you are coming Ada dear, your fiery spirit is what we need to keep the lads in line."

"Mmm!" she mused. "There are six women in this group amongst all you men. I will take charge of their needs. Also, we will organise the meals collectively. I assume Noach, dear, that you wish our evening meal to be a communal one?"

"Yes I do, I ..."

"Right, so leave that to me and Sede. We will also take care of the domestic chores, as we usually do," she sighed.

"Thank you Adataneses, I very much appreciate that," Noah added more formally.

"Now the rest of you..." Turning to Tarah he said, "You are taking charge of the camels and pack animals with the help of the attendants. Make sure they are corralled or secure every night and get plenty of food and water. We will have enough animals, so you can give one or two of them a rest from carrying a load for a day. Give each a rest in turn. I'll ask Joktan to look after the horses, since they require special treatment."

"I'm looking forward to the challenge," said Tarah.

"I'll take charge of setting up the camp with tents and shelters each night grandfather," offered Gomer.

"Yes, good, Gomer, but make sure everyone pitches in to help. That's an everyman job."

"Cush, would you take charge of security and hunting please. Keep us supplied with fresh game for the meat eaters amongst us. Make sure the party is safe at all times, scout ahead and round the sides. There are not only natural hazards and wild animals, but sadly there are brigands and others who would like to rob us. I have an uneasy feeling all may not go well on this journey. No one is to mention that to the others though."

"Happy to do that," replied Cush gruffly.

"That leaves you Arpachshad to be in charge of all supplies. Make sure we don't run short, and advise Cush when they need to hunt for food. Work with Ada and the women. You can organise bartering with villages we meet on the way. All the goods I have brought are at your disposal."

"With pleasure, grandfather," answered Arpachshad.

Later that afternoon another message arrived for Noah by a caravan passing through the village.

In the evening the men and women and a few younger people, none of whom were under fifteen, who had come with their families all gathered at Shem and Sede's camp. There was quite a throng now with the extra family members, attendants and other staff. After a generous supper of breads, fruit, some meat and other delicacies together with plentiful wine, the group of 42 people sat around as comfortably as they could to listen to Noah address them as he said he would.

Eber and three assistant scribes sat close to Noah to capture what he said, as they would continue to do with every important discourse he gave during the journey. Their task was to transcribe his words on to parchment made of animal skins. For it was essential to keep for posterity what Noah had to say, and for it to be added to the scrolls already written, so that later generations would know the truth of bygone times.

"It is good to see you all here tonight," Noah began. "I am sure that by the end of this journey some of you will have forged close relationships that will last you a lifetime. I am glad there are some young people here too. It's a very good thing, because I want you all to share what we experience on this journey with as many people as you can in future."

He paused as he usually did and looked over the group before him. He let his gaze rest briefly on each face in turn as if he was remembering each one and speaking to each individually all at the same time. There were a group of three, however, who avoided his gaze and whom he did not recognize.

"A man was stabbed last night," he began, "this is not a good thing. It is a very bad example of what this new world has become in such a short time. It was never meant to be this way. Once long ago there was no anger, misery, sickness or death, and that is the way Elohim meant it to be.

"You all know the creation story, which I have already written down in some detail on the scrolls I have given each of you my sons, so I will not speak of that tonight. Only to say that on the seventh day Elohim rested from his work of creation, and right there at the beginning he instituted a day of rest and so should we. Work six days, and rest for one. In our expedition we will journey six days and rest on the seventh. On that day we should honour our Lord.

"May I ask a question?" ventured Tarah, feeling more relaxed and a little bolder in this large family group.

"Certainly, my son."

"I have noticed as you speak of God you often use different names for him, why is that?"

"Everything I say to you on this journey is true and for your insight and edification. These are the names of God or if you like His attributes, His very reason for being and the reason he created mankind was in order that he could manifest all these attributes toward his people, his creation. He is El Shaddai, God Almighty, all knowing, all powerful and everywhere present. Adonai, Elohim, Lord God, Creator and Father. And we are his sons and daughters, and he dwells within each one of us by His Spirit if we let him. He is the very beginning of all things and will be with us to the last. He was at the beginning and is and always will be. He who guides us, teaches and corrects us. He is all these things and more. He is all things to all people throughout the earth. Remember well everything I say."

Many simply stared amazed at the profound authority Noah gave to these words. Others were nodding in agreement, and still others shaking their heads in unbelief. Noah saw them all.

"Each night when we come together like this I will tell you more of my, no, our journey through life. No doubt you thought I was going to preach to you again tonight. Yes, I can see it on some of your faces," he laughed, "but no, I have a lot to talk about over the weeks ahead and that's enough for tonight. Have you all prepared yourselves for the journey ahead?"

A murmur of assent rippled through the group.

"Good, this journey will not be easy. There will be hardships that I cannot foresee. You will need to expect the unexpected, but Cush and his team will watch over us and keep us secure. Ada, Sede and the women will deal with the domestic chores and no doubt keep all of us men in line."

A snigger of laughter from the men followed, but there was a serious nodding of heads from the women.

"Arpachshad will look after the supplies, making sure we have enough water, food and anything else we require. Gomer is in charge of setting up and taking down the camp each day. It will be arranged in a circle for safety from wild animals. Now everyone, and I mean everyone, is to help in that endeavour. Setting up and taking down will be much more efficient and quicker with everyone helping. Tarah, our lone traveller from the east, is in charge of the camels and pack animals. He and the attendants will feed and water the animals at night and see to their safety and needs. Joktan and his crew are taking care of the horses. Are there any questions or suggestions?"

There were one or two which Noah dealt with to their satisfaction. He then outlined where they would be going and points of interest along the way. There was always the chance with a long caravan of many people that a small group could become separated, so it was Noah's concern that they should be able to find their way back to the main group if such a thing happened.

He told them the route they would be taking would start heading north, with the coast of the great sea to their left for the first few days. Then they would travel toward the village of Baalbek, working their way inland. They would cross many hills and valleys, rivers and streams, although at this time of year many of these would be dry beds on which they would travel because they made good pathways. They would pass by small lakes and oases and often be able to rest on the outskirts of villages. Always on the seventh day the whole caravan would be required to rest. And later still, there was the mighty Euphrates River to be crossed followed by skirting a much larger lake and travel into the mountains where the Ark had come to rest.

Noah explained how early that morning and again later today he had received messages from Elam and Asshur, the sons of Shem and Sede, as well as Tubal, another son of Japheth and Ada, who planned to meet the caravan at Baalbek, which should be reached before the end of their first week of travel. They were coming from the direction the caravan was heading, so it was understandable that they would meet with the caravan, at some point, heading in their direction.

He then went on to say, "Much of what we need to do will be revealed to us on the way. We can't think of every contingency at the beginning. Don't worry. Go to your tents now and think about all I have said. Have a good rest. Tomorrow at dawn we head north."

As the people dispersed to their camps and beds in the light of a full moon, Noah approached Ham and Cush. "The incident last night has left you a man short Ham. Cush said you may need to hire another."

"Yes, we have dealt with that," replied Ham. "In fact, we have taken on three to replace him."

"Three?"

"Yes. They are three brothers and all good hunters. They heard what happened and came to the camp about midday. As they were heading north anyway, they offered us their services and they do not wish to be paid. They will simply accompany our group and will leave us at some stage. Cush will add them to his hunting and security party."

At this point Shem and Japheth joined the small group.

"Well, that is rather convenient," said Noah, "a man is violently attacked and immediately there are three who offer to take his place, and who just happen to be handy at attacking and killing? You said your man was stabbed and no one knows why?"

"My thoughts exactly, and I told father as much," added Cush. "I will use them, but I don't trust them. I shall keep a close eye on those three."

"Were they at the gathering tonight?" Noah asked.

"They were briefly," said Cush, "but they were not interested in what you had to say and left soon after you began to speak."

"Were they the three on the extreme left at the back wearing black robes?"

"That's them."

"Is there a problem father?" asked Shem.

"Perhaps," said Noah, "they would not meet my gaze. I feel a storm coming."

"A storm?" queried Ham.

"Trouble ahead in some form. I have a feeling the events of last night may not be the last. We must be careful and watchful. As you know, there are those who oppose many of the things I say or suggest. It's possible someone may wish to interrupt this journey too," sighed a weary Noah.

As they dispersed a light earthquake shook the ground.

The next morning, though they were eager to get away, they

were delayed by one or two things that had to be sorted, but Noah patiently accepted them, knowing from experience that early in a new expedition travel delays often occurred. As the journey proceeded he was confident that they would get into a routine and things would settle down.

At mid-morning they left the outskirts of the village and headed north, Noah in the lead with Shem's camp behind, followed by Japheth and Ham bringing up the rear. The day passed without incident but more slowly than Noah would have liked.

‡‡‡

Later that evening he addressed everyone once again, as he would do almost every night from now on to tell everyone his story.

"And so my children," he began, "I will now take you back to the days of my youth, back to the days before the great flood, where I lived in a land of beauty, where we enjoyed a relatively easy life unlike the harsh environment we have today. Here we struggle to have a life filled with a lot of sweat and tears, contending with an ever changing climate, storms, earthquakes, volcanic mountains as we now call them and all manner of hardships. It was not like that in those days. In fact, it was a very different world.

I will begin with one particular day I remember well as a young man. Our family, father, mother and my brothers and sisters, all of us took a trek up the great hill behind our village simply to enjoy the view and spend some time together."

A wistful look came over Noah's face as he continued, "I remember, it was such a beautiful day …"

FOUR

The Ship

*The Land of Havilah Before the Great Flood
It is the year of the World AM 1080 and that many years
from the time of Creation*

A group of eight persons stood on a rocky outcrop overlooking the valley and river below. The sun was glowing brightly behind a misty haze in the distance. As usual it was not too hot in the middle of the day, and only a slight breeze accompanied the group as they made out features of the landscape below them. After a heavy morning dew the ground nearby had dried out by midday, but in the absence of much wind a cloud of misty vapour still hung over the thick jungle in the distance on the other side of the river.

Springs from within the earth watered these lands, as no rain fell and any lakes and rivers that existed did so from springs of water welling up from inside the earth, as well as the heavy dew of the morning. The river below likewise was fed by springs further up in the distant highlands of this relatively new world. It was beautiful in its simplicity. Light clouds floated high above the coast to the east and west of this vast land, and to the south as far as the eye could see there was nothing but blue sparkling ocean. Here, light clouds brought gentle mist to the coastal areas and sometimes further inland, yet there were vast areas in the centre of this vast continent where no rain fell and the growth of vegetation was dependent solely on the morning dew and many underground springs.

There were no destructive storms in this placid world of gentle breezes, making it a pleasant place to live. Only the higher central area presented any challenge to life. Thus the people of this world enjoyed a rather comfortable existence for quite a long time.

The group watched dozens of birds flitting about. Some were many hued while others were mono coloured. Small lizards and insects scuttled in and out of waist high bushes, and the group of five men and three women were careful not to trample on them as they scampered over and about their feet. A large animal viewed them without alarm from another stone outcrop only a few cubits away. It merely sniffed the air in their direction, turned round slowly and ambled away.

"Oh! Look what a beautiful red and purple butterfly this is," Hebe cried as it rested on her arm.

"It's all beautiful," said Lamech her father and the senior member of the group. "The birds, flowers, bushes, trees and animals are plentiful, and the fruit from the plants and trees is so delicious to eat. Everything here is abundant. The forest canopy is so thick over there we can hardly see the river below in places because the trees are so enormous and their shade covers so much of the ground beneath them. It's simply beautiful to behold."

"Havilah is a lovely land. I wish I could see it all one day," said Hebe as she bounced on her toes and clapped her hands with excitement.

"Well, you have plenty of time to do that," continued Lamech. "You've only just passed your twentieth year, and you, Dinah, are only fifteen, so you both have a great many years ahead of you. When you've lived as long as I have you will have seen as much as there is to see."

"But Papa, you are so old. The other children say that when you get too old you die. When will that happen to you?" asked Dinah.

"Oh my dearest," laughed her father, "I've been on this earth a little over 200 years. Adam our ancestor lived to be 930 years, and Seth, his son, who died not long ago was 912, so I expect I have many more years ahead of me and so do you all."

"Will we all die one day?"

"Yes it appears so. We wonder if Elohim our Creator God meant it to be so, but sadly that's what happens to us eventually. It's the result of the sin of mankind. But even then we will be with Adonai, who has prepared a place for us to go to after we die."

"Will that place be beautiful like this?" asked Dinah, full of questions today.

"Even more so, my dear," her father replied.

"I think this is as good a place as any to stop for our midday meal," added Betenos, Lamech's wife and the mother of the family group, who had all started to find places to sit and relax after their morning trek up from their village.

"If you follow that river you will eventually come to the sea about one day's sailing along the coast from here as it winds its way to the south and west," said Noah, who was wrapping his bread around the food his mother had passed to him.

Meanwhile Betenos was making sure all the family were getting plenty to eat and drink of the food she had brought with her.

"I'd really like to take a boat up that river from the sea and see how far I could go," mused Noah as he took a second bite of his meal. "It's such a beautiful valley,"

"Well," remarked Lamech," that could take you a few days my son, and once you pass that bend we can see down there you might just have to contend with a few rapids and waterfalls along the way."

Beyond the river the jungle stretched far inland west and north, forming a natural barrier between Havilah and Shulon, the next inhabited land some twelve to fourteen days sailing from Ophir, their village. There were some coastal villages between, but the hinterland was dense forest containing a multitude of animal and bird life. There were no roads or tracks between the villages, as the forest was impassable, the only way to each was by boat and sail.

"Tell us of your journey inland, Noach, that you made with Irad and Hazo last month. We haven't had a chance to catch up on that," asked Lamech.

"They are good friends. We got on well together and made good time. We saw no one on the way out as our trek was through uninhabited country. As you requested father, we were looking for fruit-bearing plants that we don't have back at the village, and we eventually found a few and brought them back as you know. We also saw many animals and birds of course, but it was all very uneventful. I love seeing small birds flying about in their carefree way, but especially the majestic flying lizards which are ugly up close, but magnificent in flight, they are so huge. Before we found the fruit trees and brought them back we also saw a family of behemoth and that was about the only thing that was frightening, really scary in fact." He emphasised this in order to scare his younger sisters.

"Oh tell us please, what happened?" an excited Dinah asked.

"It was as we were working our way through an area of large trees and plants with huge, spiky leaves, walking slowly and carefully. We climbed this ridge and heard what sounded like a large animal growling loudly in the distance. We clambered down the other side toward a stream and could hear the sound of a waterfall nearby. When we came out of the jungle suddenly into a clearing by a small lake there they were on the other side near a waterfall cascading into the lake. There were three of them.

"One was a huge male with his equally fearsome female only slightly shorter than him and their young one. Well, did they create a scene! Obviously protective of their baby they growled and snorted at us. We were well over two hundred cubits from them on the other side of the lake, but even so they were not happy with us being there and no doubt would have charged around the lake to get at us, but we turned around and got out of there smartly to avoid what could have been a bad outcome for us. They're magnificent beasts from a distance, but fearsome up close. Ironically, I've heard they are quite afraid of humans apparently, especially when you yell at them.

"But tell us father, they weren't always aggressive like so many animals are becoming these days. I understand that in times past all animals were quite comfortable near people, because we didn't kill them then. Now of course, the fallen ones, the Nephilim and others hunt them, sometimes just for sport. They don't even eat their meat but simply take their heads as trophies."

"Oh, that's horrible!" exclaimed Hebe.

"You're quite right," said Lamech. "We're told that in the days of Adam and for many years after the creation all creatures were friendly. They were all vegetarians as we are too, although not everyone is now. In those days people didn't kill animals for sport or food. Of course, we have always kept domestic animals for milk and such, and when they get old they died and we used their hides for protection and clothing and other things. Sometimes they were killed but never for eating. Since those times life has changed, and as you say, a few people do now kill animals and experiment with eating their meat. Of course the Nephilim, ever since they came into this world, have always killed and eaten them. They are the ones who have influenced these people to eat it. Most of those people live in other lands, but I regret to say this custom is now creeping into our beautiful land of Havilah as well."

"What does meat taste like?" Dinah asked.

"We do eat fish and eggs Dinah," replied their mother, "so perhaps it's like that, but has a stronger taste I would think. Really, we don't need to eat meat because we have enough vegetables and fruit to go along with the milk, butter and cheese from our cows and goats, eggs from the chickens and bread from the grains of course.

When the men go fishing in the sea we also get all kinds of fish and seafood as well."

"Why can't we women go fishing as well?" asked Hebe.

"No reason at all," replied Noah.

Tem followed up on his older brother's statement. "So when are we going fishing again Noach?"

"Tomorrow would be good," added Baruch, Lamech and Betenos' second born son.

"No, my sons," their father responded, "we need to repair the fencing around the fields to stop the stock wandering off. We've neglected that task lately."

"But if we all pitch in and get that job done I don't see why we can't go fishing the day after tomorrow, and you can join us father," suggested Hem, but his father demurred.

"I should like that very much, but I think our repair work will take at least three days even with all of us contributing."

The group then sat quietly for a time, eating their meal, enjoying the view and the wildlife around them. Then, becoming bored, the three younger brothers, Baruch, Hem and the youngest Tem, scuffled in a playful fight with one another while Noah, his parents and his sisters watched with amusement.

Suddenly, Noah spoke out what he had been considering for some time, "I want to sail the ocean all the way to the south, as far as I can go."

"What?" exclaimed everyone at the same time.

"Yes, I want to explore what is beyond the horizon, along with the coastlands that lie to the west and east of the sea. I was discussing this with Irad and Hazo on our trek last month."

"But you are only 23 years of age Noach, and you want to explore beyond the horizon! No man has ever done that," his father Lamech exclaimed.

"Well then, isn't that a good reason for doing it?"

"You'll get lost!" cried Hebe.

"And who would you take with you?" added Betenos in a worried voice.

"Anyone who wants to come with me," Noah replied. Maybe Irad and Hazo, and perhaps even Hanoch, Hazo's brother."

"I'll come," said Hem, "and I will too," added Baruch. "Me three," said Tem, unwilling to be left out.

But Lamech stated flatly, "None of you are going anywhere and that's final!"

"But …" said Noah and got no further when he was cut off by Lamech.

"I said no!"

"I think it's time to head back now don't you think, my love," Betenos suggested to Lamech, tilting her head to one side and lifting her eyebrows as she often did when she was directing rather than asking her men to do a job, or when she was reminding them of something they had forgotten.

"Yes, my dear. We need to be back before sundown. Methuselah has asked to speak to us tonight and as our Elder he is to be obeyed. We mustn't be late for hearing what he has to say to us."

As the family worked its way back down the trail to their village Lamech and Noah fell behind out of earshot from the group just as Lamech intended.

"I said 'no' to you just now, Noach, so as not to alarm your mother and sisters by what you want to do. No one has made a sea voyage like the one you have in mind. Some say there is a large southern continent at the bottom of the world. Maybe there is and maybe there isn't. There may be other great islands instead. Is that what you are thinking about exploring my son?"

"Yes father, you've been reading my mind."

"No. It's more a case of what I've been expecting of you, to come up with an expedition like this. As you've grown into manhood you've made it clear your heart is in or on the sea. I can hardly keep you away from it. That's the reason I sent you inland in search of fruit trees last month, to give you another perspective of what life could be for you. But I see where your heart lies. You have become very proficient at sailing along the coastlands to the west and east of here, and I hoped this alone would fulfil your ambitions. However, it's clear this is not the case. I don't fully understand why, but I believe Adonai is with you in what you want to do. So, tell me, how do you mean to carry out your plan? Have you thought things through?"

"Yes I have. I need to build a boat, a ship, much larger than the ones we use for trading up and down the coast. But that's not all father, and hear me when I say I would also like to explore this whole world as we know it. What I mean is, I believe that if we set sail in one direction and just keep going, eventually we will arrive back at our starting point … from the other direction!"

"Oh my, that is a magnificent concept!"

"Has it ever been done?" Noah asked.

"Not by any of our ancestors that I'm aware of. I've heard of how some from other lands have attempted to explore the extended coastline, but I really don't know if any of them were ever successful in my lifetime, and my father Methuselah has never mentioned it. It would be a huge undertaking my son."

"I know, father. That's why we'll need a large ship to store the necessary supplies for a lengthy undertaking, as well as to provide living quarters for several men and women to sail her."

"Why would you want to take women?"

"Simply because they're as capable as men. Besides, if men are left on their own for long periods in confined spaces they end up fighting one another. Women may have a calming effect on them."

"Well, I think if you take women it could have just the opposite effect with the men fighting over the women."

"Mmm, perhaps you may be right on that one."

"Yes, well, I've been around a bit longer than you Noach."

As they walked slowly toward their village in the late afternoon, taking in the scent of the herbs and flowers that were so plentiful in their chosen habitation, Lamech thought how good life was here in Ophir, but events in the rest of Havilah and the world beyond were causing him concern. Nowadays there were so many falling away from honesty, justice and common sense.

Then Noah spoke words that gave him hope. "I've had dreams, father. Lately Elohim has been speaking to me in them I am sure. Often as I walk along on my own, and even when I am quietly just sitting and looking at the sea I feel sure he wants me to undertake this great work and support me in it."

"Perhaps. I hope you are right," said Lamech.

"Will you support me in this undertaking father?" said Noah hopefully.

"I am considering it, but let us talk some more, with Methuselah and others who are experienced on the sea. I won't let you take all your brothers. I know they would be keen to go, but it's a risky business and anyway, they're needed here to help run the estate. I'm determined about that. If we agree to let you do this you can choose only one of your brothers to accompany you, someone you can trust and work with. Build your ship at the river mouth, which is far enough away so that your mother won't know what's afoot until it's time to tell her. Once the journey is set to go she won't hold you back I'm sure. But if you tell her now your ship may never get built. This is a word of wisdom from someone older."

"Haha, thank you father! Would you consider coming yourself?"

"I'll think about that, but I probably won't because it would stress your mother too much. However, I'll certainly help you plan it. There are a lot of things we have to consider."

Later that evening Lamech's family and many others gathered

around Methuselah in the mild evening air at the village meeting place. This was outdoors where they often gathered, for there was no need to shelter since both days and nights were almost always pleasant for people to meet, to conduct their daily business and be entertained. Their speaker was a handsome man, despite his rough and rugged countenance, brought about by hard labour working in the fields all his life. A man of the spear – people said of him that in his earlier days Methuselah had been a warrior defending his homeland from marauding savages and those who sought to steal from others instead of settling in villages peacefully. Although he was getting close to four hundred years of age Methuselah wasn't the eldest in the village, but as their appointed priest of Elohim he was their leader and the one they turned to for spiritual guidance.

The villagers who gathered were dressed in all kinds of clothes in different shades and colours. Most of them were loose fitting in the style of the day. Lighter leather foot coverings protected the feet of most, but those who came from tending the fields and undertaking heavier labour wore thicker leather boots. The evening air did not require head coverings, but during the day the ever present sun obliged them to do so in places where there was no shade. In the cool of the late evening shawls or a light leather jacket and one piece garments with a hole for the head were often worn. These were woven or knitted using animal hair, fur or wool. Their usual daytime clothing was also knitted or woven both from animal products as well as the fibre of plants growing abundantly nearby.

On this night they gathered expectantly for something important Methuselah had to say to them. But before he spoke the crowd was entertained by Hebe, Dinah and three other villagers playing sweet music on their pipes and stringed instruments. Betenos, Edna, Methuselah's wife, and a few other local ladies also sang a joyful song of thanks that almost everyone joined in singing, for nothing brought the village of Ophir together more in harmony and unity at their regular weekly gatherings than when they sang about what they had accomplished. And all of this took place each week under a myriad of stars twinkling in the calm, beautiful night sky.

"That was such lovely music. Thank you, one and all," Methuselah began. "And now friends, neighbours and family, people of Ophir, this is an important day, a memorable day. For those of you who were living and remember it, this was the day nearly one hundred years ago when Enoch, our great patriarch and priest of God left us. As you all know, he never died but was simply taken up by Elohim into his heaven. Even though he was not living in this village when this happened his disappearance has been a talking point for the whole world ever since.

"It's very good to see so many young people here tonight, and as is our custom, although we meet weekly, there are times when we celebrate special occasions. Tonight I wish to share with you the creation story, the history of our people and the events surrounding Enoch's departure, especially for the young ones who have joined us since last year.

"I was a witness to Enoch's departure, but the creation story and what came after was well before my time. This information was handed down by Enoch and his forefathers in much the same way as I will share it with you tonight."

At this point some of the older people got up to leave because they had heard this story many times before.

"Please wait my friends," Methuselah said, "I know I am not an eloquent speaker and story teller, but please stay and indulge me," he called after them. "At the end of my message tonight I have an important announcement to make that may be of interest to everyone, including you."

The people then settled in to listen to the creation story, and many of the young ones who were hearing it for the first time were fascinated by the words of this ancient seer.

He told them about the creation, how Elohim shaped the heavens and the earth in six days and rested on the seventh, the story of Adam and Eve the first people to populate the world and the garden of paradise called Eden where they first lived. And how God provided all they needed to live in a perfect relationship with himself.

"Where is Eden?" asked Dinah, his granddaughter, as she was still in her mood of asking questions like earlier in the day.

"Well, we don't know dearest Dinah. Many think it is somewhere in our land of Havilah, or perhaps Shulon, because that is where Adam and Hevah lived after they were put out of the garden. Others think it may be far away, but no one can see it or go there, because mankind has been shut out of that land."

"Why were they shut out?"

"Yes, dear, I was about to tell you that. And so it happened this way…"

Everyone present was fascinated as they always were as Methuselah expounded the story of creation and that of Adam and Eve whom they knew as Hevah. Apart from the young ones, they had heard it many times, but it always got their attention as to why the world was as it was and not what it should have been. It was a sobering lesson as to why they should follow and obey God, whom they called Adonai, rather than follow their own inclinations. Having shared why Adam and Eve were banished from Eden, Methuselah then shared with them how he came to Ophir.

"Now I wish to continue with the story of my family and yours. Adam died in the year 930 in Shulon where he lived all his life. In fact all our ancestors lived in the land of Shulon. It's where I was born like some of the older ones here. Many of you are descended from other children of Adam and Hevah and those who came after them. Others drifted to other lands, but our story belongs mainly to Shulon and my family. As I have just explained to you Adam and

Hevah were expelled from the paradise of Eden and had two sons, Abel and Cain, soon after they began living in Shulon.

"After many years of happiness a terrible thing happened. Cain murdered his brother and naturally their parents were devastated that this could happen in what up until then had been their beautiful peaceful land. They were naturally very unhappy for some time, for they knew that it was their disobedience to Adonai that had brought this upon them. After a while two daughters named Azura and Awan were born to Hevah, but no sons, and they longed for another one to replace Abel.

"Eventually Hevah gave birth to Seth, and from that time on they took life head on and were happy once again. In all, they had six more sons and many daughters. Seth married his sister Azura and they had a son called Enos. He in turn took his sister Noam as his wife and they also had a son they named Kenan. This is our lineage, and I trust many here tonight are descendants of these men and women. Some of you may also be descendants of Seth's brothers and sisters.

"There was another line of people from Cain. Many years after the death of Abel, Cain took Awan as his wife and they had a son Enoch and many other sons and daughters. Later still Cain moved to Nod and built the first large town and called it Enoch after his son. I mention this, to point out that there was this Enoch of Cain, who should not be confused with Enoch my father who came later.

"You may ask what happened to Cain. Shortly after Adam died it is believed that Cain was killed when a stone dwelling fell upon him and crushed him. By a rock he killed Abel and by rock was he slain they say. So Cain's line lives on in another land. I don't think anyone of that lineage is in Havilah, but it's possible, and no doubt in years to come people will intermix as the population grows.

"But back to our blood line of Seth. Kenan took a wife named

Mualaleth and they had Mahalel. Naturally each generation produced many more sons and daughters to whom many of you are no doubt related, but I cannot speak of all of them, otherwise we would be here all night. Many moved away from the land of their birth to settle in others and populate various parts of the world.

"Mahalel took his second cousin Dinah as his wife, the daughter of Barakiel, who was in turn the daughter of his father's brother and so his full cousin. Dinah gave birth to Jared, who married Baraka, also a cousin of his, and they had Enoch, my father. Enoch married Edna, my mother, who was a daughter of Danel his cousin, and she gave birth to me exactly 400 years ago. Yes, it's my birthday today also."

With that statement the village stood and clapped and sang a short song in honour of their patriarch. "Thank you, but enough, enough. You honour me, all of you," said Methuselah.

They then took their seats and quiet descended upon the small community once again.

"Now back to my story. Eventually I married my dear wife, also named Edna, daughter of Azriel, who sang so beautifully for us tonight. Some years later we decided we were no longer safe in Shulon because people had abandoned their faith in Elohim, Soon after my grandson Noach was born our entire family, including Jared and Baraka my grandparents, myself, Lamech my eldest son and family, my daughter Ruath and her family together with my younger son Hamor all moved to Havilah. Jared and Baraka with Hamor and his family settled in nearby Shur as you are probably aware. My mother Edna lives with Jared and Baraka and the rest of us found this lovely village of Ophir to live in. But Rakeel, one of our sons decided to stay in Shulon.

"We built our homestead on the land we negotiated with the elders here and now just thirty years later we are fully part of this community. Others have come also, and instead of what was then just a tiny village of about twenty people, today we are over three hundred.

"Now, before we retire and I make my announcement, hoping you will be patient with me just a little while longer, I wish to speak briefly of the time of Enoch considering today is Enoch's day. He is the person who has had the greatest influence in our world and the community about us. In fact, everyone who followed Elohim respected Enoch. As we know, the Lord God took Enoch to himself. Enoch never died!

"Since that day disorder and confusion has broken out among the people of the world. It is as if a part of Adonai has left this earth and we are obliged to deal with the consequences, especially in other lands but in parts of Havilah as well. We are not immune here in our village, and our family and you here and some in Shur are the only ones it seems who continue to minister God's love and commandments, to encourage and warn the people. It is so important to spread Elohim's message of love to the people of other villages and lands, because, if they continue to ignore and disobey their Creator, disaster will come upon all of us. Many, it seems, are not listening to what we are telling them.

"I have been our family patriarch for the past hundred years since that day Enoch left us, and soon after arriving here the elders made me your head for which I am immensely proud. When Enoch left, his priesthood seemed to pass to me as his son. It was not formally given to me, and I feel I have been minding it for when the right person comes along. I do not think I am suited to this task. I am a man of the land rather than one who should attend to your needs. I believe the time has come for me to pass it on to someone more capable. I suggested to Jared, Enoch's father in Shur, that he take on this role, but he declined as I thought he might. However, he has suggested someone who has also been on my heart, and so what he said was confirmation for me."

At this point Methuselah stood as the people realised he was about to make an important statement. He waited as the hum of conversation subsided and then continued.

"Tonight I am making a declaration to convey a decision I have not taken lightly, one to which I have given much thought and prayer. Therefore, on this day in your presence I hereby pass on this priesthood and ministry I have as priest of Adonai to my eldest son Lamech. Please come Lamech, and stand before the people so that I may pray for you."

At this a murmur of assent rippled through the village gathering, confirmation again for Methuselah that he had been guided correctly and that his choice was well received. In the brief ceremony that followed Methuselah prayed for Lamech, placed his hands on his head and shoulders and committed him to God's blessing and anointing, followed by a short instruction in what his duty was before Adonai and the people.

After this the village group broke up and made their way to their homes individually, in couples and family groups, chatting excitedly about the appointment of their new village leader.

Later that evening at their residence located just a half hour walk from the village square, Methuselah, Lamech and Noah sat together in the courtyard discussing the day's events. The rest of the family took themselves off to bed or occupied themselves with other things.

Like many others in the village the homestead housed the entire family of three generations. It was a U shaped structure built of rock and plastered on the inside with an open end facing the sea. Each family had their own quarters but frequently came together for meals and socialising in the grand hall located on the north side near the road. Visitors were often entertained here as well. The women had made the homestead comfortable with tapestries, curtains and floor rugs, while the men furnished it with all manner of crafted fittings and furniture made from the many different woods available in the surrounding countryside. It was a comfortable home for the three families and fifteen people who lived here.

Methuselah and Edna had their own quarters on the upper floor of the grand hall. To one side of the hall in the west wing their daughter Ruath and her husband Kor lived with their two sons and daughter. On the other side of the hall Lamech and his family had what they called the eastern wing. Behind the hall and opening out on to the courtyard were service rooms where the families prepared and cooked their communal meals. Smaller service areas were located in each wing for when the families wished to dine alone or entertain their guests.

Life was pleasant in their village and nearby Shur. The land was fertile and there was good timber and stone nearby for building. Each village was connected to the sea with jetties and wharves for handling the larger trading and fishing boats. The principal industry of the area was farming, both in animals and a variety of crops, because the soil and climate were very suitable for raising all types of fruit, grains, vegetables and livestock. Produce was traded up and down the coast and there was fish for local consumption.

Some of the people studied sciences and mathematics, while others were inventors who created all manner of useful tools and appliances that were sold and traded abroad. Jewellery and handcrafts were also exported, since gold and precious stones were abundant in Havilah and the country around Ophir, but lacking in other lands that prized them.

The village of Ophir sloped down towards the southern sea that stretched far away to the horizon and beyond. Anything that lay beyond this was unknown and mysterious, and thereby gave rise to a lot of speculation as to what might be waiting to be discovered.

So it was that Noah dreamed of going where man had never gone before, to explore the sea and the lands that lay beyond that horizon, if in fact there were any to be found.

"A ship you say Noach?"

"Yes, grandfather, it needs to be a larger one than our coastal vessels, because we need to provide sleeping quarters and storage of food and the like for many weeks at sea, rather than just the one or two days we now spend in our trading and fishing boats."

"And you want to explore and discover unknown lands?"

"Yes, I've dreamed of this since I was ten years old."

"What if there is nothing out there? No one that I am aware of has ever found other lands beyond the horizon."

"Then it would be good to find out wouldn't it? I believe Elohim wants me to do this and fulfil my dream."

"That's true," added Lamech. "Ever since he was a boy I couldn't keep him away from the sea. What do you think father? Is it a viable proposition?"

"Well, we won't know if it will enhance our trading until Noach discovers whatever is out there has to offer."

"You're saying I can do it?"

"No, your father and I are weighing the risks, dangers and inconvenience with whatever prospects your venture holds. It'll take you and those who sail with you away from trading and working the estate and their other responsibilities in the village. You could be away many months. And apart from your coastal trading duties you are also in charge of the vines. Who'll care for them while you're away? And no doubt you'll be taking several crew with you as well."

"Yes. I was speaking about it to Irad and Hazo this evening, and Hanoch his brother is keen to go with me too. I think it'll take us a year to build the new ship in between our other duties, so we have plenty of time to plan the expedition."

"If we agree to what you're proposing, I've said he can take one of his brothers also, but only one," said Lamech.

Methuselah continued, "So there will be five of you. Will that be enough? I suppose you can add others as required. Well, it sounds like a grand plan and Elohim is certainly a great influence in your life Noach, so as far as I'm concerned I'm of a mind to agree with what you're proposing."

"That's wonderful. Thank you, grandfather."

"But it's not my decision. Not after tonight. Lamech is now the head of the village and it will be his decision, not mine. Your first community decision I would think, Lamech?"

"Thank you father," Lamech chuckled. "You've certainly timed the handover well. I was hoping I could lean on your judgment, but it seems it's up to me now. All right Noach, build your ship. But I make three stipulations. It must be done in between your other duties and in your own time. You are not to speak of this arrangement with anyone except those who are involved in building the ship, and it must be built in a hidden part of the river mouth. Lastly, don't choose who is to be your brother on the voyage until you've tested all of them and found the one best suited to the task. I'll help you with that. So at the start, for the first few months at least, only the three of us and your three friends are to know everything we've been discussing."

"I'm humbled and very grateful to both of you and Elohim also," Noah quickly replied.

"Oh, and I want to add a fourth requirement. If what you're planning becomes known and your mother or anyone else for that matter finds out about this before the time we believe this voyage should be revealed, I reserve the right to terminate the whole venture."

"We'll be very careful father, and thank you again, both of you."

"Actually Noach, I can show you a well-hidden place by the river mouth that has ample timber and plants nearby," added Methuselah. "You'll need to build your ship of light yet strong wood, and your sails will have to be huge and gossamer thin, because our sea breezes are always light. Once you're away from the land in the deep ocean you may find conditions are very different to what you are used to in coastal waters."

"Yes, Grandfather."

"Well, you have a lot to plan and think about Noach, but tomorrow I need you to help with the fences and railings on the farm." Lamech then dismissed the small group with "See you all in the morning."

It was a long time before Noah closed his eyes that night as a thousand and one ideas raced through his mind, but eventually he slept the sleep of a contented and happy young man. At last he had an opportunity to prove to his family and the village that he could achieve something that no one else had dared to do. He would build his ship and sail beyond the horizon.

And so he did.

FIVE

Beyond Havilah

Three Years Later
AM 1083

The sea was calm, so calm in fact, that it was like a mirror with not a breath of wind to disturb its surface. They were becalmed again! To Noah, standing in the prow of his ship, it seemed as if he could simply step off it and walk across the flat sea. He knew of course, it was just an illusion. The other four members of the *Discovery*, so named in the hope of where it would take them and the lands they might discover, were also bored with nothing to occupy their day.

"Noach, we've had enough", shouted Baruch his brother from the ship's stern, as he clambered over ropes and other tackle to where Noah was standing. "Enough is enough. We've been out here for six weeks now and have hardly gone anywhere. There's no sign of land, our food and other supplies are getting low, the men are bored and our fresh water is half gone with no way of replenishing it. If half the water we took on board has been used up we're going to need the other half to get back home."

"Yes, Noach, added Hazo, "we all agree with Baruch. We know your heart was set on this voyage, but it hasn't worked out."

"We've only made about twenty days sailing in these light breezes, by my reckoning, based on the distances we travel along the coast." Hanoch, the technical expert among them, spoke up. "Yet we have been out here 42 days! The winds are not as strong out here as they are near the coast. At the moment the sails fill for a few minutes then stay flat for an hour or more. We're only moving a few cubits every hour at this rate."

"My friend, it's time to turn back now," said Irad, the last member of the crew to speak.

Noah listened to each of the crew as they spoke. Frustrated and disappointed, he realised that what they said was right. Looking toward the horizon ahead he reflected for a time on their situation. '*O Lord I have failed you. Why did you bring me out here when you knew this would happen? Was it to test me? Surely I heard your voice correctly? Is there anything out here at all? I felt so certain you were leading me to undertake this voyage. Just give me one day more. Please Lord, show me if there is land to be found out here.*'

In his disappointment Noah prayed, standing in the bow and looking towards the horizon as he had done each day for the past week while his men looked on hopelessly. After a short time he turned back to his crew and said, "You are all quite right, it was foolish to do this."

"No, it was not foolish Noach," said Irad, attempting to comfort him. "We've gained a lot of knowledge and experience from what we've been doing. We now know the ship works well when there's a breeze, so we can try again some other time or maybe look for a different challenge. Perhaps we need to invent a better kind type of forward motion than this light air gives us."

"Well," Noah replied, "at least we've tried and you have all supported me wholeheartedly. I've decided what we'll do. Let's wait and see what the rest of this day might reveal. We might see a bird indicating land is near or receive some other sign, but if nothing turns up we'll turn the ship about and sail back to Ophir."

‡‡‡

The *Discovery* had actually taken more than two years to build, rather than the year Noah had estimated. It was forty cubits long and twelve wide with two great masts. These supported two large billowing sails and two triangular ones designed to get the maximum thrust from light winds, and there was a great S-shaped rudder constructed of strong timber with ropes and pulleys to make steering easier. Many weeks were spent trialling *Discovery* out on the ocean before Lamech and the elders allowed the crew to sail away on their voyage.

Noah and Lamech had decided that Baruch was the best choice of Noah's brothers to go on the ship with him. While Noah was away Hem would have to take over the elder brother's responsibilities, and especially as his heart was on the land rather than the sea. Tem was keen to go, but at seventeen they considered he was too young. This meant that Baruch, who would turn twenty two the day they sailed, was the obvious choice.

When it was revealed what they were about to do ten months before their departure Betenos and the other mothers were horrified, and it took a day of explanations and assurances by Methuselah, Lamech and the *Discovery* crew, before they calmed down to a point of reluctant acceptance. Others in the village were excited over their prospects, however, and wondered what might be out there to discover.

Many helpers were willing to assist in putting the final touches to the largest ship they now had in the village. To them it wasn't Noah's ship as much as it was Ophir's. If anyone built anything of consequence it was deemed to belong to the whole village since they were a close community. So it was that *Discovery* became Ophir's great seagoing ship of exploration. Eventually *Discovery* was ready for its great voyage with the whole village and nearby Shur turned out to see them off.

‡‡‡

Hem ran as fast as he could, in his haste knocking over a basket of fruit in the village square much to the vendor's annoyance.

"Hey, watch where you're going! Here, help me pick all this up."

"Sorry master Pen, I have urgent news for my father."

"Ho ho, all right, better not keep Lamech waiting."

Breathless, Hem raced through the entrance of the house through the hall, the kitchens and courtyard, jumped the fence into the field of grapes and shouted out for his father Lamech who was tending one of the grape vines.

"Calm down lad. What's got you so excited?"

"It's Noach father, they're back! I can see the ship on the horizon."

"All right my impetuous son. If they're that far out it will be a while before they reach the village wharf. Let's gather everyone together and give them a good welcome."

As *Discovery* cruised slowly into the dock with Noah at the helm all five of the crew stood waving and the villagers cheered and shouted their excitement in return. Eager hands then took the ropes thrown them to secure the craft. In the same way that the voyage began the whole village now turned out to welcome them back, shouting and laughing and clapping. Young girls and women squealed with delight, while many more were simply relieved and glad that all their men were obviously alive and well.

Irad was the first off, quickly swallowed up by family and friends, then Hazo and Hanoch got a similar welcome. Lamech, Betenos, Hem, Hebe, Dinah and Methuselah climbed on board the ship to hug and slap the backs of Baruch and Noah, while Tem and other family members waited on the wharf for their turn.

"Oh, my sons, I am so relieved, your mother is happy again," cried Betenos with tears running down her cheeks as she hugged both her sons before anyone else had a chance to greet them.

"You made it back in one piece I see."

"Yes father but…"

"You didn't find anything did you?" smiled Methuselah.

"No grandfather, father, no we did not," sighed Noah.

"Never mind, we've organised a banquet for you in the village square tonight to celebrate your safe return," Hebe said with glee as she gave her elder brother, then Baruch a lengthy hug.

"Come now, we have a lot to talk about," shouted Lamech above the loud animated greetings of everyone present.

"You go with your father, Noach, we'll secure the ship and finish what needs to be done," said Irad as he led the crew back onto the ship to do this. They could unload what was needed tomorrow.

Later at home all the family gathered around Noah and Baruch in the grand hall to hear their story before they all went into the village for the banquet.

Shaking his head Noah said despondently, "We failed, I failed them."

"No son, you didn't fail," said Lamech, "look at the experience you've all gained and how you have gone further than any man I know."

"You went beyond the horizon for many weeks, and that has to be an achievement in itself," added Methuselah.

Everyone had questions that neither Baruch nor Noah could manage to answer, because there were so many of them coming at them from all directions.

"Did you see any whales or a leviathan?" asked Dinah excitedly.

"Yes, we did," answered Baruch. "We saw one with a long neck looking at us wondering what a strange craft was doing in its ocean. We also saw many whales spouting their steam and dolphins and sharks that swam around us. The dolphins liked to play and jump out of the water ahead of us. It was amazing."

"Whales blow water out, silly, not steam. Even I know that," laughed Dinah.

Throughout the rest of the day, at the banquet that evening and in the days and weeks that followed, the five intrepid sailors were often called upon to tell their stories of what the world was like beyond the horizon.

‡‡‡

Thirty-Six Years Later
AM 1119

The village of Ophir prospered over the next several years, both in trading and reputation, because the voyage of the *Discovery* became known throughout Havilah and beyond. As the crew now used *Discovery* as their principal means of trading, not only were they able to convey more goods and stay away longer to reach ports further than they had traded before, but even 36 years later those on that memorable voyage were often called upon to tell their story in ports far and wide.

Despite Noah's responsibility on the family estate for tending the vines and berry bushes he was often able to get away on his ship. In this way he became the leading trader for Ophir and the nearby village of Shur. He kept Irad, Hazo and Hanoch as his permanent crew when they were available and from time to time added other men from both Ophir and Shur. All three of his brothers had responsibilities on their family estate too, yet when the opportunity presented itself he took each of them with him on his trading excursions, as well as Lamech, Methuselah and other family members including his sisters, much to their delight each time.

Many years earlier Methuselah had discovered a deposit of gold in a stream near their home, and its location was kept a closely guarded secret within the family. Further deposits were later found by other villagers as well, along with gems and precious stones resulting in a thriving jewellery and ornaments industry, the products of which were traded up and down the coast. Merchants also came to Ophir to seek and barter for its treasures. It thus became known as *the Village of Gold*, and in the course of time Noah's family became quite wealthy. Nevertheless, this wealth would bring heartbreak to their community in years to come.

Despite the disappointment of his exploration to the south Noah had never given up on his other dream of sailing along the coastlands of the entire world, reckoning that by sailing east he would eventually return from the west. In his down times he often thought of how and when he might achieve this.

"I don't believe it would be any less dangerous than our excursion to the south," he told the group of elders headed by Lamech, whom Noah had asked be assembled to hear his plan. "When we sailed south we had no point of reference, no land to guide us and were completely on our own. But with this proposed voyage, though we will be at sea, the land will always be kept in sight to the left of us."

"But to what purpose?" asked Methuselah, while the other men mumbled their agreement to his question.

Smiling, Noah replied, "because it's there, and because it has never been done before. It will be an opportunity to map the whole world we live in. We will discover other lands we know nothing about. It's a chance to find other places to trade with and a mission to take the knowledge of Adonai to people who have forgotten him."

"These are commendable ideas," remarked another elder.

"Yes, I am impressed with your dedication," said Jared, Methuselah's grandfather.

"You have proved yourself a capable sailor, you having done more than anyone," added another elder who along with Jared had come from Shur for this important meeting, as men from their village would most likely be included in this new venture. Wherever Noah and *Discovery* went it would impact on Shur as well as Ophir.

"How long will it take?" asked Lamech.

"No doubt I will have the hardest time convincing you on this point, gentlemen. I will be honest. We simply don't know for sure, although many have tried to estimate just how big our world continent is. I would guess it could take us about two years but it may be longer. We don't know what we will come up against. There are too many unknowns. Another complication is that we would not have *Discovery* for trading all that time, although we have two new ships now, Shur has another one and a fourth is being built as we speak."

"Yes, replied Lamech, "I realise that, but while that is true, Noach, it will keep the men you take away from their other tasks. Others will have to take on those responsibilities."

"I know that father, but I think it is time now that my crew and I should concentrate on trading and exploring. Our other responsibilities should be given to others. I am sure Tem can take over mine."

The elders then discussed all this for some time among themselves out of Noah's hearing while he waited patiently for their decision. Eventually Lamech stood up and beckoned to him. Noah looked at his father expectantly.

"Noach, bring yourself and your crew to us tomorrow at mid-afternoon. Each one is to present to us their reason for going and what they expect to achieve. You must also give us the names of others that you have considered taking. Their families will need to be consulted. I won't have anyone going if it may cause upset or division in a family or this village."

"Thank you father, I am so glad you ..."

"Noach, this is not a statement of approval from us, this is simply the next step. We will give our final decision once we have heard you all tomorrow. That is all for now."

The following afternoon the crew of *Discovery* presented themselves to the elders of Ophir and Shur. There were six other hopefuls as well, including Baruch, Noah's brother, and one woman. Before the elders interviewed each one in turn Lamech, with Betenos who had suddenly just joined them, took Noah aside from the group.

"Why is Hebe here?" he asked

"She is coming with me."

"No, she is not!" stated Betenos firmly.

"She is not a child and can make her own decisions. She is a good sailor and wants to come. She has the right attitude, and I know it will work."

"Hebe, come here please," her father beckoned. "Noah, go back to your men. I'll join you again shortly."

"Yes?" Hebe responded curtly as she approached her parents.

"You are not going and that's final!"

"But I want to go mother. Noach and I relate well together. We're close as brother and sister and would look out for each other. It's a good idea."

"I need to get back to the council and listen to the men making their submissions, otherwise we'll be here all night," said Lamech. Turning to Betenos he added, "Take Hebe aside and talk some sense into her."

"Mother, I'm 56 years old and am capable of making my own decisions."

"You should be looking for a husband!"

"I don't want a husband, I like sea adventures. I've been on three long voyages with Noach and many short ones already. We've done it before and I want to be with Noach again."

"Hebe, you've been a strong-willed daughter all your life, and I know very well your father won't be at all pleased with what you're proposing. Oh, Hebe, you are distressing me terribly, and I will miss you so much!" cried Betenos, her eyes filling up with tears.

"We will come back," said Hebe stubbornly.

"You don't know that."

"We trust in Elohim."

"And Dinah will be married before you get back."

"Yes, I know. She was naturally saddened that I won't be here for her wedding but she understands. I did suggest to Noach we could delay sailing for another year, but he's made up his mind that now is the time to go."

After further consideration the elders approved the voyage. The crew would consist of Noah and nine others including Hebe. She simply would not take "no" for an answer, and in this was supported by her grandfather Methuselah who saw her dedication and drive and talked the other elders round in a discussion that lasted most of the night.

The decision was announced to the whole village at a special gathering the next morning, when Lamech told everyone that Noah would take *Discovery* on a round the world exploration to search out new lands and people to trade with and hopefully also encourage many lost souls to turn back to God. Those accompanying him would be Irad, his second in command, followed by Hazo and Hanoch his already established crew. Assisting them would be Iro, Phar, and Lexar from Ophir, and Thirsk and Ari from Shur. When he announced that his daughter Hebe would also accompany them there was a great deal of murmuring because her inclusion meant that Baruch had missed out. Two from the same family was quite enough on what would probably be a long and uncertain voyage.

When they were ready to leave two weeks later the whole village of Ophir turned out at mid-morning to see the departure of *Discovery* and her crew as they sailed away to the east heading for Shur. Here, they docked an hour later and picked up their other two crew members, and the farewells were repeated as they departed east once again, sailing out of sight with the setting sun behind them, and leaving people not knowing when they would be back, or in fact, if they would come back at all.

For provisions the crew initially took plenty of fruit, vegetables, grain and other food as well as enough fresh water to last a month. They were expecting that they could easily trade for more supplies as they sailed along, and by rowing ashore in their smaller boat take water from the many streams that flowed into the sea. They took two goats for fresh milk and some chickens for eggs, and planned to eat a lot of seafood on the voyage as well. Water from the ocean could be used for washing and even cooking as it had only a slightly bitter taste, but although it could be drunk in very limited amounts, as it was not very salty in these early years, the fresh water obtained from the rivers on land was preferable.

For the next three weeks they sailed known waters and called into familiar ports where they shared what they were undertaking and traded what they could. Shortly after they reached the border of Havilah, and after another two weeks they came to a land they had never seen before, always keeping the coast in sight to the left of them. At times mist would cover the sea, but they were still able to navigate using the sun, as they could always determine where it was in the sky. At night they had the stars to steer by, since the sky was usually clear. Hanoch also used a magnetic instrument to show them where north was. Thus they could not get lost.

One day they put into a bay with hills surrounding it. The only flat area was at its far end behind a pebbly beach. Huge trees and thick jungle covered the land right down to the water except behind the beach where there was a clearing. As they drifted slowly into the bay Iro took soundings to check the depth of the water, which was so deep that they got quite close to the shore before they could drop their large rock anchor and come to a complete stop.

It was still, very still. Beyond the beach they saw a village where smoke, presumably from cooking fires, rose from huts. There were sea birds about squawking a welcome or perhaps a warning to these interlopers in their bay, but otherwise it was utterly quiet. There was no sign of animals or people. The silence was uncanny.

SIX

Nephilim!

oah went ashore with Irad, Hazo and Phar in the small rowboat. They took some hides and pottery with them which were always good for trading. The small boat glided through the gently lapping waves and slid onto the pebble beach with a soft crunch. But even before they stepped out of it they became aware of a change of atmosphere. There was a sense of something being not quite right. They could see nobody in the village, no movement at all, not even of domestic animals, and that was very strange. Noah got out first followed by Irad and Hazo. They left Phar with the boat, as they always left someone with the boat for safety, and walked slowly up the beach and onto a well-worn path toward the village. They left their trading goods in the boat, as it would be clumsy to carry them before they made contact with the villagers.

"This doesn't feel good," Hazo whispered as he walked ahead.

"Why are you whispering?" Irad asked.

"It just seems strange. It's too quiet, it's not natural."

"Very strange," said Noah. "We aren't carrying weapons if the people are hostile."

"We don't know that. They may just be away at a gathering up the valley. It could be anything," said Irad hopefully."

They kept on walking slowly toward the first of the huts. They noticed these were made of rough timber and straw roofs, not nearly as well built as the houses in Ophir, and there was still no sign of any domestic animal or people. The strange quietness continued.

Suddenly a shrill cry pierced the stillness. Seabirds that had been nesting nearby screeched and took to the air flapping their wings wildly as if they were being pursued. But the cry was not directed at the three men walking toward them. From behind low bushes either side of the village several males who had obviously been hiding and watching the four sailors come ashore came charging at them shouting and screaming in high shrill voices. They were not clothed decently like Noah's crew but were practically naked. They were tall, broad shouldered and armed with mallets, clubs and spears shouting at the top of their lungs as they rushed down toward the shocked seamen.

"Nephilim!" shouted Irad. "Back to the boat quickly!"

They ran. Hazo had been slightly ahead of Irad and Noah as they walked toward the village and had been distracted by something when the screaming giants revealed themselves, so he was some way behind Noah and Irad as they turned and ran for safety. Although Noah's group could sprint faster the Nephilim had much longer strides. They also had the advantage of surprise and were on Noah's men before they were half way down to the beach. Phar had seen and heard what was happening and already had the boat in the water for his friends.

Tragedy struck when one of the villagers threw his mallet and hit Hazo on the back of his left knee. He cried out, stumbled, tripped and fell headlong onto the pebbled beach. Noah told Irad to keep going for the boat which he did and very clumsily threw himself into it while Phar tried to keep the boat steady.

Noah turned to face their pursuers. He was tall for a man, but was disadvantaged by the slope of the beach and the taller, angry adversaries who were bearing down on him.

"We come in peace. There is no need for this!" Noah shouted when they were about twenty cubits from him.

At this, they stopped and stared at him almost as if they were in awe of him because he had been bold enough to confront them. Then one of them growled.

"Men are not welcome. We don't want you here," he shouted. "But if you come we will kill you and make a good meal of you!"

Noah realised there was no chance of negotiating with these savages. One of them with an ugly scar running from his left cheek to his empty right eye socket, probably the victim of a violent brawl at some time in the past, simply grabbed Hazo's hair, pulled him off the ground, cut his throat and then threw him to one side, his blood splattering on the pebbles of the beach. He then turned and continued his pursuit of the unwanted seamen with his fellow villagers.

But by now Noah was at the boat, which Phar had pushed into deeper water. Noah had to take great strides in the water before he fell into it, cutting his leg in the attempt, as Phar and Irad rowed away from their angry pursuers.

Being taller and stronger, however, the angry Nephilim could wade in deeper than Noah and his men and almost managed to upset the small boat. The leading one grabbed the stern and started pulling the boat backwards, but Noah grabbed an anchor stone at his feet and smashed it down on the hulk's hands as he gripped the wood, breaking off some of the planking. Noah then threw the stone as hard as he could at the demon's head, fracturing it. The fearsome creature screeched and let go, grabbing his forehead, and Phar and Irad were able to pull away on the oars as fast as they could, finally reaching the safety of the ship exhausted and very shaken.

The rest of the crew on *Discovery* had already raised the anchor and set the sails and were turning the ship as the three survivors got back on board. They hauled the rowboat up into the ship, sacrificing some of the pottery they had taken ashore as it fell out of the boat into the water. They then wasted no time getting out of the bay.

But poor Hazo. He was the first crew member Noah had ever lost. Hanoch was inconsolable and so was Irad, Hazo's close friend. Hebe was weeping as were others. Shaken and wary, they took some time to compose themselves before they could talk coherently about what had happened. In all their travels this was the first time Noah had lost a man and the first time he had ever been attacked. It might not be the last time, for they realised that this journey had turned out to be far more hazardous than they had expected.

While Hebe finished dressing Noah's wounded leg as she still sobbed now and again, she managed to say what was on her mind.

"I think next time you go ashore you shouldn't take all the experienced crew, Noach. If we had lost all of you there is no one skilled enough to captain the ship and sail it home."

"Yes, you're quite right. We learnt a lot of lessons today," sighed Noah.

"I don't know what to say, Hanoch. Hazo was a much younger man than I. He died far too young. This was a bad business. I am asking myself, what have I brought you to?"

"It's not your fault Noach, we knew the dangers," replied Hanoch, red eyed with weeping.

"Perhaps we should turn back. Maybe we shouldn't sail any further."

"No Noach, it's not what Hazo would have wanted. You would shame his memory if you gave up now and turned back. I'm sure he would want us to go on and finish this quest," a still very upset Irad replied.

"Yes, Noach, we must go on," sobbed a very sad Hebe.

"We are with you whatever you decide Noach," added Ari.

Hazo's brutal death had put a damper on their journey, and *Discovery's* crew would never be able to forget it, especially for the way it had happened. Yet they continued to sail on, always heading east. Now, however, they were cautious every time they looked for water or other supplies on land. So they carried on, but with sadness in their hearts.

‡‡‡

For the next month they saw several villages in the distance. Coming close to shore it was obvious they were occupied by more savage Nephilim and consequently kept the ship at a safe distance, calling instead into unpopulated bays for fresh water and enough vegetables, fruits and nuts to see them through to the next time they needed to land. There was always food from the sea to sustain them as well. By doing this they had no more trouble from these people.

Passing by this land of high hills and forest that reached down to the water all along the coast Noah and his crew ventured ever onwards in an easterly direction. Many times as they followed the coast, however, they would encounter a long peninsula or great arm of the giant continent as it protruded far into the ocean, and then they would find themselves going south for many days and even weeks, before they could turn north again and resume their easterly bearing. Then there were other times when they saw distant islands to investigate and circumnavigated them. All this was recorded by Noah with the help of Lexar and Hebe on a great parchment of animal hide. In effect it was a great map of the coastlands of their world.

After the land of rolling hills and forest and their navigation of a third long peninsula that appeared to be uninhabited, they came to a land where the country was moderately flat with grasslands and plains. Every so often they would see small villages along the shore, many of which they avoided, but occasionally when they sailed close to them and the people in them seemed friendly and inhabited by people like themselves they would land and make contact, share details of their journey, engage in trading and sometimes stay awhile. They had no problem communicating with these people as everyone in this world spoke the same language.

In this now godless world as it had become they would share their knowledge and love of God. They were aware many of the earth's people had forgotten their Creator or replaced him by worshipping idols, land formations, the sun, moon or stars. It was a hopeless task for Noah and his crew, because the people's fall from God was so entrenched that they were simply laughed at or sent on their way with a warning not to come back. This was very disheartening for Noah. Time after time the crew were rejected, yet they comforted themselves in the knowledge that their goal was to circumnavigate their world and they were at least achieving that and this was a good thing they were doing.

They frequently ventured inland for several days at a time, exploring the terrain on foot when it appeared safe to do so. They never did this with the whole crew, and often Noah would let one of the others lead the search for fresh water and food supplies or for finding anything worthwhile or unknown to them. After many months of doing this they concluded that wherever they went the whole world continent they were exploring was much the same. Broad plains were interspersed with thick forests where they came across unique groups of plants or bushes from time to time. Rivers, streams, lakes, high hills and rock formations, often with majestic waterfalls dropping from them, were abundant. The weather was comfortably warm too. Frequent coastal mists were also there from time to time to moderate the heat of the sun.

The world they were exploring was also brimming with life. There were sea birds and land birds, small and great. Magnificent eagles with wide wing spans and huge flying lizards soared in the sky, along with all kinds of small or flightless birds of many colours. Butterflies and a myriad of insects also flourished among the trees, bushes and ground. In the sea there were great whales and all manner of other marine life like rays, sharks, small and large fish, jellyfish, sea horses and other creatures. There were also plenty of different animals, some with long necks and others with massive legs and bodies. Small, active ones dashed here and there, while larger ones were not disturbed by contact with the crew in a world where humans hardly ever ventured. It was a really beautiful place.

Lexar, who was quite the artist, and Hebe too, drew pictures of all they saw as often as possible on anything they could use like wood, leaves, stones and parchment. In this way they eventually became the ship's scribes by majority agreement. Sometimes they even carved details of significant discoveries on the ship's side, deck and sleeping quarters.

‡‡‡

One Year After Leaving Ophir

Discovery sailed past many lands unknown to the crew and then, eleven months after the tragedy at Hazo's Cove, for that is what they named it, they came to a wide river after taking several weeks to pass an unbroken jungle which seemed to be uninhabited. Almost immediately after the river mouth they came across broad flat grasslands where there were a few villages and then found many more along the coast. It was obvious that these were much better constructed than anything else they had encountered since leaving Ophir. The buildings were also similar in style to their own in Havilah, and some even more so, with three storeys. Most were built of brick and stone with tiled roofs.

By this time *Discovery* was short of supplies, and so on one particular day they pulled into a reasonably sized village by the sea. Noah brought the ship into a substantial dock made of large stones set firmly in the shore and with a solid wooden deck on top and thought to himself how good it would be to have such a solid wharf in Ophir. As they tied up the ship they were greeted with many stares from the local people, but not in a hostile way.

"Greetings! We haven't seen your ship before. Where are you from?" shouted one of the local men as he caught *Discovery's* ropes to secure her to the dock.

"From Havilah," responded Noah.

"Havilah! That's almost the other side of the world," he replied.

"Yes, we've come a long way," said Noah as he climbed on to the wooden planking with Hanoch and Iro.

"But who are you? And why have you come to our village?"

"My name is Noach. We left Havilah about a year ago and are exploring the world continent and trading as we go. Who are you?"

"Noach? I haven't heard of you. I'm Kaylin, the master of this port."

"What is this place?"

"The village of Koa."

"But what land?"

"You don't know where you are? This is the land of Nod. Tubal-Cain is the king here."

"Tubal-Cain? I have heard of him. Is this where he lives?"

Laughing out loud, Kaylin enlightened Noah. "Oh my friend, you don't know much about this land do you? Tubal-Cain lives in the great city of Enoch, not this small coastal village."

"In a city you say?"

"Yes, of many thousands of people."

"Where can I find this city?"

"You must travel several days eastward along the coast until you come to the port of Myrna. Then it's a two day journey inland. The River Myrn may take you some of the way, but you won't get all the way up the Myrn in that ship. You'll need a much smaller one."

"May we barter for some water and supplies from you and then we can be off again by this evening?"

"Oh, stay as long as you wish. This dock isn't needed for another two days. Exploring the world you say?"

"Noach, look what's coming down that road in this direction!" an agitated Hanoch said urgently but quietly in Noah's ear so that Kaylin couldn't hear him.

"Ah yes, it has been my dream for many years to sail around the known world. But is it safe here for us?" Noah said in surprise, "this um person coming toward us, isn't he Nephilim?"

"Yes, but don't be concerned. They live amongst us."

"They live with you?" Hanoch said incredulously.

"Who are you?" Kaylin asked, curious at Hanoch's question.

"I am Hanoch, and my brother was killed by one of these creatures early in our journey."

"He won't harm you. They're friendly. In fact, they're a great help to us because they have knowledge and skills we don't have. They've helped us build our great cities."

The Nephilim did not approach them, but busied himself with some goods piled a few cubits from where they were. He then picked up several boxes of them and carried them away.

"What's in those boxes, feathers? How can he carry so many?"

"They are very strong people."

"But they are not people are they, I mean they're not human?" argued Hanoch.

"Well, we accept them. As you can see they are quite useful." Kaylin was now becoming somewhat irritated at Hanoch's tone of voice.

"Please forgive my crewman," Noah said. "He's still very upset over the loss of his brother. We came in peace and meant no harm."

"That's fine. Like I said, you can stay a few days if you wish. The market is some way up that main street if you want to trade, and I can arrange for some water to be brought to you. How much do you need?"

The *Discovery* did stay two more days. The crew took turns in small groups to explore the village and do some bartering in the market square. They were always cautious and avoided engaging with the few Nephilim they encountered on their walks. They noticed that the Nephilim were always quite intense in a determined way, and that they never smiled or laughed like the other villagers. It seemed to Noah they were happy to mingle with the villagers, but he wondered what life would be like if they ever became the larger population here. Wanting to know more about them he approached a market stall owner and asked how long the Nephilim had been there.

"Oh, ever since I can remember. But there were only a few back then. There are many more now."

"Are they increasing in number?"

"It's interesting that you ask that, because, yes they seem to breed much faster than we do. I mean they often have more children. They take the fairest of our women because none of our men can stand up to them. Their height and grossness is too much for us. In many ways they're uncivilised, and that disconcerts many of us. Yet they seem peaceful enough. However, I still don't completely trust them."

"Interesting," muttered Noah as he walked back to his ship. Later that day he told the crew they would continue their voyage the next day at sunrise. "I'd really like to visit this great city we've heard about. Perhaps we could meet this Tubal-Cain."

"Is that wise Noach, is it safe to do that? He may enslave us. I've heard he's not a friendly person," Hebe said with concern in her voice.

"We shall see," he answered.

Several days later *Discovery* sailed into the Port of Myrna. Noah was greeted in much the same way as at the previous village, with people incredulous that they had come so far. Noah asked the port official if it was possible to stay a while, whether they could travel to Enoch and if it was possible to meet with Tubal-Cain. When the port official, Jubal, was curious as to why Noah would want to meet their king Noah suggested that what he had achieved on this voyage could be of interest to Tubal-Cain.

Noah did not want to make a long journey inland unless he could arrange a meeting with the king. He therefore asked if there was any way of ensuring this would happen and Jubal suggested that an individual named Kurt, who was one of the king's officials and often travelled between Enoch and Myrna, might be able to help them. Jubal sent a runner and summoned him.

An hour later the Nephilim arrived!

SEVEN

Tubal-Cain

Three villainous looking characters stood on the dock eye-ing Noah's ship. They had protruding foreheads, high cheek bones and very long hair. If you were seeing them for the first time, ugly would be the word to describe them. They were enormously tall and well-muscled with huge hands and strong well-formed legs. Metal studded boots were on their feet, they wore thick leather tunics embossed with bronze plates and carried large swords at their sides. Two of them carried a sheathed knife in their heavy belts. These were soldiers, mighty warriors indeed. Their faces were coated with coloured dyes, one red, the other yellow and blue. The one who was their spokesman had his face streaked with all three.

"Jubal said you want to go to Enoch and visit the king," he shouted at Noah who remained on *Discovery's* deck, not wishing to venture too close to these fellows. "I can take you there."

"Are you Kurt?"

"Yes man, I am."

"Why are you dressed like that with swords?"

"We are here in Myrna on the king's business, we are his soldiers. But what is that to you, man?"

"My name is Noach."

"I call you man. Do you want to go to the king or not? We are leaving now."

Hebe whispered to Noah, "You must not go dear brother. I don't trust them."

"I know sister, do not fret," Noah whispered back. And then to Kurt he shouted, "No, I would rather that you take a message to the king on my behalf."

"I might if you make it worth my while."

Noah then offered Kurt some gold which he accepted and in return Noah asked him to give King Tubal-Cain his message.

"Wait here fifteen days man, and if you have not heard from us or the King by then be on your way. You will no longer be welcome here. If you stay beyond that time it may not go well for you."

With that Kurt and his men trudged off into the town and presumably set out beyond it on their way to the king.

"Eww I don't like them at all," Hebe shuddered. "But I do see how women could be attracted to them. They're so big and strong and well, very masculine."

"But they're ugly!" protested Lexar. "Surely you aren't attracted to them too?" he added, with a touch of jealousy, as he was quite fond of Hebe.

"Oh, no not me, I'm just saying that women like strong men. They're not so bothered about whether they look handsome or not."

"Humph! No wonder this world is going crazy and violent," added Iro.

"I don't trust them either, but I am interested in meeting this Tubal-Cain," said Noah as he walked below deck to attend to what he was doing before they arrived.

Ten days passed without either incident or very much activity. On the eleventh day after the soldiers had left many of *Discovery's* crew happened to be in the town centre when suddenly people started rushing to the main road through the town, shouting excitedly.

"What's all the excitement?" asked Phar, throwing away the sweet fruit he was eating and running with the rest of the crew toward the excited throng.

A passer-by answered, "The King is coming!"

"Oh, we better get back to the ship," said Thirsk. "He has most likely come to see us, we'd better warn Noach."

Eventually the king's retinue arrived at the dock area. Tubal-Cain with six of his soldier attendants, this time men rather than Nephilim, approached *Discovery* where Noah and his crew were waiting for him on the dock beside their ship.

"Greetings King Tubal-Cain, welcome to my Ship," said Noah, bowing to him in respect.

"So you are Noach, the great seaman?" smiled Tubal-Cain as he walked up to Noah. The king was a thickset man of obvious strength yet somewhat shorter than Noah, who he was obliged to look up to as they regarded each other.

"I had heard of you even before my soldier Kurt informed me of your arrival. I knew of your earlier great voyage to the south that failed, and now you have come to my land. Why have you done this?"

"We come in peace. Our mission is a simple one, but a long and dangerous one as well. We come from Havilah, and my plan is to sail right around this world of ours. When we left Havilah we sailed toward the rising sun and by my reckoning should return home eventually from the west. My earlier mission to the southern ocean was simply to discover if there was land there but there was none. It was not a complete failure, because through it we gained a great deal of experience."

"It was a noble venture. We have lands to the south beyond the horizon. We have been there and found small islands yet to be inhabited. I am interested in the design of your boat and would like you to take me there. I want to show you the islands and you can show me how your craft sails."

"Well, I suppose we could consider that."

"This is not a request, it is an order. You are in my land and I want to sail in your boat."

"It is not a boat, it is a ship."

"We have larger ones."

"When did you wish to sail?"

"Now."

Noah looked at his crew who simply stared back unable or too scared to say anything in the presence of this man dressed in kingly attire who demanded respect.

"Who is this fair maiden?"

"This is my sister Hebe."

"Hebe? Ho ho! I have a sister about her age too. She's not as beautiful as this one, though. And who is this short man?"

"His name is Ari. He is one of my crew."

"Fine, Hebe and Ari will be guests of my, ah, retinue while we are gone."

"Why is that? They're part of my crew and I need them with me."

"Again, it's an order not a request. Your crew might throw me overboard, so they will stay here as security. I'll have two of my men accompany me also."

"I said we come in peace."

"That may well be. We shall see. Now show me to your cabin which is now mine for this voyage."

"I'll stay in place of Ari," suggested Lexar, finding the courage to speak up.

Tubal-Cain glared at him. "No one questions my orders! I suggest you give this man a whipping captain."

There was nothing Noah could do to question the demands of this powerful man with his large army and formidable escort, and no doubt the whole town supported him as well. So it was that Noah took Tubal-Cain on board and they sailed south once again beyond the horizon. Unbeknown to Noah, Hebe and Ari were confined in the town gaol for the duration of this excursion.

It took just a week of sailing in the ever present light winds to reach the first of the islands that Tubal-Cain wished to visit. This time, however, they had a helpful sea current to assist them. In all there were six islands. It took three days to sail around the two large ones and four more for the smaller ones. All were uninhabited, and Lexar added their location to his grand map of the world. On the two larger islands they observed animals unlike any they had seen on their voyage so far or in their homelands of Havilah or Shulon. Nor did Tubal-Cain recognise them, since they were not found in the land of Nod either. Their features were noted in the ship's log, and as always Lexar drew pictures of them as he did for all the creatures they observed. They then sailed back to Myrna, but this time it took eleven days to do this against the current.

Much to the surprise of Noah and his crew there were no incidents or conflicts with the king and his men. The two groups settled into an uneasy truce together where they talked about all kinds of things. Tubal-Cain explained to Noah the design of tools he had fashioned from iron and bronze, along with weapons for warfare, He suggested improvements Noah could make to *Discovery* such as fitting iron or bronze under the waterline of the ship to strengthen it. Noah pointed out, however, that iron would rust and bronze would slow the ship down considerably.

Noah also bravely broached the question of where the king stood in his relationship with God. This was the only time the atmosphere on board became tense. The king growled that he would have nothing to do with a God he did not believe in and stormed off to his cabin.

After a voyage of thirty days as *Discovery* was once again approaching Myrna Tubal-Cain suggested they should enter a bay near the town where there was a wharf they could tie up to.

"It doesn't look as if there is a good passage through there, Noach," said Irad. The water is a lighter colour and I don't think it's deep enough for us."

"I think it best that we head back to the main dock as before Your Majesty. I don't think my ship will be able to navigate that bay."

"Captain, I am not asking, I'm telling you that's where I want your ship to go."

"But we may run aground!" cried Irad.

With a nod from the king his two attendants grabbed Irad, holding their knives dangerously at his throat.

"You will do as I say!"

What weapons Noah had were securely locked below and out of reach, so in this tense situation he had no option but to obey the king's orders. Subsequently, as they entered the bay *Discovery* ran onto a sandbank and lurched to a sudden stop which cracked the forward mast. The mainsail was disarrayed, timbers were split and broken below decks, and water began flooding in. They were fast aground and *Discovery* was so damaged it was not going to be usable for some time.

A very angry Noah confronted Tubal-Cain. "You did that on purpose. What was the reason? Why did you do this to us?"

Smirking, the king answered. "Now I have you where I want you captain Noach, master of the sea. You're not such a great sailor now, are you?"

"But I told you this would happen if we sailed into this bay, and you forced my hand. Now let my crewman go."

"Ah, it's sad how accidents will happen to inexperienced sailors," the king said. He laughed as he nodded to his men to let Irad go free, but they kept their knives drawn.

Forcefully, but with a benevolence that only king Tubal-Cain understood, he had *Discovery* hauled onto a dry dock available in this ship building port. Here, Noah was able to obtain a new forward mast and replace the damaged planking. Tubal-Cain even had a bronze sheath attached to the bow and part way under the ship to strengthen it. All this naturally took a great deal of time and resources. Paying for the repairs and accommodation rented outside the ship while it was being overhauled cost Noah a sizeable proportion of the trading goods he had brought with him on the voyage as well as much of his gold and precious stones. This then was Tubal-Cain's purpose for keeping them here. However, Noah was grateful to learn that Hebe and Ari who had been prisoners in his absence, were unharmed and had been treated reasonably well before they were released.

Although he was detained longer in this land than he would have wished, Noah, Hebe and Lexar were able to travel to the city of Enoch with an escort provided by King Tubal-Cain. They stayed there three days and brought back many iron and bronze implements made in Enoch to be used back in Ophir or for trading during the rest of their voyage. This cost him more gold and precious stones which were eagerly accepted in barter, since these were not as plentiful in this land. Tubal-Cain's advisers who accompanied Noah's small party everywhere they went, ostensibly for giving advice on purchases, were able to glean from the unsuspecting Lexar, unbeknown to Noah, that Havilah was rich in gold and precious stones.

Eventually, after three months of repairs, *Discovery* and her crew were able to leave Myrna. Although Noah had his ship and crew back safe and well, and was now much wiser to the evils of the world, he knew also that he had been fleeced of wealth far in excess of what their accommodation, food and repairs were worth. He was understandably glad to be leaving the Port of Myrna.

'O Adonai, you have sent me on this voyage of trials and tribulations. Yet I trust that you will bring us home safely. You are teaching me much and no doubt you will require more of me, but I pray, even if you wish

to make a fool of me from time to time, spare my sister and my crew, for I am totally responsible for them.'

Sailing ever on, *Discovery* continued her voyage to the east, with Noah full of faith, fearless and with anticipation for what was yet to come.

EIGHT

A Vast Land

After leaving the land of Nod, as the crew of *Discovery* sailed onward for many months, it became apparent to Noah that this vast world continent was much larger than he first thought. In fact, shortly after leaving Myrna while doing some calculations with Hanoch he realised they were probably not even halfway on their journey.

They passed many lands thick with vegetation and teeming with the wildlife they had observed many times in their journey. This world was truly a paradise of God's creation. Meeting people and inevitably coming across a few Nephilim as well, they were wary now and knew when to keep their distance. Villages and coastal towns they came across were well settled and prosperous. Many had constructed large and fine buildings for themselves. Cities with large populations were spread throughout the earth.

Whenever they came to a village or town that was welcoming they befriended the people there. In this way they interacted with many different groups of people, sometimes whole villages and towns, addressing them in public meetings or privately in families or small groups. Noah and his crew spoke about God to them and told them why people needed to seek him to ensure this world would survive.

"We inherited disobedience to Elohim and we need to repent of that," Noah would tell them.

Nevertheless people were proud of what they had achieved; they lived a good many years, seemingly forever and had no need of a God they could not see. Most would listen with respect or out of politeness, but others would ask them to leave the next day. A few appeared to understand and desire to do better, but the demands of their daily lives forbade them to change. Still others were fearful of the rising tide of lawlessness in the form of murders, gangs of men attacking small villages, raping and pillaging. But rather than make a stand against them they were too often content with appeasing them. Other groups wanted to change the known laws to the point where everyone simply did as they wanted. "Why do we need laws?" they said. Noah observed all this and it grieved him that he and his crew could not persuade them or appeal to their consciences. If they were unable to convince the people of a better way, at least the crew would be able to bring home many good concepts and ideas to improve the prosperity of Ophir and Shur.

Sometimes they ventured inland with the ship, especially when a wide river presented itself, but most times they went on foot. This was never with the whole crew, but Noah made sure that everyone had a chance at some point to explore and enrich their knowledge of their world. The crew so often marvelled every time they saw animals, birds and even insects seemingly at play. Frequently they would come upon creatures large and small that had no fear of man because the surrounding land was uninhabited by humans. At these times the crew delighted in being so close to them that they could even touch or stroke their fur or feathers in some cases.

Once they left Nod the earth continent extended further to the east. It seemed endless. After another two years of sailing without further major incidents, however, they realised they were heading south rather than east, all the time keeping the coast in sight to their left. They had crossed a middle or central line of the globe as Hanoch calculated, for they were aware the earth was a sphere just like the moon, and although they intended to always sail east it was now apparent to them they were far to the west in relation to their home base at Ophir albeit on the other side of the continent from their homeland, and even further south than they had reached on their aborted voyage forty years earlier. But to their left the earth continent stretched on seemingly forever. Yet it was the same land, one huge continent that extended across the north of the world, but now by their reckoning far into the southern regions as well.

‡‡‡

Four Years After Leaving Ophir
AM 1124

Eventually, after another year they passed what they realised was the most southerly point of the land mass and found themselves sailing north again. But even this southern coast extended for many days' sailing before they recognised they were heading that way. Surely this great land must bring them home soon. But with still many more months of sailing ahead of them, always breaking their onward journey to sail around any islands they saw in the distance, they wondered how long this voyage was going to last.

Hebe and Lexar worked together with Noah, inscribing everything they encountered. In the course of mapping this great world they had become very close, warm and friendly, to the point where Lexar realised they had been on this voyage for over four, nearly five years now and he believed it was time he spoke to Noah privately one evening.

He knocked on Noah's cabin door, and after a few preliminaries of sharing some of the day's events Lexar broached what he wanted to say to his captain and master.

"I, ah, that is we, I, ah, mean Hebe and I while we have been working together inscribing all we see, well we have become quite close. I feel it's time, well I need to ask you …"

"Yes, I see you work well together, you have done well. Do you need a break perhaps, let someone else assist you? Iro could help you," Noah interrupted Lexar, because he had a habit of prolonging a request or conversation longer than was required. Noah assumed he understood what Lexar needed and cut him short with what he thought was a solution.

"No Noach, I mean sir," he said, stumbling now into formality and becoming nervous as he knew Noah was intolerant of those who were indecisive.

"What is it man, spit it out."

"We wish, I mean I wish to get married."

"Married?"

"Yes sir, I would like to have Hebe for my wife and I thought I should ask you first."

"You mean you haven't asked her yet?"

"Well, er, no."

With a great sigh Noah replied softly and a little more kindly, "Well, Lexar, I think it best you go and talk about it with her and if she says yes, then you have my blessing. But on one condition."

"Oh thank you Noach, ah, what is that?"

"You don't get married until we get back to Ophir."

"Of course, that was my thought too."

"Good, man. Now be off with you, your meeting with Hebe may very well be more difficult than this one. Don't expect her to say yes right away."

As it turned out, that is exactly what happened. Although she liked Lexar Hebe had never actually looked upon him as the man she might marry. However, she told him she would consider his proposal. She did this warmly and with care so as not to disappoint him.

Lexar was disappointed she did not say yes immediately, but was resigned to letting her decide when the best time would be to give him her answer.

Meanwhile Lexar told himself that Hebe needed time to think about it. After all, they had never actually spoken of marriage before, so it probably had come as a surprise to her. He was of no doubt she would eventually say yes. After all, they worked so well together.

After two weeks and without receiving an answer from Hebe, because the subject never came up while they were working, and with Lexar too shy to prompt her, he became rather anxious and so confided in his friend Iro.

"You are a scribe with no muscles, and women like men who are strong, decisive and do dangerous things. You need to impress her with something brave Lexar," Iro advised him.

From that time Lexar sought to impress his lady with an act of bravery.

As for Hebe, she realised she was not getting any younger and should be married as all women were expected to be. She was independent, yet she did desire the company of a man to love and have children by him.

'Stupid woman that I am,' thought Hebe, 'I love my brother and Long ago when I was young I thought perhaps I could marry him as they once did. But it is not done so much today. It is a silly thought and I should forget it and marry a good man. Lexar is a lovely man. Should I marry Lexar? I could do far worse. He's a good man.'

At this point in their journey the crew of *Discovery* realised they were headed in a mainly easterly direction once again. Thus in consultation with the ever calculating Hanoch, Noah was quietly expectant that they might very well be near the end of their journey. In fact, two days after his meeting with Hanoch, the coastline started to have a familiar look about it, and after another two days there was a shout from Irad sitting at the cross trees of the forward mast.

He often sat up there to view the sea ahead for any obstacles or shallow water.

"It's Shulon!" he shouted. "We've done it."

"What, where, how do you know," several of the crew shouted back at him as he tumbled down the mast. Noah came running up from his cabin with a great grin on his face. "Yes, I recognise this coastline," he said.

"That range of hills in the distance," said Irad breathlessly "I recognise them. There's a river just this side of them and a village beyond. It's the last village of Shulon to the west before the great jungle that we've been sailing past these last few weeks."

"Yes, you're right. We've done it people," laughed Noah "this means we're only a few weeks away from Ophir, as Shulon is to the west of Havilah."

Great excitement and back slapping, hugs and a buzz of excitement followed for the rest of that day. In fact, their spirits were now lifted permanently as they realised they had accomplished what they set out to do, and very shortly they would be home again.

"Five years, it has taken us nearly five years."

"It's not over yet Noach," laughed Hebe.

"No, we must keep alert still, even though we're now in familiar waters. We still have some way to go."

Later that day they made their way to the mouth of the river and the tiny village of Ako at the very edge of Shulon.

Coming into the wharf at Ako, *Discovery* pulled gently alongside. It was always one of the stronger lads such as Thirsk or Phar who grabbed the heavy rope that secured their ship to a wharf or landing place and heaved it over the side to eager hands waiting to receive it. On this occasion, however, with the excitement of reaching Shulon and the words of Iro on his mind, Lexar wanted to be the one to throw the rope and impress his lady.

He got hold of the looped end and gathered a few extra lengths as he had seen the others do, almost overbalancing with the weight as he did. He then did what he always saw them do and unsteadily heaved it up and out to the men on the wharf. However, one link of the rope had caught around his left heel and consequently Lexar was pulled off the deck by the rope as it snaked out over the water and he ended up in the sea between the ship and the wharf, floundering in the water with the rope twisted about him.

To his dismay and embarrassment a dozen or more spectators and all *Discovery's* crew were beside themselves with laughter. Eventually all was sorted out and he was hauled dripping and red-faced up on to *Discovery's* deck. Hebe smiled at him sympathetically and made a move toward him, but Lexar was so embarrassed by his mishap that he simply walked away to his cabin with his head down.

It was not the grand entrance to Shulon that Noah had imagined either, but after things settled down he spoke with a village elder.

"Greetings, Noach, it's been a long time since we saw you here last," Ako's village elder said as he welcomed Noah and the crew on the small wharf.

"But we saw you come from the west. There's nothing there, so how did you come from that direction?"

Smiling Noah replied, "Well, actually we left from Ophir nearly five years ago and now we are coming home."

"I, ah, don't understand."

"My crew and I have sailed right away round the whole of the earth continent. We left Ophir and sailed east, and now we are returning from the west.

The man simply stared at Noah dumbfounded.

"It really is a big world and there is so much to explore. There are no villages west of here for many weeks of sailing. You are the first village in Shulon as you obviously know, and I can confirm there is only jungle far to the west, at least from what we saw from the ship."

"Well, that is amazing. What an achievement! We'll have to celebrate your return."

All the village gathered that evening to celebrate and hear of all the marvels the crew of *Discovery* had seen. In the village square and all during the festivities of their return Hebe sat beside a very quiet Lexar. By now he had bucked up a little when no one made any further mention of his mishap, but he was too embarrassed to speak of it with Hebe.

When the celebrations were over the crew made their way back to the ship and as they walked along Hebe took Lexar's hand in hers. At this he looked gingerly sideways at her but did not trust himself to say anything.

"That was very brave of you, what you did today. It didn't turn out the way you expected, but you gave all of us a good laugh and we don't love you any the less for it."

"Really?"

She said nothing more but held his hand until they arrived at her cabin door. It was then she turned and looked up into his eyes.

"Do you still want me to be your wife Lexar?"

"Wha … Oh um of course," His words were getting jumbled again. "Oh I mean yes, yes of course I do."

Hebe gave him a gentle kiss on his lips, turned and went into her cabin shutting the door.

"Wait, I, we need to talk."

Hebe's door opened a crack and with the most beautiful eyes he had ever seen she smiled and said, "In the morning we will talk about our life together. Sleep well, my love."

Lexar was not sure how long he stood there until Iro came along and asked "Are you all right friend? You look as if you have seen an angel."

"I have," he replied as his heart sang for joy.

Over the coming weeks their accomplishment was repeated

many times in several villages as they came to them. They had traded with them in previous years and were now calling in on them again on their way home. There the crew recounted their achievement and did a little trading as in most places they had visited on their travels.

Yet again in Shulon, so close to Havilah, they hoped the people here would be more receptive to God than those they had left behind in other countries. But alas, the same ignorance and pride seemed just as strong here as well. They only wanted to hear about Noah's adventures on the sea and all about the great continent they had discovered.

Over the following days Lexar and Hebe were often seen close together in conversation, but only Noah knew their secret that would be revealed once they arrived in Ophir.

It was a special moment when they sailed into their own land Havilah from the west. A sense of deep satisfaction, knowing what they had achieved and the significance of what they had done settled upon them. They had done what they set out to do, and no one before them had. The exhausted but proud crew of *Discovery* were well prepared for the welcome they would inevitably receive when they reached Ophir and Shur.

NINE

Coming Home

AM 1124

Lamech's eyes were still very good despite him being over two hundred years of age. In this period of earth's history this was considered youthful and nowhere near middle age. He was relaxing in the pleasant afternoon sun in the courtyard of his family's homestead, enjoying a meal of dried fruit, cheese and wine, all of which was from his land. Sitting with Betenos his wife they gazed over their grapevines that sloped down towards the sea. They had often done this, enjoying the fruit of their labours and looking out to the west for more than a year now.

"My dear," said Lamech encouragingly, "we must not give up hope. There is every reason to believe they are all alive and well. We don't really know how big this world is. We must trust Adonai to bring them home safely one day."

"I know my love, and I should trust in Adonai, but it's been two years since those monsters from the other side of the world came and raided our village. I want to believe, but this mother's heart is not at peace. I worry so much for them."

"Well, we know Noach got to the land of Nod because they mentioned his name. We must keep waiting and hoping. Look, you see that dark speck way to the west and out at sea? That's a ship. It may even be them."

"So you've said many times my husband, only to be disappointed when it's only another trading vessel."

They sat there for an hour longer and were then joined by other members of the family one by one. Suddenly Lamech jumped up from his seat and shaded his eyes as if to make him see more clearly.

"What is it father?" asked Hem.

"That ship doesn't look like any of the trading vessels we have or that call in here. The sails are different. Do you see that?"

As the vessel got closer over the next half hour more members of the household joined them and each had something to say. But no one said what they were all thinking and hoping until it was beyond doubt.

Finally Tem said, "I'm climbing on the roof of the implement shed to get a better view." He did so and a few moments later he shouted, but was drowned out when Lamech and Hem realised what the vessel was and they all shouted at the same time. "It's *Discovery*, it's them! Noach has done it. They're coming home!"

Lamech's family, running and stumbling in their haste to get to the town centre, alerted the town's people and once again everyone who could headed down to the dockside to welcome home their world explorers. A runner was despatched to Shur to alert them as well. What followed was a celebration never to be forgotten and often spoken about over the years to come. Once again a great feast was held to welcome the weary explorers home. The entire village of Shur joined with Ophir to celebrate.

Before the celebrations began, however, joy turned to shock and heartbreak when Hazo's family and the two villages realised that not all of them had returned safely. Hazo's mother was inconsolable and held on to his brother Hanoch the entire evening as if she might lose him as well.

During the celebration Lexar got up and uncharacteristically for him made a speech during which he formally asked Hebe to marry him. When she accepted, the celebration which had been loud up till then became even more ecstatic with their news.

For the next few evenings the people gathered in Ophir's town square so Noah and the crew could tell everyone about their adventures. While the festivities continued, it was decided that as they had travelled together for five years there was no need to delay the wedding, so within three days of their formal betrothal Lexar and Hebe were married at one of the evening village meetings. Lamech did the honours. Lamech and especially Betenos were very happy their daughter was now married.

Just as it is in every culture this was a good excuse for even more merriment. Yet it was also tinged with sadness as the elders of Ophir and Shur in turn told Noah and his crew of the tragic events that happened while they were away.

Using his authority Lamech had forbidden every villager to mention to any of Noah's crew the tragedy that had befallen them two years earlier until he and the village elders had determined the right time to do this. In a private meeting with the crew, the day after Lexar and Hebe's wedding, Lamech and the elders explained what had happened.

"You say that this monster Kurt and two of his henchmen came and raided our villages and he knew my name?" Noah responded angrily to what the elders had just told them.

"Yes Noach," continued Lamech. "They came unexpectedly, and at first because they mentioned your name we thought they were peaceful even though they were so huge and ugly. They told us you had sent them to trade, but it was a lie."

"It certainly was a lie. In fact, I never actually spoke to Kurt very much, and he would never address me by name. I mostly interacted with Tubal-Cain and his advisers who were men not Nephilim. How did he know where our villages were?"

"Apparently one of your crew told them. They also told them there was a lot of gold here. That was evidently what they were after."

Like everyone else Lexar had been following the discussion calmly, yet with mounting anger at what these Nephilim had done. Now, when Lamech mentioned that they had been tipped off by one of the crew, he went crimson with guilt and embarrassment and coughed involuntarily. He put on an innocent expression as the whole room turned in his direction.

"Do you know something about this Lexar?" asked Noah incredulously.

"I, ah no, I never spoke to Kurt."

"To someone else then? Perhaps it was the advisers when we went to the city of Enoch? You were very friendly with them as I recall."

Groaning with guilt Lexar started to whimper, "I never realised, I thought they were helping us, showing us all manner of things in their city. They asked about Ophir so I told them. They must have told Kurt…"

"Oh Lexar, they were deceiving you. I knew that might happen, I should have warned you," said Noah.

"You did, and I am so stupid," said Lexar, crimson with embarrassment and shame.

"All right, there is no point laying blame on you now. What's done is done," said Lamech, calming the room down as it buzzed with chatter.

"So they burned down some houses. Was anyone hurt?" continued Noah.

Taking a big sigh as all the elders became unsettled, Lamech added, "there's something we haven't told you yet. I asked all the people and especially your mother not to say anything until the festivities were over. We didn't want to spoil your homecoming."

"What do you mean, and what has mother got to do with this? Why are you all very tense all of a sudden?"

Intuitively Hebe spoke up with mounting anxiety as she asked the elders, "Why are Dinah and her husband not here? I assumed he had taken her to his village after they were married. I asked mother but she wouldn't tell me and kept changing the subject. I have a bad feeling about what you are now going to tell us."

"Dinah? Did they do something to Dinah?" Noah growled, as he and Hebe became very troubled, realising by the reaction of Lamech, Methuselah and the rest of the elders this indeed had something to do with their younger sister.

"He took her," mumbled Methuselah with a long sigh.

"What?" shouted Hebe.

"All right, settle down. I'll explain and don't interrupt," an exasperated and clearly saddened Lamech attempted to take back control of the conversation.

"He demanded our gold and we would not give him any, nor would we trade it when we realized he was becoming aggressive. So that's the reason, we believe, he became angry and started smashing things. Then they burnt two houses down as we told you and the next day they stormed up to the homestead. Methuselah and I were not there, neither were Baruch, Hem or Tem. Kor and Ruath were away at the time as well.

"Dubrich, Dinah's husband, stood up to them and naturally tried to protect his wife when that monster took a liking to her as soon as he saw her."

"Oh, this is horrible," cried Hebe.

"Yes it is. We've had two years now to get over this, but let me continue. He simply took out a knife and cut Dubrich's throat with one swipe according to one of the witnesses. He then grabbed Dinah who tried to break free, screaming and kicking. They are huge beasts and soon had her controlled. There was nothing she or anyone else could do. We had no weapons. Then they left with her. They have taken her with them to Nod no doubt."

"And you all did nothing!" shouted Hebe.

"What could we do? These were soldiers trained to kill. They were so tall and threatening and we would have had no chance against them." A saddened Lamech slumped into a chair from exhaustion in trying to explain.

"I'll go and bring her back," exclaimed Noah. "I know Tubal-Cain. He can be reasonable if untrustworthy at times. I cannot believe he would have done this to me or my family, and to our village on purpose. Kurt probably did this on his own. They haven't come back with a larger force have they?"

"No, but it's so dangerous Noach."

"I have Adonai with me. I'll negotiate with Kurt, take him some of the gold he wants. Dinah is more precious than gold. Who will come with me?"

The whole crew volunteered, but he declined their offer.

"No, you men have done enough, you must stay with your families now. I'll take a fresh group of men and get her back."

"I'm coming," said Hebe.

"No, Hebe you definitely are not," Noah said firmly.

"This is all my fault," Lexar said. "You must let me go. As you said, I was too friendly with the king's advisers."

"All right Lexar. I'll consider your offer, thank you," replied Noah.

Later that evening Lexar looked at his new wife, knowing that she probably hated him now for what he had done. He felt so miserable about this, but when Hebe wrapped her arms around his neck sobbing, he realised she didn't hate him at all.

When she had controlled herself she said; "I don't blame you in any way. You weren't to know what you said would be used against us and were only doing what you thought was best. But I don't want you to go. I don't want to lose you too."

"I have to do this my dear, I believe it's what Noach would expect of me and besides, I couldn't live with myself if I don't do anything. I've never been a strong man, but please let me do this to prove to myself I can. I love you and I want to do this for you and for Dinah."

"You really don't have to, but being a man, if you must, you must."

Noah was reminded that the Nephilim were fallen ones and not men. The elders had told him that Kurt had indicated it took two passes of the moon to travel to Ophir, so this meant Noah and his group would be away for at least four or five months on that reckoning. It had taken a whole year to sail there previously, so that was not an option. He therefore told the elders he would take whatever time was needed. Noah wasn't keen to take Lexar with him because he wasn't as strong as the other men, and Hebe said she didn't want him to go either, but told Noah he needed to be included for his own self-respect.

A week later Noah set out on the journey from Ophir with horses and ten men. As the group left the homestead Lexar turned and waved to Hebe, who in turn waved back, sobbing quietly so that he would not notice.

Ten weeks later the small band crossed into the land of Nod having traversed that part of the continent. The journey was not direct, as they needed to circle round a huge range of mountains stretching far into the interior. In that immense area they saw many creatures that enjoyed the cooler temperature of the higher lands, along with different plants to those that grew in the coastlands. At first they travelled along tree-lined valleys of streams with waterfalls, followed by the grasslands of the lowlands, beyond which were the mountains. And finally, they encountered more jungle until they eventually entered Nod.

Almost immediately they ran into a large group of Tubal-Cain's soldiers while still a long way from the city of Enoch. After explaining who they were, whom they had come for and showing their eagerness to reach Enoch, they were told sternly that they had no business to be in Nod and were to return the way they had come without delay.

But without accepting the soldiers' rebuff, Noah pressed them to say where he could find Kurt or his sister. One of the soldiers said he knew what had happened to the girl, and with the permission of his captain he told them. He remembered how about two years earlier Kurt and his two sidekicks had come into his village on their way back to Enoch. They confessed what they had done to her while they were drunk.

"Dinah is dead, then?" an angry Noah asked.

"If that is her name, then sadly, yes," replied the soldier.

"How can you be sure?" Noah asked hopefully.

"There were only the three of them. If the girl had still been alive she would have been with them. It's a remote area here with no other villages between ours and the great jungle you've just passed through. There is nowhere else she could be, and I have no idea where her body might be. They also showed us her jewellery. They were actually angry that their whole journey to your land only got them a few items of jewellery."

"We're sorry," said the officer. "These are dangerous lands. It's best you not come any further. The king may very well decide to raid your land if you cause trouble here. I think you're a peace loving people and we have a strong army, many of whom are Nephilim. You would stand no chance in a battle."

Despite this information Noah was keen to push on, but his men persuaded him with some effort that with Dinah dead it wouldn't achieve anything, except the probability of their own deaths and another, much more serious, attack on Ophir.

Up to this point Lexar had held his own on the long march to this place. Despite his slight build he had kept up with all the others and never lagged behind at any stage. Noah was quite impressed with his brother in law now, more than in all the time they had spent on the voyage together. Lexar had shown determination, steadfastness and a quiet intelligence. But now uncharacteristically he became deeply angry, presumably because of all the trouble he imagined he had caused. This anger had been building up in him these past weeks because he knew this trouble was all his fault, and he was now determined to do something to alleviate his guilt. He wanted to impress Hebe and show he was as strong and brave as the rest of the men. Without permission or warning, in his anger and without thinking, he rushed at the group of soldiers standing a few cubits away, yelling and throwing his fists in the air. He was unarmed. One of the soldiers reacted instinctively, raised his bow and shot an arrow deep into Lexar's chest. Lexar's momentum carried him forward where he somersaulted once and lay crumpled on the ground, his eyes open to the sky with his arms outstretched. His life taken from him.

Shocked, saddened and angry, but realising revenge for his death was not going to solve anything, Noah and his men buried Lexar where he lay and returned to Havilah.

It was not the homecoming Noah had hoped for after his world-wide voyage. His earlier achievement was now replaced with self-guilt and grief at having incidentally caused the death of his beloved sister, her husband and his devoted scribe and brother in law, as well as that of Hazo near the beginning of the voyage on *Discovery*.

A wiser, more knowledgeable and determined Noah now faced an unsettled and unknown future.

TEN

Naamah

The Land of Havilah – 395 Years After Noah's Great Voyage
AM 1520

By now the village of Ophir had grown from a small peaceful backwater into a bustling port city, where countless trading vessels and fishing boats came and went each day. Wharves and docks now lined the shore where 400 years earlier one simple wharf sufficed for the weekly vessel that serviced the area. The population had also increased greatly from natural births and people who chose to settle in Ophir, opening businesses and exploiting the many deposits of gold, gems and colourful natural stone available for mining in the surrounding area.

Buildings of every kind had spread around the original village which now reached almost to Shur, so that the two together were now considered a single port city of paved roads and walkways. All the buildings had roofs of tiles or iron thanks to the knowledge of working in bronze and iron gained from Tubal-Cain.

Many of the structures in Ophir were adorned with all kinds of features in bronze, both ornamental and utilitarian. Iron windmills with great bulging sails to catch the light airs pumped fresh water through a network of pipes into every home, and for the past 200 years a sophisticated system of getting rid of waste products had made life much more pleasant for its inhabitants. Iron poles with cupped heads containing oil lined the town streets, and each evening the lamplighters came down the avenues in their carts with ladders and drums of oil to light the lamps on these poles for the people taking their evening strolls.

Ophir was now not only a great trading port but also a rich manufacturing centre for jewellery and craftwork in gold. As in many other towns, villages and cities across the world, all manner of metal, glass, pottery and wooden products were manufactured in foundries and workshops. The surrounding countryside was farmed for animal products such as milk and cheese, along with many varieties of food and other products the animals provided whether dead or alive. The growth of vegetables and plants was so prolific that those who farmed the land could expect at least three crops, and in some cases four, each year. There was plenty of work for everyone and therefore plenty of supply. No one in Ophir, or for that matter in the rest of this world, ever went hungry.

The land produced many commodities. There was leather from hides for clothing and footwear, protection and beauty. Woven products came from fields of flax, cotton and other plants. Clothing was made from the wool, fur and hides of animals. Other products were manufactured from the sap of trees, cropping areas and orchards. Paved roads carried goods on vehicles pulled by horses, oxen and other domesticated animals to inland villages and coastal areas. It was a thriving, busy, noisy, and congested land, but a corrupt one because of human greed and the lack of a regulated system of enforcing justice. People did as they pleased to a great extent, but those who chose to deal dishonestly and unfairly in life and business found that the wider community exacted its own form of justice in the finish.

Although Lamech's homestead and fields were almost swallowed up by the city in the course of time he and his sons stubbornly refused to let the land around the house be commercialised and kept it as it had always been, with its vines, orchards and some livestock. However, he had been under such constant pressure that he had given in and had sold off his fields of barley, wheat and other crops that lay to the east of the homestead, between it and the old village centre, which was now a built up area of dwelling places. The family still kept their view of the sea to the south and west.

Betenos often kept a lookout for Noah returning from one of his long voyages if he was due to arrive from that direction. Since his first expedition around the world continent Noah had done three more circumnavigations. In addition, he sailed many times to distant lands to stay a while before returning the same way. This was always with a view to extending Havilah's trade and constantly sharing his love of God with everyone he encountered.

A secret Noah kept, along with his crew of the day, concerned the discovery of a vast island continent on one of his voyages to the southernmost shores of the world. On impulse they decided one day to sail further south over the horizon and perhaps discover the fabled continent that he had been unable to find all those many years ago. After several weeks of sailing south they realised the tale of this continent was not a fable, and that in fact an island continent did exist. They spent some time sailing around it and mapping the coastline. When they went ashore briefly in a few places they discovered it was a fertile land, lush with plants of all kinds and creatures undisturbed by man. The sea was teeming with fish. For this reason the crew collectively took an oath never to reveal the location of this untouched continent to anyone. There was already more than enough land to satisfy the inhabitants of this present world without spoiling this pristine and beautiful land of the south sea by the destructive incursion of human inhabitants and what they would bring with them. They didn't even tell their families about it and kept the knowledge of it to themselves for the rest of their lives.

It was mainly because of Noah and his contemporaries' many voyages that Ophir grew to the size it did, with people coming from all over the earth to trade there or stay permanently. Inevitably this included the 'in-breds', offspring of the Nephilim when they intermarried with human beings. Many of these dwelt amicably with humans, but others did not. Many of them had a taste for meat, and so the once solely vegetarian and seafood diet of the world became a mixed one.

A frustrated Lamech and Betenos could never understand why Hebe had not remarried after the death of Lexar, nor why Noah had still not found a wife for himself. It was a mystery to Noah that his sister remained single, yet he was so fond of her and they worked so well together that he never put any pressure on her to change her mind. She, in turn, was devastated by the tragic death of her beloved Lexar. Consequently, she had no desire to remarry. Nine months after Lexar left on the expedition that took his life she gave birth to a son whom she named after his father. Benlexar grew up on the estate and enjoyed the adventures of the sea with his uncle and so it was he did not marry for a very long time. He finally married a younger woman from Shur and they had three sons but no daughters.

Discovery served for many years as a local trading vessel, but was eventually broken up and her parts incorporated into other vessels. Noah had built several more ships since then, and his present one was his largest. Irad and Phar had their own ships. Thirsk and Ari were the leaders of the fishing fleet. Hanoch, Iro and Hebe along with Benlexar Hebe's son became Noah's trusted companions and still sailed with him. Over the years many dozens of men and women came and went as crews on his ships. Benlexar's three sons accompanied their father and great uncle off and on. On many voyages Noah was the commodore of a small fleet of ships assembled for security of numbers as well as trade.

Hebe was devoted to her brother Noah and his mission to sail the oceans, and was a great comfort and companion for him in his attempts to show the people a better way to live. She was as equally committed to God as Noah, following their father and mother, Methuselah and the family patriarchs before them in their love and devotion to their Creator. Likewise, she brought her son up in the love of God. Because of their mission Noah equally had no inclination for marriage. But that was about to change.

The world's population had grown rapidly at this time because people lived to such a great age. There were now many millions of people living on the great world continent. Villages became towns, and towns became large cities with many fine buildings, while many thousands more lived in small villages in country areas. There was a great deal of good land to live on. The environment was healthy and safe, although not to the same extent as at the beginning of the world. But it was not so safe from the violent intentions of many of earth's inhabitants.

The rapid rise in population was due to a very low death rate, while at the same time women continued to give birth to more and more children. Deaths by accident were infrequent and by disease rare, although it was not uncommon for women and babies to die in childbirth. Eventually one or two here and there died each month from old age. In Noah's immediate family only Methuselah's mother Edna as well as his grandparents Jared and Baraka had died of old age in the past two hundred years. Other relatives had died by accident or in childbirth, and one of the grandchildren of Noah's aunt Ruath was killed when their outlying village in Havilah was attacked by a raiding party from Nod. These attacks were becoming more commonplace across the inhabited world as it became more and more violent in the absence of strong leadership or government to control it.

The highest number of deaths was from murder and tribal wars. More and more people, perhaps because they were now living more closely together, were found dead by another's hand when there were squabbles. This was nothing new. Ever since Cain murdered

Abel the world had descended into evil by way of murder, bloodshed and violence. It was just that this had not found its way to Havilah to any great extent until two hundred years earlier when the population began to increase significantly. Sadly, many people began to think the world was becoming overpopulated and it became increasingly popular to abort unwanted pregnancies. Some tribal groups even sacrificed their babies to inanimate gods, much to the horror of Noah and his family when they heard of this.

As often as they were able the dedicated followers of the Creator gathered together to encourage one another and remind each other of the way God desired them to live in relationship to each other and the world at large. On one such evening they were together in the grand hall of Lamech's homestead.

"There used to be so many of us," a saddened Lamech lamented. "We met in the village hall and half the village would turn up. Now it's just a few of us meeting here."

"It is very sad," Methuselah agreed. "The world is evil and corrupt. There is so much violence. Our own village has become a city of sin and greed. The people are no longer following Elohim. They are more interested in the comforts and pleasures of this world."

"I'm especially troubled," lamented an older and wiser Noah. "Everywhere I go at best I am laughed at. Sometimes they listen and then hit back with a statement that living and enjoying life is better than dreaming fairy tales. At times I'm told to go away, with threats to make my life unhealthy if I don't. Even my good friends and one time crew have abandoned Elohim for the pleasures of this world. Irad and Thirsk have taken other wives which is not sanctioned by Adonai and even more than one while their true wives languish in misery. Yet Irad is still my good friend, and I see him occasionally. Phar and Ari gamble, get drunk and get into fights I'm told. I don't see much of them anymore, and if I do, they cross the street to avoid me. It breaks my heart, as we were once so close. It seems that the closer I get to Adonai the further my friends fall away."

"We can't trust the merchants in the city markets anymore," added a frustrated Lamech. "There's bribery and intimidation when trading, and many use inflated or deceptive weights and measures. People have become so corrupt. We now have brothels where men and women go about their wanton lusts in all kinds of debaucheries. It was never meant to be this way. Even in my own house Baruch and Hem have abandoned Adonai and gone their own way now. Where they are I have no idea. My sister Ruath, her husband Kor and their family have long since departed for another life back in Shulon. At least you, Tem, Hebe and Benlexar are still with us." Shaking his head he continued, "I can't believe Hamor and his family in Shur have turned against Adonai also."

Methuselah sat hunched over with a very dejected look on his face, simply shaking his head in unison with his son as he reflected sadly on the state of the world. "Even the land and plants are becoming less of a delight to us. We work the ground hard and toil many hours each day to produce crops, but it seems each decade is harder than the one before. The weeds and thistles have become more plentiful, not less, even after all the work we do," he said sadly.

"The animal life has also changed for the worse these past few hundred years," continued Methuselah. "I've seen carcases in the forests and uninhabited plains where animals have ripped other animals apart. I've even seen one animal attacking another weaker than itself. It was never like this when I was a child."

"I won't let you down father," a now much older and mature Tem said. "Sadly, I can't say the same for my sons and daughters. They don't want to know a God who took their mother from them at an early age. But that's in the past. I'm going with Noah on his next voyage to Shulon. Surely we can find some godly people there."

"Where are you going next Noach?" asked Betenos in an attempt to lighten the heaviness that had crept into their conversation.

"In a week I'm taking the ship to Eridu in Shulon. I should be there a few weeks trading gold and gems for wheat and flour. Tem and Benlexar are coming with me, but not Hebe this time."

"My eldest son has just turned one hundred," mused Benlexar, "So he and his brothers and their sons and daughters are well able to look after my fields and vines. As my wife is no longer alive I can enjoy sailing the seas again with my uncles and look forward to the next voyage."

"I'm travelling inland to look at some wild animals with my friend Yael and draw them. I hope I don't run into your ferocious ones grandfather," said Hebe laughing.

"Perhaps my daughter should spend more time looking for a husband and Noach should do the same for a wife!" grumbled Betenos.

"Oh, mother, really!" cried Hebe.

"All right, all right it's your life."

At this the room became uncomfortably silent.

"Eridu? I have a son Rakeel there, the one who didn't come to Havilah with us. He has several daughters," chuckled Methuselah, trying to lighten the atmosphere once again. However, the damage was done as Betenos' last statement had upset Hebe. The group then dispersed and Hebe left quickly, embarrassed and close to tears.

But for Noah his mother's statement heightened a feeling of unease he had suffered from over recent months. He was not getting any younger and was starting to look his age.

‡‡‡

The city of Eridu was about the same size as Ophir. It lay nearly three week's sailing to the west, and like Ophir it was a manufacturing centre and port. Large areas of wheat were grown round about

Eridu and this was why Noah had come there to trade and supplement Ophir's own stores of grain and flour.

There was a large body of learning in Eridu. The city was famous for its astronomers, both men and women, who had built instruments to view and study the movement of the stars and planets in the night sky. There were also mathematicians and scientists who argued amongst themselves about how the world was born, what the relevance of the distant stars was, and where humanity had come from.

As they approached Eridu Noah expressed his pleasure at their early arrival. "We've made good time on this voyage Tem," he said. "Hopefully our regular suppliers will have grain ready for us, otherwise we may have to wait until it's harvested."

"Well, it isn't a problem if we do. This is such a beautiful place and I don't mind staying here a while. Do you realise we have a relative here?" Tem recollected.

"You mean Rakeel, who Methuselah mentioned? Yes, we should call on him this visit."

As it turned out, their regular supplier had already sold his crop to another trader who offered a better deal than Noah did on his previous visit. He then suggested they approach a man called Rakeel, who still had grain and flour left to sell.

"What a coincidence!" laughed Noah. "Our uncle, who we were going to visit anyway, may be the person we trade with this time."

"Perhaps it's meant to be," answered Benlexar, and Noah looked at his nephew as if he had made a prophetic declaration.

"Yes Ben, perhaps it is."

Knowing his ship was in good hands with his crew, Noah, Tem and Benlexar made their way to Rakeel's estate some way out of the city, arriving in the late afternoon.

A man about Lamech's age greeted them as they made their way up the long pathway to his homestead. He had auburn hair flecked with grey unlike the fair-haired Lamech, yet with the same blue eyes that Lamech and Noah had also inherited. Standing beside him was a lady about the same age with dark hair and brown eyes. Noah greeted them first.

"I am Noach, son of Lamech, son of Methuselah, and these men with me are my younger brother Tem and nephew Benlexar."

"Welcome to our estate, cousins, we are Rakeel and Rebe. I am Lamech's brother. All these many years and we have never met till today. Well, I did see you when you were a baby, but not since then. You are most welcome to stay with us a few days."

"Thank you, it would be our pleasure."

However, the three visitors stayed rather more than a few days due to an event that had been a long time coming for Noah. It happened this way:

They spent the rest of the day talking together and getting to know one another. Rakeel, of course, had heard much of Noah and his exploits and asked him many questions about his voyages. In turn Rakeel and Rebe spoke of their family of four sons and six daughters, most of whom had long since left the estate and were now living elsewhere. Only the youngest daughter Emzara still lived with them. She was shortly due to come in from the fields where she spent most of her time as she loved outdoor work. Rebe told Noah that Emzara was not yet married, but he didn't think too much about this unsolicited information until he set eyes on her.

Later in the afternoon Tem and Benlexar went exploring after they were invited to look over the estate and both Rakeel and Rebe retired to attend to some business, leaving Noah alone in the family living room. Thinking about nothing in particular and feeling relaxed in this comfortable home, he was gazing out the window at the fields of corn that stretched into the distance when all of a sudden a door banged open behind him and disturbed the quietness he was enjoying. He turned round and gaped as he looked at what appeared to him to be some heavenly apparition. There, standing in the middle of the room, having come to an abrupt stop after rushing through the door, stood the most beautiful creature he had ever laid eyes on.

The woman wore a wide floppy hat, and her dark brown hair was tangled and in streaks down to her bronzed shoulders. A smear of what looked like soil was plastered on one cheek and she was dressed in unkempt working clothes covered in dust. She had dark brown eyes and she was beautiful.

Now, as we have discovered, Noah had been alive for many, many years and was probably the most travelled man in the entire world. He had met many people during his lifetime, both men and women, and was not known for being reserved or ever at a loss for words. He had never to his knowledge been awkward in the presence of any woman until today.

"Who are you?" demanded the woman.

"I, ah, we came, ah, well I …" stumbled Noah.

"What? Does my father know you are here? What are you doing in my living room?"

Composing himself, Noah finally got his mouth to mesh with his mind.

"I am Noach and you must be Emzara, I'm your cousin, Lamech's son. I've come here to Eridu with my brother and nephew to trade with Rakeel."

"Yes, well, I am Emzara, but I prefer to be called Naamah," she smiled, relieved that he was not an intruder. Here, standing in her home in front of her was Noach, the celebrated hero, of whom she had heard so much, but whom she had never met until today.

"So you are Noach. I've heard so much about you," she said. And when she smiled at Noah he was smitten. "I have always wanted to meet you, and we're related."

"Yes, we are. You and your family have been here all this time, and it's taken me this long to find you, I mean to visit."

"I hope you're going to stay a few days."

"Ye – yes we plan to."

"Oh my, look at me! Oh, you shouldn't have seen me like this. I must go, I need to wash and change."

With that Naamah rushed out of the room and Noah was left alone once more.

'Did that just happen or was I dreaming? I've just met the most beautiful creature in all the world and I know I'm going to marry her. Oh, stupid man that I am! What have I just said?'

From the time of Adam when a man meets a woman and they are attracted to each other, a certain harmony takes place that both experience and they know that *this is the one*. It doesn't happen in every case, nor to most, but for Noah and Naamah it did.

Over the next few days they spent countless hours together just talking, as they had many years to catch up on. Naamah was not even born when Noah called into Eridu on his first great journey around the world, and somehow, although he had visited the city many times later, their family paths had not crossed. Noah now learnt that Naamah knew a great deal about him. She also treasured a manuscript written by Enoch himself that her now unbelieving father no longer had a use for. It contained all she knew of the Creator whom she loved and talked to, and for Noah this was music to his ears. Naamah shared with him that Emzara was her given name but from childhood her brothers and friends all called her Naamah which she preferred.

Noah could not recall when he actually asked Naamah to marry him; they simply connected and both knew instinctively within a couple of days of Noah's arrival that they would become man and wife.

So after staying with Rakeel and Rebe three weeks, not only did Noah take all of Rakeel's harvest and flour back to Ophir, he also took Naamah, Rakeel, Rebe and a few of their nearby relatives as well, because it was decided they would be married in Ophir, since Lamech and Methuselah were there and Rakeel wished to see them once again to make up for the years of not enjoying this family connection.

Twenty days after leaving Eridu they approached Ophir, excited with the news and family they were bringing with them. However, what a disaster awaited them!

Smoke was rising over the city and spreading out to sea. Charred wood and broken pieces of furniture and other articles littered the sea near the docks. On shore, buildings near the seafront were also charred ruins, doors smashed and broken wood and rubble lying everywhere. Nothing like this had ever been seen in Ophir before. When Noah and those with him finally got ashore a dejected Lamech and Hebe were there to greet them.

"We were attacked by an army the day before yesterday. They were many hundreds of men and Nephilim from Nod." Lamech explained.

"It happened as Yael and I were returning home. She left me on the other side of town and ran to her family, as I rushed to the cave where I knew our family would be," whimpered Hebe, "but I haven't seen her since."

"Yes, we all took refuge in the cave that we prepared for this very purpose after the incident with Kurt all those years ago," added Lamech.

"What of mother and the others?" asked an incredulous Noah.

"Betenos is safe, and so are Methuselah and Edna, but sadly we've lost Hamor my younger brother when they looted Shur as well. As a town elder he took it upon himself to stand up to them and they killed him. Besides him they also killed your son Kenan, Ben, who was defending your homestead. Tem's sons and the rest of Ben's family are safe." At Lamech's words Benlexar ran off groaning with anger to see to his family. Hebe was close on his heels hoping to console him, when and if she could catch up with him.

Lamech continued. "Several hundred more in the city are dead. It was a massacre. Those who could fought back died and many of our people were killed. The invaders looted, raped our women and burnt many of the wooden buildings. They also demolished as many stone structures as they could, smashing doors and laughing as they did so. They terrified people even when they didn't kill them. Those that survived were mainly the ones that ran to the hills or hid themselves. It was horrible. They've gone now, thanks be to Adonai, and we've started cleaning up."

Much later in the day all the family gathered at Lamech's homestead which had been damaged but was liveable. Rakeel and his household members were accommodated in the guest wing that had been added to the original building many years earlier. But with all that had happened there was no celebration of the family's reunion and Noah's good news that night. Eventually after another day or so helping with the clean-up and reuniting families with their lost ones, especially Benlexar, they did come together, to formally announce their great news and rekindle their relationships once more. Lamech and Betenos were very happy despite the loss to their city and family, and Noah hardly got to see Naamah as everyone wanted to spend time with her.

Hebe welcomed her future sister in law, and to her surprise the two women found they were kindred spirits and got on well together. Nevertheless, when Hebe was alone in her room that night she was sad contemplating that her close relationship with Noah would never again be the same. Her tears flowed freely when she thought about her best friend Yael, who had been raped and murdered by the raiders.

Despite all that had happened the two families took heart and put on a banquet to celebrate Noah and Naamah's marriage. It was quite enjoyable, but also somewhat subdued because of recent events. Lamech, as priest of Adonai performed the honours.

After this Noah took his new wife and her family back to Eridu and lived there for several years, taking on some of the responsibilities of running his father-in-law's estate. His sea journeys were over now and Hanoch became captain of his ship. Benlexar also captained another ship, while Tem retired to his small plot of land next to Benlexar's estate, not far from the homestead where Lamech and Betenos along with Methuselah, Edna and Hebe continued to live.

ELEVEN

Grief

*The Land of Havilah – Fifteen Years Later
AM 1535*

Burying the dead in Shulon or Havilah for that matter was not a common occurrence in this world where people lived to great ages. So it was a rather unusual affair for Rakeel's family when they found themselves burying their father Rakeel, followed by Rebe their mother just five days later. Not a day after this their sons told Noah and Naamah they had to leave and relinquish all rights to any of the family's property. They were no longer welcome, especially as they had the nerve to keep on moralising about their God. The message was short and harsh: "Enough! We want you gone."

In this way they left the estate Noah had been content to manage for the past fifteen years, and so he and his loving Naamah returned to Ophir in Havilah. When they arrived back they learned their dear grandmother Edna was very unwell and not expected to live much longer. Thus it was that just two days later she slipped away in her sleep and was buried on the family estate. All the family in Ophir gathered to comfort and support Methuselah and one another.

"People are dying in greater numbers it seems," Noah lamented.

"Well, we're all destined for death some time," said Naamah. "I didn't know our grandmother very long and I'm sorry we didn't have more time together."

"She was a good wife and support to Methuselah. She kept herself very much in the background and didn't involve herself in our lives. She was never upset or angry. Perhaps that's why she lived so long. She has done very well," Noah added.

Much later in the evening Methuselah, Lamech and Noah sat together having a long discussion in which Tem also took part. He was living alone in the home he had built for his family a fifteen minute walk along the road from the family estate. Now that his wife was long since dead and his children had moved to other towns he spent many nights visiting the family home for companionship.

Uppermost in their conversation was the state of the world. It was now steadily becoming darker, more violent, unsafe and godless, with the approval of all manner of sinful acts men and women had forced on society. It was no longer acceptable to believe in God or be who you wanted to be. Social pressure demanded that not only did a person have to accept the irreverent practices of others, but many were compelled to take part in them even against their will and better judgment. At times it seemed that long held ways of doing things were reversed so that right had become wrong and evil was now good.

The increasing godlessness of the earth weighed heavily upon the spirit of the devout Lamech, whose family and a small group of believers in the Creator God and his ways steadfastly resisted the new world order of things as much as they could.

"We must do something about the way the world is going!" an angry Lamech said.

"Well, perhaps I could take a ship around the world once again and reason with people as we went along," replied Noah. "There are still good people out there, and I promised Naamah I would take her on such a voyage."

Methuselah held up his right hand and paused a long time before he spoke. "Not this time Noach, Lamech, I fear the world is now lost. There is something I must share with you both. Now is the time with Edna's passing to tell you what Enoch my father shared with me as a child."

"What was that…?"

"Not tonight," Methuselah interrupted Lamech. "Tomorrow, the three of us, you, Noach and myself must take a walk up the hill behind the estate. There we'll stay a few nights and camp under the stars and wait on Adonai to speak to us. While there I'll tell you what was given to me all those years ago. The time has come for me to share what Enoch prophesied, and I must no longer withhold it."

That night both Methuselah and Lamech had a dream.

The following day the three men rested after climbing the hill behind their estate. All the men were well advanced in years, but still fit and healthy, although Methuselah took a little longer to climb the track than he did in his younger days.

"There's still life in these old bones, my sons. I'm not going the way of all the earth yet," he sighed as they each found a flat rock to sit on.

Here they took in the view before them, looking across the city and to the south where their own estate lay. To the west were the forest covered hills and the river winding its way between them into the great jungle that stretched far to the north and eventually into the land of Nod. Southwards the ocean stretched away to the distant horizon. As they gazed in this direction the sun rose from the east, warming the land. All this presented a pleasant picture of the land they lived in.

"I have something to share," said Lamech. "I had a dream last night, a very specific one that remains firmly in my memory. I believe Elohim has something important to say to us today."

"I also had a dream," added Methuselah. "Did you Noach?"

"No, grandfather I did not, I slept rather deeply after our talk last night. I told Naamah we would come up here today and stay a while. She agreed with me that we need to seek Elohim's direction for whatever lies ahead of us."

"Share your dream, Lamech, and then I'll share mine," said Methuselah.

"It was like nothing I've seen on earth before. There was trouble and turmoil. The seas were raging with giant waves and a strong wind was blowing, the like of which I don't know how to describe. And water was everywhere. There was some form of raft or craft as well, but all that was in the background as Noach's face filled my dream."

There was a long pause as they looked to Methuselah who was sitting with sad eyes, musing on what Lamech had shared. "I, too, had the same dream," Methuselah said eventually, speaking slowly and softly as if each word was of great importance. "Noach filled my vision, but behind him he was holding hands with others. I couldn't see their faces. Like you, Lamech, I saw the sea raging angrily, but I saw no land. God is speaking to us today my sons, for both of us to have had the same dream at the same time."

"What do these dreams mean? Am I to be lost at sea on one of my voyages?" asked Noah in alarm.

"No, my son, it's much deeper than that. Remember, last night I said I had to share a prophecy of Enoch's with you. Now is the time for me to speak about it."

"Before you share that, father, I recall that Enoch spoke of a time when God would bring judgment on this world if the people don't change their ways. We also believed when Noah was born that Adonai had a special purpose for his life. Could these things be connected?"

"They are, Lamech. Enoch was appalled that the world was turning against Adonai. We knew the line of Cain was a godless one, and we also knew his seed would intermarry with the line of Seth and the other sons and daughters of Adam and Hevah. We also thought God would protect his own name and most of the people would continue to follow him, but this hasn't happened. People have been more interested in enjoying the pleasures of this world, rather than walking with Adonai. That's why they have fallen away from him.

"Even then Adonai might have extended his grace to them, had it not been for the fallen angels who manifested themselves as human beings and did a detestable thing. They were male and took our women as their wives and so introduced living beings who were not human into this world. These are the Nephilim, the fallen ones, the offspring of the fallen angels. They in turn mated with humans, and now we have the in-breds, who are among us today in alarming numbers. Oh yes, the fallen angels brought with them a lot of knowledge and instruction to us, and many of the Nephilim are tall, strong and muscular and can perform tasks that make our lives easier. They've helped us build great structures, but they are not human. They are not the perfect beings Elohim placed on the Earth at the beginning. The world now has no doubt gained great knowledge, but instead of using it for good it is being used for evil purposes. And if the people continue to multiply at the present rate then eventually most will have non-human characteristics. Yet, as Elohim promised Hevah, he would bring a redeemer to save humanity. This person cannot be an in-bred, he must be a man. Enoch also told us the Nephilim were a demonic incursion to prevent the redeemer being born. All this Enoch knew when Adonai revealed it to him all those years ago. He also understood that at some time in the future Adonai would unleash a great judgment on the world. What and when that judgement will come I have no idea. Perhaps our dreams last night were to give us a forewarning of all this."

"That's very likely," said Lamech.

"You've heard it said that my name means 'he comes'," Methuselah continued, "but that isn't quite right. When Enoch named me he didn't want to cause alarm to those around him before the appointed time. He told me in my youth he gave me this name because Adonai had shown him in a vision that this judgment would come when I die. So my name actually means 'when he dies it shall be sent,' referring to the judgement in store for the world. This is now my 850ᵗʰ year, and though I don't know when my death will come it can't be far off."

"This is all a lot to take in," said a troubled Noah. "I am sure Adonai is speaking to us today. We must take heed of Methuselah's words."

"The time for their fulfilment is near I fear," added Lamech. "From what we've heard here this morning, and hearing what both father and I saw in our visions last night, it's my belief that you, Noach, are to have a major role to play in whatever Elohim has in store for this world."

"I totally agree," said Methuselah, confirming what Lamech had said. "I feel very strongly that you and I, Lamech, should move away now and leave Noach here on this hilltop to seek the mind of Adonai and not return to us until our God has shown him what he must do."

For the next three days a troubled Noah prayed and sought his God to answer him and confirm the prophecy his father and grandfather had shared. During this time he ate sparingly and was full of the Spirit of the Creator, in a way such as he had never experienced before. In the late afternoon of the third day he was sitting quietly on the ground, leaning comfortably against a rock, his mind clear of any thought and heavy-eyed to the point of sleep. It was then God spoke audibly to him.

My Spirit will not contend with man forever, for he is corrupt;
his days will be 120 years.

Noah could not move. He was transfixed.

*I will wipe out mankind whom I have created from the face of
the land; mankind and animals as well, crawling things, and
the birds of the sky. For I am grieved that I have made them.*

"Adonai, Lord, is it you who is speaking to me? I am overcome.
Why are you telling me these things, the least worthy of all people?
What would you have me do?" Noah asked aloud as he lay prostrate
on the ground.

Noah was aware of the quiet peace around him with no sounds
except the buzzing of flying insects, the song of birds and the gentle breeze ruffling the leaves of nearby trees and bushes, but there
was no answer from God. After he had waited for some time Noah
began to walk slowly down the pathway leading to his homestead
and family, uncertain how he was going to explain the revelation
he had received.

"120 years?" said Methuselah, his forefinger tapping his pursed
lips and frowning in a contemplative manner.

"Yes, he said that."

"Does that mean the earth has only 120 years left before Adonai
destroys it, or is it that anyone born from now on will only live 120
years?" asked Naamah.

"He definitely said he was going to destroy all living things. At
least, all that is on the land and in the air."

"What did his voice sound like?" asked Hebe.

"It was gentle, yet firm, spoken in such a way that was not to be
questioned or challenged. I simply knew what he said was true and
would come to pass. It could not be disputed, for it was the word
of truth. The voice was beyond description. I simply know in my
heart it was Adonai who spoke to me."

"I believe he has more to tell you, Noach. You must wait upon him and he will tell you what you, what we all must do," said Lamech.

"Yes, father, that's what terrifies me," replied Noah.

At that moment the double front doors of the homestead were thrown open, startling all of them.

"Tem! What is it?" asked a startled Lamech as his younger son dashed through the open doorway, breathless with running and unable to get his words out fast enough.

"Attack, attack, the city is being attacked!" he cried.

TWELVE

Grace

There are thousands of them," gasped Tem.

"What? Where?"

"All over, there's a great army. They came over the hills from the North!"

"I've just come back from the hill behind us and saw nothing," said Noah. All of them then rushed out to the forecourt, but there was nothing to be seen, although they could hear the increasing noise of destruction in the distance.

At this moment Benlexar arrived with his granddaughter Ariel, Kenan's youngest daughter. "They must have come from the northeast along the valley road. We must go and help," shouted Noah.

Despite his great age, or perhaps because of it, Methuselah assessed the situation immediately, especially in light of what they had just been discussing with Noah. "No, my family. If what Tem says is true, from what we can hear and the fires we now see in the distance, I believe it would be foolhardy for us to join in that fight. We don't have any idea what we would be up against, but I'm certain it's something terrible. To the cave all of you, immediately, and take the servants too," he added loudly.

"I won't come," said Tem. "I'll stay and protect my property with my sons."

"We should do the same," said Lamech.

"No, my sons and daughters, we won't prevail against this foe, please believe me. Already I can see this is far worse than the last time they raided us. Lamech, we know that Adonai has spoken to us, and this is not the time for fighting."

"We've got to hide and save ourselves now for what he wants us to do later," Methuselah added urgently.

"I know you're right father."

"I'm going back to my home. I need to save my livestock," said Tem dismissively.

"I'm coming too," shouted Benlexar, "but Ariel, you must go with Hebe, she'll care for you."

"No! Benlexar," cried Hebe.

"I must, mother, my sons and their families, they won't leave, I must go to them."

"Oh, this is so wrong!" sobbed a distraught Hebe.

"I'll join you," added Noah.

"No Noach, you must come with us!" the women cried as one.

"Please Noach," pleaded Naamah, "You need to be with us, to protect us."

Torn between the brother he loved, his nephew and his responsibility to his wife and elders he reluctantly went with them, while Tem and Benlexar returned to their properties and the sound of fighting came closer.

An hour later the family were safely hidden in a grove of trees some distance from the homestead, in the underground cave recently enlarged for just this purpose. Here, Lamech's entire household awaited the outcome of the fighting. In the distance they could hear a lot of smashing, crashing and breaking, along with distant rumbles and a tragic cacophony of high pitched screams from men as well as women. This made the hidden women shiver in fear, while the men became impatient and angry. Everyone was wondering how this calamity could have befallen them.

Methuselah settled himself in a chair blocking the cave entrance.

He knew that his younger men, although they were getting older, were still impetuous and could at any moment lose control of themselves and rush out of the cave to join the fight. So he made sure none of them was going to leave the safety of the cave. He therefore stayed awake at the doorway until the sun rose the next day.

Meanwhile, at Tem's small holding he had been joined by Noah's old crew who had decided to head to Lamech's homestead in order to help defend it, but finding it deserted they then ran on to Tem's place.

"Where is Noach?" shouted Hanoch.

"He went with the others. I came back to protect my home."

"Where are they?"

"A safe place, I am sworn to secrecy, I can't tell you, sorry."

"Then we will stay here and help you protect your home, but why aren't you with them?"

"This home is all I have, I chose to stand and protect it. What about yours?" "Already gone. One of the first places they attacked. We had to run for our lives."

"Who are they?"

"The same as before, brutes from Nod! But many more than last time."

Hanoch, Iro and Tem with what meagre armaments they could lay their hands on stood firm in the gateway. They had one sword, a pitchfork and a large hammer used for driving posts into the ground. They were ready to defend against what was inevitably coming at them. Likewise, just several cubits away in their homestead, Benlexar's extended family was grouped inside their large stone dwelling, also with only a few farm tools to protect them, waiting for the inevitable.

Soon after sunrise Methuselah heard groaning outside. He tentatively opened the hidden entrance, and there was Benlexar, lying wounded and near death. His mother brushed roughly past

Methuselah in her haste to get to him. She fell on her knees and held her son as he tried to speak.

"Don't talk my love. We'll take you in and care for you," said Hebe, weeping.

"No, mother dearest, I'm done."

"Don't talk, save your energy."

"They came, they're gone, all gone …"

With that Benlexar let out a long sigh and died in his mother's arms. "Oh my son, not you too! not you," she wept.

Betenos came to comfort her and Ariel also rushed out, falling down and grasping her grandfather's limp hand, sobbing. Eventually, Lamech and Noah brought Benlexar's body into the cave. There was nothing more anyone could do.

By mid-morning all was quiet outside. Lamech gave the women and the three servants in the cave orders not to venture out or open up for anyone and promised they would be back within an hour after they had done a short reconnaissance around the immediate area.

Lamech, Noah and Methuselah tentatively made their way out of the cave to look around and make sure things were now safe. They had promised themselves that at any sign of trouble they would return to the cave and wait in safety as long as necessary.

No one, friend or foe was nearby. It was clear their homestead was in ruins even before they got to it. Smoke wafted up from inside the building and most of the roof had collapsed. All of it except the wing where Noah and Naamah lived was now uninhabitable.

They quickly made their way to Tem's home where a gruesome sight met them. Not only was his stone house gutted and left a smoking ruin with only the stonework standing, but impaled on the fence were the heads of Tem, Hanoch and Iro, their blood still dripping on to the green grass below and forming red puddles. Tem's sons lay slain in a nearby field.

"Evil has engulfed us today," wept Lamech. Noah and Methuselah simply stared at this scene, stunned into silence. Then, at the homestead next door, they found the dead bodies of all Benlexar's family. Only Ariel had survived in the safety of the family shelter.

Later in the day when they realised the storm of terror had passed and the massive army of destruction had moved down the coast to the east to continue its rape and rampage, the family started clearing up what they could.

"So much evil, O Lord, when will you end it?" lamented Methuselah.

Noah walked in a state of numbed incredulity through what was once a great city that he personally had done so much to make prosperous, and now was a heap of ruins.

Ash, smoke and dust still wafted about in what was left of the city centre. As soon as the afternoon sea breeze cleared patches of smoke more would drift over the gruesome scene again. Stepping and stumbling over broken rock and burnt embers he made his way, numbed to the core by what had happened.

'Where was I when my brother needed me?' he thought. *'Hanoch and Iro are both dead now. They must have come to help me. And all of Ben's family too. How can I live with myself after all this?'*

Virtually no building in the city remained undamaged. Most of the wooden buildings were burnt to the ground and the stone ones were gutted as well, their roofs and contents utterly destroyed.

Noah kept walking and seeing it all, and yet not comprehending what he saw, for his mind was elsewhere. Eventually he came upon the old wharf area by the shore, the very place where he used to moor *Discovery*. Here, he knew was the place where Irad his old partner and friend moored his ship. What he now saw only added to his grief, for lying on his back on the wooden planks just cubits from where his ship should be, his long-time friend lay with his throat cut, his eyes and mouth wide open. With tears in his own eyes Noah kneeled down beside Irad and with his hand gently closed his friend's. He then lifted Irad's body up to his own chest and held him close, sobbing. Noah stayed there a long time.

After a while someone came and gently separated them so they could take Irad's body away for burial. Noah didn't know the person, but asked where Irad's ship was.

"They took the best ships and burnt or holed the smaller ones. There are none left," he was told.

As he trudged back to the comfort of Naamah at the homestead, Noah found out that the rest of his original crew, Thirsk, Ari and Phar, had all been killed by the rampaging raiders. They were all dead.

Naamah, Hebe, Betenos and Lamech tried their best to comfort Noah and absolve him of all responsibility for what had happened to his old crew, his family, and Ophir as a whole but Noah would not be consoled. After several days while he was still grief-stricken Noah took himself back to his quiet place to speak to his God. *"Why, Lord?"* he asked, staying on his hilltop another three days, eating nothing except some small berries, drinking from a small stream nearby and waiting on God to speak to him again.

‡‡‡

Some Months Later ...
AM 1536

"Adonai won't speak to you while you're in a morbid state of self-pity and incrimination Noach," said Lamech, scolding his son.

"Seven times I've been up on that hill waiting on him, so what else can I do?" grumbled Noah in reply.

"Noach, you're not responsible for what happened to us. Our world is God's creation. It's up to him to do what he plans to do about it. We know he has called you for something important in the future. You simply have to take your eyes off yourself, look to him and then he will show you."

In the meantime the family had rebuilt and expanded Noah and Naamah's wing of the homestead sufficiently for all of them to be able to live in it once again while they rebuilt the rest. Likewise the townspeople who had survived were restoring what they could. The city had been reduced to a town again, because tens of thousands of the people had been massacred and those who survived were facing the tremendous task of reconstruction needed over the coming months and years.

Noah prayed earnestly that night on his knees with Naamah at his side. He slept well and the next morning felt that something had changed within him. "I'm going back up the hill again dearest, I think today may be a significant one," he said to Naamah.

"I hope so my love."

Once more Noah trudged up the well-worn track behind the homestead. As he sat on his favourite rock he thought about his family who had all been together here so many years earlier. Of the eight original members only four now remained, himself, his mother and father and Hebe his sister. Of Baruch, Hem and their families he knew nothing of where they were or if, in fact, they were still alive. Dearest Dinah had been raped and murdered, and now Tem had been killed as well. He sighed and once again began to wait on his Lord. He waited all day. As evening approached God spoke to him again:

> *I am going to put an end to all people, for the earth is filled*
> *with violence because of them.*
> *I am surely going to destroy both them and the earth.*
> *So make yourself an Ark of cypress wood; make rooms in it*
> *and coat it with pitch inside and out. This is how you are to*

*build it: The Ark is to be three hundred cubits long, fifty cubits
wide and thirty cubits high. Make a roof for it, leaving below
the roof an opening one cubit high all around. Put a door in
the side of the Ark and make lower, middle and upper decks.
I am going to bring floodwaters on the earth to destroy
all life under the heavens, every creature that has the breath of
life in it. Everything on earth will perish.*

A stunned silence greeted Noah when he came to the homestead and revealed what God had spoken to him. Eventually Betenos asked, "Are you sure that is what Adonai said Noach?"

"I am afraid so, mother. It was very specific. I dare not do anything other than what he told me."

"Who will be saved?" wondered Lamech. "The ship is big enough by those measurements to take many people, but … surely Elohim does not want to save in-breds and violent people, yet He said he will destroy all mankind. So why such a large ship?"

"It's what I suspected it would be. Adonai has a plan that he has revealed to Noach. I believe he has more to say to Noach before the day of destruction," and with a light chuckle Methuselah added, "Well, you better have it built before I die, because when I die …"

"It comes!" they all shouted and laughed together, despite the seriousness of God's prophecy.

"It will be an immense size and it will take us many years to build this ship," Noah thought out loud.

Looking toward Naamah and smiling Lamech said, "Well, Noach, you better have some sons to help you build this thing."

Betenos and Hebe groaned at this statement, but Naamah looked at Noah with a twinkle in her eye as the two of them shared unspoken words of love for each other.

"I suppose we shall," agreed Noah. "A great judgment is about to fall on this land, and it seems that Adonai has chosen me to be some kind of deliverer."

After this, God extended mercy to the people of the earth. He waited another one hundred and twenty years before he brought destruction upon them, giving them, wicked, lustful and corrupt as they were, a chance to repent. Having commissioned Noah to build an Ark, he now also provided people with a period of grace in which they could turn back to him.

‡‡‡

In the course of time Noah and his family set up a camp at the river mouth to the west of Ophir near the place where they had built *Discovery*. Here they cleared a great area of forest to provide housing while they were building, as well as a place for the Ark itself to be built. They realised it would take many years just to get to the first stage of laying the keel, since a great deal of scaffolding and related infrastructure needed to be planned and built for this to happen.

Eventually, during this time, Naamah gave birth to three sons they named Japheth, Shem and Ham. The boys grew up between the homestead in Ophir and the Ark building site. They now used the river to get there, having cleared a road through the forest from the estate down to the river bank. A small boat and rafts for the purpose were built to transport people and supplies constantly between the two sites.

Ariel, the only survivor of Benlexar's family, also eventually married a godly man who joined them in the task of building the great ship. The couple had a daughter to whom they gave the name of Sede.

In his 480th year Noah had been given a commission by God Himself to build an Ark of redemption for those who were to be saved.

And so he did.

PART TWO

THE ARK

THIRTEEN

The Build

The Land of Havilah — 64 Years Later
AM 1600

The camp was astir when the lookout at the river mouth saw Noah's ship on the horizon, returning once again. Along with his preparations for the Ark, Noah had built another ship to continue trading their produce and recruit people to join in the building of the great ship and hopefully committing their lives to God. Noah had made several voyages to that effect, each time training his sons in sailing and ship handling. Shem had stayed in camp this time, but Japheth and Ham had gone with him on this latest voyage.

Japheth guided the ship into the river mouth past the lookout standing in the lattice-woven tower they had built and waving them in. He then gently brought the ship into the small dock below the camp site just a short distance up the river. On a rise further back behind the encampment the greatest of all ships ever built sat on a flattened ridge Noah had cleared and levelled many years earlier. Even though it was not yet complete its framework of beams and great, strong ribs made an imposing sight as it pointed its massive bow to the blue sky.

"It always looks impressive every time we return," marvelled Japheth.

"Yes, my son, we're making good progress with it," chuckled Noah.

"I hope all this effort will be justified," added Ham.

Noah looked intently at his youngest son. Without taking his eye off Ham he said, "Adonai spoke to me quite clearly Ham. What he said shouldn't be ignored nor forgotten."

"As you say, father."

Ham then threw the mooring line to Nadav, Ariel's husband. As was their custom, all who were in camp then came out to welcome them.

Methuselah, healthy and strong as ever, had decided to remain at the camp by the Ark almost permanently now. This great judgment of God was to be the last major event in his life and he wanted to be where the action was when it happened. Everyone kept a close eye on his health and made sure he was never in danger so that this decree of God about his life, that when he died God's judgment would come, might be delayed as long as possible. Some thought this prophecy was superstitious, but others were inclined to treat it with respect. Noah was confident he still had fifty six left of the 120 years God had stated were needed to complete the task of building the Ark.

‡‡‡

Lamech and Betenos continued to live at the homestead on the family estate which provided much of their produce. After the road through the forest to the river was cleared they had added a lot more land to their estate as well and were farming many kinds of domesticated animals. They did not do this alone as they had the assistance of local people who needed the work at first. Later on their grandchildren from Noah and Ariel were expected to spend time on the estate helping to manage it. Hebe also undertook the management of the many animals they now had. At first she spent an equal amount of time between the Ark camp and the estate, but as time passed she spent more time at the former.

Twenty years after Noah received his commission from God,

Naamah had given birth to their first child and named him Japheth. Two years later Shem was born, and three after that Naamah gave birth to Ham. Japheth was now 44 years of age and Shem 42. Like their father they were dedicated not only to God but to the destiny they had been called to. They, along with Ham, would often travel with Noah to warn others of the coming judgment and invite people to repent and follow the God of creation. They knew they were building an Ark to save as many as wanted to be saved. The ship was large enough to do this. But it was always the same; they were laughed at and ridiculed. On rare occasions one or two would indicate their willingness to repent and come to help work on the great ship. However, such people soon lost interest in doing this. Their commitment was only skin deep, and they came out of curiosity rather than conviction.

Naamah took it upon herself to raise her boys in the love of the Lord. She would tell them the stories of old, and right there in their own family they had their father Noah, Hebe their aunt, grandfather Lamech and Methuselah to broaden their knowledge and train them up in the proper way that all boys and young men should go. Naamah was very proud of her handsome, strong and courageous sons, as they had all inherited the adventurous spirit of their father Noah. They were the pride of her life, and they in turn were very fond of their mother. Hebe and Naamah were inseparable. Not only did they share similar interests and a love of God, they worked as a team on the estate and in support of their men at the Ark site. Noah's boys loved Hebe almost as much as their mother and were often in her care when younger and worked with her as they matured. From her they learned to care for the estate animals, while their mother taught them the rudiments of growing crops and vegetables as she had done on her parents' estate. They were a close knit happy family. Ham was especially fond of his aunt as he loved helping with the animals.

During the building of the Ark a man had arrived looking for work. He quickly appeared to become infatuated with Hebe and she in turn responded to his attentions. The name he called himself was Jabal. He was, he said, named after an ancestor of long ago, but would not reveal anything more about himself, his family or much of what he had done in life except to say he had farmed the land and looked for odd jobs here and there. A drifter Noah thought and though he professed to be a follower of God, Noah was wary of him as were Lamech and Betenos. Despite their reservations Hebe became enraptured with him and so they were married and now a year later Hebe was about to give birth to their child. Betenos was horrified when she was told six months earlier that Hebe was with child as Hebe, at her age, was now beyond the accepted age of child bearing.

Ariel, the only surviving child of Benlexar's family, had married Nadav who had arrived in Ophir after a long journey. Nadav said he was related to Enosh of long ago and was the son of Danath who had met and traded with Noah on his first great circumnavigation of the world. Nadav's village was on the other side of the great continent in the land of Cush. It had been his ambition to travel and one day meet the great Noah.

Ariel gave birth to her daughter Sede one month after Shem was born. She and Nadav also had three other sons. Unfortunately, these sons became unruly in their early twenties and although they spent some time on the family estate and sat under the teaching of the women and that of Lamech and Methuselah they had no interest in the godly affairs of this family. Desiring to find their fortune in other lands, they left home at a young age. Of Nadav and Ariel's offspring only Sede was dedicated to the God of her parents and ancestors. She had grown up with Noah and Naamah's three sons who teased her, and she them, through her childhood and teenage years. When she grew into womanhood she told them how she loved both Shem and Japheth, though she was very fond of Ham as well. Her exasperated parents wondered if she would ever make up her mind which man she wished to marry, or in fact, she would marry any one of them.

Hebe nurtured Ariel and then Sede, as they grew and matured, in place of Ariel's parents and grandparents after they were brutally murdered in the last raid on Ophir years before. They in turn were devoted to her like a grandmother.

As it turned out, while Noah, Japheth and Ham were away on this latest voyage, Sede and Shem spent much more time together than previously and one happy evening it was Sede who asked Shem to marry her. She had decided to be the wife of a dedicated follower of the Lord. Although growing up together she loved all three men it was Shem she said God had told her to marry in a dream. Once she made that decision she knew it was the right one. Shem had all but given up believing Sede would ever be his wife after he had proposed to her almost twenty years previously and three more times since then.

"I had to be sure," she said, "I love your brothers, but I believe you are more committed to the service of Adonai than they are."

"I am so happy you made the right choice my darling," Shem replied.

With that he got a thump in the ribs as she ran off back to camp and he was left pondering why or what he said had been wrong. However, when he got back after her she was bubbly and excited and happy and he realised that this woman and he were going to have a happy loving relationship. Her parents were ecstatic as was Naamah, Hebe and everyone else.

As usual, after a long time away there was much hugging and back slapping as Noah, his sons and several others they had brought home with them were greeted by their family as they made their way from the ship to their little village that formed the Ark campsite.

"Well, well, what have we here Noach," asked a perplexed Methuselah, "who are all these people?"

"Yes grandfather, father, we have done very well on this trip. The best ever. These ten people have made a commitment to follow Adonai and help us finish our great enterprise."

"Ten! We've never had that many before," chuckled Lamech, "and some lovely ladies with them."

Introductions were made all round and another excuse for a feast that night had everyone looking forward to that. When the excitement had died down and Noah was alone with Naamah they gave each other a lengthy embrace.

"How are you my darling?" Noah asked.

"I am fine but Hebe is struggling with her confinement, I think this baby is close now. She says it's been difficult carrying it and she gets sharp pains every so often. This one is different from when she had Ben and she needs to rest often."

"So she must. In fact, my dear, I insist you go back with her along with father, and mother to the homestead tomorrow where she will be more comfortable."

"I won't argue with you on that. Oh, I love you so much Noach. You are so caring of others."

"I so love you too, Naamah, I missed you so much. But I love my sister also as we have shared so much together."

"I know my dearest, I will look after her, I love her too. Oh, I forgot with all the excitement."

"What?"

"Shem and Sede are to be married, they finally settled the question we were all asking ourselves."

"That's marvellous," laughed a happy Noah.

During the feast that followed Shem and Sede announced their betrothal to more clapping, ribbing and cheerful good wishes. Ham and Japheth looked over at each other, inclined their heads and shrugged their shoulders as if to say, 'We knew that would happen'. They congratulated the happy couple with affection and each gave Sede the warmest of brotherly hugs.

Later in the evening the younger family members separated themselves from the elders down by the river, swimming and chatting and generally enjoying themselves, along with the group of ten newcomers who were all relatively young, none of them more than fifty. Meanwhile the older people gathered round a fire in the centre of the small group of dwellings made of timber from the surrounding forest.

It became apparent to the elders that two of the four women they had brought on the ship were more than a little interested in Japheth and Ham, and they asked Noah if he was aware of this.

"Well, I think I need to explain one or two things," he answered.

"Will they be along the lines of things are not always what they seem?" suggested Lamech.

"I expect so."

"So let him tell his story without interruptions," sighed Betenos.

"As you know we headed along the coast of Shulon like the last time when we went east into Havilah. We went to as many villages as we could and got the usual response. Oh, we traded well and got what we wanted, but our greater work of saving lives for Adonai was just as unfruitful as at other times." Noah paused, collecting his thoughts.

"Go on uncle," prompted Ariel.

"We were between towns much further west than Eridu," he continued, looking briefly at Naamah when he mentioned her home city. "We came across this group of people on a remote beach. They appeared to be shipwrecked. Their mast was broken and they waved at us. We got as close as we could and then Ham and Japheth dived into the sea and swam over to them. To cut a long story short we took them on board and back to their village. It was just a small place less than a day's sailing further west." Noah stopped for a drink to quench his thirst and then continued.

"Six of that group over there were those people. It seemed to me that Ham had taken a liking to the dark haired one there. It took us two days to get them home and we were quite cramped, but they all slept on the deck. Ham and Nae, that's her name, she has a much longer name that's unpronounceable. Well, they were inseparable, and it turns out she's always been a secret admirer of Adonai, but has kept quiet about it for fear of being ridiculed. She claims she's related to one of Adam and Hevah's daughters, but doesn't know which one." Noah took another drink.

"Anyhow, she was able to convince her friends of what Ham had told them, that there's a judgment coming on the earth and that Adonai through us is the solution to their salvation to put it briefly. Each of them made a commitment to him. I made them each individually do this. So it seems we have some converts. Still, I must be honest with you. I wonder if it's not just to please Nae and out of curiosity see what we're doing here."

"But what of the other four?" queried Hebe.

"The young man sitting next to Nae with the red hair had a sister in the next village, so we were obliged to go there also. When he told her their story she insisted on coming as well and bringing her other brothers."

"So they haven't made a commitment?" asked Lamech.

"I'm tired, sorry, I forgot to say the auburn haired one sitting near Japheth, her name is Adataneses, but we call her Ada, who apparently also loves Adonai secretly. But would you believe it, we go on a lot of these voyages and get no response, and then on this one we find two women who independently follow Adonai, although they have never met each other until now. So there we have it."

"Well, it seems that Nae has her eyes on Ham," said Hebe.

"And Ada keeps looking at Japheth," giggled Ariel.

"Really?" asked Noah. "Well someone may need to tell Japheth, for I saw no interest from him in that direction during the voyage. But I do believe Ham is smitten."

"The others all seem like nice young people," suggested Betenos.

"This is very hopeful," said Lamech. "Let's trust they are as committed to Adonai as we are."

"Mmm," mused Methuselah. "In my dream or vision that Lamech also had and which we shared many years ago, the impression I had was that very few people will accompany you on this great excursion into the unknown Noach. I know I won't be there, and I doubt Lamech and Betenos will be either. We three are past our best. There are now over twenty people in this camp including our trusted labourers and I seriously doubt if all of them will go with you."

"That's a sobering thought grandfather," replied a weary Noah.

"Well, I hope Hebe and I are included, what with all the work I've put into this enterprise," growled Jabal.

"Who goes and who does not may very well not be anyone's decision, but the Lord's," responded Methuselah.

"Humph," replied Jabal as he got up and walked away.

"I'm sorry for his rudeness, family, Jabal has a few issues he needs to deal with," sighed Hebe as she struggled to get up.

"There aren't enough huts in the camp for everyone, so I'll make sure there's plenty of sailcloth to rig a shelter for our newcomers," stated Nadav. "They can sleep outdoors, but because of the heavy morning dew they'll need covers over them."

With that they broke off and most went off to their huts to sleep. Noah, Lamech and Methuselah had a quiet word together.

"I am not sure about that man, I was never happy Hebe married him and I fear for her future," complained Noah.

"I feel much the same way my son," sighed a concerned Lamech, with Methuselah nodding in agreement. Then they too went off to sleep while the younger group talked into the early hours of the next day.

The following day Lamech, with Betenos, Naamah and Hebe, boarded the raft they used to punt up the river on the long journey to their homestead. It was a slow job travelling upstream against the flow of the river. They used oars and moving the large rudder in the stern back and forth in a sideways motion to give the craft forward momentum. Two strong estate assistants accompanied them for this purpose. There were two rafts in use while the Ark was being built. One was at the river mouth by the Ark and the other at the estate. The one returning to the estate would remain there until it was needed to bring fresh supplies back to the Ark.

As the raft pushed off into the stream Hebe stood in the stern looking back at Jabal and Noah who watched them depart. Noah had an uneasy feeling in his stomach which he couldn't understand or put his finger on, while Jabal seemed unconcerned. Noah's usual response was to wave goodbye and then go off to attend to some urgent chore, but for some reason he didn't comprehend he stayed where he was and locked eyes with Hebe until the raft moved out of sight around the first bend in the river. As he turned he observed that Jabal had long since walked away.

With Noah's return the work on the Ark began again in earnest. Its actual construction had only started about ten years earlier, although Noah had had many more years since his commission to do so. These years had been spent planning and preparing the working site and all that was to be connected with it. The work hadn't stopped while he was absent because those who remained behind were always given some job to do.

Noah outlined to the newcomers what he had in mind and what was required to complete the project. In response the newcomers had many questions for him, and it was well into the day before he was able to find out from each one what experience and talents they had and allocate appropriate responsibilities to them. The first job he gave the new arrivals was to build three huts for them to sleep in. This would give Noah a good indication of their craftsmanship and whether they had the skills to work on the Ark itself. He was not going to risk them making errors on such an important project.

The growing Ark itself sat high on logs set under the keel, with an enormous amount of scaffolding made of bamboo and other lattice work surrounding the whole structure. The shape of the Ark was plain to see now, with most of the ribs, cross trusses and major structural beams in place in the lower hull. Some of the upper hull was also in place and an observer was now able to realise the size and extent of its construction.

Work had started on the lower deck flooring and the cladding for the underside, which would eventually reach all the way up to the top of the towering sides. The siting of this great work on its supports enabled them to work under the Ark. Later when construction of the Ark itself was finished the area under the ship would be filled with sand and a massive earth construction with high walls would then be built around the ship and backfilled with water to form a small lake for testing whether or not there were any leaks. It was essential to test for any such leaks in the lower planking as there would likely be no time for doing this once the Ark was in the ocean. Furthermore, the wooden planking needed to be kept moist so that it would not dry out, crack and split. The structure also needed to settle under its own weight before the interior compartments and fittings could be built and put in place.

Each plank making up the outer hull of the ship was carefully grooved to fit snugly into the next one with resin in the joints. The planks were pressed together with a mixture of wooden screws or plugs and bronze clips that clamped them together to provide a watertight seal. The plugs were inserted in holes drilled into the timber and resin was also applied to them to cause expansion and make a tight fitting, inseparable join. Each plank was a cubit wide to keep to a minimum the number of joins that would be exposed to the sea. The large ribs and beams also were locked together with similar but larger plugs. Once again, resin applied to the hole and plug made a perfect tight fit. At the end of the Ark's construction, as a final safety measure a mixture of pitch and resin was coated over the entire surface of the structure both inside and out.

The resin was obtained from bleeding the sap of certain pine trees. When the resin had finished flowing the trees were chopped down, covered in soil or ash, and burned slowly to produce a light-weight, black form of pure carbon called charcoal. The last step in the process of making pitch was to add the powdered charcoal to the boiling pine resin. Different proportions of charcoal were added to produce pitch with different properties. Noah had used this process in the past for waterproofing and protection, and now he used the same material to waterproof the Ark.

Methuselah had taken it upon himself to manufacture the thousands of wooden screws and bronze clamps that were needed, along with iron and bronze fittings for other parts of the great ship. This was done in a neat little foundry and workshop off to one side of the camp.

In another area further upstream, great iron saws cut the timber into planks, beams and whatever other size was required. The saws were run by a clever mechanism that used the partially dammed river to send a fast flow of water that drove pulleys which in turn spun the saws. Closer to the worksite a finishing area was laid out where the milled timber was finished or dressed in various ways for further use.

Building the Ark was slow, methodical work, because it had to be done properly. There was no room for error, and from what Noah understood God required of him there would be no time to test the Ark before it was cast upon the open sea. It had to be watertight and complete without any errors immediately it was needed. Consequently, any faults and defects that came to light while it was being built needed to be removed and replaced immediately. Noah was very strict about this and his years of shipbuilding had equipped him to spot any defects requiring attention. More than once a whole section of the ship had to be taken down and rebuilt. Noah was therefore grateful he had been given so many years to finish the Ark's construction.

Because so much of the jungle at the worksite had been cleared for the project the camp was able to have a sizeable vegetable garden and keep some domestic animals for milk and other food. Most of their supplies, however, came from what was rafted down the river from the estate.

Over the next three weeks work was devoted to finishing the trusses that would support the lower deck flooring. After this the men began to install the planking for the underside and eventually the rest of the hull of the ship. Another team was set to work on dressing the timbers that would make up the flooring of the lower deck.

Noah missed Naamah and often thought of her, especially at night. He had barely had one day and night with her after returning from his voyage, so he decided he should find an excuse to go up to the homestead to visit her. He was also naturally concerned about the welfare of his sister Hebe. This would require a three hour row by raft up the fast flowing river or slightly longer if he went by ship and sea. However, it would mean he would be taking time out from the work that was needed on the ship, and so he kept putting it off.

One evening the work crew gathered round the open camp fire as they often did and plied Noah with more questions, especially the newcomers. "Why was the ship so big? How many people will you take with you in it? How will you decide who goes? Why are both ends of the ship the same shape? Why is it so wide? How do you know when this flood will come? How will you get the ship from here down to the sea?"

As the workers talked about these matters amongst themselves and saw the tremendous size of the ship they realised that the scope of this coming disaster could be very great indeed. They had thought originally the flood would be a local event, but Methuselah was insistent that the whole earth was going to be destroyed.

It was difficult for Noah and Methuselah to answer their questions and satisfy their curiosity, even when they explained how the ship needed to be a great size to ride out the heavy seas expected. They themselves did not know exactly what was coming, and because of this agreed that it was hard to plan for the future.

"All I have is the command God gave me," Noah explained. "Unless you've heard the audible voice of Adonai you won't be able to understand that I know beyond doubt what he said to me. And what he uttered is to be obeyed, not to be argued with. I have no right to question him, he is El Shaddai, God Almighty, when all is said and done, and I must simply obey his voice. He was very specific about the dimensions of the Ark. He also said all flesh will be destroyed. So it must be a worldwide event and it must be catastrophic. So on that basis I am building a vessel that can withstand the greatest tempest imaginable. I believe Adonai will give me further instructions as the work progresses. No, it will not occur this week. Even though we still have some years left I want to finish this task as soon as possible. I don't know when the Ark will be needed, but I would rather have it sitting here unused for ten years than be putting the finishing touches and filling holes as the storm rages around us."

With that, most were satisfied and happily continued to volunteer their service, although there were a few who were beginning to have doubts about the magnitude of the coming disaster and if in fact it would ever eventuate.

Meanwhile the relationship between Ham and Nae was becoming serious, and it was evident to all that here was another potential marriage. At the same time Shem and Sede were anxious to make their love for each other official. But as much as Ada tried to capture the attention of Japheth he seemed to be totally unaware of her growing love for him.

Shem and Sede came to Noah at his dwelling late one evening toward the end of the third week to tell him they felt there was no need for them to wait any longer. "We want to get married now," Shem pleaded.

"Yes, I know," Noah said. "But let us wait until Hebe's baby is born. She is having difficulty with this one and is not well. Once the baby is born and Hebe is well enough we'll have a great celebration. We may even be having a double wedding the way Ham and Nae are getting along."

"Yes, I don't think they'll be far behind us," said Sede. "We would be happy to make it a double celebration with them."

Suddenly there was a lot of shouting and noise from the direction of the river. They grabbed flaming torches and ran down to see what the commotion was all about. Japheth and Ham were down at the dock already in excited discussion with three attendants from the estate who had just arrived by raft. Noah, Shem and Sede caught up to them quickly, and Methuselah was not far behind. Others were coming out of their huts to see what all the noise was about.

"It's Hebe!" shouted Japheth.

"They won't tell us what's wrong," said Ham angrily.

"What's the urgency that you've come here in the middle of the night, Hess?" demanded Noah.

Hess, the senior attendant, drew Noah aside out of hearing of the others. "It's about your sister, Hebe. You need to fetch Jabal and come quickly." he said.

"Yes but what …?"

"The baby is coming … however … it's dying!"

FOURTEEN

Tragedy and Joy

Noah relayed the alarming news to Methuselah, and then looked for Jabal.

"What's happening father?" asked Shem.

"Tell us," demanded Ham.

"Yes, yes, your aunt's having difficulty with the birth and we must go to her. But which is quicker? Back on the raft or by ship?"

Methuselah took charge. "There is no time to get the ship ready, Noach," he said. "Go on the raft now and take Ham and Shem with the attendants. Ariel and Sede will be anxious to go also. I'll come with Japheth, Nae and Ada on the other raft in the morning."

"But where is Jabal, we need to inform him? Queried Noah.

"Probably drunk with that brew he makes," protested Ham.

Panting with exertion Nadav came running up to the group, "I've looked everywhere in the camp and in his cabin. I can't find Jabal anywhere."

"We must wait for him," said Shem.

"I know medicine. I can help," said Ada, who had joined the group and realised the seriousness of the situation. "I'm actually a doctor, I know I should have told you this but …"

"There's no time for explanations, or to look for that man," said Methuselah, "Take Ada with you and I'll come later with Jabal if we ever find him tonight. Be off with you!"

‡‡‡

It had taken Hess and the two attendants just forty minutes to row down the river to the campsite, but now they were faced with a frustrating three hour journey back. Swift eddies and currents that made a fast journey downstream now created the slowest momentum going the other way. But if all the men put their best effort in they hoped they would be a bit quicker than that.

Meanwhile at the homestead the entire household had been aroused for many hours as the situation with Hebe and her baby became grave. Earlier Hebe had cried out suddenly in extreme pain just as everyone was getting ready for bed. Then her waters broke. Hebe had already been having pains and contractions through that day and so she knew the baby's arrival was close, but she told them not to send for Jabal until the next morning. Now, however, the birth had become a fight for life, as it became apparent that it was such a difficult one, with the survival of either or both mother and child in doubt.

Two midwives and a doctor from the town remained at Hebe's bedside, along with Betenos and Naamah. Sometime close to midnight Naamah went to Lamech.

"The situation is very grave. They are doing their best, but the baby won't come. Hebe has already lost a lot of blood and is weak. You'd best send someone for Jabal, Noach and the others. I'm really afraid we could lose her."

"I've already thought of that," replied Lamech, "I have three men standing by, I will tell them to go right away."

Noah and those on the raft were anxious and impatient to get to the estate. Shem took the stern rudder while the rest paddled as hard as they could. Ada explained to all of them about childbirth and tried to ease their anxiety without promising anything.

"Hess, did Lamech or Naamah say she was dying? I want the truth, man!"

"Not exactly," Hess replied, "But they are all worried and the doctor said the situation was grave. That is what he said, grave." This naturally did not comfort or encourage them.

Ada again attempted to reassure them. "We'll know how things are when we get there, Noach. There's nothing to be gained by fretting now."

Naamah sat with Hebe, who gripped her hand so tightly, despite her weakened state, that Naamah was in some pain. But she held onto her sister-in-law nonetheless and tried to comfort her.

"I'm so weak."

"Don't try to speak, save your energy."

"Why won't the babe come?"

"She's breeched," said one of the midwives. "And we haven't been able to turn her. "She may already be in the birth canal but is unable to go any further."

"It is a girl then?"

"Yes, dear, we think so."

"I wanted a girl," said Hebe, now so weak she could hardly speak. She whispered, "I can't do this," as she lapsed into unconsciousness.

While Hebe was unconscious they conferred on what to do. "I believe we have to save the mother now, because if she tries to bring the baby to birth it will kill her," said the doctor. "I haven't ever attended a birth like this one," he added.

"Nor I," the most experienced midwife agreed.

"It hasn't been done often," he continued "since most births are fairly straightforward yet painful, but I believe the only way to save her now is to open her abdomen and extract the baby."

"I've never seen that done, and neither has my assistant," the senior midwife said.

"I have to confess I've never done it either," said the doctor. "I have done other operations of course, but none as critical as this, yet it's what we must do."

"We have to prepare for it," the senior midwife said, instructing her assistant in what to do next, as well as telling Naamah and Betenos what was required.

At that moment Hebe woke again and cried out, "Naamah? Are you there Naa...mah?" The latter half of her name was barely a silent breath.

"I'm here Hebe."

Hebe gripped Naamah's hand once again. "Dearest sister I am not … going to come through this."

"Yes, you will. We're doing all we can. They're going to take baby out through your tummy."

"I can't, I can't … I can't focus."

"Sleep Hebe, save your strength."

"I must ask you …. look after my baby for me … if I don't …"

"Of course, my sister. Of course I will," said Naamah, tears now streaming down her face.

"Jabal won't be able to, please look after her … tell Noach … not today, but later – I'm sorry… I won't be there."

Betenos heard her and was also weeping silently. Hebe then lapsed into unconsciousness again, and her hold of Naamah's hand slipped away.

The doctor needed instruments and compounds for the operation which he did not have at the homestead, so a fast rider was sent to his clinic in town to fetch a long list of the required items. It would take him about forty minutes to return with them.

Eventually, in the early hours of the morning Noah and the raft arrived at the estate dock. Noah, and his companions immediately dashed up to the homestead on the horses Hess had brought earlier, while the others secured the raft and followed on foot.

Lamech met them in the courtyard.

"Tell me father, do not hold back, how is she, please?"

"I know you want answers, Noach, Ariel, but where is Jabal?"

"We couldn't find him. Methuselah is bringing him later supposedly."

"I don't really understand what's wrong except that the baby will not come and they can't make it do this. It's best that you speak to the doctor," said Lamech, in the calmest voice he could muster, but betraying how weary he was with the strain of everything.

"I want to see her," pleaded Ariel.

At that moment Naamah came looking for Jabal but only finding Noah, Ariel, Sede and the others. "She's unconscious Ariel, she won't know you're there. They're getting ready to operate on her."

"Operate?"

"Yes, here's the doctor. He'll tell you what they're planning to do."

With that, the doctor, aided by the senior midwife, explained the situation to the alarmed family group. They outlined how grave the situation was and said they would try to save both the mother and the child, although they weren't certain they would succeed. They would do their best.

"I wish to see her, just to hold her hand before you go ahead, in case …" pleaded Ariel.

"That's acceptable, but just for a few minutes. We need to proceed with the operation while she's unconscious."

"I forgot," said Noah. "This is Ada. She tells me she's a doctor from Shulon. Can she help?"

"By all means," said the doctor, glad to have a colleague, and began to question Ada intently on her knowledge and experience. Unfortunately, she also had not performed this procedure, but was experienced in small operations and wound aftercare. With her was a small bag of instruments she had brought from Shulon.

Ariel and Sede walked slowly into the room where Hebe lay

unconscious. The other midwife who had stayed with her left them to be alone with her. After they had been with her a few minutes, Noah, Naamah and their sons came to her bedside.

"Oh, Hebe, what have you done, why did you marry that man and bring this on yourself. Don't leave us my dear sister. Be strong. We are all here with you," whispered Noah.

He could say no more; words simply would not come. Her two nephews looked on helplessly. Hebe's breathing was now shallow, and her lovely face was pale though peaceful. Naamah placed her hands gently on Noah's shoulders. He nodded at her, got up and they all left the room.

"Life is what it is Noach, you can't blame her for wanting to fall in love again," said Naamah gently.

As the sun rose above the eastern horizon the inexperienced doctor with Ada and the two midwives proceeded to go ahead with the operation to save baby and mother.

‡‡‡

A gentle sea breeze wafted across the grape vines and pastures of the homestead, bringing with it the pleasant fragrances of many blossoms. Hundreds of the town folk had come to the estate and now lined the gently sloping hill above where they were to lay to rest Hebe and her baby daughter together in the earth from which all human beings had originated. Hebe lay there clothed in white, with the babe wrapped beside her, on a wooden bier over the deep grave.

Many of the mourners spoke of her love and devotion to her family, her ever present smile, and the way she was loved by all. Lamech led the service, and Methuselah spoke also of her dedication. As they did, Ariel her great granddaughter, with Nadav holding her, stood next to Noah and Naamah, deeply grief stricken. Japheth, Shem and Ham were there also, too stunned to speak, simply standing near their father in silence. Nae held Ham's arm, and Sede clutched Shem, both were weeping silently. Japheth stood alone near his family, unaware that Ada was close beside him.

Jabal was eventually found the morning of his wife's death and brought to the estate by Methuselah, Japheth and Nadav. He was beside himself with rage at not being there when Hebe needed him. But the fault was his own. He could not see that though and blamed everyone except himself. High in his condemnation was the God of Noah that he claimed to follow, however his ranting and blaming God for Hebe's death, confirmed to Lamech, Noah and the family that he probably never did believe in the God of Creation. Later that same day Jabal left the estate and Ophir on foot, not staying for Hebe's memorial service. They never saw him again.

Later, people gathered at the homestead to give their condolences and respect to Ariel and Nadav with Sede, Hebe's immediate family. They and the rest of the family, accepted them all with thanks or a silent nod of their heads. Noah, so traumatised by the events of the last two days, was also grief stricken. So fond of his sister, it was like a part of him had died.

Shem comforted Sede, and also his grandparents who were grieving immensely, and they with him.

Ham was angry and confused at the loss of his aunt and the baby cousin he never knew. He of all his brothers was closest to Hebe and expressed his contempt for Jabal, whom he never liked. He left the gathering and went away to vent his feelings. There was a great deal of crashing, smashing and destruction of things in the distance until Lamech went to stop him.

"Leave him dearest, let him get it out of his system. We can always repair what he's broken. After all, Adonai is going to destroy it all anyway," said Betenos firmly. Lamech simply looked at his wife unable to give her a reply. "You can have a comforting word with him later, as I will," she added.

"Yes, it's best that you let him get it out of his system," sighed Nae.

"Why, oh why, did she marry him," Betenos now fell into Lamech's arms crying uncontrollably. "I told her not to, and to have a baby at her age!"

"Dearest, it is not your fault or mine. We make decisions in life that have consequences. Hebe was always impetuous. She made her decision and Adonai has taken her. It is the way of the world," Lamech tried to comfort his wife.

Japheth sat alone on a bench in the courtyard, his elbows on his knees and his hands covering his face, his body swaying as he sat staring at the ground. Ada came quietly and sat beside him saying nothing. After a while as he rested one of his hands on the seat beside him, she gently took it and held it on her lap while he looked forlornly into space. After a few moments he then turned and looked at her.

"Who are you?" he asked, looking through tear blurred eyes. Smiling at his confusion and grief Ada said quietly, "I'm Ada, who sailed with you back from Shulon to help you build the Ark."

"Y'yes I know," he said, coming back to his senses, "It's just that I didn't realise how beautiful you were." When she smiled with tears welling up in her eyes as she looked back at him, then, for the first time in two days Japheth laughed.

‡‡‡

One Month Later

Work on the Ark came to a virtual standstill after the death of Hebe. A despondent Noah was all but ready to give up on the project out of remorse. Of all people, apart from his wife and sons, he was expecting to take Hebe on the Ark with them. As a consequence, after two weeks of having very little to do and getting no clear direction from Noah, all of Nae's friends decided to go back to their village in Shulon, saying they would return if things changed. Ada's brothers stayed on, however, as they saw that life for their sister was about to change dramatically.

Once again Methuselah and Lamech, together with the rest of the family, understood Noah's moods and turned him around. This time it was his sons who had the greatest influence on him. They were ready to start in earnest again on the Ark once they returned from a time of intimacy with their wives which they were about to take this day, immediately after the festivities were over, that coincidentally was the last day of the current year.

Many of the townsfolk as well as all the family, estate and Ark workers came to the homestead to celebrate the wedding celebration of Noah and Naamah's three sons, Japheth to Ada, Shem to Sede and Ham to Nae.

"I have to say, Noach," said Naamah, "that our boys have always been very close. They have shared all their major adventures together, so it's fitting that they should now all be married on the same day."

"You are so right," replied Noah. "It's good to see them do this. They have chosen well."

"Mmm, but from what I've observed it's those three lovely women who did the choosing. The boys simply agreed that they had made the right choices," she said laughing.

Noah laughed too. It was the first time he had done this in over a month.

"It's good to see you happy again, Noach," said his mother. "Things will be different from now on. It's a new beginning, a fresh start."

"Yes, mother, thank you," he replied.

In the lengthy, quiet pause that followed Noah confessed to all his immediate family around him. "I've come to realise once again that what we're doing with the Ark is not about me or Hebe, in fact, any of us. Adonai has a plan for mankind and I am his servant in it. He didn't tell Hebe to have another child. That was her choice. Every decision we make in life has a consequence, either for good or for bad. Remember that, my sons and daughters."

"So true Noach, and today you have gained three daughters," laughed Lamech. "I can't remember when we have ever seen three weddings on the same day."

"I'm so proud of you, my sons." Noah smiled humbly, for the homestead was full of happiness, laughter and joy once more.

FIFTEEN

A Magnificent Absurdity

The Land of Havilah – 50 Years Later
AM 1650

Since the death of Hebe no one in Noah's immediate family had passed into eternity until this day. It was a pleasant afternoon with a slight breeze as was often the case on the Lamech estate outside Ophir. Today Lamech's family were gathered on the same hill as they had fifty years earlier. This time it was to say goodbye to their matriarch and beloved wife, mother and grandmother Betenos, who had finally succumbed to an unknown illness she had suffered from for several years. At last, free of distress and pain, they laid her to rest in what had become the family burial ground. Betenos had lived a long, eventful life and had died a proud and contented woman. Her last words were for her eldest son.

"Don't look to the right or to the left, Noach. Keep your eyes on Adonai and he will guide your footsteps. Be true and steadfast and save our people from his coming judgment."

Other family members had been buried here over the years. They included Methuselah's wife Edna, Dinah's husband Dubrich after he was violently murdered by Kurt, the Nephilim, Tem and Benlexar's wives, and some years later Tem himself and his sons, along with Benlexar and all his family following the tragic attack on Ophir, and of course, their beloved Hebe and her baby daughter.

What no one expected was the arrival of Baruch, Noah's brother and Lamech's next eldest after Noah. He was now living with his extended family on the far side of the world in a land named Pho.

Baruch had heard from traders that his mother was ill and decided to visit the family, unsure what welcome he would receive having left so many years earlier after an intense disagreement with his father when he was denied a place with Noah's crew on his first great navigation of the world. However, with the passing of time forgiveness and reconciliation prevailed and he was welcomed back lovingly on his arrival. Baruch was able to say goodbye to his mother before she passed away, for which she was very thankful.

In the course of the family reunion the question of what had happened to Hem was discussed. Sadly, no one had heard of anything about what had become of Lamech's third son.

After Baruch had stayed with the family at the homestead for many weeks it was inevitable that he would want to see Noah's great ship. So it was that several days after his mother's funeral he came to the campsite and looked over the Ark, and while he was there Baruch and the menfolk expressed their views about the reason for building it. The women of the family had stayed back at the homestead while the men joined Japheth, who was the current duty manager at the site.

Now that the Ark was virtually finished each of Noah's sons and several workers took a turn each week to ensure the security of the ship and add some final or upgraded feature to the structure. Fitting out the interior to provide a living space for its eventual cargo had already begun, although they were still unsure just what would be required.

This particular day Baruch was accompanied by Noah, Nadav, Japheth, Shem, Ham, Lamech and Methuselah when they inspected the great vessel in its nearly completed form. As they came round the final bend of the river there was the Ark in all its magnificence, standing high on its construction site in the large clearing with the thick green jungle all around. It stood in a lake of water with a huge dyke surrounding it. A large opening could be seen on one side of the Ark, access to which was by way of a broad drawbridge that when raised would become the door to the great structure's only entrance.

As the men walked up to the Ark from the landing place they craned their necks to take in the immensity of the great ship towering above them, and their visitor was at first lost for words.

"Well, Noach, all those years ago when we built *Discovery* we thought how big and magnificent it was. But it pales into insignificance in comparison with this. Why has it got such a wide blunt bow?" Baruch said, letting out a huge sigh as he asked the question.

Before anyone could answer him, he continued with "Why so big? What and who will sail in this? Where are its masts? There is no steerage or sails. It's so far from the sea, how will you ever get it there? It seems to me that it's a magnificent absurdity!" he exclaimed, as they walked round every part of it on top of the dyke.

Laughing, Noah replied. "So many questions my brother. Come, let's go inside the Ark and I'll explain everything to you."

And Lamech added, "It's been a long and at times challenging enterprise that we've all proudly contributed to."

Methuselah likewise agreed "It's a great achievement," he said.

"But this is insanity," a bewildered Baruch responded. "You're all mad. Do you honestly believe you're doing this for some purpose? How can you be sure your God spoke to you? Where is he anyway? And how can you still believe in a God who allows such destruction and bloodshed in this world. He's abandoned us! I gave faith in him away years ago. I once believed in him, but not any longer."

"Baruch, Baruch," his father responded, "It's because we still believe in and follow Adonai that he spoke to us. We know he did, and we know his word is true."

"Bah!"

"Brother, his words were as clear and precise as those I am speaking with you now," said Noah. "That's why I know that this destruction is going to happen. The ship has been built to his specific dimensions. He was very clear as to what these were. Adonai was also very clear that this world will be destroyed. I don't know how, but because he told me to build this great ship it must have something to do with water. I believe he's going to cover the earth with a great flood. Who will go with us when this happens? Adonai hasn't shown me yet, but as you can see there's room for many hundreds of people and animals. We're hoping many people will come back to the Lord yet."

"If you take hundreds won't you be taking the wicked as well as the good? What would Adonai's purpose be in destroying this world if the wicked survive to carry on their rape and pillage in a new one?"

"Some things are still unknown to us. We are waiting for Adonai's word."

"I don't believe there will be many people in this vessel," Methuselah said in a sad voice. "I think Adonai wants to preserve other living creatures besides us, but I don't believe I will be on board."

"What do you mean, grandfather?" So they told him. "When you die it shall be sent, the judgment comes. What exactly comes?" cried an exasperated Baruch, throwing his arms in the air. "You speak of one hundred and twenty years? How many of those have you got left?"

"According to Adonai's word, you, your family, the world and all the people about us have just six years to repent and get right with him, my son," Lamech replied.

"I've heard enough. You're all quite mad. I have no faith in your Elohim and neither does the rest of the world. I've heard stories about you all these years you've been building this thing. People are laughing at you Noach, the once great seaman and explorer. They say your fame has corrupted you and you're deluded, just chasing after fantasies instead of true knowledge. You always were a dreamer as a boy," he continued.

"Look at what we've achieved by our own efforts. We've discovered so many things. We have mathematicians and scientists that tell us all we need to know. We, the people, have done this, without the help of any God. Where was your God in all this? We now build great structures and magnificent cities. You say that Adonai cursed the ground, and for centuries we worked it for little gain as you have, father and grandfather. But now we have machines of bronze and iron to do the hard work for us. People live long lives and they're happy. Yes, there is sickness, but our scientists have discovered remedies and ways of mending broken bones and curing all manner of illnesses. They can even cut out diseased or damaged parts of the human body. Scientists are talking of having machines that will travel faster, and some are even attempting to make craft that can fly in the sky. They've done all this from their own knowledge, and there was no Adonai who told them what to do.

"You talk of the in-breds and Nephilim as being evil, but some of them are beautiful people. There is a lot of intermarriage with them and no harm has come of this. Your morality is intolerant as well as making life boring! People should be able to choose whoever they want to have sex with or marry. Who made the laws you talk of and insist on? Life should be enjoyed without any restrictions. That's what Adonai created us for. Him to enjoy us and us to enjoy each other. We are free to choose our own destiny. Yes, there is evil and bloodshed in the world, but we have ways of living with that. Life is good. We are prosperous. I'm a rich man, but I see that our family estate is now only a poor shadow of what it once was."

There was a long pause as Baruch, suffused with frustration and anger, could not convince his once close family that the world had moved on from believing in myths and unseen gods. He had done his best to convince them that hard work, personal enterprise, wealth and a self-indulgent lifestyle was what mattered most to the people of the world.

On their part, the six men listening to Baruch looked at their dissenting relative with sadness as he spoke, but remained firm in their conviction of faith in divine guidance. It saddened them that Baruch and so many like him were beyond redemption. Only Ham seemed somewhat troubled as he listened to what his uncle had to say.

"Yes, you may have all those wonderful things, and where was Adonai in all of this you ask? Whether you believe it or not it was he who gave you that knowledge," responded Methuselah. "Yet you still have rape and murder, and more sickness now than when I was a boy. Many may be rich, but even more are slaves, something unheard of when I was born. There is financial corruption, greed, the strong destroying the weak and in-breds destroying the purity of humanity. There is such violence as we would never have believed possible, and as we personally suffered when Ophir was destroyed."

Pausing for a moment for his words to take effect, he continued, "For what purpose Baruch? So that you can live and co-habit and enjoy life as you see fit? You accept no responsibility for what you do and your morals are corrupt. All this is because of the fall of mankind. When Adam disobeyed Adonai and brought sin into the world he took us with him. Now we are all born with the sin of disobedience."

In a grandfatherly way he placed his hand on Baruch's shoulder and pleaded with him once more. "If only the world would turn back to the Lord God he would forgive them and perhaps they could yet be saved. Then the world would be a safe and prosperous place for all mankind, not just a lucky few. Adonai is longsuffering and has given all people as much time as possible to turn to him. Yet I believe he always knew they would not do this and so this world must suffer the consequences. It is inevitable, sadly so."

Baruch pulled away. "I loved you all once and still do but I cannot agree with you. What you're doing is all too bizarre in this modern world. I'm leaving for home tomorrow. I believe there's a ship heading west to Shulon in the morning, which should take me to Eridu. From there I can then get the overland carriage to Pho."

"We're sorry to see you go Baruch," Lamech replied. "It's been good for you to be here. We still hope you'll think about what we're doing and reconsider how you stand with Adonai. And I will send you off with a blessing tomorrow. Let us now return to the homestead and have a final meal together."

‡‡‡

One Year Later
AM 1651

Despite many setbacks Noah achieved his aim of completing the Ark well before the appointed time decreed by the Lord God. When the work came to a finish Nadav requested leave to return to his country with Ariel in an attempt to convince at least his family and close friends, if not his whole village, to turn back to the Lord. They would also search for their three wayward sons who had left many years before. Both of them would be back, they said, well before the disaster struck.

Each seventh day, the day the Creator God had decreed they were to rest, Lamech's family made it a habit of gathering together for prayer and discussion. Each time they brought an offering to the Lord in devotion and supplication to Him. They had committed themselves to this from the time when God spoke to Noah instructing him to build the Ark. They were well aware that the 120 years God had proclaimed was coming closer and closer to an end.

"Baruch did have a point," Ham noted after a pause in their discussion on what they should do now that the Ark was complete.

"What do you mean?" asked Shem.

"Well, if we are to take hundreds of people with us and there don't seem to be any lining up at the moment, won't we just take the evils of the present world into the new one? If there is no new world, what if we all perish?"

"That's a good point," answered Noah, ignoring Ham's statement about them all perishing. "I feel in my spirit that Adonai will speak to me again soon. I've felt that strongly since Baruch left. After all, he did express the mood of the people to us very well. And we've seen it for ourselves. All our pleading falls on deaf ears. We are laughed at and ridiculed."

"What of our workers?" asked Japheth. "They're willing enough to help us, but secretly I think they feel the way Baruch does. We pay them well and they do the work dutifully for us, but I sometimes hear them murmuring and making jokes about what we're doing when they don't realise I'm close by."

"I still think there will be very few people in the Ark," said Methuselah. "My guess is that Adonai wants you to take animals and plants with you to start a new world."

"That does seem logical," agreed Lamech.

"Well, we have built some stalls for animals as I suggested," added Ham. "Do you think we need to build more?"

"Possibly," said Noah, "but I'm really undecided. I will seek Adonai's guidance once again. Perhaps the time has come for me to camp up on the hill again. It seems that when I spend time there alone this is when he speaks to me."

"I have a serious question, dear Noach."

"Yes Ada?"

"I know we've spoken about this before. You have asked all three of us not to have children until we know what we are destined for. We have respected that and understand why you asked that of us. Perhaps we should have started families when we were first married, but we were young then and were enjoying life. We were building the Ark and went on expeditions to other lands, so children weren't something we thought about. But now, dear Noach, we three women are all desperate to be mothers as Adonai blessed us to be. Wouldn't it be good to have children now so that in five or so years when this comes upon us they will be strong enough to survive?"

Naamah nodded and smiled, while Noah's three sons pricked their ears up in anticipation of their father's reply. Lamech and Methuselah chuckled quietly on the side.

"Yes, my sons and daughters. I haven't neglected thinking about you. But as I explained before, we really don't know what is entailed in this great event that is awaiting us. Now, as we approach that time which is not far away, I think it would be unwise to take children so young into the unknown. Please let's be patient until Adonai speaks again. I'm very sure it will be soon."

‡‡‡

Seven days later Noah was waiting upon the Lord and praying on his hill behind the estate. He had done this three times over the past three months, but God remained silent. When the morning of the eighth day dawned, the ground was damp from the heavy overnight dew and the sun had barely risen over the horizon, Noah was preparing to return to the homestead. It was then that God spoke.

> *I will establish my covenant with you. You shall come into the*
> *Ark, you, your sons, your wife, and your sons' wives with you.*
> *And of all that lives, you shall bring two of every kind into the*
> *Ark to keep them alive with you. They shall be male and female.*
> *Of the birds according to their kinds, and of the animals*
> *according to their kinds, of every creeping thing of the ground,*

> *according to its kind, two of every sort shall come in to you to keep them alive. Also take with you every sort of food that is eaten, and store it up. It shall serve as food for you and for them.*

Noah came down, shaken, wondering yet full of faith, knowing what he now had to do and who and what was to come into the Ark. All his work was justified. God had spoken.

As he entered the homestead Noah's face shone with such a glow that no one had to be told that the Lord had spoken to him once more. The family gathered and all were there when he told them about God's message.

"Your wife, sons and their wives?" Lamech asked thoughtfully.

"Well, that is what he said to me. What am I to make of that?"

"Yes, well that confirms what I've been saying," said Methuselah. "Adonai has ordered you to build an Ark large enough to take examples of all living things."

"We can't get every animal and bird into the Ark," said Ham.

"No, just two of each kind," Noah replied.

"But there are thousands," stated Ada.

"Not every colour and variation of them. Just two of a kind so more will be produced from them," said Methuselah.

"All the insects?" This from Nae.

"No, I don't think so, not specifically, except the ones that will naturally be with us he said, just the land animals and birds. But let's not try to understand it all now. We've got a huge amount of work to do to prepare for our menagerie," replied Noah.

Lamech then said soberly, "We now know, Noach, who'll be going with you. It seems to be as I thought, I'm not much longer for this world."

Shem responded to this by saying, "you father and mother, the three of us and our wives, but what about Nadav and Ariel?"

"There are still a lot of unanswered questions," said Noah. "Things we still don't understand and I have to obey Adonai. For one thing, we have to start on fitting out the Ark's interior. Thankfully we have a few years left to do this."

"Well, family, now we know what is ahead of us, we must make plans. Among which the women and I can decide how we will furnish and decorate the Ark, don't you think?" laughed Naamah.

So they did.

SIXTEEN

Into the Ark

AM 1655

During the next four years Noah did everything that God had commanded him to do. Work started again on the interior of the Ark to have it ready for the day of reckoning that the Lord God was to bring upon the earth. Once again Noah and his sons and their wives, with the help of the few workers who still supported them, achieved the seemingly impossible by fitting out the interior of the great ship in less than the time they calculated was left to them.

A multitude of small and large structures for securing, housing and maintaining a host of all kinds of animals were built and placed in the Ark in a logical and sensible way. A huge aviary for smaller and medium sized birds took up a large portion of the upper deck. Other aviaries and enclosures were constructed for the larger birds, bats and other airborne creatures. The family living quarters were also placed here, as well as cages for vulnerable animals so they could be kept under constant observation. Large and medium sized animals were to be accommodated on the lower deck, along with their food requirements and other supplies. The middle deck was reserved for smaller and medium sized creatures, as well as a range of food, equipment and an assortment of things needed on a long sea voyage. When it came to housing each group of animals, compatibility of environments and temperaments was carefully considered.

There remained the big question. How long would they have to remain in the Ark? God hadn't told Noah. He therefore decided, perhaps prophetically, to equip the Ark for a voyage of a year. He and his sons reckoned that with the probable number of creatures they would have to take on board according to what they knew, and the dimensions God had given them for the Ark, it could only sustain a limited number of living things for one orbit of the earth around the sun.

"Two of every kind," God had said. The family understood that this instruction was given because he wanted them to breed and re-establish life in a new world. There had to be a new world if this old one was to be destroyed, and they had been chosen to build this Ark to ensure life would survive and re-establish itself. Otherwise, why set out on this great enterprise? Animals would need to be young adults, old enough to reproduce, yet young enough to do this many times over. The very large land animals, large birds and flying reptiles that survived needed to be small juveniles because of size relevant to space on the Ark and capacity to start breeding within a year. They would need to be nurtured until they became adults in order to reproduce. Most likely they would be at a disadvantage in the world to come, and their reproduction would start later than the other animals. Thus their numbers would be fewer in relation to those ready to breed even while they were on the Ark. Myriads of different insects would find their own way into the Ark and establish themselves in every crack and crevice in the gigantic structure. They would not need human intervention to sustain them although special provision may be needed for the bees.

Many months of planning went into fitting out the ship. The family's own accommodation and personal needs had to be met. They also had to ensure enough food was taken for all living creatures on board. There were countless items and matters to consider, and collectively the family worked them all out. In fact, it took three months of planning and reassessment before they even started construction of the compartments and other fittings.

All this preparation was behind them now, and they looked forward to how God was going to bring all the animals to them, because it was an impossibility for them to go searching for the right animals to populate the new world. During the last month they emptied most of the lake around the Ark, except for a much smaller area of water immediately surrounding it. This test showed them that the Ark was sound and free of any leaks, and the dry area they had created now made an excellent enclosure for the larger animals as they arrived and were kept inside a stockade built to allow them to live safely in the open air until it was time for them to enter the Ark. The lake around the Ark also served to provide a ready supply of water for the animals. It was topped up from time to time from the nearby river. The former construction areas beyond and between the Ark and the surrounding jungle were now turned into paddocks, enclosures and pens, all waiting for the arriving animals. Grass and other crops now growing in this area also provided a ready food supply. The anticipation of the main event was with them daily now.

With his hand on Noah's shoulder, Methuselah stood looking over the Ark site. "It's a great achievement, Noach. God's judgment will be soon now."

"Yes, grandfather, very soon. I'm expecting it any day now and spend a lot of time alone waiting on Adonai to speak to me again. But I wonder have we done enough?"

"To save the people?" Methuselah asked.

"Yes. Was there anything more we could do?" Noah wondered.

"You, your sons, Naamah, myself and Lamech, have spent many months while we built this great Ark, going about Havilah and other villages nearby, speaking and imploring people to listen, to repent, but they have refused. This, and the fact that the very conduct of people has become corrupt, is the reason Adonai must do this," lamented Methuselah.

"I know you're right, grandfather. I haven't been back to the estate for a while now. How is father?"

"He's the reason I came today, Noach. He sleeps most of the time, and he's getting weaker too. You should come to him before …" he added.

"Yes," replied Noah, "I must. I'll accompany you back today. Ham and Nae can stay and look after the site."

After the lengthy time it took over fifty years earlier to travel between the homestead and the building site when Hebe died, a road had been progressively built over the hills and along the eastern shore of the river to a point just a short way up-river of the Ark site. Another landing platform had been built here, and so it was now only a short journey by raft or small boat. A rope and pulley system had also been installed along and across the river, and a turn of a wheel on this pulled a person upstream.

It was only Noah's immediate family who went between the building site and the estate now. As soon as the work on the Ark was completed the few workers who had stayed on the job were happy to take their wages and go. They could no longer put up with the ridicule their peers made of them working on Noah's 'great disaster.' They had left a month ago and gone to live elsewhere in Havilah. Even they could not be persuaded to live for God.

Arriving at the landing on the eastern shore Naamah met Methuselah and Noah with the horse and cart. She gave Noah a big hug as she had not seen him in a week.

"I wonder if we can take this cart on the Ark?" mused Noah, "it could be useful in the new land." This brought a rebuke from Naamah,

"Noach, your father lies dying and your first thought is to this silly old cart!"

"Just thinking of practical things my dear. We can break it down and store it with other tools under the lower deck. Of course I'm concerned about my father. It's why I came back today, but it was a surprise to see you here."

Methuselah was riding alongside them on the horse he had ridden to the raft earlier in the day. "Is he worse than when I left?" he asked.

"Yes, grandfather, he is" said Naamah. I came to bring Noach in case he didn't come back with you."

"Should I go back for Ham and Nae?"

"Yes, I think so, the site should be all right for one day. We can take them back tomorrow."

"Let's hurry then," said Noah.

Eventually the whole family gathered at the homestead. Sede and Ada were attending Lamech who had been virtually bedridden for several weeks. Over the past year he had become weaker and weaker, until one day he could no longer travel anywhere and simply stayed in his room or walked in the courtyard. Now he was too weak even for that.

"He's asleep," said Ada.

"We don't think it will be long now," added Sede.

"Noach and I will stay with him a while. You go and have a break," said Naamah.

They sat either side of Lamech each holding one of his hands, speaking of the wonderful years they had all enjoyed together. Sadly, yet contented, they knew this day must come.

I have known many happy days in this family since I married you," reflected Naamah. "We are going to miss your father and mother, and Hebe of course, in our great adventure to come."

"Yes, I was so saddened that Hebe left us and will not now accompany us." Noah replied.

There is something else I never told you until now, Hebe made me promise her."

"What Naamah?"

Now with tears in her eyes Naamah continued. "It was the last thing Hebe said. She was holding my hand tightly and she said to me … 'Tell Noach – I'm sorry… I won't be there,' she couldn't finish, but she meant on the Ark with us."

Noah looked forlornly at his wife. "I loved her so much."

At that moment Lamech opened his eyes and smiled at them both. "Ah it is good to see you, Noach and Naamah."

Composing himself, Noah said, "It's good to see you awake and alert father. Don't exert yourself, you need to rest."

Fixing his gaze on them, Lamech said "Bah! I have plenty of time soon to rest. We all know how this ends. Now that you are here I have something to say to you both."

"Very well, father," they replied.

Holding their hands, Lamech continued, "I am so happy your future is assured. It is so good you married this woman, Noach, she has been a tower of strength to you. And you Emzara, Naamah, I have been so proud, not only of being your uncle, but your father in law as well. My end will come soon, now I wish to bless you both."

And so he did, first as a couple, then Naamah and finally Noah.

"You were our first born, Noach, and when this happened we knew you were going to achieve something special in this life. We believed Adonai had his hand on you from the very beginning. Your hair was as white as snow. It is a shade or two darker now, but you do stand out among men. When we named you, your name was to carry the meaning, '*This one will give us rest from our work and the toil of our hands arising from the ground which the Lord has cursed – Our comfort.*'

"We thought you would become the redeeming one as did Hevah those many years ago. So did many of our ancestors of their first born. However, I don't believe you are that man, although you are a man who walks with Adonai and he finds favour with you. You are a righteous one among men and your blood line is pure. It is your destiny to take your family into a new world with his guidance and blessing to start again.

"Hear me, my son, you must remain steadfast. You must continue to obey Adonai no matter how hard the way appears. You must honour him and teach your children and their children and their children. Do not disobey me. Nevertheless, sin I fear, will remain in the world and so a redeemer must come one day from one of your descendants. Adonai will declare it."

"Go now, and this I pass on to you: be a priest of the most-high God in your new land, where one day you will pass this blessing on to another."

"Thank you father I am honoured," Noah responded. "I have one thing to share with you, father, before you leave us. The third time I sailed around the world, although we didn't intend to, we decided that as we were so far south we should try once again to find the southern land, and we did. It is a beautiful, pristine, uninhabited land, and we left it so. That is the reason we told no one."

"I would not have expected anything less of you my son, well done."

Much weakened after his long speech Lamech then slept. Later in the day and into the evening he blessed each of Japheth, Shem, Ham and their wives. Then Lamech left them and that ancient world in his sleep in the early hours of the next morning. Contented and happy, he passed on having lived 777 years and was laid to rest beside his beloved Betenos in the estate burial ground.

‡‡‡

Seven Months Later
AM 1656

The homestead was closed soon after Lamech's death. Some farm animals remained, but the rest were transported to the site of the Ark. By now animals had miraculously started to arrive, and soon the various other enclosures were full of all sorts of creatures.

Even though the Ark was now finished and their living quarters were ready for occupation, Noah was adamant that they should not yet live in it. "Not until Adonai tells us to," he insisted. So they remained living in the huts that had been built at the work site. Methuselah was still with them and seemingly healthy.

Every so often a small boat would put in from the sea with people who had come to see the sad decline of the great Noah in his obvious dementia and to marvel at his great edifice to the god of stupidity. Verbal abuse and objects were often thrown at his family from the river. Noah wouldn't let anyone land at the site. In his mind the mockers were now beyond redemption. Sadly there was no word from Nadav and Ariel, and because God had not mentioned them Noah and Naamah had come to accept that somehow they had come to grief and would not join them now in the terror that was to come upon them.

It never failed to amaze the nine of them how the animals appeared to know where to come and that they were seemingly called for a purpose and had simply arrived here at the site.

"It's a miracle," said Sede.

By now everyone was busy all day and every day attending to the animals' needs, settling them into specified areas outside as well as preparing the Ark for occupation.

"We can't control the smaller birds," said Japheth, "they just keep coming."

"No matter," suggested Shem, "I'll open the flues on the roof of the top deck and they can fly in and out of the aviary."

"That will have to do. We'll simply have to let Adonai sort out which he wants or doesn't want," agreed Noah.

"Nae and I have made up plenty of the hibernation formula," advised Ham. "There should be adequate quantities of it now to keep at least most of the larger animals dormant for the duration of whatever is coming."

"Right, Ham, that's good. But make sure you get them on board before you give it to them otherwise you'll have to carry them on," Noah said laughing.

The mood this particular morning was one of anticipation and excitement, but with everyone on edge. Because of such a multitude of animals around them they now had another confirmation of what God was about to bring upon them and they realised it was close, very close.

It was then that the ground shook violently for the first time.

The three younger women screamed. The others looked around in shock and wonderment. The world had never experienced anything like this sudden shaking. It was a total surprise for the family as well as the animals around them. The birds and animals became agitated and many screeched, bleated or showed alarm at a phenomenon they had never experienced before. In all the excitement no one noticed that Methuselah had suddenly clutched his chest and had fallen to the ground. When Ada saw him lying there she ran quickly over to him.

"He's unconscious," she said. "I think it must be his heart, and the shock of what just happened has affected him."

When he came round they carried him to his quarters and he said, "my chest hurts; I can hardly breathe. What was that violent shaking?"

"We don't know grandfather, but it probably means things are starting to happen."

"Yes and this old man is starting to depart." Methuselah started to cough at his joke.

"Please rest grandfather," said Ada. "Nae, can you stay with him while I run and get my medicines?"

While this was happening Noah felt compelled to go down to the river and walk toward its mouth, a quiet place he often visited. Naamah watched him go, intuitively knowing what was about to happen next. He was several hundred cubits away when she saw him suddenly drop to his knees. After a time he raised his hands heavenward and stayed there like that for a long time as God spoke to him.

Go into the ark, you and all your household, for I have seen that you are righteous before me in this generation. Take with you seven pairs of all unblemished animals, the male and his mate, and a pair of the animals that are not unblemished, the male and his mate, and seven pairs of the birds of the heavens also, male and female, to keep their offspring alive on the face of all the earth. For in seven days I will send rain on the earth forty days and forty nights, and every living thing that I have made I will wipe out from the face of the earth.

After some time Noah returned to the site of the Ark. His whole family were standing there waiting for him expectantly, but he simply nodded at them. Nae and Sede then started to weep silently, but the rest looked steadfastly at Noah, waiting for him to speak. Naamah came and stood beside him taking hold of his hand as he gave them the message:

"It is time now. We must go into the Ark."

It Shall Be Sent

AM 1656

Two more tremors shook the ground that afternoon, which was unsettling and worrying, since they had not experienced anything like this before. The birds squawked and chirped loudly and the animals were restless and noisy. Something had dramatically changed not only at where the Ark was but across the earth as well.

Methuselah lay on his cot breathing shallowly, with all the women taking turns to sit with him. Finally Ada said what they all were thinking. "I'm sorry, but I have to tell you he's getting weaker, not better. I think his time has nearly come."

At this Noah went in to where his grandfather lay and knelt beside him. Methuselah then spoke. "I don't know what has come over me. It feels like everything in me is slowly closing down. So I suspect my time has come, Noach, after all these years. I've lived longer than any man or woman on earth, 969 years!"

"Rest easy, grandfather, save your strength," Noah gently replied.

"No, Noach, I must speak now before I no longer can. You know what you must do, and do it diligently. Obey Adonai, don't depart from his word. Now, I'm sure you have done this, but I must still ask, are all of Enoch's writings safe and secure, especially the creation story and our history including the line of Cain so that you can pass them on?"

"I have, grandfather. We have made copies of them as well, and there is also the scroll that Naamah was given."

"That's good. And now I'd like you to carry me outside so I can see the animals and all your family and this great Ark. I want to see it all, the green jungle and the blue sea before I die."

"Of course, grandfather. There is also something I wish to confess to you." Noah then told his grandfather, as he had told his father Lamech, of his journey of discovery to the southern land.

"So it is there!" cried Methuselah. "I always thought that if it was to be discovered you would be the one to do that, Noach."

The men then quickly built a platform and placed Methuselah's cot on it so he could look in all directions. By now he was only able to drink liquids and spent most of the remainder of the day sleeping, waking briefly each time a member of the family came to him for his blessing. As the sun set on this momentous day Methuselah slept with his ancestors, and the family knew their time of trial was about to fall on them.

For the next six days the loading of the animals continued throughout each day and much of the night as well until every one of them was on board and settled in its proper space. This was quite an achievement. Noah and all his family then went on board the Ark and organised their own private areas. Everyone felt a latent excitement, wondering what was going to happen next. They had dismantled the two rafts and other heavy equipment and stored all of it under the floor of the lower deck, along with their tools and anything that they considered would be of use in the world to come. Noah had ensured that some of the best grapevines and other fruiting plants along with a myriad of seeds of all kinds were safely stored on board as well.

Once everyone was on board the massive task of looking after more than 16,000 animals and birds began in earnest and would keep the family occupied for a long time to come. All through that week the earth tremors continued to increase in frequency and intensity. The mists in the sky above also began to turn inky, forming clouds darker than anything ever seen before, even blotting out the sun at times. The bright, beautiful days that people had always known became dimmer and the light breezes that were once so common now turned into intensely strong gales.

‡‡‡

People in nearby Ophir and Shur speculated on the significance of the changes in the sky and the quaking of the ground beneath them. A few remembered what Noah and his family had been telling them for a long time and they wondered if perhaps they should have listened to him. Some even decided to head to the site of the Ark to ask Noah if this was what he had been talking about. However, each day the seas got rougher and the winds blew so strongly that their light craft could not cope with the conditions in the ocean. Nor could they use the river, because Noah's rafts were no longer there. A few said they would take the long road through the forest and felt sure Noah would take them on board once they arrived on the eastern side of the river where the site of the Ark was.

Throughout all Havilah and across the world the same phenomena brought terror to the people of planet earth. Nothing like this had ever happened before.

After the first day of tremors it was clear to Nadav and Ariel that what Noah had predicted, or at least what God had told him, really was beginning to happen. Otherwise, how could one explain these strange events in the ground and sky? They had left Nadav's village over a month before and started their journey overland taking their time. Now they wished their horse would pull their cart faster. Once the tremors began in earnest they hurried as fast as they could to the nearest port in Shulon hoping to get a boat to Ophir. They were becoming desperate.

"We should never have spent so long with my family," an angry Nadav was blaming himself. "We were there for years. I knew we should have left months ago. But there was always something else to do or some activity they wanted us to share with them. It's all been for nothing, we are bringing no one with us."

"Yes, my husband it seems so," agreed Ariel. "We should have gone back to Ophir long ago. We can only hope that Adonai will delay long enough for us to get back to the Ark in time. Perhaps we didn't try hard enough to change our family's minds. We certainly enjoyed their lifestyle, and that's why we may be too late now."

Baruch looked at his brother Hem who had been lost for so many years as they stood and looked over Baruch's wheat fields. Hem had arrived in the area a week earlier and found where Baruch lived. The two men had talked at length each night since on all sorts of things relating to their lives past and present, including the death of their mother and a message that had arrived some months earlier with news of Lamech's death. Baruch had talked with much scorn about Noach and his great Ark, how sad he was thinking about it and how stupid and overzealous for God the family had become. Hem agreed with him, explaining how he kept his distance and never went back because of that zealousness.

"But what are we to make of these extraordinary events that have now come upon us and seemingly all over the world as well, all at the same time? Every day for the last four days the ground has been shaking, the sky is changing too, and the sun is now dimmer. Just what is going on, I wonder," said Baruch in bewilderment.

"Maybe, just maybe, father, grandfather and Noach were right?" replied Hem.

But Baruch was adamant. "I won't believe that until I see it with my own eyes," he said firmly.

"Perhaps that IS what we are seeing," said Hem with a troubled look.

Worldwide, people were becoming alarmed. "What's going on?" They were asking one another. Deputations sent to the governing councils overwhelmed the frightened administrators who had no answer to the question. Scientists of all kinds were equally baffled. Some thought that the earth was changing as it aged. Others argued it was because there were now so many millions of people and animals alive that it was more than the earth was designed to support.

"All our activity is causing the climate to change!" was the cry of some, while far to the south there were reports from ships at sea that what was happening was due to a large fireball in the sky that smashed into the ocean. Others simply felt there was nothing to worry about. It was all unusual but natural and would pass.

By the sixth day of God's warning to Noah earth tremors had increased in frequency and intensity at an alarming rate. High winds and dark clouds brought a fearsome noise in the heavens and the light of the sun was now totally blotted out by dark black clouds never seen before. Flashes of lightning, accompanied by thunder of a violence previously unknown caused terror and panic among the creatures of the earth, both animals and people. Violent fire from the sky now struck buildings, trees and other objects several times a day. The world and its inhabitants now knew beyond any doubt that some kind of catastrophic event was falling upon them.

Tens of thousands of people across the world attempted to repent and pleaded with whatever god they followed, or some other imaginary deity they now sought out, for they had never bothered in the past to think about what lies beyond death. Some finally acknowledged the Creator God. These were people who had listened to Noah and others and whose conscience now convicted them, but in their wisdom had decided previously to put off a decision to follow Adonai until they needed to.

For all of them it was too late.

Nadav and Ariel were frustrated and fearful, knowing they were probably doomed, yet hoping against hope that the ship they were in would get them to Ophir in time to escape on the Ark. This voyage was the worst they had ever experienced, as the winds were so fierce that already some sails had been ripped from their masts. They were not making much headway, and although they prayed earnestly they had missed God's timing as he had ordained. He knew this would be so, and therefore they were not included in the eight who would be preserved in the Ark.

Baruch, his family, and now Hem, recognised the wisdom of Noah, Lamech and Methuselah. They fell on their knees in anguish and cried out to the God of their brother, sister and father as the ground shook beneath them and Baruch's house began to crack and fall apart. But God was no longer listening to them.

At the same time several dozen people had gathered on the eastern side of the river opposite to where the Ark stood, calling to Noah to help them cross over, but he refused to do this. In truth, he no longer had a craft to fetch them. Others were trying to haul small boats down to Lamech's estate jetty on the river, but they were still a long way off. Some desperate ones who tried to swim across the wide river were drowned. All of them were shouting and crying out in fear as they realised that what Noah had said all along was now happening.

Eventually, on the morning of the seventh day some people did manage to get across the river, but by now all Noah's family and the animals were in the Ark. Noah had insisted this be done as quickly as possible, and thus had achieved the immense task of getting all on board by the evening of the sixth day. He then ordered his sons to winch the great door shut, leaving only a small gap to allow air to circulate as much as possible before they closed and secured it properly.

The shouts of people outside were upsetting some of Noah's family as they gathered in their living area on the upper deck. The ground shook violently and the Ark shuddered.

"Surely we can take these ones father?" a frustrated Ham asked.

"NO! Adonai has spoken and I will obey him."

"But this can't be right, father, surely there must be more who can be saved along with us."

"Unfortunately not, Ham." Noah replied. "You have seen and heard all that I've said as did your grandfather and Methuselah. Have you forgotten?"

"No, but I assumed others would build arks also. I never believed it was just going to be us."

"We don't have time to argue over this now, Ham. What Adonai has decreed is happening. We must obey him and obey father. We have to get through this. We must stay together and remain strong," Shem spoke sternly to his brother.

"Yes, we must stay united. We need each other to stay strong in this," said Naamah gently.

And Noah added, "We must be ready now for what is coming. It has to be today. You will see that Adonai keeps his word and what he says comes to pass. Now, we must ensure the door is securely shut."

At this moment another sharp jolt shook the ground outside and reverberated through the Ark.

"I'm scared about all this," cried Nae, but Sede reassured her. "We all are, dear sister, but we have one another."

As the men were about to descend to the middle deck to secure the door a great crack of thunder and a heavy thump hit the Ark, along with a bright flash of light, and the Ark rocked slightly.

"What was that?" Japheth shouted.

"We've been struck by one of those flashes of fire that have been hitting the trees. Check for any damage," yelled Noah.

"It's the door," cried Shem who was the first to get there. "It's jammed shut!"

"Check the seals," shouted Noah anxiously.

"There's no light showing around the door, it's been sealed shut on us," confirmed Shem.

"Adonai's shut us in," cried an excited Naamah.

"It's another miracle!" shouted Ada."

"Many miracles," added Sede. "Look at all these animals knowing to come here, and all of them perfect specimens. Only Adonai could have chosen and guided them. It's truly a miracle and now this!"

"Yes, my family," said Noah, "the Lord has shut us in. We are safe now for what is about to come. Let us pray." As they bowed their heads in reverence the Ark shuddered as a long rolling tremor shook the land around them.

In the six hundredth year of Noah's life, in the second month, on the seventeenth day of the month, on that day all the fountains of the great deep burst forth, and the windows of the heavens were opened. And rain fell upon the earth forty days and forty nights. On the very same day Noah and his sons, Shem and Ham and Japheth, and Noah's wife and the three wives of his sons with them entered the ark, they and every beast, according to its kind, and all the livestock according to their kinds, and every creeping thing that creeps on the earth, according to its kind, and every bird, according to its kind, every winged creature. They went into the ark with Noah, two and two of all flesh in which there was the breath of life. And those that entered, male and female of all flesh, went in as God had commanded him. And the Lord shut him in.

– Genesis 7, verses 11-16

EIGHTEEN

Flood

Along the entire length of the Ark's upper deck Noah had constructed a series of flued openings to allow light in and air to circulate. These were designed to be clamped shut during the worst of the tempest, but on this day Noah and his sons stood on the platform they had built to look out of the rearmost of these apertures. This was the only way they could see what was happening outside. The women chose instead to stay safely in their living area or attend to the animals. They had no desire to see whatever destruction might be coming upon them.

The first indication of a flood of water was when the river rose very quickly and alarmingly. Springs from within the earth inland had opened up and gushed skywards with such enormous pressure that they turned what was normally a narrow, swift flowing stream into a raging torrent of devastation. Likewise, far out at sea, Noah watched as giant waterspouts jetted a long way into the sky. In the opposite direction beyond the distant hills behind Ophir a great fountain of fire shot heavenwards as the first of many volcanoes erupted upon the land and in the sea. At the same time lightning flashed from the blackened clouds that had been gathering for several days, and then the rain fell. It was so heavy that they could no longer see the forest on the other side of the river, nor the waterspouts in the sea, nor the volcanic eruption. The rain became a maelstrom of water, sleet and wind. The frightful explosions and the roar of the exploding hill could still be heard however, as well as the constant and violent quaking of the ground. All this made a terrifying spectacle for the occupants of the Ark.

"Oh my, oh my, I never imagined…" shouted Shem, above the roar of the tempest, his face pale with shock as he held a stanchion to steady himself against the movement of the Ark as it responded to the quaking ground and swirling river rapidly encircling it.

"It's horrible," agreed Ham, sharing his brother's alarm.

"We always knew it would be something colossal," added Japheth.

"Yes," said Noah, "Adonai has spoken."

With that Noah shut the remaining flues and they re-joined their women in the living area. The family then sat in a circle and held hands a long time and prayed. The Ark now was rocking and swaying, but not alarmingly so. It had been built well, and its bulk rode the storm easily.

Cries from people outside were quickly extinguished as the river and sea merged. Great waves swept in from the ocean taking the earth, trees and foliage with them, and in less than an hour the great Ark started moving. With the force of the river flowing to the sea and the sea waves coming onto the land it was steadily raised, slewing one way then another. As the trees of the jungle were swept away some of the larger trees stood firm. Although the Ark swerved into them the waters were now so high that only the upper branches were crushed and there was no damage to the Ark. The swift flow of the now hugely wide river then bore the Ark with it far out to sea.

Nadev and Ariel and their ship foundered in the raging storm and they perished with it. Baruch and Hem stood in shock watching the destruction about them, knowing their death was inevitable. They were far inland and so the rising waters did not immediately engulf them. The rain, however, was something they had never experienced before, and it simply poured down on them without respite. Nearby the ground also opened up and great plumes of water shot skyward eventually falling back and creating lakes that grew until they ultimately covered the entire land. Baruch was separated from his family by a great rent in the earth where he and Hem were standing. His family rushed out of their home crying in horror and alarm and were immediately swept away by a torrent of water that had broken the banks of the nearby stream that flowed past their homestead. In the distance fire erupted from hills that he had often climbed. Baruch and Hem died together in the rising waters.

All over the earth people and animals fled the storm, the water spouts and eruptions, yet found nowhere safe to hide. Some went into caves or sheltered in their homes which were quickly swept away, but inevitably the sea and inland waterways rose and eventually covered every bit of dry land. None survived; all living things perished.

For although they knew God, they neither glorified him as God nor gave thanks to him, but their thinking became futile and their foolish hearts were darkened. Although they claimed to be wise, they became fools and exchanged the glory of the immortal God for images made to look like mortal man and birds and animals and reptiles. They exchanged the truth of God for a lie and worshipped and served created things rather than the Creator.

– Romans 1, verses 21-23, 25 (NIV)

The waters rose higher and higher. The animals and birds in the Ark reacted to this with a cacophony of moans and squawks in those first hours afloat, and Noah's family had to endure the noise as they moved among them, soothing them as best they could. They had added a calming mixture to the feed of those animals that could absorb it, but this took some time to take effect. Every part of the Ark now had to be checked as well to ensure there were no leaks, and this also kept the men busy in every part of the ship. Thankfully everything was sound.

As the Ark was driven further and further from the shore by the waves and the wind the roar of the erupting mountain became distant.

"Adonai be thanked!" shouted Japheth. "We're being driven away from all that destruction!"

Shouting was the only way they could communicate because of the sound of the heavy rain and shrieking wind. By now the whole family was in a mild state of shock, with no foreknowledge of what would become of them and wondering what it might be. Although they knew in advance that God was going to destroy and flood the earth, how this was to be done had been unknown to them. They had never experienced anything like this before and were naturally alarmed at the severity of God's judgment. Even though they knew that their Lord God would not let them perish, none of them were able to sleep for the first night in the Ark.

The next two days were to be the most exhausting of all in their year-long experience of life on board. It was the matter of getting into a routine with the animals and having time for themselves and one another. They had discussed this earlier of course, but there is nothing like the real thing, and the reality of living through the flood hit them hard. They realised for the first time that to survive and keep all the animals alive was now up to them. The choices they made each day would impact on the entire population in the Ark. Any mistake in providing food and water or inattention to the animals' needs could simply wipe out a whole species. Their responsibility was immense.

Meanwhile the heavy rain continued unabated day after day. Each family member had an area of responsibility and a group of animals or birds to care for. Noah was in charge of everything and the undisputed captain of the ship. He was responsible for all on board and this weighed heavily on him. He therefore often spent time in prayer with his Lord. Naamah, of course, was a strong help and support for him. Noah also insisted that the family pray together each night before they went to bed.

There was little time for them to rest during their waking hours. Some task was always there to be done. A twenty four hour watch was kept, and every member took their turn while the others slept. It was not that they expected any danger from outside, but if something harmful should befall any of the birds and animals there would always be someone available to deal with this. So a duty watch meant going round the ship every so often. As there were eight of them they each did a two hour watch when it was their turn during the eight hours set aside for sleep. In this way each member of the family was required to do this only every second night. The animals and birds often slept in the dark and semi dark confines of the decks and the calming mixture kept most of them docile. Some animals even hibernated for long periods of time.

Air was circulated in the Ark by various means. Vents in the roof were now kept slightly ajar, as well as small openings in the upper parts of the middle and upper decks. Other mechanisms were also used. Torches using oil in spill-proof containers were used to light their way. As the family mostly ate vegetables their food was often eaten cold, although at times they prepared a soup or vegetable stew for themselves over a safely enclosed fire and grill. Animal waste was disposed of by a clever plan devised by Noah and his sons. They had built the animal cages and compartments above the flooring so that the waste could fall through slats into a sloping trough which in turn drained the effluent into a holding tank. Its contents were then pumped out by hand each day through an outlet above the waterline. Solid waste was collected in containers and dumped out the general waste outlet. Only the men took their turn at this undesirable but necessary task. Thus the many repetitive tasks and requirements for survival in the Ark became a daily routine for the eight survivors from the old world.

As the days turned into weeks their daily routine became easier. The rain continued to fall unabated, although its initial intensity lessened as the days passed. Huge waves came and went, but the design of the Ark was such that it rode out the quirks of wind, wave and current easily. Unable to be steered, it was at the mercy of the wind and waves, but it rode up and down readily and simply moved along at the whim of the storm. Occasionally it slewed to the left or right but soon righted itself. None of this was alarming or uncomfortable to the occupants, because the sheer size of the vessel enabled it to cut through all the troughs and peaks that the sea threw at it. In fact, their journey didn't seem to be greatly different from when they had sailed in light airs in their smaller ships of days gone by.

When life had developed a routine and the family were able to relax somewhat they could now reflect on what had befallen them. One factor that did become obvious after a few days was how much colder it was. With no sun now shining in a clear sky the temperature outside had dropped considerably and this was noticeable inside as well.

"Everything Adonai said would happen has happened exactly as and when he said it would," reflected Naamah as the family sat for a midday meal after a time of prayer. They had even sung some songs and those who had musical instruments had played them.

"Yes, that's true," sighed a weary Noah.

"But it's become a lot colder than we're used to," said Sede, shivering.

"Yes, I think we've all noticed that. We shall have to make warmer clothes for ourselves, instead of putting on more layers," suggested Naamah.

"The cooler temperature doesn't seem to have affected the animals at all. They've settled in quite well, thankfully," added Ada.

"Yes, and so have the birds and bats and most of the flying creatures," said Sede.

"I think the bats have gone to sleep permanently," laughed Nae.

"And most of the larger animals," agreed Japheth.

"I think the small animals will forever run about their cages. Smaller is livelier, I think," laughed Shem.

"They probably do that to keep warm," chuckled Nae.

"So many creatures we knew of are not here though," mused Naamah, "especially the giant reptiles. Adonai seems to have left them out of our new world."

"It would appear so," agreed Noah. "But I don't think the drop in temperature outside will affect us and the animals too badly. Our combined body heat in this confined area will be enough to keep it liveable. As with everything, we need to keep an eye on all the creatures and ourselves in case any of them get distressed."

"I'm concerned about the flesh eating animals," Sede said. "Hopefully we have enough dried animal meat to feed them through this, but what if this goes bad?" she asked.

"It's the same for all the grains and dried plants, hay and vegetables we have stored. We must make sure none of it gets damp, otherwise it will certainly deteriorate and decay. If any food does get damp we'll have to use it immediately."

"Many of the flesh eating animals are in hibernation anyway, so hopefully they won't eat much," added Japheth.

"Won't they be hungry when they wake up?" asked Nae.

"You worry so much about the animals, but what about all the people we left behind? What's all this for?" a moody Ham replied. "I mean, when and if we ever do find some new land and this infernal water falling from the sky ceases, what then? How do we start again with just us and these animals?"

"I believe Adonai will tell us, my son," Noah replied. "Why else would he have gone to all this trouble, instructing us to build this great ship and take these animals on board if we were all not to start again?"

"I just can't see how we'll survive," Ham replied. "Yes, we have enough food to last a year, but if the whole world is destroyed and we find land again, what will we eat then? There are so many questions and so many uncertainties. I can't sleep at night thinking that this is still going to end in disaster."

Noah replied, "As Naamah has just said, all this has happened exactly as Adonai indicated. So I'm confident that he'll make a way for us and all these animals not only to survive but to repopulate the new world whatever it is like and wherever that may be."

"I agree with you, Noach. I know we all do," said Sede encouragingly.

"Exactly," said Shem. "We have trusted father so far, so why should we doubt him or Adonai now. And look, here we are, we've survived and we're safe and dry here. This great ship is riding out the storm with no problems. Apart from the first day I've never felt in danger, and we floated away from that eruption of fire behind Ophir and the rage of the river as it turned the Ark this way and that. Surely you must see the hand of Adonai in all this, Ham?"

"Well, I'm still not convinced about all this. I'm not sure I want to serve a God who has destroyed all those good people and all the animals. It's all wrong."

"Ham, you know why it had to be. Don't you believe that? You did, once?" said Shem, grasping his brother's arm encouragingly.

Ham pulled away and stormed off, tipping his food onto the deck in anger. Nae looked at her family awkwardly and apologetically, sighed, and went off after him.

"All this is affecting him very hard," responded Japheth. "He was upset that Nadav and Ariel didn't make it back to the Ark in time.

He was fond of Nadav. They had worked well together."

"All of us have had to come to terms in our own way with what has happened," replied Naamah. "None of us wanted all this."

"That's so true," responded Sede.

"We must stay united. Ham has always been difficult. Hopefully he'll think his way around it all. I know that he enjoys looking after the large animals. Let's get back to our duties now, and we can discuss all this again this evening if we need to," sighed Noah, as he dismissed the group.

The stress of the responsibility he now had to shoulder was evident on his tired features.

"You should get more rest my darling, said Naamah in a reassuring way. "We are all capable of carrying out our duties and Adonai has brought us this far. Trust him now for what is to come."

"Yes, thank you. You are so right my love. I do feel weary and I'll have some rest now."

Meanwhile on the lower deck Ada attended to a deep cut Ham had suffered in his leg when he had taken a kick at a damaged trough lying outside the elephants' enclosure. He had slipped on some uncollected manure and promptly fell hard against the broken trough. Ada told him it would need stitches and he would need to come up to the upper deck where there was more light and somewhere for him to lie down while she treated his wound.

"I'm sorry, Ada, I'm just … frustrated that we're confined in here for probably a year, it's …" he said.

"There's no need to explain," she replied soothingly. "Nae and I will help you up to the living area. I need to stitch the wound. The cut is too deep to heal on its own."

"Right, let's get it done then."

"Haw, haw, brother Ham, what have you done?" laughed Japheth when Ham and the two women limped into the family area.

"Okay, okay. I remember when you caught your leg in the anchor rope and fell on the deck once. What a job that was untangling you."

"Yes, I can still feel that rope burn. It lasted for days."

"Ah, have we had a little accident?" said Naamah with a laugh too.

"Yes, it appears I'm now the joke of the day," groaned Ham.

"I'm keeping his blood for the bats when they wake up," laughed Nae. Naamah glanced over at Shem, who winked as if to say Ham's tantrum was over and peace now reigned again.

Day after day as the rain continued to fall the family found things to amuse themselves with in between their ongoing tasks. In this way they kept their spirits up by playing group games, singing and playing their musical instruments, all the while attending to their host of animals and birds. And every evening they came together in prayer to keep them focused on the deliverance they owed to their God.

Then, suddenly at the end of forty days, the rain stopped and the sun shone again for the first time since they had entered the Ark. It was a welcome sign indeed, that encouraged Noah to open the flues wider. But the sea still surged and the wind still blew a gale.

The flood continued forty days on the earth. The waters increased and bore up the ark, and it rose high above the earth. The waters prevailed and increased greatly on the earth, and the ark floated on the face of the waters. And the waters prevailed so mightily on the earth that all the high mountains under the whole heaven were covered. The waters prevailed above the mountains, covering them fifteen cubits deep. And all flesh died that moved on the earth, birds, livestock, beasts, all swarming creatures that swarm on the earth, and all mankind. Everything on the dry land in whose nostrils was the breath of life died. He wiped out every living thing that was on the face of the ground, man and animals and creeping things and birds of the heavens. They were destroyed from the earth. Only Noah was left, and those who were with him in the ark. And the waters prevailed on the earth 150 days.

– Genesis 7, verses 17-24

NINETEEN

Fear and Hope

The Great Flood Continues Unabated

A t some point during the last watch of the night in the early hours of the morning the rain stopped. The pause in the constant rhythm of rain hitting the roof of the Ark was the first indication that something different was happening. By chance this particular watch was being kept by Noah. With the coming of the dawn there was the bright sun, shining more strongly than the passengers on this great ship had seen since before the tempest fell upon them. It was the first clear day of the new world. Noah confirmed the rain had ceased when he opened one of the flues and looked out onto a glistening, vast water world, and when he saw this he called the rest of the family up to gaze upon this new day.

"Magnificent desolation!" cried Noah.

Each family member in turn looked out at the calm sea and brilliant sunshine.

"There's nothing but water for as far as I can see," said an incredulous Naamah. Then everyone spoke at once with statements of wonder and amazement.

"So what now?" asked Ham. "Do we simply drift forever on this water world? Is this it!?"

"Have some faith brother," replied Shem. "Adonai didn't bring us this far, just to leave us to perish in these waters, unless he expects us and all the animals to only eat fish."

"I can't see the animals taking to that," replied Ada. "No, there must be something out here for us, some land I mean."

"We just have to float until we find it," added Japheth.

"Yes, I believe you're correct, my son," Noah agreed.

"But we have no means of moving or steering the ship if we do," exclaimed Ham, "just exactly where are we, I wonder?"

"We'll have to wait for darkness and hopefully see some stars then. That way I can calculate our position based on what coordinates we used when we sailed the seas before this flood. The earth has certainly undergone a great change, but I don't think that has extended to the stars," Noah said.

"I hope we find land soon. I don't want to become a fish," laughed Nae.

"Some of the animals on this level are stirring since you opened the flues and let in more light. Perhaps we need to shut them again so they don't become unsettled," suggested Sede.

That night when the sky was clear for the first time Noah took a sighting of some known stars, and confirmed what he thought; the position of the stars had not changed.

"It's amazing," said Noah. "Since I looked at the night sky last there appear to be thousands more stars than I ever saw before. The brighter ones I recognise are the ones whose place was known to us. Incredibly, it appears we are not so far from where Ophir used to be. We must have been drifting back and forth over only a small part of the ocean after all. Perhaps land may even be nearby. But if this water now covers all the land it may need to drain away for us to see it again."

"But where would all the water go?" asked Nae.

"I have no idea, but perhaps from where it came, from inside the earth. We shall have to wait and see."

"How long do we have to wait? Surely we can use the small boat we placed on the lower deck. It has a sail and a rudder, so we can go and find some land," suggested Ham with some degree of exasperation.

"And just how will we get the boat outside?" asked Japheth. "We can't open the door. If we do the waves will roll in and sink us, and we can't get the boat through the roof."

"It was just a thought. We have to do something! We can't just sit here for weeks and months and wait."

"Well, we may have to, my family," said Noah. Adonai hasn't given me any directions on this. The only instinct I have is that we must wait."

"For how long?" asked Ham.

"Until we find land," replied Noah.

"That could be forever," Ham objected.

"Silly, we would die before then," observed Sede.

"I don't know, you are making fun of my fears," said Ham. "You all have so much faith in Adonai, but I feel I am rapidly losing mine."

"I agree with my husband," whimpered Nae.

"It has been an eventful day, people. Let's take these concerns before Adonai together now, and then sleep on this. Perhaps tomorrow will bring some definite direction for us. Who has the first watch for tonight?"

"I do, father," said Shem.

The next day brought with it no sight of any land nor any indication of where they might end up. Neither did the next or the one after that, nor did the following weeks. In fact, it would be another one hundred and ten days before the Ark grounded on land, and even then the waters continued to cover their world. The outside temperature also remained cool despite the sun in the sky, but over the next several weeks the days became warmer as the weather of the new world that was emerging adjusted itself into seasons, rather than the constant summery environment of the old one.

For many days at a time a strong wind blew, pushing up the water into waves and swells that splashed against the side of the Ark. In all of this the people on board wondered what kind of world they had now entered. From all the signs it did not seem as if it was going to be as pleasant as their previous one had been.

Ham grew more and more despondent and fearful of their future, and his feelings eventually affected his wife's attitude as well. Japheth understood his brother's concerns, but trusted his father Noah and his relationship with God. As for Naamah, Shem, Sede and Ada, they had little or no fear that the Lord God would not bring them out of their present situation. The successful work of building this great Ark and the fact that God had used it to save all these animals and birds as well as themselves was enough to assure them that they would finally survive and start again in a new world.

Noah, with the responsibility of all this on his shoulders, naturally had periods of doubt from time to time, but he had heard the audible voice of the Lord, and this gave him the confidence and faith that he and his family had been chosen to continue life on earth as God entrusted this to them. It was not going to be easy, for there were clearly many challenges ahead. He was aware of Ham and Nae's lack of faith, which was growing weaker by the day. Yet by the very fact that they were here and enduring this long wait Noah knew that Adonai was testing them to make them stronger in their faith and trust in him.

Noah prayed, as he had done already many times during the forty days of rain, and would continue to do so daily. At times it was with his faithful Naamah by his side, and at others it was with the whole family when they met together each evening before retiring for the night.

After the excitement of the rain ceasing to fall Noah's family fell into their daily routines once again while they floated upon their world of water. Adonai was with them. None became sick and apart from Ham's accident no one else injured themselves. Unfortunately, a pair of the larger reptiles died, meaning this species would not continue in the new world.

"How did that happen?" asked Naamah.

"We are not sure," replied Ada. "Sede discovered them. They looked to be hibernating normally. I'd checked them just yesterday and their breathing although shallow was still regular. But overnight something happened. They're cold to the touch, no longer breathing, and obviously quite dead."

"All right, let's keep a close watch on the other reptiles and hibernating animals," advised Noah.

"We can use their bodies as food for the carnivorous animals," suggested Japheth.

"Very well. How are the birds and other flying creatures in the aviary?" asked Noah. "They can be rather vulnerable creatures."

"We've lost a couple of those, but many of them have laid eggs which is a good sign," said Ada happily. "I believe all of them will survive. I suppose it all depends on how long we have to live like this before we find land. I doubt that any of the birds and animals can survive in this environment indefinitely."

"Including us, no doubt," interposed Ham.

"Yes Ham, we are quite aware of that," Sede said testily.

"Hey everyone, let's have a song or two. Sede, Nae and Japheth need to practise their instruments," suggested Naamah clapping her hands to lighten the atmosphere.

"I can provide a rhythm by tapping some empty casks, I've been practising," added Ham."

"Taking your frustrations out on poor innocent empty casks," laughed Nae.

Everyone joined in her laughter, and they then had a happy hour of making music, singing whatever came into their hearts and learning a new song.

Life continued in the same monotonous way for the inhabitants of the Ark as they longed for an indication of the presence of land and a place where they would be able finally to establish a new life for themselves, hoping for a more congenial environment than the dark and dingy confines of their menagerie. Finally, after floating aimlessly for almost sixteen weeks the Ark scraped on something, slewed to a stop for some moments and then moved again a short distance until it finally settled firmly with a loud crunch on some soft earth and gravel.

"Whoa what was that!" exclaimed Japheth.

"We've found some land at last," laughed Shem. "Quick, let's look outside!"

"There's nothing to see. It is still just water!" groaned Ham.

"Let me see," said Noah, rising from some writing he had been concentrating on when the Ark crunched to a stop.

He opened two or three more flues to get a complete view all around the Ark, but there was nothing to see but water. There was no sight of any land, but they were definitely not moving at all. Something was holding them fast, although the Ark was rocking gently as the waves outside washed against it. After an hour or two there was no further movement as the great ship settled down in the place where it had come to rest. No longer did the Ark passengers feel the movement of the great ship as it proceeded across the ocean. Once again the inhabitants were disappointed in not seeing land or something they could get their bearings on, and so tempers flared once again as their frustrations surfaced.

"I don't know where we are, how could I?" groaned Noah in response to yet another negative question from Ham. "Every day, every step we take is another step into the unknown. We have to take each day as it comes. Let's stay calm. We simply have to be patient a while longer."

"Maybe we'll see land tomorrow," said Nae hopefully.

But despite her hopes it would be another seventy four days before Nae and the rest of Noah's family saw any land and then only in the distance. It was Japheth with his keen eye who alerted the company to this milestone.

"In the distance, on the horizon there, do you see that small black object? It may be a rock, and further to the north there, I believe it's a plume of smoke or steam," he said excitedly.

"You're probably right Japheth. But my eyes are not as keen as they once were," Noah responded.

"Yes, he's right father," agreed an excited Shem "It's definitely land standing out of the sea. And there's a plume of something like smoke over there."

"Let me see," added Ham. "The water is definitely lower around the Ark now. We may see the ground we're sitting on very soon."

"I agree the water has been receding slowly these past few weeks, and while we've been here the place we're sitting on has shaken several times as you are aware, so perhaps it's settling. It seems to indicate the sea is receding and the land is rising and falling as well, perhaps because of the tremors," Noah responded.

"Hopefully then, we'll see all this confounded water seep away over the next week or so. Perhaps it will start to recede faster each day," Ham suggested.

With this sighting their expectations became more optimistic. When an excited Ham opened the flue at first light in the morning two days later he saw a wonderful sight. "They're definitely islands, sharp peaks, a whole string of them on the horizon," he cried, "and that one to the north is belching smoke. I believe I can see something bright. Is it on fire?"

"Yes, I can see them now. Sharper peaks than before this flood," Noah answered. "The water has receded even more, and look below. We're sitting on a ridge of gravel extending beyond the bow. You can see how it slopes away on both sides. But there's still not enough land yet to lower the entrance door onto it. The water is still lapping close to the Ark."

"Let me see, let me see," shouted an excited Nae, with the other women standing close by and all wanting to look at this wonderful sight at the same time.

"There must have been a catastrophic disturbance going on under the water all these months. That mountain of fire on the horizon looks quite alarming," observed Shem. "We don't want to get too close to that."

Over the next several days more land became visible as the water around the Ark receded to reveal rocky uneven ground. Gradually at first and then more rapidly, the waters subsided further over the following weeks. However, the ground remained saturated. It was still not safe to walk on nor was there any sign of plant growth, at least not in the Ark's immediate vicinity. It did not help that rain continued to fall at times, and there was a period of three days when a storm brought high winds and more rain swept over their resting place. Every so often strong tremors shook the ground on which the Ark rested, leaving the occupants in a state of apprehension and asking themselves whether or not this new world they had entered was safe, or were there perhaps fresh calamities to fall upon them.

"It doesn't look like utopia," Naamah decided. "There is no beautiful forest like we had, and these violent shakes show that whatever Adonai has brought on us it is not over yet."

"No, my dear, it does not but what were we expecting? After all that flood we could hardly expect to see forests and plants with leaves and fruit. It all needs time to grow again. As for the violent jolts and that mountain of fire we see in the distance, you're right. Whatever judgment or upheaval Elohim has brought upon the earth it would appear that it hasn't ended with the flood receding," Noah answered his wife, after they had looked once more on the desolate land about them and then discussed the likelihood of leaving the Ark and moving out into the post flood world.

"It's been thirty nine days since we first saw land rise out of the sea. Tomorrow I'm going to send a raven to seek out what he may find," Noah added.

"Why a raven?" asked Ham as he and the other family members joined Noah and Naamah.

"Because he's a predator and scavenger. If there's any food for him to find out there he'll find it."

"But there's nothing out there except rocks and sludge and saturated ground. Not even any grass, nothing," said an exasperated Ham.

"We're quite high up here, and as we've seen there are often strong cold winds outside. So perhaps it's not quite suitable for growth here yet. There may be vegetation at lower altitudes where it's warmer hopefully, and seeds that were carried by the waters can take root and begin to grow," Ada suggested.

"We're alive and well," said Sede. "Each day brings new hope and possibilities, and of course, new challenges we must respond to with the knowledge and understanding that Adonai has given us."

Noah looked at his daughters in law, pausing to consider what they had said before he replied. "Thank you for your wise and encouraging words my dears, I was beginning to think I was the only one who had to keep you all focused and hopeful."

"We are all in this together father," agreed Shem. "We have supported you and will continue to do so even if our faces don't always reflect that. Whatever you do, we know it will be the right thing. Even when we make mistakes we will still learn from them."

"More wise words. Perhaps now Naamah and I can retire to a lofty mountain and let the six of you take over," laughed Noah.

"Oh no, Noach, we still need your guidance and wisdom," said

Ada, giving him an encouraging hug, which brought a smile from Naamah.

The next day as he said he would, Noah released a raven from a flue in the roof of the Ark. "Look," he said, "it's flown off far to the west."

As they watched the small speck dwindle to nothing they kept looking at the spot where it had disappeared and then a few moments later they saw a black speck in the sky once again. "It's coming back!" cried Noah, "No, now it's heading north. Look, it's circling around something and it's heading south."

Four members of the family kept watch until half an hour later they saw the raven again. It didn't come back to the Ark this time, but headed in an easterly direction and they saw it no more.

"The flood is still present apparently," Noah said, "Even though we can't see water any longer the ground must be waterlogged. Even so there must be land out there for the raven to find rest on, because it didn't come back, though it could be dead from exhaustion or else is looking to land somewhere. I'm going to wait another seven days to see if the sun and these winds dry the ground out."

A week later Noah released a dove in the same manner as the raven, which had still not returned. The family watched expectantly as the dove flew a small circle around the Ark and then a wider one and kept this up until it was lost to sight. Eventually it returned.

"No, I still don't think there is enough growth out there for the dove to find food or a place to nest, or perhaps the ground is still not dry enough. I'll wait another seven days and then send her out again," Noah decided.

"But now," observed Japheth "we can see grass or something like it growing in the valley either side of us. At least it has a kind of greenish tinge. Perhaps we'll have some fresh food to eat soon."

"Yes, I agree Japheth," said Noah. "But as you remember in the past when we sowed a new field and the seedlings sprouted how delicate they were, so we must wait some days more for the plants to strengthen, otherwise if we and the animals walk on them now we'll destroy the new growth. Besides, there will hardly be enough of them to begin to feed us all. We must wait."

After another seven days passed Naamah pointed out that the growth in the plants was quite prolific. "It's amazing how much has grown in seven days," she said.

"Yes, it's time to send our dove out again," observed Noah.

As they watched the dove fly off Nae exclaimed, "She's circling as before, she knows where to go now. She's headed south!"

The dove did not return as they watched expectantly for her. Several hours went by and only Shem was still keeping watch for her. As the sun began to set he shouted, "Look!"

"She's coming back, and she has something in her beak."

The dove, cooing to signal she had done well, landed on the roof of the Ark and hopped to Noah as he stood under the open flue. Noah reached out and took the dove in his hands.

"She has brought back an olive leaf," exclaimed Ada.

"Yes, a young leaf from an olive bush. There must be prolific growth out there now although she didn't find a place to nest. Olive shoots can sprout from damp ground, but it must either be still too damp, or else the olive plants are too small for her to have a comfortable nesting place. I'm going to wait for another seven days and then send her out once more." Noah did so, and this time the dove did not return.

Noah then waited another circuit of the moon before he took the next step and removed the greater covering on the top deck of the Ark. The family clambered out and walked around the top deck and saw that the land was now dry. They opened a small door they had made in the Ark's main entrance so they could walk on the surface of the new earth for the first time. Ham was naturally in a rush to get through the door first.

"No, not yet Ham, I know you are eager to explore the new world as we all are," said Japheth. "But it's only right that father and mother have the honour of stepping on the new land for the first time."

They then stood as a family group at the foot of the small ladder from the doorway. Noah forbade them to walk any distance from the Ark because the ground was not yet stable enough. It was simply a cautious look at the new world around them.

"So father Noach, would you say that this world is now safe for us to live in, our future is assured, and we face no further immediate danger or destruction?" Sede asked.

"Yes," he replied. "It would seem so, my dear."

Noah then glanced at Naamah, not quite understanding the women's change in demeanour at Sede's question. Nor did his sons understand why all their wives were now smiling and giggling quietly among themselves.

"I'll explain later what that was about, my dear," Naamah responded smiling.

Upon re-entering the Ark Naamah took Noah aside and asked him, "what do you expect all these animals to do once you have released them?"

With a reserved manner, expecting this to be some sort of test question he replied, "I expect them to breed and multiply and replenish this world."

"Correct, my love, and what do you think the first priority of all our lovely daughters now is?"

"Oh, is that why they were being coy just now?"

"Yes, that was the reason for Sede's question, which we women understood immediately, but left you men in the dark. Our boys will be rather active over the next few weeks I'm thinking, if they haven't already been," laughed Naamah.

"It's the way of the world," chuckled Noah, "and yes, no doubt it is Adonai's intention that we replenish this new world, both animals and humans. Our sons and daughters will populate this world, but as for us, I think our time is past."

"Oh, that is most definitely true my love."

Although the family had taken tentative steps into their new world the subsurface of the ground had been waterlogged for over a year and was still unstable. It would take another eight weeks before Noah received Adonai's permission to disembark all the inhabitants of the Ark.

From the day when the flood struck the old world until they left the Ark to populate the new world the passengers on the Ark had been in their confinement 370 days, a year and five days.

In Noah's six hundred and first year, in the first month, the first day of the month, the waters were dried from off the earth. And Noah removed the covering of the ark and looked, and behold, the face of the ground was dry. In the second month, on the twenty-seventh day of the month, the earth had dried out.

– Genesis 8, verses 13-15

Redemption

The New World
AM 1657

Go out from the ark, you and your wife, and your sons and your sons' wives with you. Bring out with you every living thing that is with you of all flesh – birds and animals and every creeping thing that creeps on the earth – that they may swarm on the earth, and be fruitful and multiply on the earth.

With these words God instructed Noah to leave the Ark. The great door was unsealed and lowered onto the new earth. The family could now go to and fro quite freely. Over time, pair by pair, kind by kind, they let the animals go. The birds were released as well. This was not done en masse, but with ample time between groups that may not be compatible. They were all glad to have the freedom of the vast new world in which they now found themselves.

The Ark had come to rest on a high ridge, with many other ridges, hills and valleys that had been formed in the immediate area sloping away from it as far as the eye could see. These provided natural distribution routes for the different kinds of animals when they left the Ark. On their release the animals instinctively made their way down the various valleys that led away from the Ark. Those that entered a particular valley eventually found themselves in a completely different area from others that had chosen another route. In this way over time the various families of all creatures discovered the habitat that suited them and flourished in it.

In these early days of the new world there was little or no danger for living things. Plant growth was rapid and lush. The days were warm, a hangover from the old world and the warm oceans, and all creatures multiplied very quickly in this new environment. Only much later would harsh living and natural depletion by predators cause the extinction of some animal species, while others which adapted better to their surroundings thrived. Just as God had brought the animals to the Ark, he now determined where they should go by the natural instincts he had created in them.

Concerning the animals and birds that were now present in multiple numbers through breeding while on the Ark and those of which they had taken on board seven pairs, Noah asked his family to take one each of the unblemished ones and keep them separate. He further instructed that an altar of rocks and stones be built near the entrance to the Ark close to the place where they first stepped out onto this new world.

"That's a fine looking altar of rocks Shem, Ham and Japheth, well done," he said.

"To your exact specifications, father," laughed Shem.

"So what are we going to do with it?" asked Japheth.

"We will make a burnt offering to Adonai for bringing us through the tempest and giving us a new life," his father replied.

"But what will we sacrifice? There is no harvest yet, nor fresh fruit or grain to bring an offering as we used to do," queried Ham.

"These are our sacrifice," said Noah, as he pointed to the caged birds and animals he had asked them to put aside.

"NO!" shouted Ham, Nae and Ada as one.

"You can't do that father," cried Ham angrily.

"Why not, my son?"

"We've nurtured these birds and animals for a year and kept them alive, and now you're going to kill them?" he continued incredulously.

"We must make a thanksgiving offering to Adonai, Ham," Noah replied, "It's what we must do, and all we have for it are these birds and animals. They must be our sacrifice."

"This is madness," Ham responded, and Japheth added, "I agree with Ham, father. We have only these few animals and birds to start again in this new world. It's wrong to put their future survival at risk by doing this."

"I love you, Noach, and I have always agreed with you," added Ada. "But it does seem folly to sacrifice these animals at this time. Surely we could simply sacrifice one if it's necessary, but all of them?"

"It's only one of each kind of the clean, unblemished ones," said Noah. "The animals that have left the Ark already in most cases were just the two of them, a male and female. Several are ready to give birth to their offspring and of the birds there are many already. Adonai expects them to survive. With the ones I have chosen we have several of each kind now, and they will be enough to breed and prosper. Adonai has begun this new world with them. Do you think he doesn't know what he's doing? He created the world in just six days and you don't think he can multiply these few?"

"Could we not wait a year and make this offering then as a thanksgiving sacrifice. The birds and animals will have established themselves in good numbers by then," suggested Sede.

"I can see you're all against me in this," lamented Noah. "We'll meet again in a year and offer a second sacrifice, but we must also make one now as we enter this new world. The things of God are not decided by majority vote. I am his priest, an honour bestowed on me by my father and grandfather who were also his priests. I was the one Adonai chose to bring all of us into this new world, and through his blessing of me he has blessed you too. I really do understand your concerns, but I believe Adonai is a God who can multiply the animal kingdom despite this sacrifice. They are his creation. He will make them flourish and us even more so because we do this. Now I ask you to stand with me in making this offering. Adonai is your God as well. It shall be done."

"I understand you, father," said Shem. "Obviously we were not expecting this, although I suppose we should have because it is proper to give Adonai a thanksgiving offering. You are, as you said, his priest, our great leader, father and patriarch. I will honour what you say and partake with you. I encourage the rest of us to do the same."

"Thank you, Shem," said Noah gratefully. "I will make one concession to all of you. I will choose only a few of these selected animals and birds to be sacrificed, not all. I trust that will be acceptable, but please understand that I am not obliged to submit to your feelings. As priest of Adonai that is my decision."

The offerings were prepared and placed on the altar, along with some wood and other combustible material gathered from the Ark. This was lit by Shem and Japheth. The family then stood around the altar as Noah offered a lengthy prayer. Some of them were quite reluctant to do this, others were sad including Ham, who held his anger inside him. Nevertheless, he bowed his head with the rest of them out of respect for his father but not for his God. The fire rose and consumed the offering, and as the smoke rose toward the clouds. God spoke…

> *I will never again curse the ground because of man, for the intention of man's heart is evil from his youth. Neither will I ever again strike down every living creature as I have done. While the earth remains, seedtime and harvest, cold and heat, summer and winter, day and night, shall not cease.*

As the animals and birds gradually dispersed across the country-side over the following days and weeks, it was a busy time for the members of Noah's family who gave each creature a final check to make sure they were fit enough to survive. Many had already given birth to young and eggs had hatched, so many more creatures left the Ark than entered it.

The day after the offering on the stone altar, as the family came together for their devotional time, one member of the family had a big grin on his face as he joined the family group.

"Well, Japheth what are you so happy about?" asked Naamah.

Ada answered, "I am with child."

"Ah, I knew. That's wonderful news, dear."

With that the women chatted excitedly amongst themselves, while the men quietly congratulated Japheth. Noah asked his other two sons how they were progressing with their expected outcomes. Laughing, they answered, "We're working on it father."

When the couples were able to explore the land nearby, and this became more and more possible as the final few of the animals and birds departed, they set up simple fences to keep the domesticated animals from wandering off. Noah gave strict orders that no one was to journey more than two hours in any direction before returning to the Ark.

"In time we shall explore further afield," he said, "but in the meantime we must be cautious since we still don't know how firm the ground is. The frequent earth tremors we feel every day indicate the earth is still settling, and it may take a long time for it to be completely stable. Perhaps it never will."

As they began to settle into their new land while still living in the Ark, God spoke again to Noah…

Be fruitful and multiply and fill the earth. The fear of you and the dread of you shall be upon every beast of the earth and upon every bird of the heavens, upon everything that creeps on the ground and all the fish of the sea. Into your hand they are delivered. Every moving thing that lives shall be food for you. And as I gave you the green plants, I give you everything. But you shall not eat flesh with its life, that is, its blood.

And for your lifeblood I will require a reckoning: from every beast I will require it and from man. From his fellow man I will require a reckoning for the life of man.

Whoever sheds the blood of man, by man shall his blood be shed, for I made man in my own image.

And you, be fruitful and multiply, increase greatly on the earth and multiply in it.

Noah passed these words of the Lord God on to his family.

"It seems that Adonai is permitting us to eat meat. I remember all those years ago Dinah asked what meat tasted like. I suppose now we shall find out," said Noah, "but not for many years yet. We should let the animal population grow."

"Yes, said Ada, "it's imperative we let the animal population grow. We must be careful not to exterminate what we have laboured so hard to establish."

"It would appear that Adonai is laying down some rules for us to live by," stated Shem.

"I agree," said Noah. "God is definitely speaking to us. We must be alert and listen for his word. He was silent during the time we were on the flood waters but now he is speaking again. Come," he said to his sons, "I feel we should make our way over to that hill, just the four of us."

Noah and his sons then climbed up the distant hill as Noah was led by God's Spirit. Noah felt that God had more to say to them. Once they were at the top they waited patiently. Although Ham felt some irritation he gave his father the benefit of doubt as he did in most things and obediently went with his brothers. Then God spoke one more time in the hearing of Noah and his sons…

Behold, I establish my covenant with you and your offspring
after you, and with every living creature that is with you,
the birds, the livestock, and every beast of the earth with you,
as many as came out of the ark; it is for every beast of the earth.
I establish my covenant with you, that never again shall all
flesh be cut off by the waters of the flood, and never again shall
there be a flood to destroy the earth.

This is the sign of the covenant that I make between me and
you and every living creature that is with you, for all future
generations: I have set my bow in the cloud, and it shall be a
sign of the covenant between me and the earth. When I bring
clouds over the earth and the bow is seen in the clouds,
I will remember my covenant that is between me and you and
every living creature of all flesh. And the waters shall never
again become a flood to destroy all flesh. When the bow is in
the clouds, I will see it and remember the everlasting covenant
between me and every living creature of all flesh that is
on the earth.

All four men listened to the audible words of Adonai as they lay flat on the ground with their arms outstretched, completely in awe.

After some time had passed they composed themselves and made their way back to the Ark to tell their wives what they had experienced. But Noah lagged behind them a little and the Lord had one final word for him…

This is the sign of the covenant that I have established between
me and all flesh that is on the earth.

They were the last words the Lord God ever spoke audibly to
Noah.

On returning to the Ark the women folk ran to meet their men.
"Do you see that magnificent bow in the sky? I have never seen a
bow as brilliant as that one," said Sede excitedly.

"Yes dearest," replied Shem. "Adonai spoke to us. We heard him,
all of us, and that bow is a sign of his covenant with us. He told us
that."

When Noah caught up with the rest of them they sat in a circle
near the door of the Ark and reflected on the words God had just
spoken to them. A very restrained Ham then spoke up.

"I'm still confused. I heard Adonai like all of you did. Although I
have doubted him, yet he considered me worthy to speak to, along
with you all. I am humbled. I don't know what to think of this. I
heard him clearly, but there is still a part of me that cannot accept
what he said. I suppose I shall have to take time to work all this out."

"It's good, Ham, that you acknowledge Adonai. Take your time
and he will guide you," replied Noah.

"I wish at this time in your hearing to make a proclamation. We
have survived a great deluge. Almost all the animals we brought
with us have survived and now departed to seek their dwelling
places. That is a testament to all your dedication and good work.
We can be proud of what we achieved, yet not by our hands alone.
We would not be here today without the help of all those sadly left
behind, who also assisted us in the building of our great Ark. But
even more so are we grateful for the provision and redemption that
Adonai, our Lord, has provided. We must always give thanks for
this day. Now, it would appear that Adonai has given me, given us,
a covenant to live by. He will keep his side of it whether or not we

keep ours. So from this day forth all those who follow us, all our descendants, must be told about this covenant and its terms must be engraved not only on our hearts and minds but on stone and parchment as well, and repeated for all men and women who follow us to know and obey from this day forth.

Adonai has impressed upon my heart these rules or laws that we must now live by. Not all will apply to us immediately, but over time they will.

We must not worship idols or images in place of Adonai.
We must not curse God.
We must not commit murder.
We must not commit adultery or sexual immorality.
We must not steal.
We must not eat flesh torn from a living animal.
We must establish courts of justice to decide the rights
and wrongs of a dispute when this arises between one person
and another.

Noah then addressed them. "Over the next few weeks we will determine the best place to set up a village for ourselves. Each couple here needs their own dwelling, and we can use timber and fittings from the Ark to do this. Where we are right now is a windswept and uncomfortable place to be, and I'm sure there are warmer and more sheltered places elsewhere that would suit us better. We must seek these out over the coming days and weeks. We don't appear to be near any large area of water either. We have a stream close by for now, but we need to be on the lookout for a more accessible and plentiful water source. We should live together in harmony as a family at least for a short time until we decide whether we will live separately in other places. But that's something for the future."

He continued, "This is an exciting time to be alive, and we are responsible for what we make of it. Let's go forth and multiply as Adonai would have us do. Naamah and I are past child bearing age so, it's up to the six of you to do this. Ada is blessed to be carrying a child, and no doubt the Lord will bless Sede and Nae very soon as well. Let's go forward as a family, unitedly, and discover our new world.

We need to begin again, and it starts today."

PART THREE

A SECOND CHANCE

TWENTY-ONE

Increase

The New World – Fifty Years Later
AM 1707

Canaan looked over the valley at the vast rows of various fruit bearing vines, sighing in frustration and anger. He was hot, tired, sore and thirsty, a very unhappy man. Not only had he argued with his wife that morning, but the task he was in charge of, pruning the vines, was arduous, back breaking work from which he could see no great benefit to himself or his family. His young wife had just given birth to their third child, another girl. He wanted a boy and he blamed her for this, despite what his aunt Ada had told him, that it was his seed that determined the gender of the children they had. What was the point of working this hard land to grow grapes and fruit so that his grandfather could get drunk once again when they harvested it and made wine? Canaan despised him. He threw his empty water jar against a nearby rock in anger, smashing it to pieces. He then dropped the work he was doing, swearing to himself, and made his way angrily to the base camp at the bottom of the valley.

‡‡‡

Fifty years had now passed since the eight survivors had left the Ark. Within a year Ada, Sede and Nae had each given birth and all of them were boys. Within two years they had each given birth again. Ada had had twins, a boy and girl. Sede and Nae each had another boy. Over the last fifty years these three women had given birth to over thirty children in all. Four of these confinements had been twins. By this time two generations had been born in addition to the eight people who came out of the Ark. The lack of disease, physical imperfections and the purity of the genetic makeup they had brought with them from the previous world enabled them to intermarry with their siblings and cousins without fear of having inherited deficiencies.

They had not given their village a name; they simply called it, 'our village' or 'home-base.' There were now over eighty adults living in it, with a further twenty or so children under fifteen years, including five infants less than a year old. The village had already expanded, with other homes built some distance away. Nevertheless, this group would remain in the general locality for at least another fifty years before they established any villages in other places.

Although they had explored their immediate region they had not ventured to build outlying villages, preferring the security of the founding village where there was an ample supply of water, good grazing and cropping land. Noah and his sons had discovered a great sea to the west and what was either a great lake or another sea to the north. They had also discovered the southern coast of another sea far to the south. In the east they had travelled many days and had discovered two rivers that Noah named the Euphrates and Tigris, after rivers of the same name in the old world. Everything beyond the rivers was still a mystery.

Most built the walls of their homes from what the land provided, using rocks and stones, and mud for bricks and tiles. Foliage was used to thatch roofs. Others preferred the skins of animals to make tents for themselves, especially if they were of a nomadic mind, choosing to move frequently to seek out nearby land to grow crops and raise livestock. No matter what the buildings were made of they had to be sturdy enough to withstand the frequent earth tremors that continued to reshape this new world. Pyramid shaped buildings with a thicker wall at the base than the top to withstand these forces were frequently built.

Ada and Japheth's child was the first male child to be born in this new world and they named him Gomer. Shem and Sede had Elam as their first born. Ham and Nae's first boy was named Cush. Over the following years Shem and Sede gave birth to Asshur, Arpachshad, Lud, Aram and other sons and daughters. Japheth and Ada had Magog, Madai, Javan, Tubal, Meshech and Tiras as well as other daughters. Ham and Nae, in addition to their many daughters, brought Mizraim, Put and Canaan into this new world.

All these children in turn had married and produced their own offspring. Two couples of the second generation born in this land added to the ever increasing population of the new world as they honoured the call to repopulate the earth at a younger age, rather than wait many years after marriage as the custom had been in the old world. Already a third generation was there in the babes of the village.

The fertility of the young men and women was such that twins and even triplets were often born. Even if no great advancement was achieved in these first few years when they concentrated on farming and working the land, at least they answered God's call to repopulate it in a very short time.

‡‡‡

At the lower end of the valley that Canaan was walking down along a worn, rocky path there was a small workplace where a stone and wooden structure stood. It had baths and vats for crushing grapes and fruit beside it, along with a lot of other pieces of equipment lying about in untidy heaps. Here the grapes were processed into wine, fruit juice and pulp for general consumption. Nearby were tents of animal skins, and even further away was a larger tent used for shelter or overnight accommodation of the workers. Another tent outside the encampment was for Noah's personal use, where he often went for privacy and prayer. However, his family had long ago realised that prayer was an infrequent activity and his quiet sampling of their produce was Noah's main focus. This was the new world's first vineyard, located some distance from the village.

As Canaan passed Noah's tent that day he was not in a very pleasant mood, and hearing the old man's snores he put aside restraint and angrily pulled open the opening to the tent with a mind to confront his grandfather about all his personal issues which had gained in strength and intensity as he walked down the valley. What Canaan now saw before him both stunned and disgusted him. He threw the flap back and stormed off to find his father Ham.

"That sorry excuse for a Patriarch and so called servant of Adonai is simply disgusting!" he cried.

"Whoa, Canaan what are you talking about? That's no way to show respect to your grandfather," replied Ham as his son approached him. "What's got into you?"

"My grandfather? I'd rather have anyone other than him as my grandfather! He's lying in his tent in a shocking state snoring his head off, while I'm working in this infernal heat, getting blisters and cuts on my hands so his precious vines will grow in order for him to get drunk again!"

"All right, my son, I can see you're obviously unhappy about many things. Come on, show me what you're talking about."

Ham then looked into Noah's tent where he was lying on his back, naked, snoring loudly and with a flask of red wine held in his left hand. He had spilt some of it over himself and the rest had dribbled out onto the ground. Ham walked away, saying nothing to Canaan who walked two steps behind him. Ham then found Japheth and Shem inside the workplace.

"I was looking for you two," he said. "We have to do something about father. He's drunk again, lying naked in his tent snoring, and it's disgusting."

"How on earth do you know that Ham?" asked Shem.

"I saw him," Ham replied.

"You looked on our father's nakedness? What compelled you to do that?" demanded Japheth.

"Canaan alerted me, I ..."

"Canaan also?"

"Yes, he found him like that."

"No, you didn't find him like that, you deliberately looked in on his nakedness, and now you are demeaning his character as well. Have you told anyone else?"

"Only Cush and Put as we were coming in here."

"What have you done? This is our father's reputation you are destroying. Everyone will know about him now."

"Well he shouldn't get drunk. Wasn't he supposed to be our Patriarch and Priest of Adonai standing up for goodness and godliness? He's a miserable failure," an angry Ham retorted.

"Father has put me in charge of this vineyard," said Japheth. "Work here today will cease. Go home, and you, too, Canaan, and tell Cush, Put and the others that tonight we will gather at the village meeting hall and have a discussion about a lot of issues that have been simmering away. Surely this will now bring them to a head."

Grumbling, Ham and Canaan took Cush, Put and the other people working in the vineyard that day back to the village, discussing many things as they walked slowly along.

"What are we to do about this?" sighed Japheth.

"First of all, we should take this shawl on our shoulders, enter father's tent backwards and lay it over him so that he is covered and we are not guilty of looking on his nakedness," suggested Shem.

"Good, let's do that." And they did.

Later, Noah shuffled into the dwelling he shared with Naamah his wife. The effects of his drinking were still apparent to anyone who looked at him.

"My dearest man, this drinking of yours will not do!" she cried.

"What's the matter now?" he responded.

"Look at the state you are in. You're not setting a good example to the family with your constant drinking."

"I'm tired, Naamah. I'm so tired. This new world has broken me. It has been much harder now than I envisioned. I expected a new world much like we had before, and we would simply carry on as the trees, plants and grass grew. But instead, it has been a long hard struggle working the unforgiving ground, along with trial and error in these changing seasons with their rain and times of drought. There are storms we never had before and intense heat we never knew. Then there are the frequent and sudden earth tremors as well. It's all so unpredictable. I wonder if we're being punished. Perhaps the ones who perished in the flood were the lucky ones!"

"It has been hard," she replied, "and the seven of us have had to face it just as much as you have. We've stood faithfully beside you, and even Ham who often disagrees with you has stood by you too. But this drunkenness of yours! Look at yourself, feeling sorry for yourself once again," Naamah continued, in her firm but gentle way. "There is no excuse for you to get drunk so often and lie in your tent naked and snoring while your sons and grandsons are working hard for you. I've stood by you in everything up till now and I love you, but I will not stand for this."

"It's not for me, it's for them and all of you and … what did you just say?"

"You were drunk, naked and snoring loudly. Everyone heard you."

"I was naked? How do you know that?"

Sighing in exasperation, Naamah explained that Ham and Canaan had come back to the village in an angry mood. She had been unable to find out what the issue was until Japheth and Shem came and spoke to her, explaining what had happened and that they needed to have a family meeting in the Hall once Noah had sobered up."

"So Canaan and Ham saw me naked and spoke of it, but Shem and Japheth covered me without looking?"

"Yes."

"Cursed then be Canaan. He shall be a servant of servants to his brothers."

Pausing for some time after he had spoken, but then without another word, Noah looked out his window at the fields of wheat and corn and the livestock in pens close by. Naamah waited patiently as she knew he needed time to come to terms with what she had just told him. She watched him as he was lost in thought, perhaps praying silently to God. After a while she saw him straighten himself to his full height from the stoop he had recently developed. He then turned with tears in his eyes and told her what he must do.

After the meeting had been progressing for an hour it was becoming more and more heated as several family members expressed their frustrations and anger. Almost every adult in the village was in attendance, since this was to be a meeting to decide a number of outstanding problems and disputes that had gone on too long and many present had wanted resolved. Japheth and Shem controlled the meeting and bravely so, otherwise it could have got out of control to the point where many of the men might have taken their anger out on one another physically.

Despite their best intentions, however, the meeting eventually descended into a frenzy of shouting and abuse that became more and more intense until the moment when Noah and Naamah entered the hall. The immediate silence that fell was deafening as they made their way to the front of the room.

As Japheth and Shem stepped aside and sat down, Noah moved to the space they had just vacated, nodding to each of them in turn, and with Naamah at his side and holding his hand he addressed all of those gathered there.

"My sons and daughters, there are three generations of us now after just fifty years in this new land. Most of you do not know the old world so you cannot compare it with what we have today. Daily life then was easy compared to the hard struggle we have had in these years since the flood. I know I have told you this before. But I say it again now to hopefully help you understand that it has been very hard for us, the eight who came out of the Ark. We had no foreknowledge of what we would encounter. For me at least it has been far harder than I would have wished for.

"Because Adonai provided a way for us to survive his judgement on the old world I rather expected he would make it easy for us to establish a new life. This has not happened. In fact, Adonai has not spoken to me audibly or by his Spirit since the first days we landed here. Due to our hard toil I put aside time praying to him in order to concentrate on surviving and providing a safe place for all of you to be born into. In recent years as we broke the land in and started to reap some of its harvest I became complacent, indulgent, disillusioned and somewhat resentful, lacking faith and losing my vision. All of this neglect is a grave sin in the sight of the Lord God. It is probably because of those sins that he has not spoken to me for many years. I have not been a faithful son to him and I have not been true to my side of the covenant he made with us.

"Today an incident happened with me that you all no doubt now know. I am ashamed, I am sorry, I have let you all down. Tonight I repent of my lack of leadership and propose a new course for your consideration. I will not force anyone to do my will. All I can say is that the one thing I have achieved and of which I am very proud is you. You are the future of this world, and we have grown into a sizeable community in a very short time. This is the greatest thing we have achieved. Yet when all is said and done we are only simple farmers and merely exist to live off the land, with no other achievement or vision to work towards."

The room remained silent in respect and curiosity as to what their Patriarch was about to say to them. Noah then outlined his plan for their immediate future;

"At present you are angry and frustrated. You are rightly upset about many things. But they are all of no consequence in the greater vision for the future of this village. You have made them into mountains because you have focused on the little things and irritabilities of life rather than having a wider perspective. We are the first people to inhabit this new world and should be looking to grow not only in numbers but in understanding of our world, making each year better than the last and not getting weighed down with day to day disputes. We are intelligent beings and can make things by reinventing the good tools, machines and strategies we had in the old world. We have a village school to teach our young ones for a start. We can do great things if we put our abilities and commitment to the task ahead. To this end we must find out what a vast world we have out there, what it can give us and how we can use it to achieve our goals.

"We have not ventured far from these lands in which we live. We know there is a great sea to the west, another to the south and perhaps another to the north. And there is also a lot more land to be discovered in all other directions. One day our descendants will live in those lands.

"Tonight you feel unfulfilled, frustrated, even angry because you are doing the same old things day after day. So let's broaden our horizons beyond this valley and the countryside round about. I therefore propose that we send out exploratory teams into the lands beyond us. Japheth, Shem and Ham if they are agreeable will each lead a group of sons and older grandsons in groups of five or seven to do this. They can spend several months exploring these lands and then report back what they find.

"The women, younger grandsons, or for that matter, any man who has no desire to face the hardships of such a venture will maintain the village, farms and vineyard. I will not force anyone to go."

"Why in groups of five and seven?" queried Gomer.

"Because when you come to a place and you can't decide to go this way or that, you will vote and the majority decision is the one you will follow. If you had an even number you might never reach a decision. But in any event, for safety's sake the final word will rest with Ham, Shem or Japheth. Their experience will determine each decision for the wellbeing of all."

"No women, Noach? asked Ada. "Surely Nae, Sede and myself can also share our experience and knowledge on such a venture?"

"For you three that's a decision you can make with your husbands," Noah replied. "But all the other groups should comprise men only, because the younger women have children and grandchildren to care for. I myself intend to travel to the south coast. I miss the sea and I long to explore the possibility of setting up a future port there. Tonight I've given everyone my thoughts for our immediate future. Decide now if this is what you want to do, and we'll meet again tomorrow evening once you have all had time to think about all this and we can discuss it further then, whether to do it or not. If the answer is negative, then we can think about something else to do. No more questions until then. Goodnight to you all."

Noah then called Ham, Japheth and Shem to himself and asked them to stay behind after everyone else had left. He asked Canaan to stay behind too. When everyone else had left he stood before them, each anticipating that what he had to say to them was not going to be pleasant.

"For what I did today, as I told the village, I am ashamed and regret the outcome," said Noah. "Yet my privacy, or anyone's privacy for that matter, is a personal thing that no other person has the right to invade, and then use this to belittle, degrade or humiliate someone. In public a man sows what he reaps, but in private his life is between him and Adonai, and no one has the right to intrude upon that. Because of what you did today, Canaan, you will become a servant, a slave to your brothers. I do not say this to punish you, but as a reflection on your character. From this time on you will be the lesser and others the greater. You have only yourself to blame for this. By way of contrast Shem and Japheth showed dignity and restraint towards me. Your offspring will also be slaves to Shem's descendants. Japheth will prosper and his descendants will occupy more territory than anyone else. Go now, my sons, and decide where you will explore if you agree with what I have proposed. As for you, Canaan, perhaps you would like to accompany me on my trek to the south coast?"

"You curse me with one hand and give me a peace offering with the other? I really don't understand you grandfather. Why are you doing this?" replied Canaan angrily.

"I don't hate you Canaan. I would like to have wished the best for you as does Adonai, but it is your own wrongdoing that has prevented you from understanding his will. Your own actions will determine your future."

"Bah, you're all quite mad. I'll have nothing to do with your God. I'll go my own way. I've no wish to travel with you."

"So be it."

"Father I …"

"No, Ham, all your life you've swayed this way and that. One day you follow Adonai and the next you're cursing him. What you did today dishonoured me, your father. I love you my son, but your sons and daughters and grandchildren will follow what you teach them. They are a reflection of you. I told Canaan just now that his actions are a reflection of his character, but they are also a reflection of you and Nae. I am not responsible for them. I do not prophesy these words in anger or for revenge, but simply as the words Adonai has impressed on me these many years."

The next evening the village came together and as one agreed with Noah's plan. Everyone was keen to increase their knowledge of the world and their future prospects and so they got right behind the new venture. Many questions were asked and answered by Noah, his sons and their wives, as well as in intelligent ways by younger members of the village. It was decided that Japheth would explore the lands to the north and west, Shem would travel east and Ham would go south and west to the shores of the great sea. Noah would take two grandsons and explore the southern coast. Ada would accompany Japheth and Nae would go with Ham, but Sede would remain in the village along with Aram, their fifth son, and Madai, Meshech and Tiras, the sons of Japheth and Ada. Their task, together with Naamah, would be to take care of the village, its farms and vineyard.

Japheth and Ada would take their sons Gomer, Magog, Javan and Tubal as well as Gomer's eldest son Ashkenaz and head to the great sea to the north, to explore along its coastline and beyond and confirm whether it really was a great ocean or only a large lake.

Shem would travel east, taking with him Elam, Arpachshad, Asshur and Shelah, who was Arpachshad's eldest son.

Ham and Nae's group comprised Cush their eldest, Mizraim and Put, as well as Seba, Cush's son and Ludim, Mizraim's son. They would travel to the sea in the south and west and follow its coastline as far as they could. Canaan couldn't make up his mind, but eventually decided to go with his family group the day they departed.

Noah would take Madai, the third son of Japheth and Ada, and Lud, the fourth son of Shem and Sede. They would explore the south coast of this extensive land as far south as the great peninsula, then back along the shore of the sea to the west of them.

The teams of explorers were all eager to set off on their travels and after two weeks of preparation they all left in their different directions on the same day. The entire village turned out to see each of them off before settling back to their various routines.

Canaan travelled only a short distance with his father and mother before wandering off alone on a pathway of self-discovery and reflection on what Noah had said, until he decided to return to the village. He then took his family with him and moved some distance away, often wandering and never settling in any one place very long.

For the village, all this was the first major exploration beyond the area they were familiar with. It would result in a foundation for the future growth and population of the world. From this time onwards the whole family were eager to expand their horizons.

And so they did.

‡‡‡

One Year Later

Month after month the village looked out keenly for their loved ones to return. By the time a year had gone by all the groups had returned safely. There were the inevitable injuries for some along the way but nothing major. As each returned they told of their adventures and kept the village enthralled as each night they related a little more about their travels.

Japheth, the most adventurous of Noah's sons and the one who had done most of the exploring up until now, was expected to be the last to return. In fact, he was the first, and reported on the cool and temperate lands to the north. After going in this direction he turned west and finally south, coming to what he thought was most likely the northern shore of the sea to the west and followed this until he found his way back to the village. He then decided to head out again to the east to meet up with Shem on his return if he could.

The next to return was Noah, full of ideas of a sea voyage and building a port or even several of them on the shores of the south sea or the sea to the west. The best place for a port was on the shore of the sea in the west, because this site was the closest to the village, only a few days travel away. He now formally named this sea, 'the Western Sea'.

Then Shem, who by chance had met up with Japheth only a week from the village, also returned. He told of deserts, another great river, mountains and an impenetrable jungle. They had crossed the river but only ventured as far as the start of the mountains and then turned south to find a another great stretch of jungle and a rich, plentiful land, finally turning back when he realised if his party had continued on it could very well have taken them many years to explore it all.

Finally, many months later, Ham and Nae wearily entered the village on a cold, wet day. They were so long reaching home behind the others that Shem and Japheth had pleaded with Noah that they should go and search for them, but he forbade this. Noah wanted to wait a full year before he sent anyone out to find them.

When they did arrive, along with the usual welcoming and celebrations and relief that they were safe, it was a joy for one particular member of the party when the wife of Cush presented him with their sixth son who had been born while he was away, and whom she had named Nimrod.

"He is a little rebel," she stated. "He would not take the breast at first, but when he did and realised it was so good he wouldn't let go!"

They all laughed when she told them this, but a century later they would no longer laugh at what Nimrod did.

Much more interesting, however, was Ham's story that was to amaze them all.

TWENTY-TWO

The Western Sea

AM 1708

Noah sat with his three sons, along with Ada, and his three eldest grandsons, Gomer, Elam and Cush, around the central table of the village hall. It was a solid block of wood, which, together with its supports, had been brought down out of the Ark. This was where Noah's exploration council consulted together about what would be the best option for exploring their world. There were eight of them, but when it came to a decision on a particular issue only seven voted, while Noah took no part. However, he did have an overriding vote on any decision if he deemed it not to be in the best interests of the village or departed from the vision of what they were trying to achieve. In this way he let his family decide the best course of action while still retaining the overall leadership.

The council realised that as their village grew larger they would need to find other lands in which to live. The valleys that had supported them up to this point had reached the limit of the amount of food that could be grown due to the changeable climate. Thus, finding a fertile area large enough to build further villages was the main object of their planning. Moreover, Noah and Japheth also hungered to explore the new, vast world that awaited their footprints.

They went over all the information they had acquired on their recent forays into the previously unknown world. The exploration teams had made some amazing discoveries, some foreseen and some entirely unanticipated and surprising. The mountainous land to the north also had large areas of grasslands, as well as a great inland sea. The vast areas of land further north possibly led to a larger ocean beyond. The climate of this area was often cool and damp. Further exploration of it would be needed.

To the east and beyond, deserts and dry hilly country gave way to great mountains from which rivers ran to the sea through vast jungles. The climate of this area varied between hot and cold, dry, wet and humid. It was a huge land waiting to be discovered in its entirety far into their future.

To the south and east, it was a mostly dry climate with many deserts, but there were also some fertile areas, especially between the great rivers Euphrates and Tigris as well as along the coasts.

Noah had selected several sites along the shore of the Western Sea as possible places for building and launching a ship. They were good prospects for ports in the future.

Ham and his team had brought the most interesting of the reports. The first major feature of importance they had come across was an immensely fertile river system that extended south far into the interior of a great land. Rather than continue their intended route along the coast of the Western Sea they followed this great river inland along its eastern shore for many weeks, stopping on many occasions to explore the surrounding land. Ultimately, after travelling many weeks they realised this vast river with its adjacent land would require a lot more investigation in the future and so crossed the river at a narrow point and proceeded down its western side northward to the coast, again diverting inland a number of times. They found great forests there and saw many animals and birds. The river itself teemed with life. It was a rich and plentiful land.

When they eventually arrived back at the sea they realised the mouth of the river was itself a great distance in width. They then explored right along the coast of this sea to the west until Ham decided that they had gone far enough and turned back for the long journey home through dry and barren inland country but a rich and well forested coastline.

The Western Sea which they had explored only in part was the most intriguing of all mysteries for Noah and the exploration teams. Was it part of an unlimited ocean, or an enormous, land-locked inland sea?

"From all the information we have gathered," said Noah, "it seems to me we should concentrate our future exploration in three areas. I intend to build a ship and sail along the coastlands of the Western Sea as it is the closest body of water to us. Doing this, I am sure, will answer many of our questions." He announced this to the group as they came to the time for making decisions now they had completed their review of the information everyone had collected.

"The second area is the vast fertile valley that lies between the rivers Euphrates and Tigris. It would appear this may provide a rich and rewarding land to live in and establish new villages as we expand in the near future."

"The third area is the great river and fertile lands that extend into the southern land that Ham's group discovered."

Japheth was the first to respond to Noah's statement.

"I agree, father, and I think that's as far as our travels can extend at this time. We don't want to spread our resources too far from here. Still, I'm eager to explore further west and north beyond the lands we've discovered already."

"All in good time, Japheth. I believe that exploring the Western Sea will not only answer many of our questions, but also open up further opportunities for discoveries to satisfy your desires."

"So, who goes where?" asked Shem.

"A good question, Shem."

"I think I'd like to explore further along the river we discovered. I'm sure Mizraim will join me in this, and we can take a few of the young lads with us," suggested Cush.

"Very good, Cush, I'll leave you to select your team and go when it suits you."

"Gomer and Elam, would you consider leading an expedition to locate good areas to farm and settle in the fertile valleys beyond the Euphrates? They could be places to build new villages over the next several years. I'm naming both of you, because I envisage that you could each lead a group with which you could explore a larger area and then make a better informed decision on the best locations."

"I'm keen to do that, grandfather," replied Elam.

"Me too," agreed Gomer.

"Now, as for the rest of us, I'd like you Japheth, Shem and Ham to come with me on a voyage of discovery in the Western Sea. Naamah will come as well, and I'll leave it to you to bring your wives if they wish to come."

"I'll always go where Japheth goes," laughed Ada.

"I think Sede is ready for a change of outlook too," added Shem.

"I'll go, but I doubt that Nae will. She would be only too happy to stay in the village, I think. After what she went through on our last expedition Nae would be reluctant to venture out into the wild unknown again," agreed Ham.

"That's all good, and we may take some of the others as well depending on the size of the boat we build. That, of course, will take some time. I have a location in mind, where forests of tall straight cedar are growing nearby, and I intend to set up camp there while we construct it," added Noah.

"I agree father, our children are mature enough to run the farms and maintain the village, so I'm happy to go with you," replied Japheth.

"So am I," agreed Shem.

"I think we women will let you build your boat and join you closer to the time you sail. Perhaps we can be employed making the sails for it. You'll need to specify the shape and size," added Ada.

"Yes, there's a lot to plan and work on over the coming months. This ship will be different from the ones we built in the old world. Trees have grown prolifically since we arrived in the Ark, but they're not as big as the ones in the old world. We'll need to select the timber carefully. Perhaps we can take some timbers from the Ark to use in our new vessel. We also need to spend time down on the coast to evaluate the winds and currents and a host of other things. It may be two years before we can set sail."

"Let's get started then," laughed Shem enthusiastically.

And so they did.

‡‡‡

Three Years Later
AM 1711

The ship glided silently through the clear blue water with Shem at the helm steering it into yet another bay. He then brought the '*Hebe*' into the wind as Japheth and Ham lowered the large stone to anchor the ship, while several others furled her sails. Five of the crew lowered themselves into a smaller boat and rowed ashore so they could explore this part of the coastline on foot. They were the first people to have done this. In fact, everywhere they went was a first, as this ship, named after Noah's sister along with her crew of fifteen, ventured into the lands bordering on the Western Sea.

Some three years earlier Noah had set up a modest shipbuilding yard and dock on the eastern shore of the sea at a place he named Ty, where there was an ample supply of timber growing in the nearby forest. This was supplemented by timber taken from the Ark and brought to the site with many other items, either carried or pulled by animals, for the construction of Noah's new ship. It took a month of hard effort to achieve this. Once the timber arrived on site Noah set about building his new ship, thankful he had had the foresight to bring many of his shipbuilding tools from the old world. These were now put to good use, along with natural products of the surrounding area that could be adapted for use in constructing and fitting out the ship so it would be as comfortable and secure as he and his team could make it. Setting about this new task in earnest, Noah and his crew had the small ship completed in a little over two years.

Naamah, Ada, Sede, and Nae with other family members had moved to Ty and formed a small settlement where they made the sails and rigging with locally sourced material and other items they had brought from the village. Many people were involved in building and equipping the first ship of the new world. It was a dhow-shaped craft some forty two cubits in length, constructed using strong beams from the Ark for its keel, ribs and masts. Local timber was used for the planking and decking. Tar, discovered and taken with them on the long trek to the coast with the timbers from the Ark, was used to caulk and waterproof the craft. It had two masts; a main mast forward and a mizzen mast aft. A larger triangular shaped sail hung between the bow and the main mast and a second, smaller one from the mizzen.

After two months of local sea trials Noah considered they were ready to set out and explore this vast expanse of water. As well as a place for constructing ships, the small tented settlement at Ty would in time become a village and the home port of many more similar expeditions.

While all this was going on Cush and Mizraim had returned from exploring the great river to the south. They had located several places that they considered would be good enough to settle in.

Nevertheless, Noah decided that the lands by the Euphrates and Tigris were the best choice to expand into in the immediate future, based on the reports brought back by Elam and Gomer. "We should stay close together and not spread around too much," he said. "In this way we can trade amongst ourselves more easily and exchange ideas and resources that will better help each community to build and grow."

Thus it was that steadily over the next few years they began to create small settlements within this fertile region.

Now, aboard *Hebe,* they found themselves in this bay of crystal clear water surrounded by cliffs of sandstone, with a thick forest of leafy trees covering the entire coastal area right down to a small beach of white pebbles. Everywhere they went they marvelled at how fast the new world had regrown, from a bare watery waste when they came to rest in the Ark, to this prolific growth of vegetation and many animals they saw along the way. Three days were spent here exploring the land beyond the shore.

The ship had left Ty three months earlier and headed south keeping the land always in sight to their left and often taking soundings from the bow constantly so that they didn't run aground in the yet unfamiliar waters. They had already spent many days exploring the mouth of the great river that Ham told them was the one his group had seen on his earlier expedition and had followed inland for many weeks. However, they only explored it where it entered this great sea. Following that, they had put into three more natural harbours before the one they were presently at.

The members of the ship's crew were Noah and Naamah, his sons and their wives, except Nae who had happily stayed in Ty, occasionally returning to the home village. In addition there were three members of Shem and Sede's family, their sons Lud and Arpachshad and his son Shelah. Of Japheth and Ada's sons there were Magog, Javan, Madai and Tiras. To make up a crew of fifteen

Put, another of Ham's sons, had also joined them. At some stage all of them to varying extents had been involved in the construction and fitting out of the ship.

Meanwhile, back in the home village the other senior members of what was now a very large family concentrated on further exploring nearby areas, especially the Euphrates and Tigris valley, as well as overseeing the production and industry of their village.

Although he allowed Ham, Shem and Japheth turns at being in charge of sailing the ship, Noah remained in overall control of the expedition. During the initial sea trials and since embarking on the voyage they had constantly learnt new skills of how to handle the vessel in the frequent changes of direction and intensity of the wind. They had correctly assumed it would be stronger than what they had previously been used to, so the masts, rigging and sails were made of much sturdier materials than in the old world. Yet for all they had learned and experienced so far they were not prepared for what was about to overtake them.

The storm hit them suddenly from out of the east. Ham had noticed a dark cloud on the far horizon but took no further notice until they realised it was spreading across the whole sea and getting closer to them at a rapid rate. As they started taking in the sails, heavy sheets of rain obliterated their view of the horizon and the way forward. In the thick of it their small ship was tossed to and fro in the towering waves. Lightning struck and thunder roared in the maelstrom of waters many cubits high, crashing into and over the deck of what now seemed a very small and paltry vessel compared to the might of the elements throwing it about.

Unable to steer a course, even with three men on the tiller, they could not control their progress and the ship was simply taken at the whim of wind and the chilling rain that cut into the skins of those on deck. Closing all the hatches, most of the crew sought safety below deck. Noah took charge and ordered that the anchor stones that were tied to the vessel be dropped into the sea to help steady the craft. Almost everyone sustained an injury of some kind, mainly bruises, as they were knocked about and many were sick. To alleviate their personal discomfort some tried to lie down. The older ones had their own small cabins with bunks, while the rest swung violently to and fro in their hammocks strung between the rafters.

With a loud crack first one stay of the mizzen mast gave way and then another. A loud boom and shudder told the crew that the mast had fallen overboard. Four men braved the storm to cut away the remaining stays and let the mast float away to avoid any more damage or the ship being pulled under. Then, as if that was not enough, another violent crack brought the top of the foremast crashing down onto the deck. Fortunately, what stays still remained attached held it so that it was not lost overboard.

The storm continued unabated for many hours and into the night, but the next morning dawned with a calmer sea, although the sky was still overcast. The ship and its crew had survived the storm, battered and bruised, but now they had been blown out to sea far away from any land.

"Where are we?" Ham wondered.

Noah answered. "I seem to recollect you asking me that on the Ark one time Ham. I would suggest we're somewhere in the middle of the Western Sea, but I have no idea how far from land we are. With this overcast sky I don't even know which is north and which is south. When we find out we must work the ship south until we find land again."

"It will be hard to do that, father, without our mizzen mast, the top of the foremast gone and much of our rigging and sails in tatters."

"I'm aware of that, Shem. We're drifting at the moment, but now that the storm is past and we have calmer water even though there are still heavy swells, we must do our best to replace the rigging and sails with the spare ones we brought with us. When we make shore again we can hopefully reset the mizzen with the spare one in the hold and repair the foremast from timber we find ashore."

"Noach," said Ada. "I've attended to everyone's injuries except yours. Now, will you please sit down here and remain still for ten minutes so that I can do something about that gash on your forehead. With all that blood streaking down your face you look like the Nephilim with their painted faces when they went about hunting and attacking people back in the old world."

"Thank you, Ada. Yes, I do need to rest I suppose."

"Yes, Noach, you do," said Naamah. "You take so much upon yourself. You're not a young man any more. When Ada has finished with you please both of you join the rest of us. We haven't eaten since yesterday and I've made some broth. We all need some hot food before you men start fixing the sails."

"That sounds very good Naamah. We need some good food to warm us up again," laughed Noah.

Eventually the wounded ship and crew found themselves back somewhere along the shoreline they had been swept away from the previous day. Repairs were made and after three weeks they continued on their expedition of discovery. Every day they sailed or stopped and walked on land, it was a new discovery for them. It was truly a whole new world, prolific in its growth and the abundance of its wildlife. Noah and his immediate family were constantly amazed at how quickly life had returned to the devastated, flooded world in which they had made a new start. For the younger ones born into this world it was simply a voyage of encountering more of the world in which they lived.

After several weeks they came to a narrow channel between two large land masses. Even as they ventured into this waterway they observed great chunks of earth and boulders falling into the sea on the northern shore. It was apparent that yet another great earth tremor had dislodged the cliff face. Obviously this was a common occurrence here, and Noah and his sons speculated that this channel over time would grow much wider not only from the earth tremors dislodging the cliffs but the great surge of water they observed running through the waterway. But where did it lead to?

"I'm keen to see where it may take us," remarked Japheth.

"It stretches away into the distance. It may be another vast river system," added Ham.

"It doesn't appear too narrow. If anything, it looks like it gets wider in the distance," suggested Lud.

"Yes, definitely. I believe we should see where it leads us," agreed Magog. "What do you say, father?" Shem asked.

"Yes, we're here to discover this new world. We should take every opportunity that's presented to us. We'll see where it takes us."

As they sailed into the channel, even with the easterly wind behind them they found the sea very rough and choppy. With the soundings they took, even though the sea was very deep, they soon realised there was a strong current flowing against them.

"What could this mean?" queried Javan whose task it was to take the soundings, a job he shared with his brother Tiras.

"I wonder," said Noah, "could there be a much larger area of water ahead of us which is flowing into this sea?"

In fact, it took them just a day with the help of a strong east wind to negotiate the current and they found themselves in another vast sea with the cliffs of the channel disappearing to the north and south the further they navigated westwards. By nightfall *Hebe* had left the land far behind and all that could be seen was open water from horizon to horizon.

"It's another great sea connected by the channel we passed through," observed Japheth.

"Yes, you're right my son, and it would appear this may even be a great ocean which perhaps spreads around the whole globe as it did in the old world. I've seen enough. I believe we should head back through the channel and continue to explore what would now be the northern shore of the Western Sea," commanded Noah. "But we shall remember this, and come and explore it another day," he added.

They spent that night in the open sea once again, marvelling at the myriad of stars in the clear sky as they often did on calm, clear nights. When morning came *Hebe* headed back through the channel, assisted by the strong current, until they could head north again, keeping the land in the distance to their left, as they continued to explore this great Western Sea.

Several weeks later they found themselves heading south again and then north. Noah realised they had sailed along a large peninsula, and with his mapping skills gained from his experience in the old world he suggested this peninsula of land was shaped like a human leg that even had a foot.

During all their travels they had seen many islands which they often sailed around and even landed on. Sometimes mountains of fire they now named volcanoes were often seen far inland, along with many islands simply erupting out of the sea. They kept a safe distance from all these. Rivers were plentiful, and great forests spread inland.

When they landed, as they often did, Ada enjoyed searching the forests and grasslands for herbs and plants that she could make into medicines. They took other plants that had not seeded naturally back in their home valleys to try to have them grow there. They had discovered a beautiful world with high, sharp peaked mountains and fertile valleys and plains. The effects of the great flood were apparent in the contorted rock formations they observed, quite unlike the more uniform shapes of the old world.

Heading north once again they encountered another storm, but this time they were prepared and had all sails furled before the tempest struck. No sooner had they come to the most northern shore of the sea than they headed south again.

Another three weeks found them at the southern end of perhaps another large peninsula where there were many islands, several of which were marked with plumes of smoke and fire. Often, while walking on these coasts and islands the earth shook violently beneath them. Yet despite that there was an incredible beauty to these lands and their waterways.

Sailing north once again and then east, they came to a narrow strip of land which they crossed on foot. Japheth was sure this was the land he had explored as he was returning from his previous expedition. It divided the Western Sea from a great inland sea that spread itself far to the north, he told them. If so, they were not far from the end of their voyage.

As it turned out they had to sail another month longer past many inlets, bays and islands until they arrived back at Ty on the eastern shore. Noah had achieved another milestone. He and his crew had navigated the entire coastline of what they called the Western Sea.

"It's such a beautiful world," laughed Sede, as they completed the last part of their great voyage and reflected on what they had achieved together.

"Yes, my dear, it is a beautiful world that Adonai has given us. The stunning lands we have seen make the valleys and plains where we live and farm pale in comparison."

The rest of the crew acknowledged in their own way what they had discovered.

"Are you happy with what we have achieved, father?" asked Shem."

"I was discouraged after the toil we endured for so many years since coming out of the Ark," Noah replied. "And I thought the new world was a harsh place that would only offer us hardship and toil. This voyage, however, has invigorated me. There is so much more to explore. I want to see it all."

"So where to next, grandfather?" laughed Arpachshad.

"We shall see, my boy, we shall see."

TWENTY-THREE

Babel

Many Years Later
AM 1799

It is now almost one hundred and fifty years since the Ark came to rest and discharged its human cargo into the new world. Now into their fourth generation in this world, more than three thousand people are confined in a relatively small area. The years following Noah's initial exploration of the Western Sea brought a prolific expansion in the number of people and the founding of several new villages and towns. These were concentrated chiefly in the area between the Euphrates and Tigris rivers. The population of the earth over the next one hundred years or so grew rapidly due to many births and few deaths, a legacy from the old world, the genetic purity of Noah's family heritage and the lack of disease at the beginning of the post flood world.

For a time Noah was continuing to make decisions that the people followed, enjoying their respect as the acknowledged patriarch of his ever expanding family. But this would not last much longer. He had directed that new settlements should be founded mainly to the east of their original village in the Euphrates valley area. But not only there, because God had decreed they should fill the whole earth. Noah therefore encouraged the establishment of settlements further out in the lands they had already explored. Some people did so and in time these would become great dynasties. The descendants of Ham, Cush, Mizraim and Put, for example, established villages along the great river in the boundless land to the south.

Other children and grandchildren of Ham, as well as those of Shem and Japheth, established themselves in the land they called Shinar in the Euphrates Valley.

At that time everyone spoke the language that Noah and his family had brought from the old world. In this way they were all able to communicate and understand one another. The result of this great expansion of people with the same language living closely together meant that they rapidly learned new skills and reinvented much of what Noah and his sons and their wives had known in the old world. Industry, agriculture, farming, building and the construction of tools and machines to make work easier was rapid, as was the expansion of knowledge. But the downside to this rapid expansion was that people came to believe in themselves and their own abilities over and above the provision and guidance of a divine being.

Once Noah saw that the growth in the descendants of those who had survived in the Ark was well established he left the management of this now great area of land, the cradle of their new civilisation, to Shem and Ham and their descendants, as well as those of Japheth, while he and Japheth explored new lands to be settled in future years. He also gave Shem and the sons of Arpachshad more and more of the responsibility for the people's spiritual growth and welfare. However, the aspiration of most people was more towards their desire for enjoying the fruits of their labour and what they could achieve rather than worshipping an unseen God. Because of the rapid growth in numbers and settlements being established close to one another inevitably friction arose in time and these severe disagreements impacted on the wellbeing of what was initially a peaceful worldwide community.

Ham never again sailed or journeyed with Noah on any long term explorations. Instead he and his sons spent their time exploring the vast southern land as well as establishing villages in Shinar.

Shem and Japheth travelled on expeditions to the Western Sea on several occasions until Shem and Sede decided their destiny lay in managing the new areas of settlement in Shinar on a permanent basis. With the support of Arpachshad they also attempted to prevent the many hundreds of new settlers from neglecting or ignoring their Creator God. They did this by encouraging these people to worship God, rather than by paying reverence to figurines and other tangible objects that people were beginning to say were more believable, because they could be seen and touched, as opposed to believing in an unseen God who had to be worshipped and believed in by faith alone.

Noah and Japheth continued to explore more of the Western Sea in *Hebe* as well as many lands to the west and north, which they covered on foot or by horse, donkey and camel, along with their wives Naamah and Ada, who were their constant companions. Japheth and Ada also led teams to other lands on a number of occasions. Both he and his father Noah had an insatiable ambition to explore more and more of this new world. Noah and Naamah's great age was not yet a determining factor in whether they were fit enough to carry on this work, for they seemed to stay as strong and healthy as they had ever been, although they were just a little slower in their movements and reactions.

On one of his voyages in the Western Sea Noah spent some time in a bay on the western coast of a long peninsula. He remarked to Japheth that he thought this was an ideal land to retire to. "When I'm old and can no longer travel I think I'd like to live here, grow grapes and make wine. It's a sure way to have my sons and grandsons visit me if I can supply them with wine," he chuckled.

"I would have thought you are already old enough to retire from your labours, father, but you just keep going. You are amazing. But, yes, it is a good place. There's warm weather, plentiful rain when you need it, good soil and deep water for ships to come and go. It's a long way from Ty though."

"In a hundred years many of our sons and daughters may very well be living here, Japheth."

"You expect to still be alive then?"

"Adonai willing Japheth, Adonai willing."

Noah and Naamah were now living permanently at the port of Ty. Although there were still no villages or habitation across the sea with which to trade he used the port and village as a base for his frequent explorations by sea. Inevitably Noah suggested that he repeat what he first did as a young man and be the first to circumnavigate this new world.

He planned to build two new ships larger and more durable than *Hebe.* He and Naamah would take one and Japheth and Ada the other, and then embark together upon the most adventurous, possibly dangerous and ambitious voyage of all time. They would circumnavigate the world as much as was possible, using the same method they had always used, sailing continuously with the coastline in view to their left. They realised this new world land mass was far more broken up and dispersed than the one in the old world and that this voyage would take several years. Many discouraged them from such a venture and warned they might never return. Noah as always dismissed their fear, for he was such a man of faith and ambition and with the confidence of so much experience behind him, he was determined to be first once again.

Noah and Naamah named their ship *Dinah* after Noah's younger sister who never lived to enjoy having a family and joining them in this new world. Japheth and Ada named theirs *Athena* after a daughter who had been killed tragically by a wild beast before she was sixteen years of age, the first tragedy of its kind in this new world.

In the year of the world, AM1799, the ships *Dinah* and *Athene* set out from Ty with thirty eight souls on a voyage of discovery that would have great significance for the future colonisation of the new world.

‡‡‡

Four Years Later
AM 1803

Seventy years earlier a young man named Nimrod, the son of Cush, made a name for himself as a mighty hunter. He had grown up an impetuous youth, fearless and extremely rebellious of his parents, grandparents, their patriarch Noah and generally at odds with the world about him.

'He has a bad spirit,' people said of him; 'an anti-Adonai spirit.'

Nevertheless, God blessed Nimrod with a strong, tall, healthy body and many skills, including the construction of buildings and use of tools. He was also a great hunter of game and a strong leader. As he grew up his peers looked up to him and his leadership was never questioned.

When wild animals had been harassing the settlements near where he lived with his family, Nimrod, his brothers and companions hunted these animals and the danger they posed to the villages soon disappeared. This made him very popular. A story that circulated at that time but was not verified except by those who were with him, told how he fought one of the giant behemoths and killed it. These rare animals seldom came near civilisation, but if they did people said Nimrod would kill them. Many scoffed at the story which had become legendary, saying it was only to boost his image, because Nimrod was prone to exaggeration and not infrequently told tall tales.

Now, at ninety one years of age, he was chief of a village he had founded and named Babel. It was already well populated and was becoming even more so rapidly, for word of his strength went before him and people flocked to what they presumed was the safety of a strong man. Nimrod had been given authority earlier by his father Cush and grandfather Ham, and his very character and temperament emboldened him further to take charge in any situation in which he found himself.

As a respected, fearless leader who stood up to anyone who disagreed with him, Nimrod's temperament was such that he did not avoid frequent fights throughout his life. He always won them, which is why he enjoyed taunting lesser men. He had even established an army of fighters to be ready to deal with an attack from some other village, though such an event had never occurred in the new world up to this time because most people lived in harmony with one another. Nimrod's action made some outsiders think that he might be spoiling for a war with his distant brothers and cousins. People were aware that strife had been frequent in the old world and now it seemed that Nimrod was determined to bring that evil into the new world too.

An incident arose when a village nearby named Kish, north of Babel on the banks of the Euphrates River, was taking water from the river to irrigate its vines and fruit trees. Nimrod was angered about this, as he believed they were taking most of the water and that was the reason the flow of the river through Babel had been greatly reduced during the past six months. He therefore led his army against Kish, attacking the village without warning and killing all its men. After abusing its women and taking them and their children as spoils, he used them as slaves in the building of the great city that he now planned. When word of this became known Nimrod's reputation spread as being not just a hunter of wild animals and a builder of a large town, but now as the feared hunter of men as well. News of this massacre got back to Cush and Ham as well as Shem.

Shortly after this Noah and Japheth made landfall at a place far south of Ty on what they called the Sea of Reeds. They had sailed along the coast of the entire southern land and it had taken them three years and three months to get there. Being only several days journey from their starting point they interrupted their world voyage for several months before continuing. Shem made the journey to greet them on learning his father and brother were nearby.

On hearing from Shem what had happened to the village of Kish, Noah angrily demanded that Shem take him to Babel to confront Nimrod. They would locate and take Ham and Cush with them as well. Japheth would meanwhile take the opportunity to change some members of the crew, replace one young man they had tragically lost overboard one night, and make repairs to the ships where needed.

After a long journey Noah and the patriarchs rode into the town of Babel. When they reached Nimrod's residence which he was transforming into a palatial living area they confronted him. Being the same height as Nimrod, Noah stood silently looking him in the eye, while Noah's sons stood behind him except for Ham and Cush who had moved to stand near their offspring. The two men stood silently, staring each other out, waiting for one or the other to speak. All about them remained silent as well for an extended time, the only sound was from small birds flitting about them. Then Noah spoke.

"This is an evil thing you have done Nimrod! What can you achieve by bringing violence into this world?"

"You have no authority over me, old man. This is no longer your world. It is what we do with it, and we do as we please."

"Adonai …"

"Bah! Don't speak to me of your God. With my consort Semiramis and our son Tammuz we have educated people here to show them a better way. We have discovered our earth mother who gives birth to her man child. We will worship what we please. Go away old man, you have no authority here."

"Adonai has blessed you with many talents, Nimrod, and this is how you repay him!"

"We are building a great city here. We have clay which we bake into strong bricks and tar to bind them together. We will build a high tower, high enough to reach the clouds, then even further to the heavens and even then we will not see your God, for he is not there! We will build it so high that if ever your God sends another flood we can escape it! We will do greater things than you ever did, greater than your old world, greater than your God. We will be invincible!

"The people don't want to follow your rules, you timeworn old man, your covenant, the decree of your God. Nor do they want to risk their lives in strange far off places. They wish only to live in these lands with me as their king. Already they call me Sargon. I am simply doing what the people want of me. I am giving them peace and security!"

"You were a rebel from your birth. What you are doing here is an act of defiance and rebellion against Adonai, who has promised never to send another flood."

"We don't believe you!"

"I can do no more. You have the spirit of Cain and you are lost. From now on you will be known as Nimrod, the rebel. You have rebelled against your fellow man and worse still, you defy Adonai who will judge you and all of you who rebel against him."

"Go your way, old man. Sail the seas and follow your fantasies. No doubt you'll fall off the edge of the world anyway, and we'll be rid of you." With that, Nimrod turned on his heel and left them to make their way back home.

All this was a matter of great regret to Noah, Shem and those who agreed with them, not only because of the rebellion, arrogance and disrespect that Nimrod had shown toward Noah. That was evil enough, but it was the fact that Cush and Ham had made no effort to support them. Noah did not hesitate to tell Ham what he thought of his reluctance to lend his support, but Ham simply looked at his father and said nothing. How sad it was that after all they had achieved together their world had come to this.

After repairing and replenishing their ships, Noah and Japheth continued their great sea voyage, while Shem went home to his village and his loving Sede. Eventually God spoke again, but this time to Shem, one night some months after he returned from seeing Noah off on his journey of exploration. On a quiet still night while he gazed at the myriad of stars in the heavens as he often did, Shem prayed: *"Lord what will you make of this Nimrod, the evil he has brought to the earth? The great tower he is building. This is in defiance of you. Judge him Lord in your righteousness."*

While he prayed he had a vision. A man came and stood before him, one like a son of Adam and he spoke to Shem:

> *Behold, they are one people, and they have all one language,*
> *and this is only the beginning of what they will do.*
> *And nothing that they propose to do will now be impossible*
> *for them. Come, let us confuse their language, so that they may*
> *not understand one another's speech and I will scatter them*
> *across the world.*

Shem awoke and found himself alone. Was it a dream he just had, or had God actually spoken to him? He walked over to the place where he had seen the man in his dream stand and there in the dust he could clearly see a man's fresh footprints. Shem prayed *"O, Adonai you have come down and spoken to your servant. Now I know you are Lord over this new world."*

Nimrod built his great city and attempted to build his high tower, but over the next several months and years a strange thing happened. People could not understand why their gods were causing all manner of obstacles to delay the building of the tower and the city. Men stayed away from work and their initial enthusiasm for building the great metropolis waned. For the first time illness infiltrated the densely populated city and the workers stayed home too weak to work. Many drifted away to other villages. Earth tremors hampered their work frequently. Confusion reigned as building calculations turned out to be wrong or incomplete. Nimrod had men executed if they made mistakes, yet all to no avail. Morale got lower and lower over time. People eventually became incoherent and started speaking different dialects others could not understand. "It's the gods! We need to appease them!" they said, and they made all manner of offerings to them, but this did nothing to change their obstacles and morale.

The building of the tower took longer and longer to add one level to the next until, after eight years, work on it stopped altogether. It sat there for many years unoccupied, a monument to men's rebellion and attempt to make themselves greater than God. Eventually earth tremors levelled it to the ground.

Nimrod gave up on his tower. Undeterred, he rebuilt the village of Kish and then went on to found Uruk and Akkad in Shinar, Nineveh and many others. Over time these villages would grow to become great cities.

‡‡‡

Many Years Later
AM 1820

Seventeen years had passed since Noah's failed confrontation with Nimrod. In the meantime Noah, Japheth and their wives had continued on their exploration of the world. Because of their lengthy absence many of their close relatives had now all but given up hope of seeing them alive again and presumed they had come to grief, while more distant relatives had given up on them longer still, angry that so many young and able men had most likely perished with them. For them Noah was a figure of the past, and now the future of the world was in their hands. Men and women alike had become more and more devoted to their new gods, rather than the one Shem and his sons tried to convince them to honour.

Shem and Sede, however, had not given up hope. Having grown up with Noah and Naamah and survived through many perils, they knew how Noah's tenacity and the commitment and abilities of Japheth, Ada and Naamah would keep them safe. They had no doubt they would return, most likely when they were least expected, and so it turned out to be.

Late one afternoon at the time of year when trees start losing their leaves the inhabitants of the village of Ty saw a sail on the horizon. Then they saw a second sail and within two hours the word spread and a fast rider was sent to Shem's village to inform him that Noah had returned.

Two days after the ships *Dinah* and *Athena* arrived at their home port Shem greeted his father, mother and brother with tears of joy streaming down his cheeks. Sede and Ada fell into each other's arms weeping as well, while Noah and Naamah hugged the adult grandchildren who had come with Shem to greet them. The news then spread rapidly to Ham and his children and the rest of Noah's extended family. Many of those who had sailed with Noah and Japheth now travelled home to their villages in Shinar or elsewhere, confirming they were still alive and recounting to their families the adventures they had experienced.

Eventually Ham came to Shem's village with some of his sons and grandchildren. Then, along with many of Japheth and Shem's sons, daughters and grandchildren they spent an entertaining two weeks listening to the amazing stories the intrepid explorers brought back with them.

Noah spoke of a vast world as big as the old one which had been virtually one huge continent. This new world however was divided into many great lands with seas and oceans around them. Countless islands were now scattered across the face of the earth, with even more of them erupting out of the sea as they sailed by at a safe distance.

They had seen great areas of forest, jungle, grassy plains and desert areas where nothing grew. There were vast mountain ranges with sharp peaks, evidence of the violence and suddenness of the great flood, and quite unlike the rounded hills of the old world. There were wide, long rivers, as well as fast flowing narrow ones, high waterfalls, lakes small and large, and narrow inlets deep enough for ships to sail in, but narrow and treacherous to navigate due to fickle winds. Beautiful bays with sandy or pebble beaches had also often sheltered the two ships from storms and violent weather.

They told their listeners of many places with good soil suitable for future villages, and lands with pleasant climates for growing crops. Far to the north, however, it was too cold to live, and the great southern land Noah had discovered in the old world that was thick with vegetation was now rapidly becoming a land of ice far too cold and dry for anyone to live in.

The world was still recovering from the flood, since many volcanoes were still throwing rocks, debris and fire violently into the sky. These lands would not be habitable for a long time to come, or at least until the eruptions stopped. It was not just the lands near Shinar that erupted with fire and frequent earth tremors. This was still happening everywhere they went, they told their enthralled listeners.

"The land to the east of us is vast, the largest landmass, that together with our lands and the great continent to the south we estimate is probably the largest land area in the world, formed from the heart of the old world. The eastern lands have many mountains, valleys, rivers and jungles of vegetation.

"Beyond the eastern lands is the greatest of oceans, then a mass of land that stretches from the far north to the far south without a break. It divides this world in two. Here also is a great mountain range that appears to form the backbone of the entire land from the top to the bottom. Once again, there are more rivers, valleys, plains and jungles. To the east of that great land which lies closer to the west and north of our lands there are still more lands mostly covered in forest. Here, also, are many lakes, rivers, lower mountains, plains and rolling country. Its climate is much cooler and wetter than what we are used to.

"Yet we barely explored enough of the new world to know what lies beyond the coastlands of these great continents and islands. There is so much more to explore and discover," laughed an exuberant Noah as he spoke at length to a captive audience.

He was often interrupted by Naamah or Ada with additional stories, and also by Japheth who had often gone off with some of the young men to explore inland from the coasts. They had some amazing stories to tell.

"It's extraordinary," Japheth said, "how the animals and birds and all manner of creatures have spread so quickly over the world. It's as if they took the first opportunity they had to get as far away from human beings as they could. Many times, either at sea or jammed up against some coastline, we saw vast rafts of rotten vegetation, tree trunks, soil and other debris that we assume were left over from the flood. Most of these floating islands had regrown vegetation on them, and it was easy to see how this would have taken root on the barren land once the waters subsided. Some of these floating islands we saw at sea even had animals living on them. So again, this could be one way the animals have spread so quickly from land to land and island to island."

Noah then explained that with such a long voyage over so many years in a world now dominated by seasons both hot and cold, storms and drought, and all manner of physical dangers from unstable ground and wild animals, it was inevitable that tragedy would strike now and again. This was the reason why six adult men and a young man just eighteen years of age were tragically killed during the years of their exploration. Two were swept overboard. The young man was trying to prove his maturity and bravery when he got too close to an eruption on an island while trying to gather the yellow sulphur that they had found was useful for medicine and in other ways. Two men were also killed when they disturbed the territory of wild animals, and another died in a fall from an unstable cliff. On another occasion one of the men was walking along a beach enjoying the waves as they came ashore, splashing over his legs and surging back out again. This was something everyone enjoyed doing from time to time. Suddenly, he cried out in pain, as if he had stepped on something sharp. Those with him then pulled what appeared to be a small sea creature with spikes out of his foot which then bled profusely. They had to carry him back to their camp as he was unable to walk. His foot, then his entire leg had become swollen. He was in great pain and eventually a fever took hold of him. Ada was unable to cure him and could only give him something to stem the pain which apparently had little effect. He died in agony two days later.

No women died throughout the entire voyage and eight children were born. In all they lost seven men but gained five girls and three boys.

Later, at a quiet moment, Noah took Shem aside and asked him, "what has happened in these lands in our absence, Shem?"

He replied, "Nimrod continues to grow stronger. He now calls himself Sargon as you would expect. His high tower came to nothing as you said it would. But he has determination, I'll give him that.

He has founded new villages and created a one-man government over all this. What he says becomes law, and it's not based on Adonai's covenant with us. The people either love him or fear him, but either way they follow him and his rebellion against God grows stronger every year. Most people don't want to hear about Adonai. I'm afraid they are falling away from the time they are born. Their parents simply aren't interested in teaching them of the Lord.

"But Adonai came, he spoke to me, he came down and spoke to me!" Shem said, a glow coming over him, as he continued to tell Noah of the vision he had received and how Adonai stated he would scatter the people across the world and confuse their language. He continued, "an amazing thing has happened even in the time you were away. People in villages remote from Babel and those nearby have started to speak different languages over the last few years. Many of them are now communicating in words none of us understand. It's happened just as Adonai told me it would."

"It's the work of the Lord. Adonai is with you Shem. But I wonder what the future holds? I'm not sure I want to be part of it," Noah replied with a long sigh.

"You remember young Peleg, my great grandson, the son of Eber, the grandson of Arpachshad? He came and saw me after your meeting with Nimrod," Shem continued. "He asked permission to assist those who were afraid of Nimrod, because their lives were controlled by him due to the debts they owed him for the charges he levied on them. When they couldn't pay Nimrod he took their land and dwellings, and now he treats them virtually as slaves. Peleg has become very bold having sailed with us and is prepared to stand against Nimrod and those who want to enslave others.

"He has asked permission to take these people away in groups and explore north, south and east for new lands, so they can establish themselves well away from Nimrod's tyranny. I said of course, and in partnership with his brother Joktan, many of the young men and women have supported him. He has become quite popular, and now people are seeking Peleg out to find them new places to farm and establish villages. A lot has happened while you were away," reflected Shem.

"So through Peleg the world will be divided into many nations in the years to come. With Ham establishing villages in the southern lands and you very much in control here, it seems that people are finally spreading themselves throughout the earth. This is very good," said Noah.

"With what Japheth and I have discovered and talked about on many an evening," he continued, "we are determined to provide people like Peleg and others who want to live in new lands the means to do just that. We intend to build more ships and have people found colonies around the whole earth. We have located many good places to do this. It will be our mission from now on, or at least Japheth will head it up.

"My dear Naamah is encouraging me to settle down in a quiet place and enjoy the rest of the days that Adonai may give us," said Noah. "She tells me I have done enough, and now it's time to pass the governance of this world to you, my three sons."

"Gladly father, although I think Nimrod has other ideas. He would never submit to me," said Shem.

"He is a rebel and history will confirm what I am saying. Sadly, due to the way of men he will most likely become more famous than you or Ham or Japheth," replied Noah. "People will remember his exploits while we are forgotten. With his new religion, he is the one that Satan will use to continue his evil plans to deceive mankind in this beautiful new world. I fear it may very well be the beginning of the end," lamented Noah.

So it was in the generation of Peleg that the people of the world were divided. Groups of people settled themselves in distant lands and consequently, as their language changed over time and without communicating with other groups, new tribal and ethnic people and languages along with various types of government were established.

TWENTY-FOUR

Noah's Land

AM 1850 – AM 1952

After five generations in the new world there was a population of well over twelve thousand. Small groups of people had spread in many different directions, sometimes even by way of a sea journey in one of Japheth and Noah's fleet of ships, or else trudging overland to seek out new fields to farm, grow crops or hunt animals. In the land of Sin far to the east a small community had established itself, and many other lands to the north and east of Babel had also been populated. Enterprising and resourceful people had explored even to the furthest places, literally to the ends of the known world. Over time they would develop into different people with different languages, and because of the climate and environment they dwelt in, even their appearance would begin to differ from others.

To the south along the great river and near its entry into the Western Sea many communities were founded. But Shinar and Babel to the east was where the greatest concentration of people and progress took place. It would later be said that this was the place where civilisation began.

Over the next hundred years the earth's population increased to well over seventy thousand, perhaps even as much as one hundred thousand. Many small settlements founded in the early years of the new world were the start of what would become in time great cities, nations and even empires and ethnic people groups.

During this time Japheth and Noah spent many years exploring the earth. They sometimes stayed for a time in various places, leaving behind them a permanent community when they travelled on further. Eventually Japheth, Ada and their offspring ventured north and west to seek lands to settle in. Noah and Naamah constantly sought out new areas to establish communities, sometimes living on their own with Japheth's ships calling in on them frequently.

One such land was far to the east or west depending on which way they travelled. On the other side of the world from Shinar and located in the Great Ocean lay a land that the descendants of people who would later come to live there would name *Nukuroa* after the great man himself. Noah and Naamah lived here for ten years, far away from all the issues that beset Shinar, leaving the governance of the new world to their sons and grandsons along with Nimrod, their adversary.

Noah and Naamah loved their island home. They avoided the larger of the two main islands with its erupting volcanoes, choosing a smaller one off the coast of the northern island, where there was enough land to grow crops, keep a few animals and catch fish. With its beautiful beaches and warm pleasant climate, it was in Noah's own words, "So much like the old world that I wonder if one of those island rafts didn't drift ashore here and spread unique green plants. It's a veritable little paradise with almost all the physical features I've observed in this new world compressed into these remote islands. This beautiful place is like Adonai's own land."

For Naamah, these were perhaps the happiest years of her marriage to Noah, because she had him virtually all to herself, uninterrupted by travel to far places or being intensely occupied with a particular project that consumed his time or thoughts. When they did travel anywhere Naamah was always at Noah's side and they shared all their activities together.

They enjoyed a restful existence, perhaps for the first time in their long lives. Only working and producing enough to feed themselves and the half dozen younger people accompanying them, gave them time to reflect on what they had achieved. In their daily prayer before their Lord they sought his purpose for the rest of their lives, however long that might be before they went the way of all the earth, for it was already apparent to them that the life span of human beings in this new world would not be as long as it was in the old.

They swam frequently in the waves that broke on their sandy shores, enjoying the warmth of the waters. At times when the wind and currents combined to create huge waves they would body surf through them and then be carried swiftly onto the shore. They particularly enjoyed swimming with dolphins because when these were present there were no dangerous sharks around. They also enjoyed the company of all kinds of birds, many of which did not fly. There were no large wild animals in this utopia and no poisonous snakes either to be wary of. This was truly a safe paradise compared to the rest of the world.

Noah and Naamah laughed here as they had never laughed before, sang to each other, and spent many intimate moments together. This blissful existence was seemingly God's reward for the years they had devoted to his service. They were very happy.

When God eventually showed them where he wanted them to go next he put a desire within their hearts to return to Ty and then seek out Noah's bay on the peninsula in the Western Sea that he had discovered many years earlier. They felt they should retire to this place which was much closer to their families than their island paradise so far away across the world, so they did this on one of Japheth's voyages, leaving their paradise uninhabited for they knew not how long.

In the course of time Noah and Naamah came to live in his bay on a sunny shore of the Western Sea, accompanied by a great grandson named Timnah and his family. Noah built an estate here and planted his vines of choice. Eventually others joined them, and as he had predicted many years previously, several of their offspring now lived there as well. Their retirement estate became a small village and once it was established Timnah and his family travelled in search of other lands to live.

Naamah and Noah lived peacefully and quietly tending their vines, along with a few domestic animals and gardens. Naamah had finally convinced Noah to settle down, enjoy life and not get involved in the affairs of the rest of the world now far enough away that they could not be drawn into reconciling disputes. He had done enough for this new world that had expanded and enriched itself, but now had sadly become a place where some of the inhabitants fought amongst themselves for superiority or the best tracts of land. No longer did Noah concern himself with their day to day governance. In fact, he began to enjoy not being in charge or the centre of attention any more. He was now finally willing to let younger men and women take on the dangers and challenges of exploring their world. Then, in Noah's 886th year tragedy struck.

‡‡‡

AM 1942

Naamah had always been a resourceful woman, intelligent and loyal to her Lord God and her family. Stubborn when she wanted to be, she never compromised her beliefs or morals. Naamah enjoyed her garden and grew many varieties of vegetables for Noah, herself and their small village. In the old world for many years she had not only managed crops on her father's estate, but also Lamech's farm and crops when the men were busy building the Ark, along with Hebe, her sister in law. Over her many years she had become proficient in a wide range of skills.

Her happiest times now were when, with Noah, they walked inland and searched out a stream or waterfall, or else climbed a hill and looked out over the green forests and distant snow-capped mountains. They also enjoyed walking hand in hand along the shore near their village. From the rocks and timber near at hand Noah had built a small but comfortable cottage with a stone floor and thatched roof. Their vineyards surrounded the village and covered the sloping land up behind their home. It was a gentle climb from the beach to their cottage with an entryway where they could sit and look out over an uninterrupted view of the sea.

Once a year Noah and Naamah made the voyage to Ty, staying close to land whenever a storm looked likely. The village was proud of the small coastal ship they used for trading and getting supplies. The young men of the village were its crew.

When Noah and Naamah were in Ty and the nearby lands where their immediate family lived they were able to visit with Shem, Sede, Japheth and Ada, and occasionally with Ham and Nae if the last named made the long journey from where they now lived to greet their father. This last time Noah and Naamah travelled to Ty they had enjoyed a happy reunion that included some of their grandchildren and other offspring.

Naamah had been feeling unwell on the journey home, which was unusual for her as she was a seasoned and proficient sailor. Yet she didn't feel her body responding to the movement of the sea in the way she was used to. They arrived back at their settlement on an unusually wet and blustery day.

By now the men of the village had built a small jetty where boats and ships could tie up instead of rowing small boats to and from the larger ships in the bay as in previous times. It was wet and choppy, and getting off the ship was somewhat precarious as the plank they used to step from the ship to the jetty was not only wet and slippery but moving about quite noticeably.

Noah had already gone ashore while Naamah attended to putting the last of their belongings into a haversack for one of the young men to carry ashore. Suddenly she felt a sharp pain in her chest. She stopped what she was doing and stood still for a moment breathing deeply, and then the pain passed. She then sat down on a chair nearby.

"Are you all right my lady?" one of the crew asked respectfully as he came into her cabin to take her haversack.

Sighing, Naamah replied, "oh yes it's nothing. It's just that I'm not as young as I used to be."

"Can I help you ashore?" he asked.

"Yes, thank you, that would be nice."

As the small ship rocked awkwardly against the stanchions of the jetty, the walking plank also moved up and down. Although one end was secured to the ship, the other end was moving about unsteadily on the jetty, but not so much that the younger people could not negotiate it comfortably. When it came to Naamah's turn she found that she was having difficulty focusing as she went ashore, as she was somewhat unsettled after the event in her cabin. The plank was too narrow for someone to walk beside her so her assistant walked in front of her sideways down the plank holding her arm. It was awkward with the movement of the ship and consequently he did not have a tight hold of her.

As Naamah negotiated the swaying walkway she was unsteady on her legs then, having almost reached the jetty the sailor stepped off the plank and lost his grip on her. At the same moment Naamah lost her footing on the plank and fell into the water between the ship and the jetty.

Without thinking of his own safety the sailor dived in after her, and another man nearby seeing what had happened jumped into the water as well. Their main concern was that she would be crushed between the thick piles of the jetty and the moving ship.

Both men got to her at the same time. Ignoring the nearby ladder, as they could all be crushed on that if the ship swung that way, they swam with one arm each, holding Naamah between them, to the beach some fifty cubits away.

Getting to the shore the men fell down exhausted, while Naamah lay between them. It was then they realised she was lying on her back very still.

"She's not moving; was she knocked out?"

"I don't know, what should we do?" they cried.

By this time four others had run down to the beach to help. One was a young woman who knew what to do. She turned Naamah on her side and some water gushed out of her mouth, but there was no response from the unconscious woman. She then turned her onto her back and started to push on her chest, but nothing happened at first and then with a gulp and some more water exiting her mouth Naamah coughed and groaned.

Someone had gone to fetch Noah and he came running as quickly as he could to the shore where Naamah lay barely conscious, her eyes closed and breathing very slowly.

"Naamah, my dear can you hear me?" cried an anxious Noah.

"She's not responding," said the young woman. "Help me and I'll sit her up. That might help."

They got Naamah into a sitting position, but she was far from responsive so they laid her back onto the beach again. Then she opened her eyes and looked straight into Noah's.

"You …" Naamah coughed.

"Don't try to talk dearest, we will get you back to the cottage."

"No, I …hard to breathe, pain in chest … You ha… you have the most beautiful … blue eyes my darling."

"Naamah don't …"

"Sorry, so weak … I can't, Noach I …"

"No, my love, we will take care of you."

Barely able to hear her, Noah held Naamah in his arms and kissed her gently on the lips and held her tightly, his head against her neck. Naamah's last words to him were, "… take care my love."

‡‡‡

Noah was alone again. He mourned the loss of his beloved partner and wife deeply, but he was not depressed. He had experienced too much of life to be miserable and understood now what God wanted of him.

'We are born, we live for Adonai and we die. This is the way of the earth, the way of God our Creator and my destiny,' he told himself.

Although they were informed of the death of their mother soon afterwards, Noah's sons were unable to visit him until almost a year later. It was the first time all three sons and their wives had travelled to see him in his village. When they arrived all of them expected to find a morose, lonely old man, but to their surprise they found him quite cheerful.

"I am going to build another ship," he told them.

"NO! Father, you have done enough, you are not as young as you were," exclaimed Shem.

"Ha! Fooled you all didn't I?" Noah laughed.

"What do you mean Noach?" asked Sede.

"I'm not going to build it myself. I'm going to have the shipyard in Ty build one for me to my specifications. They need the ship we have at this village for supplies and trading, so if I'm to indulge myself I must build another."

Ham groaned, "and just what will you do with it father?"

"I can't just grow grapes and make wine for the rest of the days Adonai grants me. I love the sea too much. There are so many islands and bays on the mainland between here and Ty, so I've decided to do a little more exploring."

"Well, father, you'll need a crew," added Japheth.

"All arranged. Some young men in our small village here want me to show them how to sail the seas and I'm happy to teach them so they in turn can explore this great world of ours."

"Very noble father," sighed Ham.

"You are not a young man any more Noach," said Ada. "You must take care. Naamah's heart gave out, and yours may too if you do too much."

"Yes, dear Ada, I understand, but I feel fit and strong still, just a little slower in my movements. I promise as soon as I feel unwell, as Naamah had told me she was, I will stop. Until then I intend to keep seeking what Adonai wants to show me until I drop."

‡‡‡

Over the next ten years Noah enjoyed short voyages to many islands and coastlands nearby, relishing the chance to pass on his knowledge and skills to the young men and women who came to him. By this time as he was now back in the habit of praying daily with God, he felt compelled to take one more expedition of significance.

He wanted to gather together as many of his sons, grandsons and their offspring as were willing to join him. Noah's plan was to take them on a journey overland to the Ark, and on the way tell them his story. He wanted to have the details written on parchment for the generations to come so they would know what happened throughout his life.

Noah sent summons and invitations to his sons and to their sons and daughters by ship and land, inviting them in turn to bring as many of their families with them as they wished. He informed them that they were to take part in a life changing journey that would impact them for the rest of their lives. They were to be prepared for this to last for several weeks.

Noah made a promise to himself: *'I will also attempt to make up for how I have failed Adonai and expound to my offspring the way of righteousness and fellowship with God and what he requires of future generations. I have had a vision from Adonai that there is a man I must invite to join us. The Lord has shown me that this is the man through whom He will bring salvation to this evil world.'*

And so he did.

Passage to the Ark

Some Months Later
AM 1952

Noah had gathered as many as possible of his immediate family and their offspring together to accompany him on this, his final great journey, to visit for one last time the Ark that had brought just eight of them into this new world. They had all assembled at the port of Ty on the east coast of the Western Sea where Noah had begun his worldwide travels. After loading their supplies on their pack animals the large company left Ty the day after they were obliged to replace one of their hired men who had been so viciously wounded the previous night that he was unable to travel with the company. It was suspected that the three black cloaked strangers who volunteered to travel with them may have been responsible for this attack.

The expedition headed north from Ty with the sea to the west as instructed by Noah, camping under the stars at night wherever and whenever he decided it was a good place to stop. The first village they came to was Baalbek, four days into their journey. Here their numbers grew to forty nine when they met up with Elam and Asshur, sons of Shem and Sede. Elam, their eldest son, his brother and their families lived to the north of their route, so it was easier for Noah's group to come to them. Tubal, a son of Japheth and Ada, also joined them here. He had actually settled in the lands near the resting place of the Ark and had travelled south to meet them. Tubal himself had founded a large village which already was being called *Tubilsi,* meaning Tubal's city. Tubal and his two attendants were planning to guide the other travellers directly to the Ark once they passed the Euphrates River, because they knew the way better than anyone now that the landscape had changed considerably since Noah and the other sons had last been there.

At Baalbek they were only four days into their journey, but already Cush and his team of riders who protected the group as they travelled reported to Noah that they were becoming suspicious of the three strangers who had joined them at Ty.

"Even now at this early stage of our journey we are having problems with those strangers," said Cush gruffly.

"What's the problem?" asked Noah.

"They will only ride together in a group. They have very good horses which are so much swifter than the ones you bought in Ty. I use them as scouts, but they don't go where I want them to. They just make up their own minds about which direction they ride each day. It's always out of sight, as well, so I never know exactly where they've been. However, they find their way back to camp again each night. But they report nothing of what they've seen or tell me where they've been."

"They look after their own horses and won't put them with the other animals at night, and they won't let me anywhere near them either," commented Joktan.

"I've seen dust far in the distance to our rear and then out to the east, but still behind us," mused Noah. "I wonder if that's them or some other travellers we don't know about."

"Do you think they're meeting with other people that are following us?" asked Shem.

"Anything is possible," Cush replied. "They're simply not forthcoming with any information, so I find their whole behaviour suspicious. They keep very much to themselves, and it would be better if they left us."

"Do you need more men?" asked Asshur. "You can have one of mine if you like."

"And two of mine as well," added Tubal. "Actually, I insist on this. They're my best trackers and will be invaluable in guiding us to the Ark across all the many hills, valleys, streams and rivers in between."

"I'm very glad to accept them," answered Cush. "In fact, when we get to the high country ahead I suggest you take over my role, Tubal, because you know the country far better than I do."

"Yes, of course, I'm available to help at any time. Why don't I ride with you some days if that's acceptable to you?"

"All right. It's a good way to get to know you, cousin."

Having just discussed their suspicions a mild earth tremor shook the ground where they were standing, and it seemed to be a warning to them of trouble ahead.

Some days later the expedition reached the village of Ebla. Here the company of forty nine was reduced by one when the body of a livestock attendant was found stabbed outside the camp. He was discovered early that morning as the expedition was getting ready for the day's travel, and no one had seen or heard anything amiss during the night. This prompted Noah's sons and grandsons to gather on a hill overlooking the camp and to share their thoughts and concerns.

"It could be just another coincidence," said Noah.

"Perhaps roving bandits came across our camp in the night and one of the animal herders found himself in the wrong place," suggested Cush.

"Well, it's not going to stop us. We'll bury him here and move on," said Noah.

"Shouldn't we question those three dark-cloaked men who joined us?" asked Tubal.

"No, I don't want to alert them that we may suspect them, if it is them," Cush replied.

"Perhaps we need to simply keep our eyes and ears and wits about us," added Shem. "If this happens again we'll know then it was not a coincidence and someone is intending to harm this expedition."

"Good thoughts my sons. Yes, let's stay close together and watch out for one another. No one is to go outside the camp from now on unless they are with two others," added Noah to end the discussion.

As the men were dispersing to break camp Ada and Sede marched up the hill to Noah looking stern. He saw them approaching and let out a groan, much to the amusement of the other men who quickly walked away.

"What is it this time, my dears," Noah asked in a kindly manner before they spoke, judging from their facial expressions that they were going to complain to him yet again about something that needed to be done.

"Some of the young ones are becoming very tired as they walk. They're getting sore feet and blisters, because they're not used to long marches," a breathless Sede explained after climbing the hill.

"Yes, and one of the servant girls is with child and well on her way to having it. She says she 'did not know,'" an exasperated Ada added.

"And you want me to…?" But before Noah could reply properly Sede interrupted with, "can we use some of the pack animals that are not carrying loads to carry them, Noach?"

"Of course you can. The animals do need a rest now and again from carrying loads, but tell Tarah I said they could ride on them starting today and the days after until they get fit. You'll need to share the lifts around. Those that need to can walk some of the time and ride some, but eventually I expect them to walk all day like the rest of us. The animals need a rest too."

"I think the servant girl will need to ride some of the day every day from now on," said Ada.

"If she must. And stop fluttering your beautiful eyelashes at me both of you. I don't need to be bribed," said Noah.

With this, laughing, the women walked away to speak to Tarah.

'*I may be old Lord, but I'm still learning patience,*' Noah shared his thoughts with God.

The expedition marched on towards the east until they rested near the village of Aleppo. They were starting to move inland now, leaving the coastlands behind as they travelled to higher and more uneven ground that made the going slower. Everyone seemed happy enough on the surface and they were getting used to the long days of walking, but nevertheless there was a current of unease in the camp. Since the livestock attendant had been killed they had noticed the dust of what was probably a large band of travellers far behind them. At worst it could be a band of robbers stalking them, waiting for an opportunity to attack and rob Noah's people of their possessions.

"I should take a group and investigate," suggested Cush.

But Noah demurred. "No, that would leave us undermanned and more vulnerable. Besides, we're still on the main trade route. It may be nothing more than another group of traders, so your effort could be wasted."

Another consideration arose from an argument that had broken out between a few members of Ham's camp and a few in Shem's. An issue had come to a head at the end of the evening's gathering as they sat around drinking and conversing. Mizraim and Ludim had voiced their frustration over the way they were always the last in the expedition to depart and remained in this position throughout the day as well. They complained that Shem's camp was always first, and this meant that they were always walking in the dust of Shem and everyone else. Joktan, Peleg's brother, and some of his attendants had laughed at this and unkindly told Ham's people to get used to it because that was their lot and true station in life. Tempers had flared at this slight and much shouting and waving of arms resulted.

Shem and Ham, along with Elam and Asshur, waded into the angry group to calm things down. When it was explained what all the fuss was about Ham commented, "they have a point, Shem."

"Well, they could have brought the issue to us or Noach instead of letting it build up so much resentment between them. We can easily settle this. I think the whole thing is childish on both sides for men as advanced in years as you are," replied Shem. "Joktan, I find what you said extremely ignorant and offensive. You should apologise."

"Yes, I'm sorry for what I said. We all had drunk too much, and I guess it got away on me. I apologise."

"Accepted," replied Mizraim testily.

"Fine," said Ludim in the same tone.

"What I suggest, Ham, is that tomorrow your camp lead out followed by Japheth's and then mine. Noach always chooses his place as he will tomorrow. Each day we can change it around. Perhaps Japheth will lead out the following day."

"That seems fair and acceptable," agreed Ham.

"I think we have more to worry about from that pillar of dust following behind us than this," grumbled Tubal.

"I tend to agree," added Cush.

Shem went to Noach's tent to inform him of the arrangement they had reached, and Noah agreed to this with a wave of his hand as if the matter were a trivial one.

"Are the women happy, Shem?" he replied, as this was a more pressing concern for him.

"It would appear so. They've not made any complaints and they seem happy enough despite the rigours and discomfort they have to put up with. As you know they have suffered much worse than this."

"That they have. Our women have been wonderful. They've been a great support to us all."

"They certainly have, good night father."

The expedition travelled on to the east from Aleppo, often camping in the wilderness. The next village they reached on the banks of the river Euphrates was Karkemish. "We will stop here two days to replenish our stores and give the animals a good rest, not to mention ourselves," Noah said. "That will be long enough for the group following us to catch us up, we can then have a good look at them and determine their intentions."

Within the hour Cush and his team rode in from scouting the local area. With him were the three dark-robed strangers who had volunteered to ride with them. This time, however, they had their hands tied behind their backs and their mounts were led by Cush's men.

"What have we here Cush?" Noah shouted as Cush rode up to him.

"An interesting development, Noach. Could we please have a short rest, a drink and some food, and then I shall tell you everything you want to know." While the three were tied to their mounts and watched by others, Cush and his team sat in a circle with Noah, Ham, Shem, Japheth and almost all the senior men.

"We knew you would be stopping at Karkemish, and so it wouldn't be a long journey for us to catch up with you if we took a little detour," Cush began. "Perhaps Tubal would like to take up the story as it involves him directly."

"Cush suggested we take a closer look at the travelling band behind us," Tubal continued. "We decided to circle around them to the north and the south. Cush went north and I went south. As it turned out my group was the closest and we came upon them sooner than we expected. We hid behind a ridge before they saw us and watched them for a time as they were breaking camp."

"But what of these three that you have tied up?" Noah asked impatiently.

"Yes, sir, I was about to tell you. While we were watching these others break camp, who should we see but our three friends leaving as well and heading east to catch up with our expedition. They had disappeared overnight and had not caught up with us the previous day in keeping with their usual habit." Tubal paused and looked across the group of men before him.

"Go on," prompted Shem.

"Naturally we took off after them and followed them. Eventually they caught up with Cush and we came riding in behind them. You should have seen the guilty shock on their faces when they realised we had been following them and they couldn't escape either way. Between Cush and me we extracted their story, ah, with a little gentle persuasion."

"I don't want to hear about anything violent," growled Noah.

Cush then took up the story again, "It seems they are spies for this other group. Our suspicions have been confirmed that it is stalking us. What they refused to tell us, or perhaps what they don't know themselves as they were only recruited back at the village where we started, is why that band of misfits is following us."

"How many are there?"

"About twenty, and they are all well-armed."

"So could these three be responsible for the killings in our camp?"

"Again, we couldn't get them to confess to that, but perhaps you may like to question them."

"Bring them here," Noah ordered.

Despite some intense questioning by Noah and his sons they could get nothing further from the three strangers. Finally, frustrated by their obstinacy and in an uncharacteristic fit of anger Noah gave them three choices. He could behead all three now, make them his slaves, or they could tell him what he wanted to know. Not wishing to die or become his slaves they finally opened up. The leader of the three spoke.

"It appears those who are following you were sent by a close relative of yours, master."

"I have many relatives. Go on."

"We do not know what they intend to do to you exactly, but I'm sure it is unpleasant. They say you are searching for an ancient ship. I heard them say 'when we have done with that and them we will get our reward.' They refused to reveal anything more, but threatened us with our lives if we told you. So now we are fugitives!"

"I see, I thought it might have something to do with our journey."

There was no honour or benefit in killing the three captives. When their bodies were found this would only alert the gang pursuing Noah's group that their plans were now known. Nor were the captives useful as slaves since they would almost certainly do all they could to escape at the first opportunity. Noah therefore let them go and told them to head north to avoid meeting with the gang again. But he warned them that if they disobeyed and were seen by Noah's scouts in or near their pursuers' camp at any time in the days ahead they would be judged guilty of murder and would be immediately executed if they were again captured.

The three strangers were then released with their mounts, escorted some distance north of Karkemish and sent on their way. They were never seen again.

"It seems this group of men following us has been recruited to do us some harm. The question is, who is the close relative?" remarked Japheth.

"Yes, I wonder if they intend to damage the Ark and us in some way," mused Noah. "I wonder if ..."

But Noah cut off what he was about to say and went silent as he looked over toward Cush and Mizraim, who seemed agitated as they discussed something significant between themselves out of the hearing of the others.

"Is everything all right Cush?" asked Noah.

"Oh, ah yes, just a family issue, nothing to worry about. We'll work it out."

"The trade route we are following goes north from Karkemish on this side of the river, so if that band follows us across the Euphrates we will know they are intent on doing us harm, and that will confirm what these three have just told us," said Tubal.

Later that night after Noah's evening discourse Cush and Mizraim approached Noah. Cush spoke first, "We have something we need to tell you Noach."

"Well, by the look on your faces it's either bad or very bad. What's on your minds?"

"Well, not so bad, grandfather," Mizraim replied. "We have decided to return to our lands and families, and will not be continuing with you to the Ark. Please understand that we are not against what you are doing, Noach."

"I, we, have enjoyed your talks about the time before our father was born. But as you moved into the flood and life after that, well, our father Ham has told us about that and this new world where we, ourselves, have lived most of our lives," added Cush. "Tubal will now lead you across the Euphrates and into the high country as we already agreed."

"Our father Ham and Ludim will continue with you. I believe Ludim is interested in the construction of the Ark which he will use in building his fleet of ships. They will inform us on their return of what we don't know from your account, and you yourself have said you will provide a written history for our sons and daughters to read as well," Mizraim concluded.

"Well, my sons, I'm sad to see you leave. I have appreciated your help and company on this journey so far. But I know that your first commitment is to your families so I will bless you and send you on your way. When will you leave?"

"The day after tomorrow, grandfather."

"Then after tomorrow night's discourse I shall give you my blessing in the company of your relatives."

Well after midnight, when the camp was asleep except for the sentries, Tubal surreptitiously made his way to Noah's tent as he had asked him to. They were in quiet discussion for over an hour.

The next evening when that time came Noah blessed Cush and Mizraim:

"Cush and Mizraim, you are among the first to be born into this new world, you will be blessed, you will grow into great nations, and dynasties will come from you. You shall build cities along the great river of the Land of Ham and elsewhere. Go and fill that unlimited land, and may your children prosper."

On the third day after arriving at Karkemish Cush and Mizraim and their attendants made their way south. Shortly after leaving Noah's camp they were delayed for a short time by a certain group of travellers who happened to be following.

Noah and his party crossed the mighty Euphrates, carefully fording the now shallow river as it was the dry season, and headed northeast. Before they broke camp Noah had a quiet word with Shem, Sede, Japheth and Ada.

The mysterious band of twenty armed men followed them across the next day.

TWENTY-SIX

Peril Along the Way

A week further into their journey, on the seventh day, the expedition rested in a valley near water. The region was known as Edessa. By this stage, the way was becoming more and more rugged as they travelled higher and higher into the interior. At times rain and storms hindered them, and it was getting noticeably cooler in the evenings.

Noah stopped the group in mid-afternoon rather than the usual hour before sunset when they were alarmed by a moderate earth tremor that went on and on. Rather than continue up the valley they camped where they were to ensure their safety from any dangerous aftershocks.

"We'll camp here overnight," Noah said. "It could be dangerous to continue along this valley even though it's a short one and there's more level ground on the other side. There's too much danger from falling rocks if we go on. With a company as large as this inevitably someone will get hurt."

"That's wise, father," Japheth remarked.

"We can make up time on the flatter ground," added Tubal who knew this route better than the others.

"So what do we make of the misfits who are pursuing us?" said Shem.

"We'll have sentries posted in groups around the camp all night, as we have done since crossing the Euphrates," Tubal replied.

"Do we need to increase them? I'm beginning to feel uneasy. They just seem to be waiting for an opportune time to attack, and this valley might suit them best," Joktan suggested.

"I agree," Noah said. "Make the sentries up into groups of three and relieve them every two hours instead of four. I saw a couple of them falling asleep last night."

"It will be done," answered Tubal. "I must insist that now all the men agree to take a turn at sentry duty no matter what their position is."

"Perhaps we should do it tribe by tribe," suggested Ham. "It will make for easier communication and changeover if we do it that way."

"We are all agreed then?" asked Tubal.

Everyone gave their assent and worked out a schedule for the sentries over the next few nights. As dusk settled over the camp no one spotted the four spies on a nearby hill watching the camp intently and noting where each group settled. Later that night a full moon rose over the area, providing ample light over the rough and rocky ground for anyone who wanted to attack them.

Their mood had been somewhat lighter this particular day after Noah's discourse of the previous night. Then, with the added participation of Japheth, Ham, Shem, Sede and Ada, he had talked about the happy occasion when his three sons married their wives and added details of humorous events each couple experienced on their intimate time away immediately after their wedding ceremony. This lifted the whole expedition out of their sadness of the previous day when Noah had then delicately told of the tragic death of his much loved sister, Hebe.

Over the next two weeks Noah's expedition crossed the highlands where the daily journey became much slower. By now they had reached a high plateau known as the Amid and at this place they rested for some days on a level area surrounded by snow-capped mountains in the distance. A week earlier the camp had been spellbound as Noah, Japheth, Shem and Ham, Sede and Ada told the story of the flood waters coming on the earth and the great destruction that followed.

Here they rested again for a few days before continuing further into the high country. Since the last earth tremor there had been several more, but none of them were alarming enough to make them feel unsafe or want to abandon the journey.

The mysterious band of travellers following them kept their distance, but always stayed within a day's ride. Tubal was frustrated by their presence and asked permission to take a group of men out to confront them. Noah agreed to this, provided it was only to speak to them. Any hint of violence or confrontation was to be avoided.

Tubal accordingly took twenty six men with him and headed off straight to the place where they were last seen. They did manage to catch up to those who were following the expedition, but when they saw Tubal and his troop in the distance they turned and fled. Tubal then pursued them for two hours before discontinuing the chase and came back to camp none the wiser as to why the expedition was being followed. The posting of sentries around the camp was continued.

By now most of Noah's group had grown used to the daily march, rough going as it had become, and few grumbled and wanted to return to their home villages. Their anticipation of seeing the Ark and the enjoyment they took from Noah's nightly discourse, which by now was becoming a story everyone looked forward to, banished any dissent. Each night the travellers sat spellbound as Noah, Shem, Japheth, Ham, Sede and Ada shared about what they had experienced during the long wait for the great flood waters to subside, and their stories gave rise to many questions which made these times longer. Besides, no one now wanted to turn back for fear of running into the band of unknowns behind them, being captured by them and probably endangering their lives.

Some time later Noah's weary expedition had now reached the heart of the high country. Noting how hard it had been over the last few days Noah then declared a three day rest for everybody.

"We have actually made good time despite our setbacks. But because I made allowance for them we now find ourselves with not too far to go compared with how far we have come," Noah explained to the group at their evening gathering.

"Are you sure we are heading in the right direction?" asked Ham. "This land is unfamiliar to me."

Noah replied. "Yes, Ham, you're right. I must confess we have taken a roundabout route to the Ark, but not too far out of our way."

"You mean we didn't need to go through all these valleys and highlands?"

"I had hoped it might dissuade our friends from following us and whatever mischief they were up to. After our little disturbance at Karkemish Tubal and I had a long discussion and we decided that we should not take the more direct route. It was his idea that we should go this way in an attempt to disorient our pursuers and hopefully lose them. However, that doesn't appear to have worked. The direct route would also have most likely brought us into contact with other traders and travellers we thought we would be better off to avoid. We would still have had many hills and valleys to encounter whatever route we chose."

"Well, I hope you know what you're doing and that it makes all this extra travel worthwhile. Why weren't we informed?" Ham grumbled.

"I wanted to avoid arguments and delays due to a prolonged discussion on which way to go. We did agree to let Tubal take us by the best route, because he knows this country better than any of us. So for the sake of expediency we, I, made a decision to go this way."

"It may be of interest to you all, not that it affects our journey very much, but you may have heard of the great volcano that is erupting north of here?" Tubal said, changing the subject to divert the conversation.

"It's been active for many decades, growing larger and grander as the years go by. Almost every year there is a major eruption which adds more height to it and alters the surrounding country. People stay well away from it. The reason I mention it is that people are already calling it Mount Ararat, perhaps in memory of the Ark, or perhaps because now it is the highest mountain in this eastern high country region we call Ararat. But it wasn't always so."

"Ah, that would be a problem in generations to come, would it not?" suggested Shem "I mean, if that name becomes permanent then future generations will think that's where the Ark landed."

"That's quite possible, Shem," Noah said. "I named the region where we came to rest 'The highlands or mountains of Ararat', because the tops of the ridges where we came to rest extended over a large area. As the flood receded and formed valleys and highlands there were many high places and mountains to be seen. I didn't name them all individually. Now other people are confusing that name I gave with only one mountain rather than the area where the Ark lies. But perhaps that's a good thing since the Ark is in a remote place and well preserved I hope."

"I'm still bothered by this band of misfits following us though," grumbled Japheth. "Shouldn't we confront them once and for all? There are many of us, and we could surprise them by invading their camp at night or very early morning?"

"I'm not a fighting man," stated Tarah.

"Nor I," added Gomer.

"Well, not all of us are. Some will need to stay in camp," Japheth said.

"Yes, Japheth. It has been on my mind, and I'm sure many of you have thought the same," Noah replied. "I think the next place we rest would be the right one for this. After all, it will be our last major camp before we make our final journey to the Ark. We are about to cross the upper Tigris, then we will be close to the place where the Ark rests and will make a semi-permanent camp. That's where we'll stay for a month or so and from there we can make several visits to the Ark. We are nearly there!"

Noah's caravan crossed the Tigris at a narrow part of the river without incident and they were now encamped in a pleasant valley near a supply of fresh water, feed for the animals and wild fruit trees laden with a ripe crop. This was a bonus in what was otherwise an unproductive land. It was a fertile area and had the promise that, in time, a village might be established there and enjoy the produce of the surrounding valley.

"It's a good place to camp, father," Shem said.

"Yes, Shem. We have water and the surrounding land can provide for us for the time we spend here. There's game to be had here as well."

"Is this it? I don't remember this area at all," queried Ham.

"Of course it is. We may not have travelled down this particular valley Ham, but don't you recognise that high peak in the distance?"

"Ah yes Japheth, now that you point it out, it does seem familiar."

"As I said, we'll camp here a while. Rest now, and perhaps we'll make our first journey to the Ark in a few days," Noah said.

"I want to go tomorrow."

"You would, Japheth. I expect nothing less from you. But no, we will rest the animals not to mention all our weary travellers. The climb up to the Ark is steep from here and we need everyone to be fit again to enjoy the journey."

"And our friends? When will we pay them a visit?" asked Japheth.

"Again, Japheth, we must make sure their intentions are other than peaceful before we confront them. They may simply be following us to the Ark for their own purposes. We will avoid any confrontation until after our first visit to the Ark." Noah was firm on that account.

Here the expedition set up sturdy living quarters to withstand the occasional high winds and earth tremors, and provided fenced areas for the animals using materials from the surrounding locality. Gomer did an exceptional job of supervising the construction of the camp by all the able bodied members of the expedition, and Noah commended him for his efforts.

Late on the afternoon of the day following their arrival all members of the camp saw an alarming sight far to the north east. Everyone wondered what it could be and decided it was probably a dust or sand storm such as were frequent in other parts of the known world.

Joktan, Tarah and others quickly herded the livestock towards some nearby caves to protect them. Others stood, watching the dark mass of cloud coming towards them, totally unaware of the danger it posed. As it got closer it became apparent that it was nothing like anything they had ever seen before. Toward dusk it was almost upon them, and at that point they suddenly realised the danger they were in.

"It's ash from a volcanic eruption! The mountain to the north has erupted and is spewing its ash and debris toward us. Everyone into the caves, quickly!" shouted Tubal.

Tubal, because he lived closest to this area and was familiar with the land, its vagaries and dangers, had been their guide since crossing the Euphrates, so he was the first to recognise what was happening to them.

"We must hurry before it's upon us, otherwise we may choke to death!"

No one argued as they followed the animals, and soon everyone was sheltered in the now crowded caves. These were not extensive, but did give enough shelter to the entire group so long as they stood or sat closely together. They realised they could not possibly survive in such a cramped state for any great length of time, as they had no food and little water with them in the rush to get to safety. They wondered how long the eruption would last, and Tubal could not reassure them about this. "Sometimes the volcano erupts for days on end, while other times it's for just a few hours," he told them.

The ash fall lasted the rest of the evening and into the night. It was strangely quiet, for there was no strong wind or storm, simply a faint smell of sulphur and the falling ash which floated lightly down much like snow. As they were a great distance from the mountain they heard the explosive thunder only faintly and were not alarmed by it, but what dust and ash did penetrate the caves made life rather uncomfortable. Thus the large group of travellers spent a cramped and unhappy night, hungry and thirsty, wondering what was happening outside and if they would be able to survive this event when they were so close to their goal.

TWENTY-SEVEN

The Reason I Brought You Here

When dawn came they saw that the eruption had ceased some time during the night and there was now a relative calm. It was cold, much colder than before the eruption, and this they realised was due to a haze that covered the sky, blotting out the sun's warmth.

The ground was covered with a fine layer of ash up to their ankles in most places, but in others it was almost half a cubit deep. The tents and dwellings were all standing, but were covered in a pale grey ash. Its removal took the group the rest of the day to make the campsite liveable again, and during this time the few women and their servants got cooking fires going and watered both people and animals.

"This will make the journey to the Ark much harder, won't it, Tubal?" asked Japheth.

"I'm afraid so. Three things are likely now. If a wind gets up it will blow this ash around like a dust storm and make walking or riding through it impossible. If it rains now, the dust will turn into a quagmire of slush. Even if nothing like either of these happens it will still be hard going, like walking through fresh snow, and many of you haven't experienced that," Tubal explained.

"We'll just have to do the best we can with whatever is presented to us," Noah grumbled. "We've come all this way and are only a few hours march from our destination, although it's steep country from here on. Turning back or giving up now is not even an option. We will press on, hopefully, tomorrow I think, as waiting any longer we may face another eruption."

"I don't think we should take the whole camp to the Ark, father. It would be too hazardous with that many people after this ash fall."

"You're quite right, Shem. We'll take a smaller group and create a pathway through the ash for the others to follow. We'll camp at the Ark, and they can join us the following day."

"That's a good idea, grandfather. Perhaps I can lead the second group. I can follow your tracks," suggested Joktan.

"Yes, Joktan. I'm happy for you to do that. But I'll send Japheth back to meet you so that you don't get lost. There are a few valleys between here and the Ark, and you may very well take a wrong track if the pathway we make becomes obliterated for any reason."

"I'll stay with the camp, because there are a few things that need repairing after the ash. I'll come with Joktan's group," said Gomer.

"That's all good. You must each decide what to do, but I'd like Ham, Shem and Japheth along with Sede and Ada to join me in the first group."

"I haven't been feeling very well, Noach, and after our experience of last night I feel even worse. I'd prefer to stay here another day and come in the second group if I feel well enough, but I insist Shem go with you." Replied Sede.

"What of our friends following us?" asked Japheth.

"They will have been affected by the ash as well. I imagine their intentions have been dampened somewhat, so I don't think they'll bother us for a while," said Noah, scratching his chin and beard contemplatively.

Unfortunately for Noah, his assessment of the situation was not correct. Having sheltered in a valley close by in larger caves than Noah's group, their pursuers were far more rested. Even now three of their number were observing the activities of the camp from a concealed location high in the rocks across the nearby stream.

"Tonight," said Noah, "We'll gather together once again. I'm not sure why I'm saying this, but it could be the last time we're all together. Since we will go our various ways after visiting the Ark it may be the last time I have the opportunity of speaking to you as a group. I have some things left unsaid that now need to be spoken. We will gather as we usually do after supper."

Noah sat on a log facing the travellers who had accompanied him on this expedition to the Ark. The sun had finally set on their campsite. He looked at each of his family and companions, pausing momentarily on each face as he often did before he started on the evening's discourse. A waning moon rising over their gathering provided a soft light and made the evening that much more pleasant. It was as if the moon itself was fading away in the same way their journey was coming to an end. If it was to be their last gathering together this was very appropriate.

"I have told you many things over the last several weeks," said Noah. "I hope you have found what I said interesting and stimulating and trust you will not forget this journey. Tomorrow some of us will go to the site of the Ark and the rest of you will follow the next day.

"The reason I brought you here on this journey was not just to view the Ark and be assured that what we experienced really did happen. Tonight I want to explain the reason this had to be.

"In the beginning Adonai, God our Creator, prepared a perfect world and gave it to us. No doubt he was looking forward to sitting back and enjoying, observing and communicating with his faultless creation. There was no death, sickness, anger, jealousy, theft or murder, and all the other corrupt things we have inherited. An unspoiled world was his plan, and so it should be even now and in the future. But it was not to be.

"Our dear ancestors Adam and Hevah were in fact the only humans to enjoy this paradise on earth. They walked and talked with Adonai every day for just a short time, or perhaps even several years, we simply don't know how long. They enjoyed all its beauty and perfection until they met with a challenge, which God allowed to test their commitment and love of him. Sadly they failed this test. Disobedience to God and self-will overcame their perfect relationship with him, and through this, sin entered the world when they succumbed to the deceptions of Lucifer, the beautiful fallen angel, who had become Satan and the devil on earth.

"Adam and Hevah were expelled from the Garden of Eden, and no one could ever go back there. Eventually, they had two sons, Abel and Cain. All was well as the boys grew to manhood. In due course the sin that had come upon the beautiful earth reared its ugly head in the form of murder. Oh, no doubt anger, jealousy, temper tantrums and a score of sins that we are all guilty of had been apparent many times already, but this act which brought death to Abel has remained as the clearest evidence of Adam and Hevah's disobedience. Cain murdered his brother Abel essentially over nothing more than envy.

"Cain was banished from his parents' presence, but not completely, because he took one of his sisters as a wife and moved to the land of Nod. Adam and Hevah called the land they now lived in Shulon, as I told you earlier in our journey, and had many more sons and daughters, one of whom was Seth, our ancestor. As you all know, many generations passed and many more people were born into the world. Even though sin was at work corrupting a fading paradise, it was still a beautiful place, even more so than this world we now live in. I can bear witness to that. Eventually a man named Enoch was born, who grew to become perhaps the closest man to God since Adam walked with Adonai. But Enoch did not live to a grand old age like the rest of us. One day he was there and the next he was gone."

"How is it that Enoch was just taken?" Tarah asked, with others in the camp circle murmuring their interest as well.

"Ah, that's a good story. I wasn't there. It happened before I was born, and so I heard it this way from my grandfather Methuselah and my father Lamech.

"On their rest days our family gathered with others in their local village as a group, just like we're doing here tonight. Jared and Baraka, Enoch's parents, along with my grandparents and Lamech my father and Betenos my mother, with other members of the family including their children would listen to Enoch telling them what God had laid on his heart.

"One evening they were together as usual, had just had supper and were waiting expectantly for Enoch to speak. He usually sat while he did this, but this time he stood up and both my father and grandfather said he just kept going – up! A light descended and surrounded him, nothing very dramatic. My father thought for a moment the moon had merely shone through a crack in the roof, but Enoch simply ascended, disappeared, and was seen no more. They all rushed outside to look for him, but he was gone! No more Enoch, and they never saw him again. They could only say that Adonai had taken him.

"At that time it was obvious Enoch was chosen by God. He was not afraid to speak out and proclaim God's truth. It was he who first started writing things down, to use characters for writing and conserving knowledge. He preserved all this on parchment, animal skins and even stone. He was the God-appointed spiritual leader of our community and perhaps the only holy prophet of God in the world by this time. He simply spoke the word of God and they all knew it was from Adonai, because it was powerful yet loving, intelligent and simply truthful and accurate. They would often sit together and call upon the Lord, praying for the salvation of the earth, to somehow restore it to the paradise it was at the beginning. That all disappeared and was lost when Adam and Hevah ignored or disobeyed the Creator's one simple rule.

Don't touch or eat of the fruit of THAT tree.

"Sadly they did, and now we and all human beings will live with the consequences of that one act of defiance. This is an important truth. It was not the forbidden fruit they ate so much as it was the fact they disobeyed Adonai, and we have been disobeying him ever since. The Creator gave them a choice, gives all of us a choice, but they failed! Sadly, we continue to do so, yet one day …?"

"Where is this going father?" growled Ham.

Ignoring him, Noah continued. "Which is the very reason I sent for you to accompany me on this journey, so that I could tell you this truth before I am taken from this world. I want all of you to know what happened in the past from the beginning and why God allowed the great flood to destroy the world as it then was.

"When eventually Satan's fallen angels manifested themselves in human form and mated with the women of the world they gave birth to creatures that were no longer human but corrupted. Their makeup was no longer what Adonai had created them to be. When there was also a rise in violence toward one another, with murder, rape, theft, tribal wars, and simply because mankind now had virtually no concept of God, Adonai was grieved he had made us and the solution to all this was to destroy mankind, as we have shared with you in great detail.

"Unfortunately, we are still born into sin through the fall of Adam and Hevah and will continue to do so. Although Adonai destroyed the corrupted people of the earth in the flood the seed of sin has continued with us. None of us are inherently good, we are all tainted with sin. We cannot help it. We don't necessarily desire it or seek it, we are simply born with it. We are what we are.

"I believe a redeemer is coming to save the world from its corruption. One day there will be a saviour, someone who will take this world back for God, and Satan will no longer be its prince. Adonai cannot risk human beings being corrupted with the seed of fallen angels. His saviour will have to be a pure human being. Whether you believe this or not, it's a truth from Adonai that cannot be argued against. You may try, but God will have the final say.

This is the reason for the flood, for the Ark and all that has happened. It is the responsibility of our family to see that Adonai's covenant is preserved. This was given to us when we left the Ark. But nevertheless, evil has prevailed once again in this new world.

"It is my prayer, I ask you, I beseech you, that you follow righteousness, truth and justice, putting aside anger and hatred, for this will eventually be the death of you, of all human beings. These are hard words and I know not all of you can accept them, but some of you will. The world's future depends on those of you who do.

"Yes, there is a spiritual world unseen by us, but all around us and in God's heaven are good angels as well as the fallen ones who have a great influence on the minds and souls of men and women. Adonai is all-powerful, all-knowing, and everywhere present, yet he allows Satan to have some influence over you, but only if you let him. Adonai does this not to permanently hurt or torment you, but to make you stronger so that you may have a closer walk with him by resisting Satan's attacks. My family, this is what I want to impart to you. You must worship Adonai only, not the sun or moon, or idols, or other gods, they have no life in them!"

At this point there was a low murmuring from Ham, Ludim and others, while many sat in awe, soaking up everything Noah said. Tarah, however, was now feeling rather uncomfortable and wondering if in fact he wanted to stay to the end of the expedition, because the words this great man was speaking were the very things he and his father were guilty of. '*But I must not feel guilty. We are entitled to decide for ourselves what we believe in. Surely Noah's God would not condemn us for seeking out and honouring his own creation like the sun and moon?*' Tarah thought to himself.

"Do not think that Adonai will forgive you or take you to his heaven if you worship these things," Noah continued. "Yes, he created the sun and moon and the clay that you make idols from, but they are lifeless objects and do not have life in them as we know it. Adonai is a jealous God, but also a loving one, who wants only the very best for all of you. You must not worship these things. He cannot help you if you do."

Feeling very uncomfortable and glad it was dark so that no one would see him reddening in embarrassment, Tarah almost gasped out loud when Noah spoke those words. *'Can this man read my thoughts?'* he exclaimed silently.

"Adonai desires a people set apart to be holy before him. Be holy as God is holy, the opposite of sinful – God's holiness is so magnificent it is indescribable – angels praise his holiness eternally. He wants you to have fellowship with him and he makes it easy for you to come to him and pray, not to wait for him to come to you, for you can come to him. If you reject him he will not push you away. You are the ones who are walking away from him. You are all Adonai's children and he wants so much to commune with you as he did with Adam before he disobeyed him."

Ham interrupted Noah, saying, "you are telling us that images men created from the talents your God gave them, as well as the sun and moon which he also created do not speak to us, yet this God of yours doesn't speak to us either!"

"Oh, Ham, my son, if only you would tear down that barrier of unbelief that keeps you from Adonai! He does speak in many different ways to those who seek him and fear him, who respect, obey and worship him. You, yourself, have heard him speak. You cannot deny that.

"If you are feeling uncomfortable, or even guilty now," continued Noah, "it is not my words but Adonai's Spirit that is speaking to you. Listen to him, change your attitude and turn back to him."

Tarah groaned within himself, desperate to get away or for Noah to finish, but he knew that was not likely to happen. Yet something within himself was touched by the words his ancestor was speaking.

"Enough of my preaching for tonight," said Noah. "I have spoken to you as a priest of God. Whether you accept him or not he is still the life source of the universe. Enoch had the authority of high priest of Adonai while he lived, then Methuselah took over this role once Enoch left. Methuselah soon passed it on to my father Lamech whom he believed was closer to God, and my father in turn passed that authority to me just before he died. I now have the honour of being a 'priest' to whoever will listen to me and follow Adonai. It has been a hard road and responsibility for me to carry all these years, and I must admit I have not always been as totally obedient to it as I should have. This journey we have undertaken is an endeavour to make amends for the times I have fallen short. Very soon I will pass my task on to someone else."

"Who will that be?" asked Gomer.

"I will reveal that soon, my son, very soon."

TWENTY-EIGHT

The Ark

Early the next morning Noah, his sons Japheth, Shem and Ham along with Ada, Arpachshad, Asshur, Eber, Peleg, Tubal, Ludim, Ashchenaz, Tarah and seven other young men made their way from the camp into the foothills close by and were soon lost to sight by those who remained. Apart from Ada no other women accompanied them, as they deemed it safer for them to follow with the larger group the next day. Sede kissed and hugged Shem, and those staying behind waved farewell.

'That was an unusual thing to do,' Tarah thought, because they would all see one another again the next day.

Noah, his sons, Ada and two others rode horses while the rest walked alongside them, taking care over the ash covered ground. They also led a few donkeys laden with tents and their related equipment, food, and the water they needed for a short-stay camp at the Ark. It was hazardous going over the grey-white ash from the eruption which masked many unseen rocks and hollows. While the ash lay thick in a lot of places, in others it barely covered the ground. Here and there larger rocks broke the monotony of the ash covered countryside.

Although the final leg of the journey to the Ark was not long, there were some rather steep sections with several ridges and valleys to cross. This made for slow going, but eventually about midday the weary travellers beheld a wonderful sight.

"Oh, how beautiful! There she is!" exclaimed Ada as they stood on the last ridge and saw the Ark towering above them from the next ridge just a short distance away.

The group stood still to view the magnificent spectacle. The fourteen men who had never seen the Ark gasped in awe, and a babble of excited chatter broke out as they all gave vent to their emotions.

Tubal, the only member of the group to have previously seen the Ark, although he had not been one of its crew exclaimed, "It looks like a ghost ship covered in ash! It's so stark and grey."

"It's huge, even larger than I imagined," said an awestruck Eber.

"Let's make our way to her, but be careful," warned Noah. "There are timbers lying about that we left on our last visit here and other unseen items we could trip over."

As they came closer it was obvious that several earlier eruptions had penetrated the Ark's interior and partly covered up the entrance that had been left open. The side facing the erupting mountain had ash and debris up almost to the level of the second deck, while a few creepers and tangled vegetation attempted to grow over it, in this highland, where not many plants grew. Holes in her sides from where Noah had taken planks only added to the Ark's sorry state. Once she had been magnificent, but now it was clear she was steadily deteriorating.

"The top deck appears to have caved in here and there," Japheth observed.

"Yes, and much of the interior has rocks, mud and ash which must have come from earlier eruptions," added Ham.

"None of this damage was evident the last time I was here," said Tubal. "So all of it has occurred over the last five years."

Despite the damage to the structure of the Ark and the ash and earth which now covered it inside and out, there was still much for the group to explore. Although most of the animal pens and other fittings had been used by Noah and his family to construct their homestead and various other buildings in the first few years of the new world, there was still plenty left for the younger men to explore, laughing with the pleasure it gave them. All the furniture and fittings from these living areas had long since been removed. Thus the once great Ark was now mostly an empty shell compared to the grand vessel she had once been.

"She served us well," lamented Noah.

"It's sad to see how she has deteriorated, but I suppose we expected that when we abandoned her," Ada remarked sadly.

"It was certainly well constructed, grandfather. I can see now why its construction took you so long, just as you told us," said Peleg.

"I don't think we could ever build anything quite like this again," opined Ludim.

"Well, my nephew, we'll never need to," laughed Shem.

"From what we can see, it's obvious to me that over time the whole structure, magnificent as it is, will eventually be covered in material from that erupting mountain," observed Ashchenaz.

"I have to confess," said Tarah, "from the stories I heard as a child and from others before I met you, Noach, and even while you were telling us your story, I doubted that this was even real. But today I've seen it with my own eyes. It's far greater than I imagined, and I now see that all those birds and animals could have easily been housed in here. It's a magnificent achievement and I'm immensely impressed. Above all, I believe you now, Noach."

"Thank you, my son, I knew you would be. This is why I brought all of you here. With all the unbelief in the world today I knew that once you saw this you would believe and know that what we said happened, really did happen."

They then set up a small camp with the tents. This was done inside the Ark just in case there was another eruption, and this would provide them with more protection from it. The winds at the top of the ridge where the Ark sat were quite strong and chilling, as in recent years each season was becoming cooler than the last. Sheltering inside the Ark simply made their campsite more comfortable.

"Father, Japheth and I have found the old altar on which you made that first sacrifice but some of its stones are missing. Do you still wish to use it again as you said you might?" queried Shem.

"I do, and for some reason I have a strong inclination to do that right now today, and not wait for the rest of the expedition tomorrow. Perhaps we can make another offering once they get here tomorrow, but I want to do this today at sunset."

"What are you offering father?" asked Ham.

"The young goat we brought," he replied.

Ham swore. "I thought we were going to have a fine roast from that goat tonight!"

"It's a shame the animals have to be sacrificed. Sede disagrees and tries to tell me otherwise, but you must do what you must do," Ada murmured sadly.

"But you understand why, don't you Ada?" said Shem softly. "It's an offering to Adonai. He has given us so much, even our very lives, so it's only a small token compared to all we've received from him."

"I could accept the sacrifice more if we could eat it as well," said Ham cynically.

"Well, the goat could very well have been killed and eaten anyway, but as a sacrifice it must be consumed on the altar completely," added Shem.

"Take some of the abandoned timber and shavings that lie around inside, plus any you can find outside, and prepare the altar ready for firing. I will make the sacrifice," directed Noah.

Then, once the stone altar was repaired and the men had added wood on top Noah slew the goat and laid the body on the altar. The fire was lit and the sacrifice was consumed in the flames. Noah then prayed a lengthy prayer aloud to God as the sun began to set in the west, with the nineteen other members of the group standing around him respectfully.

The evening that followed was an enjoyable time for everyone. A few more Ark stories were shared over their meal and then they retired for the night. It was a special evening for Japheth and Ada, who sought out the personal space they had occupied during the flood and slept there that night in privacy with their memories.

The morning dawned bright and clear. The wind had dropped and it was quite a pleasant sunny day. At mid-morning as arranged Japheth, Peleg and Tubal set off to meet the remainder of the expedition who were to join them by midday. Meanwhile the rest of the group walked around the site looking for souvenirs and items of interest. Some carved their names in the planks and ribs of the Ark.

In the middle of the afternoon Noah and his party began to feel uneasy when the rest of the expedition had not arrived and started to wonder if something had gone wrong for them.

"They may have left late in the day because they had a lot more people to get organised," Shem suggested.

"No, father, I feel something is amiss," replied Arpachshad. "They didn't need to pack up all the tents, as there is still plenty of room inside the Ark if they wished to stay overnight. They were to be here by midday. Something's wrong. I'll take a few men and meet up with them, perhaps …"

"There's a rider coming!" yelled Tarah. "He appears to be taking no thought of the ground under him, as he's riding so fast. I fear he brings bad news!"

The rider, Joktan's son Jerah from the main camp, galloped up to them. "I followed your tracks; I got lost but found them again," he gasped in obvious urgency.

"What is it lad, is there trouble?" shouted Noah.

"Y.., Yes, the camp is being attacked! I wanted to stay and help defend it but my father, Joktan, ordered me to ride and tell you. So I set off and after about half an hour Japheth found me. He rushed off to the camp, ordering me to ride and inform you, but I got lost as I said and then I …."

"How long ago did they attack?" demanded Shem.

"About five hours ago or more."

"The others, are they ..?" Shem got no further.

"There were dozens of them attacking. We stood no chance. I'm sorry, I think they're all dead."

"We must go …" Noah began to order their departure.

"No, father," said Shem. "You're too old to hurry or fight. Ham and I will go with Asshur and Ludim, along with Jerah here on the remaining horses. You stay with Ada and the rest. We'll send for you when we know it's safe."

"Shem, I need to come. There'll be wounded!" Ada insisted.

"I'll stay, take my horse," offered Ludim.

"Go quickly my sons and daughter."

As they rode off Arpachshad looked at Noah, reading his mind he whispered, "We're not going to wait, are we grandfather?"

"No, Arpachshad, we'll give them a few minutes because they're faster than us. They'll quickly get ahead and then we'll follow on foot."

As he stood looking back at the wonderful vessel he had built, most probably for the last time, a tear came to Noah's eye, for he remembered so many things from the past and the people who had died along the way, never able to accompany him into the new world. But he was also thinking of the desperate situation he was about to face. Noah then turned and walked along the ridge, not looking back, as the others followed him.

TWENTY-NINE

Canaan

The Previous Day

Canaan gazed down on the camp from his hidden perch among the rocks on the cliff face that overlooked the stream and Noah's camp beyond. He then spoke quietly to his three sons, Sidon, Heth and Amor. "Ah, it seems like they're splitting up. Yes, twenty of them are heading for those hills. Good. Now it will be easier to attack the camp. We'll do that when Nimrod's men arrive. It shouldn't be long now. I'd like to attack at sunset."

"Are you sure we have enough men, father? What if they're well armed and experienced fighters? They know we're here," cautioned Heth.

"Ha! They have very few weapons and they're not fighting men. Besides, my brother Cush told us that when he met with us after he left them, on his way back to his homeland."

"Yes, but he also warned you, pleaded with you, not to do this thing, since many of them are good people," Amor said.

"Are you scared now? Don't you want to fight? Remember, we came here for a purpose. If we do this Nimrod will make me a governor of our lands, and then I'll have complete control over Shem and his people. We're going to attack them and I want no more arguments."

"How will we attack them, then, father?" asked Sidon.

"I can stand on that rock jutting out over the stream and direct the attack from there."

"How will you do that?" demanded Amor.

"By shouting," Canaan replied.

"Yes, I suppose you're getting too old for fighting," added Heth. "Best leave it to us."

"Watch your mouth, you upstart! I know what I'm doing. Now, each of you take five men. Sidon, you cross the stream down there, Amor further upstream there, and Heth, for your impudence, you can take the centre which is the most dangerous spot if they are armed, though I doubt they are. All of you will then attack on my signal. Nimrod's men will probably do the same on horseback from the south, so just watch you don't get under their hooves Sidon."

But Nimrod's men did not arrive that day.

Shortly after Noah and the rest of his party of twenty left, Gomer thought he saw movement in the rocks across the stream from the camp.

"What did you see?" asked Joktan.

"I'm not sure, some movement I think. It may have been a wild goat but – no, wait, look, did you see that?"

"Yes, you're right. There are men up there spying on us. It must surely be the group who've been following us for so long. Now that we've split up we're more vulnerable if their intentions aren't friendly," said Joktan.

"I very much doubt that they're friendly. Otherwise, why don't they come and talk to us instead of spying on us."

"We need to warn the others in the camp to be on the lookout for trouble. Gather what weapons we have, make sure every man has one, and get the women away to safety. They could attack at any time, now or perhaps at sunset. Then again, they might wait until dawn tomorrow. No matter when, we must be vigilant at all times."

With that the camp began to set up defences against a possible attack, not openly, but making sure their weapons were ready at hand. The men encouraged the women to move into the caves for safety, but Sede refused to go and insisted on cooking their midday and evening meals with the help of her assistants. "No band of brigands is going to upset my day," she said. "I've seen and survived too many dangers to be bothered about a few spies across the stream."

Joktan organised the older men, interspersing them around the camp with numbers of younger men, who were ostensibly in working or conversation groups, but actually preparing for any eventuality. Joktan encouraged them to discreetly make spears from the branches of nearby trees, especially those with straight hard wooden stems and any thin hardwood growing by the stream. Joktan was well skilled with bow and arrow, and so he and a couple of others made arrows for all their bows, as well as slings for throwing stones collected from the stream. Others, including the women, placed concealed impediments near the mouth of the main cave so they could quickly erect a barrier as a means of defending themselves. If they were attacked, this was their defensive plan.

But no attack came that day.

Nimrod's band of twenty five heavily armed men, helmeted and clothed in thick leather for protection, arrived outside Canaan's camp at midnight. A troop trained and focused on killing, they made contact with the two sentries that Canaan had posted south of his camp. Canaan and his three sons then came to talk with them.

"Nimrod has ordered me to assist you in destroying the Ark as well as killing as many of Shem's offspring that we can. He said we are to spare Ham and Japheth and their families, but how do we know who is who?" asked Akkad, Nimrod's son and leader of the band.

"I know them and I will direct you," Canaan replied.

"My friend, when my men's bloodlust is aroused and they start killing, they will just go on and on. They aren't going to stand around like fools politely asking each person whose family they belong to, and then killing them or waiting for you to tell them what to do. They just kill. Wake up man!"

"Ah well, collateral damage can't be helped, just don't kill Ham. We believe the three of them Ham, Shem and Japheth went off with Noach this morning, so it's mainly Shem and Japheth's people who're here. Ham only had Ludim and one or two others accompany him from his family on this journey from what we could see, and Ludim went with Ham as well. Their servants or workers don't matter. So kill them all I say."

"At dawn?"

"Yes, at dawn. I'll stand on a rock jutting over the river, which you will see clearly at daylight. When I blow my horn we will attack from that side of the stream and you can attack on horseback from here."

Spitting what he had been chewing onto the ground Akkad replied, "we look forward to it."

Overnight most of the people in Noah's camp slept in the main cave, but Sede, who refused to be intimidated, slept in the large central tent along with Elam, Gomer and two of the servant girls. Joktan had set a rotating watch of four pairs of men discreetly about the camp, relieving them with replacements every two hours.

The next morning when the sun was still well below the horizon but brightening the sky, Akkad's men were roused and readied themselves for the fight ahead. The same happened in Canaan's camp as well, although Canaan himself had slept in and his son Heth had to come and give him an aggressive kick to wake him up. Realising he had no time to eat anything, and that he had lost his men's respect for oversleeping from the stares they gave him, Canaan made his way quickly to the jutting outcrop and his men got themselves into position to attack.

Canaan looked down at the camp which appeared peaceful and quiet with no visible movement. Thinking to himself that it would be an easy victory, since they would catch the camp unawares and it was therefore unlikely they would lose any men themselves, he blew his ram's horn.

Amor and his men immediately moved out of their concealment and started to wade across the stream. Sidon and his men did the same, but Heth waited a few minutes, since he had the shortest distance to cover. By doing so he expected all three groups of men would be in the camp at the same time.

Akkad with a shout headed his men on horseback toward the camp. As they were travelling faster than the men crossing the stream they were the first to attack the campsite, yelling their battle cry, which gave Joktan and his defensive team a few moments' warning, as well as the camp's sentries who saw Canaan's men advancing from one direction and the troop coming down on them from another..

"Horsemen! We didn't know about them!" Gomer shouted across to Joktan.

"We'll take care of them, you look after those coming across the stream. I'm sending ten men to help you."

Joktan called to his son Jerah, "take one of the horses, follow Noach's tracks and tell them we're under attack. Go as fast as you can!"

"But father, I want to help fight …"

"GO, now!"

Gomer got ready to defend the camp with spears, swords and knives against the first of the attackers to reach them from across the stream. His defenders also had a few slings. This was to protect Sede and the women who were now realising their danger and making for the cave. Gomer's men were already using their slings to hurl stones which briefly slowed the advance of Canaan's men. But then they rallied and came running full tilt at the defenders.

Akkad's troop of horsemen was also bearing down on the camp

and had already despatched the two southern sentries simply by chopping down on their necks and virtually severing their heads. The sentries stood no chance and died before their bodies hit the ground.

Sede was hurrying her women attendants along, not running ahead of them to save herself, but making sure they were all getting to safety. Elam was with her to protect his mother, and as a rider came at them with a spear ready to strike them he stood his ground hoping to stop him with his own spear before he reached them. But the attacker threw his spear first and Elam was slow to react. Sadly, when Sede pushed him hard out of the way the attacker's spear caught her full in the chest. She gasped, collapsed and fell to the earth.

Elam, infuriated beyond measure, screamed after the horseman as he tried to ride away, threw his own spear at him and by chance, for Elam had never thrown a spear in battle before, struck his enemy in his lower back. The spear exited through his stomach with blood and entrails disgorging over his horse's mane. He fell off the horse, his foot caught in its stirrup, and was dragged through the camp screaming before he died.

"Back! Get back here to the cave!" yelled Joktan.

Gomer and his group of men ran toward the safety of the cave, but being the eldest of all of them was slower and Heth caught up with him, stabbing him in his left side. Gomer tripped and fell and lay still. Canaan's men came on, yelling and thirsting now for blood, seeing they had an advantage. Elam, realising there was nothing he could do for his mother except save himself, ran to the shelter of the barricades, took up a sling and stones and proceeded to inflict as much damage on the camp invaders as he could, enraged and filled with a boldness unlike his usual mild self.

Meanwhile Canaan watched the battle from his rock, not moving to join the fight.

One of Sede's women made it to the safety of the cave and its barricade, but another was struck down just as she got there. Joktan despatched her assailant with an arrow through his throat. He then killed two other horsemen with accurate shots, while the men around him threw spears and used slingshots with sharp stones. Many of the attackers were now on the ground wounded and dying. The intensity of Joktan's defence had destroyed the momentum of Akkad's attack, and Canaan's men were beaten back from the camp by a shower of spears, arrows and stones.

Four more of Akkad's men were wounded and retreated, one falling off his horse, rolling twice on the ground and then lying still. The same fate befell Canaan's men, several of whom ran off or limped away wounded. Three of them were left lying motionless on the ground.

The defenders did not get off lightly either. Two of the men behind the barrier fell to arrows and then Joktan was struck twice as well. He kept rallying the men and shouting orders, but eventually collapsed from loss of blood. Madai, a son of Japheth, then took charge. They fought off Canaan's men bravely and struck another one down as he limped away. Suddenly there was a horn blast, but this time it was from Akkad, and the attackers retreated to the edge of the camp out of range of the defenders' arrows. During this cessation of hostilities Madai ordered several men to bring Gomer and two other wounded men back behind the barrier.

Canaan had now finally crossed the stream and was involved in an angry exchange with Akkad at the southern end of Noah's camp.

"You fool, you incompetent idiot!" Akkad was red faced with rage. "This was supposed to be an easy kill. A walkover. My orders from my father Nimrod were very precise. I was to assist you but in no circumstances was I to lose any men. If only a few of them had been wounded this might have been acceptable, but I've now lost five men dead and even more are wounded."

"I was told they had no weapons," pleaded Canaan.

"They probably did have only a few days ago, but today they had an armoury! They knew you were coming, and they were prepared."

"I don't know how, I …"

"Bah! You probably gave yourselves away. You've had weeks to assess their strength. You could have raided them and taken their bows and spears, but no doubt you were enjoying your campfires and the taste of the meat you killed, while getting drunk on the ale you carried. We're finished here. You can complete the job yourself if you want to, but Nimrod will hear of this for certain. He's a hard man and will punish me severely. As for you, you can forget any payment or reward he offered you."

Before Canaan could argue further Akkad turned his mount around, rallied his men to put their dead and wounded on horses and left the camp, never to return.

"He's right, father," an exasperated Heth voiced his anger. "We should have attacked them earlier and we gave away our position in the rocks because of our carelessness. Then, when we came to fight you stood up there like a sentinel preserving your skin while your sons and men died for you."

"Oh, shut your mouth Heth, you're always complaining. What do you mean my son's dying, where's Amor?"

"Lying over there by the barricade, probably dead!"

"We've come too far to give up now. We don't need Akkad and his bunch of misfits. We can take them. They've suffered casualties too. We'll rest for a bit and then attack them in force. I'll lead the fight."

"But will you? What about Amor, we need to rescue him," Sidon responded.

"I haven't seen him move after he fell, and he had a bad head wound. I think we've lost him," Heth said with disgust.

Canaan now had fifteen men left standing. Three of these were wounded, but were still strong enough to fight. After a half hour's rest and tending to the wounded Canaan ordered another attack, a final one that he believed would give him victory. He would then deal with Noah, Shem and the Ark.

They attacked as a group rather than splitting up, yelling and filled with rage for revenge. They were just fifty cubits from the barricade when Japheth, Peleg and Tubal came riding into the camp. Assessing the situation immediately they attacked Canaan's band from the rear.

Tubal deftly leaned down from his fast galloping horse and lifted a spear stuck in the ground. As he got closer to the melee he threw it at a man who turned in shock to see the three horsemen bearing down on them. It was the last thing Sidon ever saw as the spear caught him in the left eye, throwing him violently backwards onto the ground with the point of the spear through his skull and embedded in the ash covered soil slowly reddening with his blood. Japheth jumped off his horse and grappled with Heth who was also taken unawares and tried to fight back, but Japheth had picked up a bronze sword and thrust it through him.

The fight was over very quickly then. With the death of Sidon and Heth mortally wounded the fight went out of Canaan's troop and they pleaded for mercy. They were quickly rounded up, tied up securely and made to sit in the centre of the camp while they awaited their fate.

A short time later Shem with Ham and their group arrived. By now the dead had been moved out of the sun into one of the caves, while the wounded were being attended to in the large central tent. Sede's body had been laid on its own in the smaller of the two caves.

Japheth quickly went to Shem to tell him what happened before anyone else did. He was naturally inconsolable at the death of his beloved wife. Japheth went with him to Sede's cave where Shem spent a long time by his wife's side holding her hand and murmuring to her in a soft, loving way. Japheth ordered two of the young men to stand guard outside and let no one except Ada in until Noah arrived.

Being the practical woman she was, Ada chose to put aside her own deep grief for her beloved Sede while she attended to the wounded of both sides. The most serious casualty was Gomer who was clinging to life. Joktan had the shaft of an arrow in his shoulder and a long cut on his scalp and Heth had lost a lot of blood from his serious wound. Ada stitched this up and he would live. She attended to several others with the help of the women who had been ministering to the wounded before she got there. Apart from Sede they had lost six dead, including the young woman who had been the one who had found herself with child at the start of the expedition.

Ham was beside himself with anger. He had no idea why his son Canaan had conspired to kill his brother and wreck the Ark. Elam and Javan had to restrain him from taking out his shame and anger on Canaan physically.

"We will have a council when Noach gets here and decide what is to be done with them," Japheth ordered.

Eventually Noah and the rest of the group that had gone to the Ark arrived back in camp and were told and shown what had happened. Noah stood at the entrance to Sede's cave, paused a few moments and then approached Shem. He put his hand on Shem's shoulder, helped him to stand then hugged him for a long time, saying nothing. Eventually he sent everyone out of the cave, sat down on a rock nearby and then he and Shem conversed. A little later Ada came and also hugged her brother in law. She had a soft blanket with her, which she laid over Sede, kissing her on the cheek as she did so.

Noah looked at his grandson, now a mature, some would say elderly man, and shook his head. "Words fail me, Canaan. How could you stoop so low as to orchestrate this murder? Like Cain, your greed and jealousy has brought this on you and all of us. I warned you that there are always consequences from the decisions you make. You had no sons at first, then Adonai gave you more sons than any of your brothers. You had eleven of them, two now lie dead at your feet and one is terribly wounded. He will be lucky to live. Your eldest son, Sidon, is dead, yet there is not a scratch on you. This is how you repay Adonai and your family."

Canaan hung his head in shame and remorse.

Walking over to where the others were gathered Noah then addressed his second born son. "Shem, you have lost your beautiful Sede today. What judgment do you wish to fall on this excuse of a human being?"

"My sorrow is great and almost unbearable, but I do not seek revenge. That won't solve anything. Canaan is disgraced in front of his surviving sons and family, when they hear of it, as well as banished by Nimrod no doubt. That is punishment enough. He must live with this for the rest of his life."

Noah then said in dismissal "Ham, take your son and do with him as you will, there will be no revenge killings or executions here today, although we are in our God-given rights to do so.

"Canaan, your people will not overcome Shem as you planned. You will serve him all the days of your miserable lives and the generations that follow you as well. Be gone from my sight, I don't wish to see you again."

Later that day they buried the dead, including Amor and Sidon, and piled rocks over their graves. As for Sede, they laid her body on flat river stones covered only by the blanket that Ada had placed over her. Ada and the women also laid flowers growing by the stream around her body. They then sealed off the small cave where she lay and that became her tomb.

THIRTY

Blessings

It took a few days to come to terms with all that had happened. Ham and Ludim left the camp the day following the attack, taking with them Canaan, the remainder of his group and their attendants. Heth was carried on a makeshift litter using animal skins as a bed and with four men to carry him. He would live.

Since they left so soon Noah was able to bid them only a brief farewell. Neither Ham nor Ludim wanted his blessing. Either because of his gross embarrassment as to what his offspring had brought into the world, or simply because he no longer believed in the God of his father despite all that he had seen and shared with Noah during their journey in the Ark and this new world, Ham never again spoke or met with his father or brothers to the end of his days.

Noah gave a blessing to each and every surviving member of the expedition, encouraging them once again to follow the words and warnings of his message about the Lord God.

His exhortation and blessing to Japheth and Ada was a long one, prophesying that a great many of their descendants would become people groups throughout the world, that their offspring would inhabit the far reaches of the earth and that many nations would come from them.

"Be true to Adonai. Pass on all you have seen and done to your family and all you meet. Go in peace and prosperity, and may the Lord God always be with you."

Japheth later led a second and final expedition to the Ark for those who had not yet visited it and wished to do so. From there they all went their separate ways. Eventually Japheth and Ada settled in a land to the northwest and visited their patriarch and father from time to time and would be there to bury him, as would Shem, when Noah's time came.

Before Japheth left again for the Ark Noah asked that they all bear witness to the blessing he would now give Tarah and Shem.

"Tarah, I asked you to come on this expedition, knowing full well that you and your father do not follow Adonai. I pray that you will take to heart what you have learnt on this journey and think on it even though you have not yet decided to follow him. I trust that you and everyone here will teach their children about Adonai so they will pass faith in him on to their children. Many may take my story and twist and change it, but I trust that you will hold true to what I have shared with you.

"Tarah, you will have sons and I believe, at least Adonai has shown me in a vision, that not you but one of your sons is destined for great things. That is what I meant when I said that the summons to this journey was not exactly about you. I doubt now I will live to see your son and speak with him as I would like to. So I must impress upon you the importance of what God would have me say to the generations that follow. I can do that only through you, and trust, no, command, that you pass on to your son what I have shared with you.

"I cannot say whether it will be your eldest or youngest child. That is for Adonai to show you, but whoever he is, I have no doubt he will be a leader among his people. Adonai has shown me that in time a redeemer will come to free this godless world from its sin and restore God's world to what it was created to be once and for all and finally. Without that hope this world and its inhabitants are already doomed. I don't know how, when, or who, but somewhere in the future God will restore all things. I believe the Lord has shown me that your descendants will have a decisive part to play in that.

"Take these scrolls and two extra donkeys to add to the one that came with you in order to carry them," Noah laughed. "Have a safe journey and may Adonai bless you and your father Nahor to the end of your days.

"Now Shem, tragedy has come upon you when you least expected it. It's time for you to settle in the land you've chosen. Your duty from this time forth is as we discussed in the cave with dear Sede's body resting before us. I told you what you had to do, and you have agreed to take on that responsibility as Adonai leads and guides you, for he has shown me you are his chosen priest for the days that lie ahead.

"And so my son Shem, as it was passed from Enoch to Methuselah and then to my father Lamech and finally to me, I now bestow the Priesthood of Adonai on you. From this day forth you will be known as Priest of Adonai and Almighty God. May everyone in this gathering be witness to this blessing?"

There was a shout, then a cheer, and the whole camp erupted in applause and appreciation. Japheth and Ada hugged their brother. Even Tarah was impressed. However, Noah was somewhat uncertain whether such revelry was appropriate at such a solemn moment. Yet it was an excuse for a celebration, and so their departures were delayed an hour or so as they took the wine casks off the pack animals to celebrate.

Eventually, Japheth left with those who were going to the Ark. They would later return to the camp and then make their own way home. Japheth and Ada took Gomer with them on a stretcher, and two other badly wounded men to ensure their recovery, along with Ashchenaz, Madai and Javan.

Tubal accompanied them for a short distance until he headed

north to his village. Joktan, with one arm in a sling, was able to ride with his father Eber, his son Jerah and brother Peleg and head home to their families.

Noah and Shem retraced their steps to Ty, accompanied by Elam, Asshur and Arpachshad with all their attendants.

Tarah went back home in the same way as he had left, a lone traveller.

"It's not that they choose to sin, Shem," Noah reminded his newly appointed priest of God as they rode side by side toward the setting sun. "It's because we're all born with a sinful nature. A child doesn't have to be taught to be disobedient, for example, but they do need to be taught how to be good. If people don't believe that, if they have no understanding of this, then they won't realise they need to repent to be made blameless or righteous before Adonai. They will continue in their incompleteness if you like, until circumstances and eventually death overtake them. We are responsible for the decisions we make in life, and we reap the consequences of them. We all fall short of Adonai's standard, even though we endeavour to do good and achieve happiness. This is why there's need for a redeemer to come one day to restore all things to what Adonai intended for our world and our lives to be.

"This new world gave human beings a new start, but already we have failed. Do what you can, my son, to turn the hearts of a rebellious people back to Adonai."

They were going home.

‡‡‡

There were no more great adventures or journeys of exploration for Noah for the rest of his life. He lived peacefully, contented, reflecting on his accomplishments while he tended his vines, gardens and livestock in the little village he called home with the sea his constant companion. As long as he could he would go on short treks or sea journeys to marvel at the world God had given him. Occasionally when they could Shem, Japheth and Ada, would continue to visit him, along with many who would come to seek his wisdom or listen to his story.

Noah survived longer than anyone in this new world, only his grandfather Methuselah and Jared in the old world lived longer than he did. He died at the grand old age of 950 years, having made a significant contribution to the new world in its rebirth. Noah was laid to rest beside his Naamah in their little village by the sea.

God looks down from heaven
on the children of man
to see if there are any who understand,
who seek after God.

Epilogue

May I share with you dear reader, a man came to Shalem. He is a descendant of mine. I met him when he drew near to me with his band of devoted men after defeating King Kedorlaomer and rescuing his nephew in the land where Adonai had brought him some years previously.

He was a person of great wealth with many herds, flocks and servants. The Lord had blessed him. He was also a man of faith and righteousness, and I saw that Elohim's hand was upon him. He came to honour me and he did. I then went to his camp and blessed him. I laid my hands, one on each shoulder, as I faced him and looked him in the eye.

Abram, Elohim has looked upon you favourably and has brought you to this land as it was prophesied to your father Tarah by Noach and witnessed by many. The Lord has given me this word for you:

> *"Blessed be Abram by El Elyon, God Most High.*
> *Creator of heaven and earth.*
> *And blessed be Shaddai,*
> *Who delivered your enemies into your hand."*

Abram in turn gave offerings to me and would not take them back when I offered to return them, but rather said that what he gave was never his, as this was an offering to the Lord through me his priest. To take it back would be to dishonour God.

So I fed him, his men and sent him on his way telling him that his was a destiny that would influence the world to come for many tribes and generations. I told him I remembered Shem, the son of Noach, and with Noach's story inscribed on these many parchments, scrolls, and maps, the history that Noach had compiled through his scribes recorded this revelation.

"I now pass these on to you," I said, "for I perceive you are the man who must be their caretaker for posterity. Make copies and give them to your sons and their sons and daughters so that in times to come people will know how the world began, the struggles we have endured, and the people great and small who shaped this world and brought us this far. How Elohim takes care of those who serve him and the consequences when they do not. These scrolls tell not only Noach's story but the story of Adonai and his love for men and women, as well as our human response to him and the relationship of person to person. Take them with you to every place you settle and ensure you share them with every generation that follows.

"At some time in the days, months or years to come Elohim will meet with you and show you what he will do through you. Keep watch, for you may entertain an angel of God unawares or even the Lord Himself.

"I am of the past, you are the future. Go in peace and be a prophet of truth, faith and righteousness."

I did not encounter Abram again. He in turn journeyed to his lands a little mystified at what, or more to the point how, the Lord was going to do what he had promised through him as he had no heir and was, by the standard of these latter times, well advanced in years.

As priest of Adonai I can tell you that every generation since the disobedience of Adam and Hevah has hoped their first born son would be the redeemer that the Lord promised at the time of that fall when he spoke to Satan and judged him with a curse:

"And I will put enmity between you and the woman
and between your seed and her seed;
He will crush your head and you will strike his heel."

From the time when Hevah gave birth to Cain and said: *"I have given birth to a man child – The Lord."*

It was her hope that her son would be the one to restore them back to the paradise they had lost. But he was not.

Again when Noach was born and his father Lamech said: *"He will comfort us in the labour and painful toil of our hands caused by the ground the Lord has cursed."*

But, as is often the case, it may not be the first born son or daughter that the Lord blesses or chooses to favour but another instead. Of Noach's sons Elohim chose Shem, and of his sons it was to be the third son Arpachshad, then Eber, then Peleg and eventually to Tarah and now through Abram it is our hope that the promised one should come.

I am king of Salem and priest of God. I can attest to the truth of the words, events and people in this manuscript. I have kept and cherished the discourse of Noach, compiled through his scribes on their last expedition when they visited the Ark for the final time. What was my part in this story? The Lord changed my name and authority as appropriate to being His Priest. As for my parentage, I no longer look to the past but to what Adonai will establish in the future.

If Shem lives in me, then I am the only one now living of the eight that survived the flood in the Ark. All have passed on. Arpachshad died just a year ago. Shelah, Arpachshad's eldest son, and Eber his grandson still lives, but in this world as Noach predicted the lifespans of our descendants have become shorter with each generation. Consequently, Peleg, Eber's son died some time ago, actually some years before Noach did, Peleg's son Rue died thirty years later and his son Serug after him. Nahor died before these last two, his father and grandfather. I mention these men, for they were the direct descendants of Tarah, Abram's father who you met and who has now also passed into the next life.

Noach left our world one hundred years ago, a great servant of Adonai and the sea. I preserved these words so that you could read them in order to know how life was, where we came from and where we have been. Noach's words are true as seen through his eyes. He was buried where he requested, behind his cottage near the sea in a village now named … well, perhaps it's best to leave him in peace and that place shall remain his own.

This is Noach's story as I have related it. I trust it has blessed you and will encourage you to allow Adonai, the Lord, do great things through you also.

אוב העושיה
Melchizedek

Author's Note

Often throughout my life I have been fascinated by the many different features that line our coasts, inland valleys and mountain ranges. Here are all kinds of rock formations, layers of soil and various kinds of debris even in the forests. There are also many fossils to be seen in museum collections or along the sea shore. I have frequently thought to myself, *'If only these rocks and fossils could speak, what a story they would tell!'*

I believe that much of what I have seen in this way is a snapshot, evidence if you like, of the great flood that covered the globe and the catastrophic upheaval that, along with the ice age that followed, reshaped this earth many thousands of years ago.

In this narrative I have attempted to combine Biblical truth with scientific evidence, along with historical events and the legends of many people groups throughout the world, while adding from my imagination as well to create a story those rocks and fossils might wish to tell us.

There are many themes running through the story of Noah. A perfect world became an imperfect one through the disobedience of human beings, and the promise of a redeemer to take us and the earth back to the paradise it was created to be at the beginning.

A long, healthy, genetically pure and disease free life for the first people to inhabit this planet became one of seventy to eighty years and perhaps a few more for some, while earth's inhabitants succumbed to genetic decline and many kinds of illnesses and diseases.

An earth which is young. The assertion that it took millions of years to form the earth and its early inhabitants indicates that those who make this claim simply do not know for sure as they are guessing, and this "evolutionary truth" is questionable and very bad science.

Even though God gave human beings a second chance through Noah after the flood and the earth was repopulated it did not take long for the influence of Satan to infiltrate peoples' worldview, culture and beliefs once more. Through the rebellion of Babel (Babylon) human beings were once again headed for destruction due to their dismissal of God and replacing him with other religions. All anti-God religions and beliefs originate in Babel. God then needed to raise up another people who would in time bring forth a Messiah to redeem them from the inevitable consequence of their sin, unbelief in the Creator God and replacement of him with earthly gods and self-indulgence, which is in effect the worship of Satan. This is what people need to be saved from.

Rather than work backwards using a B.C. timeline, I started my narrative from the beginning of creation, about 6,000 years ago, and worked forward from there. Hence the use of AM (Anno Mundi, the year of the world). AM 1 is the year of creation and the first year, the beginning of the human race with Adam and Eve.

Human beings were intelligent from the very beginning and learned to bring progress to the world around them rapidly. The pre-flood world was far more advanced than history and science credit. The same applied immediately after the flood, as Noah, his sons and their wives would have brought that earlier knowledge with them. Most likely they had manuscripts containing knowledge and techniques, perhaps written on animal skin, and so human beings learned to write far earlier than historians and archaeologists would have us believe. From a height of learning and sophistication the rest of history to this day has all been downhill. The many ancient and enduring structures found throughout the earth, that modern technology cannot replicate, is one proof of this.

Many place and character names as well as attributes of God are in Hebrew or its English equivalent. It is my contention that a primary form of Hebrew was an early, if not the original language of the earth and may very well have been the language of the pre flood world.

Dinosaurs lived among people, and although many were lost at the time of the flood, several were taken into the new world on the Ark. I have alluded to them without making them a major focus. However, for me the evidence is overwhelming that they were there in the pre flood world and brought into the new world from there.

I maintain that human beings began exploring the post flood world and its seas almost as soon as they were able to. Noah was obviously a man of the sea and had built ships in the old world. He could never have been able to construct such a vessel as the Ark unless he already possessed such knowledge. Furthermore, since he lived a further three hundred years after the flood he would have been eager to explore the new world. I am sure he did.

This is a novel. The main characters are real people, Noah's family, including the patriarchs before him, his sons and those mentioned as his offspring. They actually lived. Wives' names mentioned in Genesis are given, while a few come from legend or historical accounts. Others are fictitious, as are his siblings and other wider family members. Minor characters are fictitious and are there to strengthen the narrative.

It is probable many of the early patriarchs, especially Noah himself, later became gods and heroes in many cultural myths and legends of the present world. Poseidon, Neptune, Zeus and Jupiter, appear in those of Greece and Rome, while Seth, Horus and Osiris are in Egyptian mythology, to name a few.

When searching for the '*wife of Noah*' I found she was given many names from different sources and consequently I gave her both the name of Emzara and Naamah.

The day to day or year to year events of Noah and his family, apart from what the book of Genesis reveals to us, are conjectural. Some accounts taken from the Book of Jubilees and Josephus may also be historical.

Noah's story is one of faith, endurance, hardship and discovery. Many may disagree with the time lines and sequences in my story and might like to write Noah's story differently, but to my mind what I have done fits comfortably with what might have been, what was, and what is yet for us to discover.

I trust you enjoyed it.

– Paul Christian

The Case for the *True* Story of Noah and the Flood

The story of Noah and his flood is known worldwide. Whether you believe it actually happened or for you it is simply a myth, this epic adventure of a man and his family, a ship and how they survived a worldwide catastrophe has inspired many books, films, discussions, debates and scientific discovery down the years.

If you don't believe it actually happened, however, then, apart from many geological, anthropological, archaeological, historical, and literary manuscripts that testify it did indeed happen, how do you account for the fact that there are over 300 versions of this event to be found in the histories of many cultures across the world?

Numerous people groups that were isolated for centuries have preserved stories of a man, a ship and a catastrophe from which they survived and told them to explorers and missionaries before they had a chance to be influenced by their visitors. In other words, they already knew the biblical story.

Here, below, are just a few of the accounts of a great flood that these groups preserved.

The Epic of Gilgamesh

The Gilgamesh Epic is a 4,000-year-old poem from ancient Mesopotamia that tells a story similar to the Biblical account of the flood in the time of Noah. Here is an edited summary:

Gods named Anu, Enlil, Ninurta, Ennugi, and Ea decided to flood the earth. They were sworn to secrecy about these plans, but the god Ea revealed the plan to Utnapishtim through a reed wall in a reed house. Ea commanded Utnapishtim to demolish his house and build a ship, regardless of the cost, to keep human beings alive. Ea instructed him with precise dimensions, 120 cubits square with six decks, telling him to seal it with pitch and bitumen. Utnapushtim then assembled craftsmen and built the ship.

When it was complete a feast was held after which Utnapushtim's entire family went aboard along with his craftsmen and "all the animals of the field". He also loaded the ship with gold and silver.

A violent storm then arose, terrifying the gods and causing them to retreat to the heavens. The female goddess, Ishtar, lamented the wholesale destruction of humanity and the other gods wept beside her.

The storm lasted six days and nights, after which "all the human beings turned to clay". Utnapishtim wept when he saw the destruction. After his ship came to land on Mount Nimush he released a dove, a swallow and a raven. The dove and swallow returned, but the raven did not. Utnapishtim then opened up the ship and all the passengers left it.

You will observe the similarities between this and the Noah account in Genesis – God (gods) flood the earth – a man is instructed to build a ship with precise (although different) measurements – sealed with pitch and bitumen – the family go on board together with all the animals – a violent storm – the destruction of humanity – the ship comes to rest on a mountain – a raven and a dove are sent out – the occupants of the ship survive.

Many claim the Genesis account was based on the Gilgamesh Epic because this was written before Moses wrote Genesis. However, Moses' account is far more realistic, readable and scientifically accurate. Throughout history there have been many accounts written after earlier ones, where the later accounts proved to be more accurate than the earlier versions.

The Miautso People

The following is from a translation by Edgar Truax of the oral traditions of the Miautso people of China. ('According to the Miao People', *Impact*, April 1991, Institute for Creation Research, El Cajon California)

The Miautso were an early people who regarded themselves as descendants of Japheth, and who also remembered some of the other early patriarchs whose names appear in the Genesis record. Christian missionaries discovered this information in the form of ancient couplets that this people possessed.

They were also in possession of surprisingly accurate recollections of the Creation and the Flood. Some of their records also coincide almost exactly with the Genesis record. Having originally settled in what is now the Kiangsi province of China from where they were later driven out by the Chinese, they claim that they are not themselves of Chinese stock. This is borne out by their insistence that they are descended from Japheth of Indo-European descent. Their oral traditions have been preserved by the fact that their history was faithfully repeated in full many times at important events such as funerals, weddings and other public occasions.

They speak of Adam, whose name in their language means "earth" or "clay", the substance from which he was created.

They also mention Se-the = Seth (Adam and Eve's son) as well as other names in the generations of Adam such as Enos, Cainan, Mahalaleel, Jared, Enoch and Methuselah, Lama for Lamech, and Nuah for Noah.

In the Miautso account Nuah was a righteous man who was

commanded by God to build a great ship. The release of the dove from this ship is mentioned along with a graphic and somewhat horrifying depiction of the flood itself and the subsequent drying out of the land.

Lo Han is their name for Ham, Lo-Shen for Shem and Jah-phu for Japheth. Cusah is their name for Cush, Messay for Mizraim, Elan for Elam, Nga-shur for Asshur, and Go-men for Gomer.

Ancient China

In addition to this, a descendant of Ham, in fact his grandson, a son of Canaan, who fathered the Sinite people could have journeyed to China. If this is correct these people seem to have retained a belief in the one God of Genesis, as their most ancient script on oracle bones indicates they knew or followed many of the events of Genesis up to the time of Babel. An interesting example of a connection with the account in Genesis is that the Chinese character for ship, 'chuan' 船 comprises three radicals meaning "vessel" (the first character), "eight" (the second character), and "people" (the third character). This points to Noah's ark, which contained the eight original people who were their ancestors. (See creation.com/images/pdfs/tj/j19_2/j19_2_96-108.pdf)

Polynesia

"In the time of Nuu, (that is, Noah) the flood came upon the earth". Hawaiian tradition relates how Nuu Mehani escaped the flood and re-peopled the earth, that overwhelming disaster which is mentioned in the Hawaiian Kumulip Chant. (Abraham Fornander, *An Account of the Race*, 1969, I, 94)

New Zealand Māori and Moriori genealogies and traditions mention names such as Nu-nuku, and Nu-kumaitore. These names are similar to the Hawaiian Nuu, believed to refer to Noah as mentioned in the previous paragraph. Is it possible they were influenced or have originated from the time of Noah?

‡‡‡

To sum all this up, ancient cultures world-wide record common traditions that speak of 'a great flood' at some time in their history. Whilst the details may vary from culture to culture they refer to similar features and individuals.

Many describe a single person or family who survive a world-wide flood which was sent (by whatever entity or god they believe in) to wipe out an evil generation. Often specific animals and people that were saved by way of a wooden vessel are mentioned. They also often specify certain animals and especially birds that were sent out to seek new land while the floodwaters were still over the earth.

Many of these stories are found in places that have never experienced local floods in their regions. For this reason it is very unlikely these 'legends' are based on local flooding events. It is more probable that they are retelling stories from an original worldwide destruction by flood waters that took place in their distant past. At the same time they mention Noah and his family, albeit often changing their names as their own specific ancestors.

It is often claimed that the Bible copied Noah's story from some other source. We have already mentioned that the 'Epic of Gilgamesh' was written before Moses compiled Genesis. However, it is quite likely that the former took its story from Noah's account which he would have passed on to others and which Moses eventually wrote from, for this is better written and more plausible. Unfortunately, Noah's specific account has been lost or yet awaits discovery.

Whatever the case this narrative attempted to relay to you, the reader, a likely way in which Noah did in fact record this epic and the events that transpired before and after the great flood. It also showed how this account could have been preserved and how eventually Moses could have had access to it, through Abraham's descendants, Jacob / Israel and his sons, in order to compile the book of Genesis.

Earth in Upheaval

*A Brief Scientific and Geological Overview of
What Happened to the Earth During Noah's Flood and
That Continues to the Present Day*

As the flood waters rose on the ancient world many physical changes took place across the globe beneath the oceans and across the land. Catastrophic earthquakes and widespread volcanic activity changed the face of Noah's old world permanently. During the entire year that the flood and its immediate aftermath prevailed over the whole globe many other mechanisms produced destructive, constructive and re-constructive consequences. What had probably once been a single massive continent and ocean world was split apart, forming several separate continental land masses and thousands of islands dispersed among new oceans and seas.

The rapid rise of water may have covered the whole planet within days, but most likely within weeks due to the heavy rain that fell and the large volumes of water that gushed explosively from within the earth. There are various reasons why the rainfall was so strong and persistent.

The water that fell as rain may have come from the canopy of water above and surrounding the earth, as described in the first days of creation. This possibly formed a layer of protection from the brilliant sun in the atmosphere, thereby giving the entire earth a uniform and mild to warm climate that was free of storms and extremes of heat and cold created by strong winds and sea currents. At that time a mist rose from the ground overnight and left on it a heavy dew in the early morning to water the ground. Springs of clean fresh water within the earth also fed rivers and streams, providing water for plants to grow and people to use. Consequently, the earth enjoyed a mild climate and was a very pleasant place in which to live. All this changed dramatically forever when the flood came.

Alternatively, the excessively heavy rain may have simply been caused by a build-up of natural water vapour in the clouds in the weeks before the flood to an extent previously unknown in the old world by some unknown reason.

Another way the water could have rained down so intensely and continuously was when the fountains of the earth burst forth. These could have resulted from the catastrophic earthquakes opening up cracks in the subterranean earth and sea floor that enabled the release of great reservoirs of water and pushed them skyward in great volumes which then in turn fell back on the earth as rain. The forty days and nights of this rain were probably a combination of all these and possibly other unknown forces as well. Any meteors that may have fallen on the earth during this cataclysmic reshaping could also have added to the destruction, or even possibly initiated the whole catastrophe.

The land did not become completely flooded immediately and may have taken several weeks to do so. This would have enabled people to take shelter until such time as the flood eventually overcame them. Such a gradual but nevertheless devastating extinction of life would explain why there are very few human fossils from this time, since fossils require some kind of sudden covering for their preservation. Wildlife, on the other hand, faced with the change in the world order would almost certainly have panicked en masse and blindly rushed to their destruction not having the intelligence to devise ways of alleviating their plight.

When the waters burst forth, covered the planet, then later

receded, large continental movements and catastrophic volcanic activity were instigated and continued to increase for a time. Enormous forces were released, thrusting the mountain ranges upward and creating vast caverns in the deepest oceans as a result of the breakup of the pre flood supercontinent and rapid subduction of the oceanic crust into the earth's mantle. This would have been so rapid and catastrophic that it could have been measured in metres per second. When the granite rock within the mantle was thrust up forming the new continents, in a start and stop series of events, this would have resulted eventually in the creation of high mountain ridges and the solidifying of the new continents, which in turn would have caused the floodwaters to drain back into the ocean basins we know today.

The rapid movements in the earth's crust and the violent volcanic activity they caused both contributed to the destructive earthquakes. Yet neither the Ark nor anything else floating on the surface would have scarcely felt or been affected by them because the ocean itself would have absorbed the effects of the strong shocks and tremors. Large swells or surges were all that was to be seen or experienced on the sea.

During the flooding stage great swathes of preflood rock, mud, sand and earth were layered over the surface. This occurred frequently with greatly varying times between each layer. The thickness of each layer also varied depending on its locality and composition. The titanic forces involved compacted this material in varying densities depending on the particular material involved and the pressure applied to it. Anything that was once alive that was caught in these layers was quickly fossilized due to the suddenness with which it was covered and compressed.

Deep basins were filled rapidly with sediment and the outflow from volcanic activity. Swift currents in the ocean changed in direction and intensity with the raising and lowering of the land, allowing the heavier sediment to drop in the lower areas while rapidly scattering debris and lighter material over the higher ground. Tremendous tectonic forces twisted and bent rock and layers of sediment in a variety of geological forms, many of which would be set in place for thousands of years.

Early in the flood the once abundant vegetation that covered the earth was stripped away along with the animals and birds, insects and every form of life that lived on it. As the waters rose animal tracks showing how many creatures tried to outrun the rapidly rising water were preserved by being rapidly covered in sediment and pressurised. In the same way many animals, their eggs, insects, crustaceans and sea life together with individual tree logs and plants among others were perfectly preserved as fossils. Although immense quantities of fish and sea life perished in the storms that swept the old world, enough survived to replenish the oceans of the new.

Vast areas of foliage were quickly covered and buried under pressure forming fossilized deposits. Other swaths of foliage both large and small were formed into island rafts by the wind and sea currents. Most of these log and vegetation rafts would eventually sink and be rapidly covered in sediment and, again under pressure, were turned into enormous deposits of fossils. Wherever great quantities of them were pressed together they formed vast areas of coal, oil and gas.

Where rafts of logs and other vegetation stayed afloat for the duration of the flood they preserved many insects, microscopic life, seeds and bacteria. Even very small animals may have survived and rode out the flood this way as such rafts served to transport these life forms all over the new world. In such a compact state it is possible that even plants grew from seeds or sprouted new life, having water, light and oxygen available, all of which are the elements needed to sustain life even on the great oceans. If these rafts kept floating on the ocean currents for up to a hundred or even two hundred years 'bumping' into one land mass after another as sea currents carried them about the planet, then life forms may have been transported from one area of land to another.

When the heavy rain finally ceased after forty days, the torrential rain having caused the rapid rise of flood waters over the earth, there was a period of another one hundred and ten days when the flood waters continued to rise at a slower rate. The fountains of the deep probably continued to pour forth great volumes of water, while at the same time great land masses were sinking, twisting and rising in different locations.

At the end of the one hundred and fifty days the water reached its peak and rose no more, as when the tide turns and there was a brief time of relative calm before the waters began to ebb. This may have lasted as little as a few hours. The forces creating the fountains stopped at this point and cracks and fissures in the earth's surface under the flood then began to take back the great volumes of water that had been poured forth earlier.

When the flood began to recede the ebbing water caused widespread erosion on the new continents and vast plains were created. As the water receded still further these wide flows became channels that eroded the land even more deeply, creating many valleys and canyons, which later gave rise to rivers and streams.

As the continents were uplifted the waters retreated and formed the oceans. A small part of them was evaporated by the sun, which was much hotter now because the filtering cloud canopy of the old world was no longer there. The new climatic conditions caused clouds to form and new weather cycles to begin. There was a combination of rising land together with falling ocean basins to enable a world of water to drain such a vast amount in the two hundred and twenty days that the storm took to finish its catastrophic work.

Nothing of the old world remained. All that had happened combined to give the new world its continents, islands, deep oceans and high mountain ranges. Ongoing volcanic activity would also add more mountains and depressions and even islands in the sea as the years went by. On land the plains, plateaus, valleys, rivers, streams, waterfalls and all manner of geological features were set in place permanently by this great catastrophe. The many layers of earth and twisted rock formations laid down during the flood can easily be viewed to this day in eroded valleys, canyons and shoreline cliffs across the entire world.

At the end of the flood when all the water had receded the formation of the new earth did not cease at that point. Ongoing volcanic activity and later an ice age was to follow that would add further changes to the landscape. With continued earth tremors and plate movements the earth would continue to change, albeit less severely and with diminishing frequency than the dramatic and rapid changes brought about by the flood.

When it came to climate, uniform weather and temperature of the old world gave way to a new climate with extremes of heat and cold in different areas. At first, the intensity of the tectonic forces and extreme volcanic activity would have increased the warmth of the sea, whereas the average land temperature may not have changed noticeably as there would as yet be no ice at the poles. As the decades rolled on, however, it would become apparent that some areas of this new world were a lot cooler and others warmer, and the weather in general was more extreme and unpredictable for its new inhabitants.

The warming of the seas during the flood created a warm climate in the first years of the new earth. Both vegetation and animal life benefited greatly from this hangover of the old world, and consequently growth was rapid in both plant and animal life. Birds and animals bred prolifically, often having more offspring at a birthing or hatching than their later descendants would enjoy. Trees grew rapidly, along with all plant life. The sea teemed with life, far more than on land, because not all marine life was destroyed by the flood. This proliferation and rapid growth of life continued for at least two hundred years before the earth's climate changed as the seas, due to lessening undersea volcanic activity, began to cool rapidly. The ice age that then followed created even more distinct land formations and environmental changes.

The data source for this overview is taken mainly from *How Noah's Flood Shaped the Earth* and www.Creation.com. See references on the following page.

References

The book of Genesis – Moses – Sinai – C15th BC
The Genesis Account – JD Sarfati PHd,
Creation Publishers, Georgia, 2015
How Noah's Flood Shaped the Earth
MJ Oard & JK Reed, Creation Publishers, Georgia 2017
www.Creation.com – various articles & videos
Dr Andy Woods – *Sermons*
Sugarland Bible Church, Texas 2021-23
Antiquities – Josephus – Jerusalem AD 93
Dictionary of the Bible – WM Smith 1863
Annals of the World – Ussher – London 1650
Book of Jubilees – Israel c150BC
newcreation.blog/
what-is-the-truth-about-noahs-flood-in-the-bible/?
en.wikipedia.org/wiki/Mount_Judi
en.wikipedia.org/wiki/Urartu
Google Maps
Holy Bible ESV – English Standard Version
www.biblegateway.com
Holy Bible NIV – New International Version
Tyndale House Publishers Wheaton Il 60189

Plus much more reading from many sources

Acknowledgements

There are many people who encouraged, enquired about my progress and generally supported me in this mission of writing a narrative of the life and times of the Patriarch Noah. Some who had more than a little input in helping me achieve this include:

My friends Dan and Gina, for their support and suggestions.

Dianne, who has done a sterling job of proof reading.

Pastors Ian and Brenda Clark, formerly my Bible College tutors, for their advice and editing of the final version.

Each of them provided very honest and critical feedback, resulting in a far more readable story than the account I originally wrote. While details of the story itself did not require significant changes, their suggestions enabled me to restructure it better.